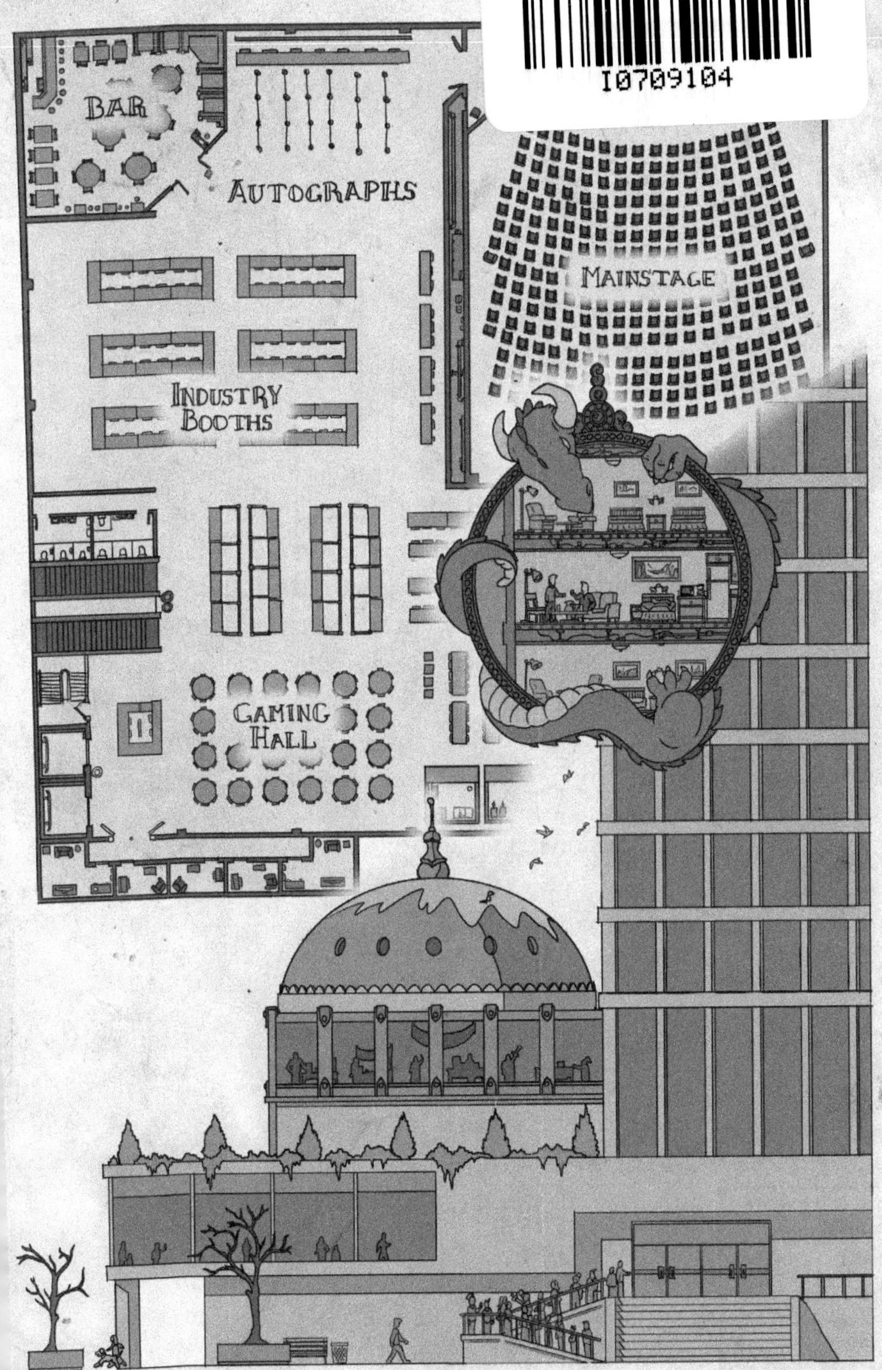
BAR
AUTOGRAPHS
MAINSTAGE
INDUSTRY
BOOTHS
GAMING
HALL
I0709104

The Silenced Tale
Book Three of The Accidental Turn Series

Cover design by Ruthanne Reid and Rodney V. Smith
Edited by Kisa Whipkey (2017) and Donna Frey (2024)
Book design by Brienne Wright
Map by Christopher Winkelaar

Electronic ISBN: 978-1-7381485-1-6
Paperback ISBN: 978-1-7381485-2-3

PRAISE FOR THE SERIES

"Being a part of a family, however unconventional, is an integral theme of Frey's clever, adventurous, and endearing Turn novels. [...] The thought-provoking story discusses the stereotypical role of women in fantasy novels, but more focus is placed on the characters' struggles with their familial roles and relationships, creating depth and commonality."
—Publisher's Weekly

"I started reading and was captivated. This superb novel grabbed me from the opening sentence, and never let go. [...] The whole tale is several clever twists on the oh-so-familiar fantasies we've read before. I want more. *Books* more".
—Ed Greenwood, *Forgotten Realms*

"Let me start by saying [...] that I think that J.M. Frey's *The Untold Tale* is the most important work of fantasy written in 2015. It may be the most important work of fantasy written this decade, but I'll have to get back to you on that in 2020.
—Dr. Mike Perschon, *The Steampunk Scholar*

"INSANELYAMAZING! The Untold Tale tears apart the tropes of heroic fantasy and gives back what we need: true heroes, true love, and the astonishing realization that yes, real people are magical."
—Julie Czerneda,the *Night's Edge* and *Trade Pact* series

"This story is nothing short of fun, unexpected, and a little bit queer. If you're interested in a Science Fiction/

Fantasy undertaking with all of the ingredients of a queer anthology, *The Untold Tale* is for you."
—Dallas Barnes, *Pink Play Mags*

"It's easily the strongest I've read in the last year. [...] The fictional world = real world trope isn't the only one Frey twists, however. She also plays with the ideas of the hero and heroic adventure, feminism, gender roles, and the role of the narrative itself, in innovative – and occasionally cheeky – ways. This novel has the potential to appeal to a great many readers, across genres."
—Violette Malan, PhD, *Dhulyn Parno* Series

"If I could mark this as 10/5 stars, I would, but that's impossible, so 5/5 it is, with much hearts and swoons. [...] *The Untold Tale* is delicious, each word meant to be savoured, breathed in, nibbled at, full of hidden delight and wonder. Frey has a beautiful writing style - all at once slightly old-fashioned and delectable, whilst also being modern and quick-paced. It's tongue-in-cheek and it's serious. It's like an epic fantasy and a modern YA all in one. It is a book for every bookworm or geek [...] But most of all, it is a book for writers - and Frey delivers."
—Ana Tan, *A Tsp Blog*

"John Scalzi did Redshirts. He poked fun at a beloved symbol of geekdom, and we loved it. Frey has done the same for the sacred fantasy tropes and it's fantastic. An empowered woman of color, thrown into the chauvinistic world of the epic fantasy today's geeks were weaned on, serves as the perfect narrator for a critical and wonderful look at fantasy in the modern world."
—Leah Petersen, *The Physics of Falling* series

THE SILENCED TALE

J. M. FREY

For Stephanie Lalonde, my first convention-buddy and
my greatest, and truest friend. You have been such a
rock, and such a wonderful source of fun. I love being
a fan with you.
Let's never stop

#ConClusion3
#CannotWait
#SoEXCITED
#ToKTReveal
#BlackOut
#TheatricsOrReal
#OHEMGEE
#BinkyLives
#WereYouThere
#WhatWasInTheWater
#ElgarReedIsOurKing
#EpicCosplayOfEpicness
#GotABitTooEpic
#RememberTheFallen
#ISurvivedConClusion3
#GeekArmy
#WeAreOurOwnHeroes

ONE

he phone call from the Smithsonian Museum is the first indication that something's off. There's a little dancing red star beside his calls icon, indicating a voice-mail waits for him, when he gets off the plane from Victoria. He listens to it in the cab ride home, frowns, blinks a little, then listens to it three more times. The content doesn't change, though he imagines the curator's voice gets more and more hysterical with each replay. The upshot is this: his typewriter, the old race-car red Olympia De Luxe his aunty gave him, has been stolen.

It's a bummer, but he'd donated the typewriter because he didn't need it anymore. And frankly, as far as he's concerned, they can make up a fake to put on display. Nobody will ever know the difference if they don't publicize it. Why they told him it had been stolen at all is the bigger mystery. It's not like he has a spare for them to borrow, or any leads on where the lost one is. No one's tried to ransom it *back* to him.

"We're very sorry," the curator says again when he calls her back, juggling his carry-on, his house keys as he unlocks his front door, and his wheelie suitcase. "We just have no idea what happened."

Elgar jams his cell phone between his ear and shoulder as he sheds his dripping coat and muddy boots. He leaves his suitcase and carry-on by the front door, only half-listening to the curator bumble her way through more apologies as he sifts through the mail that's waiting on the table in his front hall. His assistant, Juan, has been in to feed Linux and drop off the correspondence needing his attention. In pride of place on the top of the pile is the latest in what feels like an unending, torturous series of contracts to read and sign back to Flageolet Entertainment. Elgar sets it back down in disgust.

Outside, the mushy gray of a late Seattle winter drizzles on. Elgar paces over to the window as the curator works her way up, verbally, to whatever it is she wants to add to "your typewriter's been stolen." *That* information should have been the climax of the scene, and he can't think of what might be more important than theft. Poor narrative structure. If the curator was one of his MFA students, he would dock marks for rambling. Being circuitous. Wordy. Loquacious. Palaverous.

He stares out the window at the slush-flakes falling onto the quiet muddy mess of his backyard as he muses on synonyms. The curator keeps talking. Elgar blinks and frowns. "Wait, back up. What did you just say?" he asks, checking back into the conversation.

"It disappeared," the curator mutters, clearly ashamed to have to say it out loud a second time.

Weird things are just a part of Elgar's life now. And while a theft like this might be par for the course for an internationally best-selling author, what she'd said is… well, new. No, not new. It's… *neoteric.*

Any other time, Elgar might have assumed it was just an overzealous fan. That happened sometimes. Quite a lot, actually. Elgar's old apartment in the co-op housing complex he'd been living in with his aunty when he began writing The Tales of Kintyre Turn in the late seventies had been broken into enough that the landlord of the unit had put bars across the windows and doors. He uses the place as storage now, instead of renting it out.

But this is really neoteric.

"It just disappeared," the curator repeats a third time, distraught and desperate to fill the empty air when Elgar remains silent.

Right. There are crazy fans, and then there's... this.

This right here is a completely different brand of crazy. The new kind of crazy he's still trying to get his head around, a year after he'd been introduced to it in a hotel bar in Toronto. This is the kind of crazy he thought he'd just left behind in Victoria after a week-long visit with the Piper family—his family, in a way that goes much deeper than blood.

"We reviewed the security camera logs," the curator promises. "But there was no indication of who committed the crime. Or... or how, actually. It just sort of... vanished?" she finishes. "Kinda just blinked out of existence on the footage, really."

"*Poof* kind of vanished?"

"No, no poof. No explosion. Just... blink. In one frame of the footage, not in the next. The police think it might have been a fancy digital splice-job."

"Huh," Elgar says, a strange sort of displacing numbness settling in his fingers and toes, crawling up his limbs. "And, uh, when did this happen?"

The curator makes a distressed sound. "December twenty-ninth," she admits, and it sounds like she's saying it through her teeth. "We only waited so long to tell you because we thought... well, we thought we would have figured it out by now. I mean, about how it happened."

"No, no, it's okay," Elgar says, trying to sound warm and soothing when every short hair he possesses is standing upright with a frightful chill. "I understand. Is there, uh, is there anything you need from me?"

"Not at this time, Mr. Reed. I just, ah, I just felt that it was about time you knew." She sounds shamed and small. "And I apologize, again."

"Okay. Thanks for calling," Elgar says, and then stares in blank horror at his smartphone as she disconnects. He sets it down on the windowsill and rubs his arms through his thick sweater. A brush against his leg, sudden and unexpected, makes him yelp and step back. An indignant feline howl replies. Elgar catches sight of an angry marmalade blur as it streaks out of the living room and into the kitchen.

"Linux!" he calls after the cat, guilt instantly surging up to squeeze his still-frantic heart. "Aw, sorry, buddy! You scared the crap out of me."

Linux meows angrily. Elgar finds him sitting primly on the counter, where he knows he isn't allowed to be, licking his tail.

"Did I step on you, buddy? Sorry, I'm a dick."

He reaches out, grabs Linux carefully by his scruff to keep the cat from bolting, and runs his fingers across the cat's tail, checking for swelling or breaks. Linux protests with hisses, laid-back ears, and a harsh rake of claws against Elgar's inner wrist.

"Right, I know, I deserved that," Elgar says with a wince. "But I'm a big guy, Linux. There's an awful lot of me to come down on you. Let me just check, okay—ow! Shit! Ungrateful little asshole!"

He lets Linux go, satisfied that the cat is whole, if supremely pissed off at him, and washes out his new battle wounds. Linux yowls at him again and speeds away toward Elgar's office. Probably to sit on his laptop and glare.

Elgar had bought one of those kitty-friendly desks, where the underside is a wooden maze of tunnels for the cat to sit in, with a comfy, pillow-lined basket beside the keyboard. It was meant to keep kitty feeling entertained and comfortable while you were working, rather than neglected. Linux uses the tunnels and the basket sometimes, but whenever Elgar leaves the room for a cup of coffee or to answer the call of nature, he inevitably comes back to find the cat spread out over his laptop, eyes slits of contentment as he rubs his fur in between the keys and soaks in the machine's heat.

Whether or not the laptop is on doesn't matter. Linux is envious of how much time the machine gets and tries to get his body between the keys as often as possible.

A sudden thought grips Elgar's lungs in terror. His chest freezes up, breath punched out of him. *What if my laptop has vanished, too?* He rushes to his office, clutching his sluggishly bleeding hand, and stops in the doorway. His lungs burn as he sucks in a breath to shout.

"Linux, move!"

The cat raises his head and grumbles unhappily. Elgar crosses his office and shoves his hand under the furry creature, who hisses and snarls, but refuses to be budged. Underneath him, Elgar's fingers skim the cool metal casing of his computer. He sags, bending down to press his forehead against Linux's fuzzy belly, overcome with relief.

Linux bats at his hair, but with claws sheathed this time. Elgar rubs his nose against the cat's tum, and Linux gives up his anger, sprawls back, and enjoys the bizarre petting. After a moment, Elgar's joints feel sturdy enough for him to straighten.

He keeps backups—both paper and digital—in a fireproof safe in the bottom drawer of his filing cabinet, and he checks this, too. Everything is where it should be. The correct number of CDs and memory keys still sit atop the early-draft manuscripts filed neatly under them. He locks the safe, and then the filing cabinet, and runs his hands through his puff of white hair, relieved and annoyed at himself in equal measure.

If it really was actual, real magic that stole his old typewriter, then it hadn't reached here. And really, he chides himself, if there was some sort of magic intent on stealing his work, or his tools, then everything would have vanished months ago, the same time as the typewriter.

The same time that everyone else's books were disappearing.

Still...

He doesn't want to worry Forsyth unnecessarily; Forsyth would drop everything and come to Seattle for him. Maybe he'd even get on a plane, though he despises the things. No, better to go to the more prosaic of the pair first. He glances at the clock on the wall. Lucy will be at work by now, so he goes back out to the living room, grabs his phone, and calls her office.

"Professor Piper, UVic," she answers on the second ring. "Hello?"

"Hey, Lucy, it's me," he says.

There's a slight pause on the other end of the line, a hesitation that he wouldn't have noticed if he hadn't been listening for it. It's taken Elgar a few visits to Victoria to work out why it is that Lucy always seems uncomfortable around him, why she never totally welcomes his presence in their lives. It's not that Lucy Piper doesn't like her husband's creator. It's the fact that Elgar Reed is the living reminder that, at some base level, the man she loves and the child they have created together are not real. They live, they breathe, they can touch and be touched, they have preferences, they laugh and cry and bleed. But they are not, at their most base, of her world.

And there is always the terrifying possibility that something might happen—in the world of the books, or to Forsyth and Alis, or to Elgar himself—that will make everyone she holds most dear blink out of existence. They've had more than one wine-fueled evening of sniffles and honesty since the Pipers returned from Hain. And Lucy's chiefest fear is that, when Elgar dies, as he eventually must, her husband and daughter might go with him.

The truth of it is that, even though it's through Elgar's imagination and pen that the inhabitants of *The Tales of Kintyre Turn* have gained sentience and access to this realm—what Bevel Dom has dubbed the Over-realm—no one actually really knows how or why the Deal-Maker magic works here. Especially when no other magics do. Forsyth's potions are just herb soups, his runes nothing more than lifeless scratches in the dirt, his Words of Power nothing but blurred mumbles.

Which means that, no matter how hard Elgar tries to work at their relationship—and he does try, despite any accusations anyone might level at him about his being narcissistic, self-important, and high-handed—there is always an unavoidable undercurrent of tense animosity on Lucy's end. A fearful wariness.

And he can't blame her. After all, what Elgar thought up had hurt her.

"How was your flight?" Lucy says after a quick breath. "You must have just got in."

"I did. It was fine. Same as always. Listen, uh… I have a strange question for you."

"Yeah?"

"When you were, um, there… Forsyth said that the Deal-Maker was destroying totems, right?"

"…yeah," Lucy says, and Elgar can hear the worry creeping into her voice just as clearly as the squeak of her office chair as she sits up. "Why?"

"Was… was there ever any attempt on a totem from *The Tales of Kintyre Turn*?"

Lucy is silent for another moment, and it's just long enough that the chills return.

"Lucy?"

"I didn't really see it, myself," she answers slowly, her voice low and scared. "I didn't get much chance. I was, uh, unconscious for a lot of this bit, but... Forsyth said he saw your typewriter."

"The red De Luxe?"

"Yeah. Blasted apart. Like, by lightning. The Deal-Maker was a weather witch."

Elgar's stomach drops out. He'd only ever written one weather witch into the books; he knew exactly who Pip was referring to. "Shit," he says, and even to his own ears it sounds strangled. "Solinde?"

"I never learned her name."

"It's Solinde," Elgar says firmly.

"Elgar, what's happened?"

"I... the Smithsonian called. Apparently, my typewriter vanished. Back in December."

Lucy goes silent again. "I see," she says at length.

This is why Elgar likes his pseudo daughter-in-law so much. She's clever. Cleverer than him, at any rate. She catches on to things faster, understands the depths of things more. She even found things in his own writing he hadn't realized he'd put there in the first place. She'd written a whole PhD thesis about it. (It had been a bit horrifying to read, if he was honest—made him feel naked in ways he hadn't experienced since his first weeks as an MFA student.) But she's smart, and he doesn't have to spell things out for her, which he likes.

"And it didn't come back when the books returned?" she prompts.

"No."

"And the rest of your... your stuff?"

"Right where it should be. Thank god."

"Huh."

"Yeah, huh."

There's a shuffle and a thump from the other end of the line, and the sound of papers being moved around. "Okay, well, I guess there's nothing else to really worry about. Nothing else is missing, nothing's happened. It's been quiet."

Another silence, telling and tense, echoes down the figurative line from Canada.

"Do you ever worry it won't be?" Elgar asks, the confession blurting out.

"Do *you*?"

Another telling pause. It sounds like she's waiting for him to confess more. And, to be honest, there is more to confess. For all that Lucy is cleverer than him, Elgar is also not stupid. He knows that she doesn't have a very high opinion of his social graces. And for all that he likes her, Lucy Piper, quite frankly, intimidates him.

She's exactly the kind of woman that had made him a sweaty, nervous mess when he was a young geek. She's self-assured, intelligent, speaks two languages, and sometimes seems to be sneering down her pert nose at him. He'd been frustrated and angry when women like Lucy overlooked him in favor of asshole jocks who treated them like garbage. He told himself that "nice guys finish last," that women only wanted jerks, and then wrote a world where people like him, people who didn't fit in, people like Kintyre Turn—who didn't want to conform to what other people told him he should want—won the day. Where people like that got to be the hero, were free to behave however they liked, and got whatever they were entitled to have, because they strove for it. A world where women threw themselves at the Good Guys, and rewarded them with the sex, the servitude, the wifely submission that they deserved, simply by virtue of being Good Guys.

A world, Lucy had told him in the strongest language, and more than once, where being a woman completely *sucked*.

In the end, it turned out that Elgar had written the perfect romantic lead... he just hadn't made him the main character. Women like Lucy Piper were looking for men like Lucy Piper: confident, generous, thoughtful, self-assured, compassionate. People who treated women like people instead of rewards for leveling up. People like Forsyth Turn.

Elgar knew this. Well, he knew it now. But it was sometimes difficult to relinquish old habits and prejudices. And if he was honest with himself, he'd admit that Forsyth Turn, his own creation, intimidated him, too.

Sometimes, it was hard not to feel like a slow child while trying to follow their rapid-fire, jargon-filled conversations. Sometimes, it even made him feel resentful. They did their best to explain when they caught him staring down into his cup—tea, wine, beer, or the strange liquors Forsyth kept bringing home, trying to find replacements for the nonsense ones Elgar had made up, which Forsyth missed terribly. But even that made Elgar feel stupid. No, not just stupid... *puerile*.

He was glad he'd already written all three books of the *Shuttleborn* trilogy, because there were days when just thinking about Lucy's pursed frown of distaste made him snap his laptop closed and waste his work-time watching junk TV.

It makes it hard to write when you know that there are people in another world who literally suffered because of what you did, that there are people in this world who are disappointed with your every attempt. And as excited as Elgar is that Flageolet Entertainment has picked up the Kintyre Turn series and is in the midst of pre-production for the big television adaptation, he also secretly fears that if he has any hand at all in writing the scripts, those changes will affect Hain, Kintyre and Bevel, Wyndam and Pointe, Forsyth and Alis.

Initially, he'd asked to be present in the Writers' Room, to work as the story consultant and maybe write an episode or two. Now, the most his agent has managed to get him to consent to is an agreement that he'll read the scripts from home. He'll send in notes and suggestions to keep the characters recognizable and the setting accurate, and otherwise remain hands-off.

He doesn't dare do anything more.

And Lucy's question—a simple, loaded "do *you?*"—makes all of this old self-loathing, resentment, and worry swirl into a hard ball behind his larynx. He swallows, trying to banish it back.

"Maybe I worry a little," he says. "But I... I don't want to waste every minute worrying, you know?"

Lucy sighs. "Yeah, yeah, I know. I get it. Look, I... I don't think there's anything more to this. I hope there isn't, anyway. And you're right. There's no point in getting worked up if it's nothing. It happened months ago. I mean, years might have passed over in Hain by now."

"Is that how it works?"

"Honestly?"

"Yeah?"

Lucy snorts. "I have no fucking clue."

Elgar catches himself chortling, and presses his palm against the rain-cooled windowpane in front of him. The laughter feels good. Feels like it's pummeling the fear, cracking it apart piece by piece, pounding it into silky ash.

"The first time I went, I was there for nearly a year, but only a few weeks had passed here. The second time, we were there for well over a month, and it was only eight hours. And yet, time had passed in Hain at the same rate it had here—it had been about two years for them since Forsyth and I left, too. It's a weird sort of slipstream thing, I think. Time passes at the same rate, unless a Reader is present? I don't know."

"It's something to think about."

"To be fair, I try not to," Lucy admits.

"Sure," Elgar allows. "Okay."

"Listen, I'll bring it up with Forsyth, and if he thinks it's something to be concerned with, he'll call, okay? Otherwise, I think you're travel-tired, and worn out, and this hit you harder than you thought it would. I think you're good."

"I'm going to back up everything I've ever written by emailing it to myself, anyway," Elgar says.

"If that makes you feel better, then do it."

"Okay."

"But I think you're fine. I think this was a one-off."

"But..." Elgar says, and then hesitates. There's a corner of clear tape on the window, from when he and Juan had plastered his living room with the concept sketches Flageolet sent over, and he picks at it now with his fingernail. "What if... what if it actually isn't nothing?" Elgar asks again, voice small and doltish in that way that Lucy's confidence and insight always makes him feel.

"Then something else will happen. And then it will be a pattern. We can decipher a pattern."

The tiny triangle of tape comes away from the glass, sticking to the pad of his finger. "That's true. Though, I thought two was 'a coincidence' and three was 'a pattern.'"

Lucy chuckles. "You have the best spymaster in the known world on your side here, Reed. Two's enough for him to find the pattern. If there is one. There might not be. But if there is, we'll figure it out. Trust us."

"I do."

"Okay, then."

"Okay."

They both linger on the phone, listening to each other breathe. It's cowardly. Elgar's too afraid of his own fear, of being alone with his admittedly vast imagination, to want to sever the call and, with it, his only connection to someone who understands.

"Elgar. You're *fine*," Lucy says eventually, and her voice is warm, comforting. She's lost the haughty distance she sometimes has when he's surprised her. "I promise."

"Okay."

"Okay. Go get some sleep, all right?"

"All right. Bye."

"Bye," she says, and ends the call. Outside, the perpetually gray clouds open up again, and the world is pummeled in earnest by the rain.

FORSYTH

Pip comes home smelling of her time after school at the gym. The look on her face and the fact that she did not shower before she came home says clearly that she is bursting to inform me of something. She crooks her finger at me, bidding me follow even as she entreats me verbally to go in the opposite direction.

"Hey, Freckles," she says as she drops her satchel and coat on the bottom stair in a heap, a practice she knows I find frustratingly slobby. "Pour me a glass? Then come up?"

Both confused and intrigued, I rise from where I was reading the newspaper on the sofa and head into the kitchen to provide Pip with her requested libation. While I'm there, I pour a second glass for myself.

"*Bao bei*," I call through the door of our en suite when I have the requested after-work wine in hand. "Why did you not shower at the school?"

"Come in," Pip says. "I want to have this conversation

face-to-face."

I oblige, and my wife sticks her hand out around our shower curtain for her glass. Amused, I pass it to her and sit on the closed lid of the toilet. The shower wall has a small window in it that looks out over our backyard, and the light of the sunset behind Pip throws an extremely enticing silhouette against the curtain.

"Mmm, shower-wine," she says. "Way better than shower-coffee."

"I know it is 'date night,' but surely you can't be *this* eager, can you?" I chide.

Pip pokes her head around the curtain, her hair a froth of suds, and waggles her eyebrows at me. "I wasn't before, but you did bring me shower-wine. Wanna climb in?"

"Absolutely."

Pip quaffs her wine and hands her empty glass to me, a Malbec mustache painting her upper lip. I lean forward to kiss it away, then quaff my own wine. Pip leers at me as I strip off my day-wear—a pair of warm, stretchy yoga pants and a freshly cleaned hoodie.

"Oh, you spent the day commando. Such thoughtful foresight," Pip comments as I step into the spray. She slides her soapy hands over my shoulders and down my back to grab a double handful of her most favorite part of my physical assets.

"Alis was with her grandparents all day," I say, grinning at her eagerness. "And I didn't have to step out to the store, so I thought there was no point in making extra laundry for myself."

Pip gives my backside a firm squeeze to show me just how much she appreciates my thoughtfulness. I return the favor, and soon things are slippery, and soapy, and lovely.

"What conversation did you want to have face-to-face?" I ask between kisses, and Pip makes a face.

"No, no, I'll tell you after. Not while we're naked."

"Pip," I say, backing off a little. "Whatever it was, you thought it urgent enough that you chose to come straight home instead of showering at the university."

"It'll *keep*," Pip promises, pursuing my lips again.

But now I am curious, and curiosity has always been a more potent addiction than desire. "Then why the initial rush?"

"I didn't want it going around and around in my brain while I was showering there." Pip steps into me.

I step back again. Pip pouts. "What is it?"

"It will keep," she insists, and makes up the lost space between us. This time, I do not back up. Instead, I let her have her way. Her delightful, delightful way.

Soon we are dressed in naught but our bathrobes and cuddled into one another on the sofa before the electric fireplace, our wine glasses and the bottle both waiting on the coffee table. We doze until Pip jerks in my arms and nuzzles her nose deeper into my naked chest.

"Umf?" I ask softly, running my palms down the texture of her back. Pip says nothing, but cringes and wriggles again. I've never known her to be jittery in bed—normally, she flops into her preferred position, on her back with one hand over her head, and stays there until morning.

My wife is a deep sleeper. If Alis cries, it's generally I who hears the crackle from the baby monitor first. I wouldn't say I'm an especially light sleeper myself, but the noise of an Overrealm city at night is more than I'm used to. I'm not entirely comfortable with trying to sleep in a soundscape that doesn't resemble a wide, dark countryside dotted with moonflowers and barrow lights, the tinkling bell-laughter of fairies, and the plaintive songs of lonely Kiss-Me Frogs at twilight.

I don't think I sleep as deeply as I used to, at any rate.

Perhaps Pip's uncomfortable. The sofa is narrow, and I suppose using me as a mattress isn't ideal. I don't think I've grown any sharper—rather the opposite. The delicious foods and lack of sparring partners in the Overrealm has served to make me doughier, certainly, but Pip says much more comfortable for a cuddle, too. Perhaps she pulled a muscle during her workout. Perhaps her back hurts.

Still, the curiosity pulls at me, and I run my palms down her scars a second time. Pip huffs and tenses up, eyes screwing shut and fingers clenching in the fabric of my robe. How intriguing. She is waking now, making little noises that I remember from her time at Turn Hall, when she fought the return to wakefulness and pain.

Seeking to soothe, I run an appreciative, comforting hand along the exposed skin at her shoulder, and snuggle forward to kiss my favorite little leaf on her nape. Pip sighs in her sleep, uncoiling, and wedges herself on her side against the back of the sofa. This serves to turn her back away, protecting it, and I wonder if she even knows she has done so. She pulls my arm around her waist, clutching my hand like Alis clutches her stuffed lion, Library. I resist the urge to prod at her scars again. If she is genuinely hurt, she will tell me. Otherwise, I will not torment her for my own interest.

Our legs tangled together, ankles knocking, I watch as she drifts toward wakefulness.

"Mmmm. That was a nice appetizer," Pip says, grinning up at me cheekily.

"And for the main course, you will tell me what had you so upset today?" I ask, sitting us both up.

Pip heaves a sigh, flopping back so her head is in my lap, her legs akimbo on the sofa, theatrically petulant. She looks up at me through the fringe sticking to her forehead with residual dampness, and I cannot help the chuckle that such a sight presents.

"You sure know how to spoil a mood, *bao bei*," she complains. But then she goes still. "Elgar called me."

"Oh?" I ask, wondering what it is my Writer could have said that was important enough he had to call my wife as soon as he got home. Or, for that matter, that hadn't occurred to him while he was here. He'd only left this morning. I haven't even washed the sheets in the spare room yet.

"What about?" I ask. "Something to distress you, obviously. No, not distress. It wasn't that urgent. Concern, then?"

"It's not anything really hinky," she says, stretching and getting more comfortable on my thighs. Any discomfort in her back seems to have vanished, or at least, she now finds it ignorable. "Just... well, his old typewriter has vanished."

I frown, throwing my mind back to where Pip said the typewriter was located. Yes, a museum. Or, it appears, *not* the museum. "Ah, so it was not a totem, but the actual machine? Interesting."

"Yeah," Pip says. "And he called me because he didn't want to worry you. But I promised I'd tell you about it anyway. And that we would look into it, if there was anything worth looking into."

My wife's instinct may be correct, and I tell her as much.

Pip sits up, nodding as she pours us both more wine. Then she turns to face me, curling her bare feet under my thigh, tapping one fingernail against the bowl of her glass. She is clearly trying to figure out how to phrase something, and I am patient until she has found the words she seeks. Meanwhile, I watch as she flexes her shoulders and wriggles in her seat, readjusting the lay of the robe against her back. Hmmm, perhaps not so ignorable as I thought.

The scars could not be hurting her—they are long ago healed and Pip is religious in her regime of stretching the skin gently, treating it with creams and oils to keep them supple. It is less vanity and more a desire to ensure that they do not pain or cripple her later in life. So perhaps it is something muscular, something gained from her increased hours at the gym these last few weeks.

I decide that, later tonight, I will give her a massage with some of her skin oil. That ought to take care of both potential reasons for her discomfort. And it will very likely lead to other things that will help her take her mind off it.

Finally, Pip finds her words. "Elgar thought that... maybe totems were disappearing again," she confesses. "I told him it was all done, but now I can't stop... I mean, it's stuck in my head, you know?"

"I see," I say, reaching out to take the wine from her hands so I may fold them between my own and kiss the tips. "And now you have thought your way into a small panic."

"Just a small one," Pip allows. "But I... I dunno. He's concerned that it might not be over, and... to be honest? I'm not certain that it is."

Ah, and here is the root of the problem. I draw my wife against me, resting her head against my heartbeat, and kiss her crown. It seems to soothe her, when she's been thinking too long or too much about my origins, to have this reminder that I live, I breathe; that I am here.

"But I could also be spinning fantasies," Pip admits quietly. She swirls her fingertip through my extremely sparse chest hair. "I don't want to get anyone worked up if I can help it. But I thought I should at least mention it."

"Just to see if I've noticed anything else... hinky?" I ask.

Pip grins up at me, that lovely, blinding smile of sheer girlish delight that she gifts to me whenever I master the phrasing of some new idiom or jargon from her world. "Yeah."

"Nothing hinky," I vow. "All has been quiet."

Pip winces. "That's nearly inviting hinkiness." She reaches out and brushes a tender thumb over the thin white scar on my left cheek, the last signature that Boot-knife ever left on someone's flesh.

"Oh?" I tease, leaning down for a kiss, which she willingly offers up. When I move back, my wife curls her fingernails against my nape and fails to let me go.

"Mmm," she says into our next kiss. "Almost as bad as 'what's the worst that could happen'? Or 'I'll be right back.'"

"Ghastly," I agree, sipping at her lips. "But no worries. My story is not a horror thriller."

"But it *is* a fantasy," Pip says, and lets me go to sit up. Her expression, when I finally have the chance to study it, is the sort of blank calm she employs when she is trying to keep others from seeing her inner turmoil. I would resent that she is even now not telling me all that is worrying her, if it wasn't for the fact that I can parse the language of her inward-rolled lips and the tightness of the lines around her eyes so well.

"And what does that mean, dearest?" I ask, sitting up as well. "What trope am I missing?"

Pip reaches across me to retrieve her wine glass. She takes a sip and, as she swallows, seems to come to a decision. "I... I think we might be in the eye of the storm here."

"The eye of the storm?"

"The calm in the middle of the hurricane."

I raise my own glass to her. "I know what this idiom means. I just don't understand how—ah. Yes." I sip, too, for now I have thoughts of my own to consider, to chew on.

Pip winds her hand around mine, threading my fingers with her own, squeezing as if, any moment, the proverbial hurricane will descend upon our house and rip us apart.

"You believe that there is some adventure yet to be had, some danger left to ford?" I ask softly, squeezing back.

"The thing is, *bao bei*," Pip whispers. "Fantasy novels usually come in trilogies."

TWO

ELGAR

The next week is a flurry of video-calls with LA, apologetic cat-cuddles with Linux, catch-up meetings with Juan, and daily chats with his agent, Kim. With the press and the fans both dying to see what's next from the "fantastic imagination" of Elgar Reed, the danger that news of the TV series might leak is high.

The principal casting calls have started to go out, but the production company wants to keep a lid on the series for as long as possible. It's unconventional, but the idea is to release *all* the news all at once, in a big sort of social media info-bomb that will, they hope, make the series the main topic of conversation for a few entertainment news cycles. Honestly, it's all just a bit too modern and busy for Elgar, so he just does as he's asked and keeps mum about the whole thing. After all, Elgar is a firm believer that spoilers, well, spoil things.

True to point, things were nearly ruined at the beginning of the week, when a casting agent's assistant—a dumb millennial with a celebrity ladyboner—posted a photo of the call for Bootknife on her social media. It was caught quickly and yanked before any of the major outlets seemed to get ahold of it, but Elgar didn't have one ounce of sympathy when he'd heard that she'd been fired the next day—confidentiality contracts exist for a reason.

The assistant's flub means they have to consider throwing nosy fans and media types a bone in terms of *Shuttleborn*, though. So, to the already busy week, Elgar adds a back-and-forth with the publisher, who wants to keep a tightly clamped lid on the text of the book, and has no stake in whether or not Flageolet's secret is spilled.

It takes three calls, and a "please, please?" wine basket sent to the whole marketing team, but the publisher is eventually persuaded to post the first chapter on a social reading site to kick off the marketing drive and keep fan attention on *Shuttleborn*. Hopefully, that will satisfy anyone poking around Elgar and draw them away from digging further. It sort of feels like he's thrown *Shuttleborn*'s Tristan and Vana to the wolves to keep Kintyre and Bevel safe, and he tries not to think too hard about what it might mean that he's now imagining the afterlives of characters he hasn't yet met in person.

And so, once again, Elgar doesn't spend any of his week actually *writing*. He barely has time to *think*, and spends more time eating sandwiches over his keyboard than Juan is really happy about. It isn't until he gets another call from the Smithsonian curator to explain that they'd found a similar model of typewriter online that he even remembers the weird chill her first phone call gave him.

"Do we have your permission to put the replica up and note it as such?" the curator asks, being annoyingly thorough with whatever checklist she's clearly got on her end.

"What will you tell people about the one I donated?" Elgar asks back.

He can't exactly hear her shrug, but it's clear in her voice when she replies: "Well, you know, artifacts have to be taken out of displays all the time, to be cleaned, or repaired, or repatriated."

"I'm not a nation asking for my plundered antiques back," Elgar hisses, a strange frisson of fear at the memory of the machine's disappearance crawling up his spine.

"Honestly, no one will kick up a fuss that it's not the original," the curator soothes. "Until we find it, this is the best we've got. Is it okay?"

"Yeah," Elgar agrees. "Right. Yeah." Because what else can he really add?

He almost tells her not to waste their resources looking for an artifact they'll never recover, but decides against it. What can he say, anyway? *"Oh, I spoke with one of my fictional characters via email, and he told me that the Viceroy's weather witch mother sucked it into the novels I wrote and destroyed it in a twisted plot for vengeance."*

No.

Fantasy writers are given leeway to be eccentric, but there's a line. And talking about your characters as if they're real people in the real world is where it's drawn. Even if you *are* talking to your characters because they're real people in the real world.

Instead, he gives the museum's scheme his blessing, promises not to talk about the theft publicly (but also not to deny it if the truth comes out), and then spends the rest of the afternoon dutifully scritching Linux as he backs up all his work by emailing the digital proofs to his own address. True, it puts them one step closer to letting hackers at the manuscripts, but one step further away from losing everything forever in case of...

Well, just in case.

Maybe Elgar only notices the man in black because he's already unsettled and jumping at shadows. Maybe it's all the paranoia over the loss of his typewriter. Maybe it's the fear of the Deal-Maker magic that has proven—twice—that it can reach into this world and snatch out anything, or any*one*, it wants. Or maybe it's just because he's seen the man in black out of the corner of his eye enough times that it now constitutes a pattern, and Elgar's brain has finally started paying attention to it.

But when he leaves the house to fetch some groceries for dinner, he realizes he's being watched. And as that revelation trickles down into his brain, it's followed with the grains of another: that someone's been watching him for weeks now.

Elgar doesn't have much reason to leave his house. He's rarely there on weekends because he usually ends up at conventions then, leaving Thursdays and coming home Mondays. And the weekends that aren't spent surrounded by the glory of nerds who love his work and hotties in skimpy cosplay, he tends to fly up to visit his new family. It's only a forty-minute direct flight, and, adding the commute to the airport on this end, and the commute to the Piper household in Victoria on the other, he can go from his front door to Forsyth's in roughly two hours.

Juan takes care of the house when Elgar's away—feeding Linux, sorting the mail, even mowing the lawn and taking care of the minimal landscaping—and often has groceries and ready-made meals carefully labeled in the fridge when Elgar gets back. Elgar's pre-diabetic, and Juan takes it very seriously that his boss eat right.

He also gets a bit histrionic in that flaming, limp-wristed way that twinks like him get when Elgar doesn't get up and go for a walk at least once a day. He's started to threaten a treadmill-desk, which would make Linux spectacularly unhappy, so Elgar is trying to do better. He's even asked Juan to make him fewer meals so he'll have the excuse of walking to the grocery store six blocks away.

And it's taken him about five visits now to realize that every time he does, a man dressed all in black is sitting on the bench outside the shop.

It could be a coincidence. In fact, it probably is a coincidence.

There are lots of people who have reasons to be in the same place at roughly the same time every day. The homeless guy who opens the doors for him at the monorail station, for example. Or the same three baristas he sees at the SeaTac airport every time he flies. There are also an equal number of reasons for people to dress all in black—a lot of retail shops ask employees to dress in monochrome, and one of Elgar's writing buddies only wears black because he says it's easier to make sure his wardrobe never clashes.

Maybe this particular man in black is waiting for his wife to finish work in the grocery store at this time every afternoon. Maybe he's a businessman on a break, enjoying the outdoor air. Maybe, like Elgar, he works from home, and he comes to this bench to people-watch for an hour.

Except now that Elgar's noticed the man, it feels like his eyes are burning brands into the back of his neck. It feels like he's... not *staring*. It's more than staring. It's harder, somehow, more intrusive. Pervasive. Intense. *Gimlet.*

It's possible that this man is a fan of *The Tales of Kintyre Turn*, and he recognizes Elgar. Maybe. But shouldn't the stare feel less like a blow to the back of the head, then? Maybe he's a reporter looking to trap Elgar into giving him a scoop about the show?

No, now he's just being a dumbass.

The paranoia about the TV show leaking is starting to get to him. Elgar shakes his head, and tries to push the man in black out of his mind. But the curiosity follows him as he walks up and down the aisles. He makes a decision. He's going to talk to the man, find out once and for all if he's really here for Elgar.

Congratulating himself for choosing a pre-made salad and a steak to fry up instead of the frozen pizza that was calling his name, Elgar is quick to get back out of the store, the desire to talk to the man in black itching at the back of his skull.

He fully intends to do it, too. Until he looks up and meets the man's gaze across the sidewalk.

Elgar has written the phrase "the hate in his eyes" more times than he can count over the last twenty years and eleven plus novels. But he's never really been able to envision how that kind of visible, tangible hate would actually look.

Now, he knows.

It smacks into him, as if the stranger has launched a crossbow bolt at his heart, making his lungs constrict with terror and his whole body sway and jerk. His fists clench, sweat gathers behind his whiskers, and his knees go wobbly.

Clutching his groceries close, he clamps down on the ridiculous urge to apologize to the man—for what?—and makes the most dignified escape he can, considering his inability to run at a pace that is anything more than a mortifying wobble. He only looks back over his shoulder twice.

When he gets back home, he dumps the bags in the kitchen, double-checks every lock on every door and window, and spends an hour in his en suite bathroom searching "panic attacks" on his phone and the methods used to control one.

It's past sunset when he manages to get his breathing back to a normal level, and by then, he's exhausted by the adrenaline his body's been dumping into his system, forcing his heart and lungs to work so hard he might as well have been running a marathon. He's too tired to be hungry now, so he shuffles his way to the kitchen to put the steak in the freezer for another day, and the salad in the crisper for tomorrow.

What he finds on the kitchen counter makes him scream.

The plastic salad bowl has burst open. All across the granite countertop, a writhing, bilious wave of maggots wriggles its way to the edge, falling in fat plops against the tiled floor. Some of them burst like pustules, yellow-white, splattering into the grout.

The salad is heaving like a creature trying to escape the pile of leaves and sliced vegetables.

And Linux sits beside it, one paw raised to strike, ears back and teeth bared, whiskers and expression intent and tight. Elgar doesn't know how he knows it, but he *knows* that if Linux strikes whatever it is that's trying to escape the salad, his cat won't survive.

He swoops around the revolting, stinking pile of maggots and scoops Linux up around his middle. The cat snarls and yowls, but Elgar holds him tightly, accepting the scratches this time instead of flinching away. He doesn't let go of Linux until they're both back in the en suite. Elgar locks the door and jams a towel against the gap at the bottom. Linux prowls back and forth in front of it, hissing and snarling at whatever is on the other side.

Elgar's hands shake and bleed so badly that it takes him four tries to call Juan.

"There's—" he's able to get out, and then has to swallow hard against his own rising gorge. "There's bugs!"

"Bugs, boss?" Juan asks from the other end of the line. It sounds like his assistant is in a bar. Elgar hates to pull him away from his own social time, but he can't... he can't face the kitchen alone.

"Maggots!" he says, coughing and then biting his tongue hard. He will not puke. He will not. "All over! It's... I can't..."

"'S okay, boss," Juan says quickly. "Maybe the cleaner forgot to do the garbage disposal this week. We'll get it sorted."

"Juan, I can't..." Elgar tries again, and the lump of bile pressing against the hollow of his throat becomes a hot ball of shame and fear. "I don't..." The sob that bites off the rest of that sentence startles them both, if Juan's soft gasp on the other end of the line is anything to go by.

"I'll be there in ten minutes, boss. Okay? Ten minutes." And then, faintly, as he clearly holds the phone away from his face: "Don't worry, babe. I'll be back. Yeah, part of the job, you know? It's cool. Gimmie an hour, okay? Have another drink. Okay."

"I'm sorry," Elgar whispers when Juan comes back on the line, narrating his journey from the bar to his car, and then switching the phone to his Bluetooth speaker as he drives.

"I'm nearly there, boss. Breathe. Deep breaths, okay?"

"Okay. Deep breaths. I'm sorry."

"For what, boss?"

"Screwing up your date."

"Nah, it's cool. He was a weirdo, anyway."

"Weirdo how?"

"Doesn't read. I ask you, what kind of a man doesn't like reading? A loser, that's what. I don't sleep with men who don't own books, boss."

Elgar tries to laugh, but it comes out bubbly and choked.

"Hey, boss, hey. Keep breathing. I'm nearly there."

"Juan..."

"What's that I hear in the background?"

"Linux. He's... I locked us in the bathroom. He's not happy."

The cat punctuates that statement with a long, low yowl, hunching down and ripping at the towel jammed under the door with his teeth, trying to get at whatever's on the other side. Elgar jumps up from the side of the tub and pushes the towel back with his toe, grateful that he's still wearing his street shoes when Linux, put out, attacks his foot instead.

"You... you're in the bathroom?" Juan asks, a note of worry creeping into his voice.

"Yeah, I... Juan, I was... it was awful."

"Okay, I'm on your street now. Just... stay where you are, okay?"

"I locked the front door."

"It's fine. I have my keys."

"Maybe you shouldn't come in..."

"I'm here, okay?" The sound of a car pulling into his driveway is faint under Linux's rolling growls. The soft thump of the car door closing makes the cat's ears twitch. "I'm just gonna..." The jingle of keys sounds over the phone.

Elgar holds his breath, fear and shame seizing his lungs. He has a sudden, horrible flash of whatever it is downstairs punching across the room toward Juan. He gags at the thought of a tidal wave of maggots splashing out of the kitchen, swallowing his assistant under their slimy, pulsing bodies.

But as soon as Elgar hears the front door open, Linux's body immediately relaxes. The cat pricks his ears forward, listening, and sits up primly, wrapping his tail around his paws.

"Boss?" floats up from downstairs.

Elgar ends the call and shoves his phone in his pocket. "Juan?" he calls down. "Are you...? Is everything...?"

"There's nothing strange, boss. I mean, your salad is all over the counter. But nothing else is wrong. Good for you, by the way. Salad for dinner. I'm proud of you."

Elgar sucks on a horrible, choking breath, torn between wanting to chuckle and wanting to scream. He toes the towel out of the way and cracks the bathroom door. Impatient, Linux bolts through the gap, meowing that special chirrupy greeting he saves only for Juan, the man who always gives him a treat.

Elgar sticks his head out of the bathroom slowly, tentatively. The overwhelming fear, the funk of rotting vegetables, and the terror that something is coming to get him have all evaporated. There isn't even an after-image of the horrible, pungent stink. His house just feels... normal. Like it always feels: empty of anything but the three of them, smelling faintly of cat litter, dusty paper, and the "Clean Linen" scented sticks the cleaning company likes to hide in discreet corners.

Cautious, shaky, and exhausted from his fear, Elgar makes his way downstairs. His shoes are silent on the plush gray carpeting, but Juan is looking up at him when he makes it into the kitchen, anyway.

Juan is the epitome of what Elgar thought gay guys were—skinny, tall, with gym-earned muscles and a tanning-bed glow. His teeth are white, and straight, and perfect. His eyes are a soulful brown, and his dark hair is elegantly coiffed. Juan is never less than perfectly put together; it always makes Elgar feel a little wrinkly and schlubby by comparison. For his date, Juan has apparently pulled out all the stops. He's wearing a pair of designer jeans and a midnight blue velvet smoking jacket with an honest-to-god pocket square.

In short, Juan is the complete opposite of the gay

guys Elgar had accidentally written into his novels. Well, Kintyre is bi, Lucy had explained to him. Or perhaps only gay for Bevel, in particular; that wasn't really clear. But Bevel has been gay the whole time, and Elgar hadn't known it. Although, in retrospect, it makes sense, what with how unenthusiastic the character had seemed about bedding maidens when Elgar had tried to write the celebration scenes. Elgar isn't the kind of wishy-washy writer who bows to the whim of muses or uses mumbo-jumbo terms to describe where his inspiration comes from, but he does listen when his characters resist or seem reluctant, or just aren't working right. He always figured it had been his own subconscious telling him that something wasn't jiving. Now, he knows that it literally was another person, on the other side of the door of his imagination, digging in his heels and saying, "No!"

Juan smiles at Elgar, and pats his shoulder when he gets close enough. "See? Nothing but salad here. I even think it's salvageable." His tone is a little too bright, though, his smile a little too tight, his gestures a bit too deliberate. He's being patronizing. Whether he realizes it or not.

Elgar bristles. "I didn't make it up," he says as Juan fetches down the colander and tosses the spilled salad into it. "There was—"

"I'll check it as I wash it," Juan promises, his back to Elgar, and Elgar's frustration mounts.

"I know you think I get carried away with the things I make up, but I didn't—"

"It's cool, boss. It's cool," Juan says, rinsing off the veggies and picking through them carefully.

"It's not cool. There were bugs... maggots..." He looks at the floor, but even the splattered puss is gone. Linux circles his ankles, meowing up at him, and then butts the cupboard that holds his food cans with deliberate care.

"You hungry, too, little man?" Juan asks the cat. Linux meows again, more pitiful than the last one, and Juan sets the salad aside to dry and gets Linux his dinner, too.

"You don't have to—" Elgar starts.

"I'm here. That's what you pay me for, boss. To do stuff for you."

"Not on your off time."

"I don't mind."

"But I can—"

Juan dumps the can into Linux's bowl, and then straightens and frowns at what he finds on Elgar's face. "I don't think you can, boss. Sit." He points imperiously at one of the stools tucked under the overhang of the kitchen island. Juan always has impeccable posture, and when he's feeling imperious, it becomes downright birdlike.

Elgar sits. His face feels cold, and sort of like it's drooping, and his stomach pools somewhere around his knees when he finally settles.

"You look like you've seen a ghost," Juan says gently. He washes his hands, and then puts on the kettle.

"I feel like it," Elgar says, swallowing down the bitter aftertaste of adrenaline.

Juan sucks on his lips for a second, clearly coming to a decision about something. He sighs, shakes his head, and says: "I gotta ask, boss—did you take anything tonight?"

Elgar stiffens. "What do you mean?"

Juan looks down at the counter, clearly uncomfortable to be asking this of his employer, and traces the pattern of the granite with one perfectly buffed fingernail. "You know, like... did you get some special mushrooms for your salad?"

"I... Juan! You know me! I don't..."

"I had a boyfriend once who started in on hash to relax when he got too stressed out at work. I know you've been under a lot of pressure, boss, especially with this Flageolet stuff." He looks up, dark eyes earnest with worry.

"No," Elgar says, gripping the edge of the counter. "Never."

"You wouldn't be the first writer to use in order to get over a block, and I—"

"A block?" Elgar splutters, jerking back. The stool sways, but he manages to yank himself back to center. "What makes you think I have writer's block?"

Juan scratches the back of his neck. "Well, you haven't produced anything new since you finished *Magicwon*. I didn't want to bring it up, but Kim—"

"If my agent is worried, she can damn well ask me herself," Elgar snarls, stunned to realize that they were gossiping about him behind his back.

"She's tried," Juan shoots back. "Boss, you told her you 'weren't writing anything right now.' You've never gone so long without at least pitching something. It's been almost two full years since you finished the *Shuttleborn* series, and you wouldn't even let them publish the first book until the third book was written. You've declined every invitation to short-story anthologies, and you changed your mind about wanting to write a script for the TV series. You—"

"I know what I've done!" Elgar interrupts, frustration and shame blooming in his gut as his assistant enumerates his cowardice.

Juan slumps a little, curling his velvet-clad shoulders inward, trying to look soft and comforting. His hands flutter on the edge of the counter, and a smile pulls uncomfortably on the side of his mouth. For the first time since they were first feeling each other out, he looks nervous.

"Sure, boss, but... what we can't figure out is why."

Elgar drops his face into his hands, rubbing his forehead. The exhaustion is tugging harder now, a headache building behind his eyes. "I have my reasons, okay?"

"Which are?"

Elgar presses his thumbs against the bridge of his nose. "I... I can't..."

"Is it writer's block, boss?"

"I don't believe in writer's block, and you know that, Juan. I just... I don't have any ideas. Okay?" He looks up, feeling that a confession this humiliatingly personal deserves at least eye contact. "I have no *ideas.*"

It's a lie. And he really hopes Juan doesn't notice that. It isn't that he's drained of ideas. It's more that every time he comes up with a new world or character, he realizes that he might be harming another actual person in order to give that character enough motivation to begin the story. There's no narrative without conflict. So he cringes away from each new book that germinates in his imagination. He refuses to water those sprouts, to nurture them. Only to then have to twist and hack at them, to rip them up or cut them down.

Juan's eyes go round at the fake confession. "No ideas at all, boss?"

Elgar shakes his head as convincingly as he knows how. Forsyth despises lying, but he's a consummate dissembler by nature. Algar's wrath had taught him how to hide, and Lewko Pointe the Elder had honed it in him. His time as Shadow Hand had made it second nature. And Elgar has been studying under his creation, mostly so he could get better at handling the press. He holds eye contact with Juan and forces himself to blink slowly, not to lick his lips, or perform any of the other tells Forsyth says he's prone to.

Poker face.

"Maybe you can—"

"I'm just tired, Juan," Elgar says. "I need a break for a while, okay? I want to focus on the TV series. On my family."

"Yes," Juan says, eyes narrowing and spine straightening again. "This mysterious new family that you somehow acquired, who you never show me pictures of."

Elgar rolls his eyes. "They're real. I promise I'm not going up to Victoria once a month to score drugs."

"But how are they related to you, boss?"

"Syth's my sort of... cousin. You know, twice removed or something like that."

Juan shifts like he wants to pace or come around the counter. He puts his hands on his hips and leans back again, clearly attempting to convey that he isn't rushing or crowding Elgar, that he is waiting patiently for the rest of the explanation. Of course, he isn't patient about it at all. Even Elgar can see that.

"I, um... they reached out to me at a... con." Elgar puffs up, feeling defensive. "I like hanging out with them, okay? They're good people. They get me out of the house. I thought you wanted me to get out more, spend time with people, do more than just go to conventions."

"I did. I do," Juan says, holding up his hands, palms out, *don't shoot*. "Just... maybe talk to Kim, okay? Tell her what you told me. She's worried."

"I'll call her tomorrow."

"Okay. Okay, boss. Thanks." Juan turns away then, assembles the salad in a bowl—sans steak—and sets it down in front of Elgar with a fork. "Here. Eat up. Get some sleep. Maybe you just had a stress dream."

Elgar narrows his eyes and tries not to gag at the smell of the vegetables under his nose. They're not rotting anymore, but the smell still turns his stomach. "You mean, if it wasn't a bad high," Elgar sneers.

Juan huffs a sighing chuckle. "I'm not going to live

that down, am I?"

"No."

"Okay, boss." He pats Elgar's shoulder. "I'll lock up after me. Anything else you need?"

"No. No, I..." The childish shame is back, sliding up Elgar's back, surging out from where Juan is touching him. "Thank you for coming, all the same."

"All good, boss. It's what you pay me for."

"I don't pay you to walk out on your dates."

"Ah, now that was a favor," Juan says with a wink. "I have to go back now and break it to him that no bookie means no nookie."

"Good luck."

Juan pats himself down, making sure he still has his wallet, keys, and cell phone. His grin is brilliant, sparkling, his worry for Elgar wiped away in the face of returning to his date, for all that he says he intends to break the poor bastard's heart and blue-ball him all in one go. "Thanks! I'm gonna need it!"

Elgar waits for Juan to say his goodbyes to Linux, and locks the door behind him. Then he stands, grabs the salad, and goes out into his backyard through the kitchen porch. His trash can is in the corner of the yard, against the fence. Elgar throws the salad—bowl, fork, and all— straight into it.

FORSYTH

There is a saying in the Overrealm that the weather of the month of March either begins as a lion or as a lamb, and ends the opposite. This year, it seems, March intends to arrive as a Library Lion. For even now, in the last week of February, we find ourselves surrounded by slushy that refuses to melt away, and weather that is much like that mythical creature—large, buffeting, and leaves my hair standing up in odd wet swirls.

"Pray tell, wife, what has caused you to be so obsessed with fitness, recently?" I smile at Pip as I ask this, for she has diverted our late afternoon outing so that we may collectively glance into the window of a newly opened studio space. The printed advertisement blaring out over the high street in dayglo colors proclaims the availability of classes and personal instructors for all manner of the martial arts, including—

"Look, fencing," Pip says, pointing to the sign. "And stage combat lessons."

"I see that," I say, not bothering to turn my eyes away from my wife's face.

Below us, where her stroller has been pushed up beside the glass, I can hear Alis slapping her palms against it. Somehow, she's pushed her way out of her hateful, hateful knitted mittens. I am quite glad that they are clipped to the cuffs of her jacket, or she would have relieved herself of the burden of having mitts at all the instant we first put them on her. She must also wear her knitted toque, which she finds equally unacceptable. And I am equally glad that she is unable to untie the dongles when we knot them under her chin, or our brazen girl would be bareheaded, as well.

"Maybe you could—" Pip says, and then looks up, catches the expression on my face, and halts herself. "Don't you miss it?"

"Of course I miss sparring," I say.

"Sooo..." Pip says with a small, hopeful grin that nonetheless is too tight around the corners, shows too much teeth between her plum-slicked lips.

"So, what interests me *more* than a studio where I may practice with Smoke opening within walking distance of our neighborhood, my dear, is how you have clearly brought us three blocks out of our way in order to appear to accidentally come upon this sign."

Pip deflates. "Busted."

"Indeed." I raise an eyebrow at her, Spock-like, and add, "Fascinating," just to make her smile. This smile is a real one, for all that it is watery and a little tremulous. "Was this your attempt at being subtle?"

"Maybe?" she says.

"You'll have to try harder to trick a Shadow Hand of Hain," I scold gently, and turn the stroller back out onto the sidewalk. We resume our slow meander down the pavement, shoppers and errand-runners flowing around us like fish amid the reeds.

Pip reaches out and takes my nearest hand. I am well able to steer the stroller with one hand at this pace, so I curl my gloved fingers around my wife's and bring them up to kiss her breeze-chilled knuckles. Like her daughter, Pip dislikes gloves.

"And this failed subterfuge of yours, wife?" I say amiably, keeping my tone light so she knows that I am curious, and teasing, not accusing. "Is this your way of saying that I am getting fat again?"

Pip snorts. She whips her hand out of mine, slides quick fingers as cold as eels under my pea coat and but-ton-down shirt together, and pinches the little bubble of flesh over my hips that is caused by my belt.

"Yow!" I protest. "Pip, your hands are cold."

Grinning, Pip flattens her whole palm against the small of my back, and I jump. Alis giggles at my discom-fort, the traitor, but everything is made better when Pip slides her pinky and ring finger a little lower, dipping the pads of her fingers into my undergarments and scratch-ing lightly at the upper swell of my buttocks.

"Stop," I mutter. "Or I will be in no fit condition to remain in public."

Pip giggles, free and happy, and that pleases me.

Whatever worry brought us to the studio, it seems to have cleared now. Pip removes her hand from the back of my clothes and wraps it around my own once more.

"You're not fat," Pip reminds me. "And you never were."

"But I am far more sedentary than I used to be. You must admit to that," I point out.

"You can always come to the gym with me."

I make a face at that, for Pip knows how greatly I dislike exercise for the sake of exercise. It is repetitive, and boring. If I were to exercise, I would much prefer for it to have a point—to work on skills like fencing, or archery, or to at least include a lovely view of the countryside, like horseback riding.

"I'd... I'd *like* it if you came to the gym with me," Pip says softly, and the shadow of worry is back, like storm clouds passing across her face.

"And what would we do with Alis?" I ask.

"Dad would come to the house for a few hours if we—"

"Every day? That's asking much of Martin."

Pip blows out a frustrated breath. "It would make me feel better if you... practiced."

I am not certain how to reply to this, so I do not. True, Pip has been acting oddly since Elgar called to confess that his typewriter had vanished. Her sleep has grown lighter, and she no longer rests on her back. Yesterday, I caught her looking through a glossy booklet that she must have requested from a home security company, for it looks too grand to have simply arrived as junk mail. And now she is expressing concerns about my ability to fight.

What has Pip so agitated? Which clues have I been missing? For something has obviously happened—or is currently happening—and I have failed to notice.

"Da?" Alis asks when we are silent for more than a

few paces. She has stopped beating her legs against the footrest, and she holds Library up toward me like a tithe.

"I'm fine, sweeting," I tell her. "Though I thank you for the offer."

"Ma, Ma, Ma?" Pip leans over and kisses the much-abused plush lion on the head. "Yah," Alis approves, and returns to babbling contentedly to the toy, to the sidewalk, to the people passing by, and the small birds that flit between the trees that line the main avenue, searching the snow for crumbs.

"Oh," Pip says, as we reach a corner crossing. "Actually, can we cut left? I just want to pop into the thrift shop to see if they've got a playpen in."

"We have a playpen."

"Yeah, but I thought it would be nice to leave one in my parents' car."

"They already have one, as well."

"Well, yeah, but if there's a spare in their trunk, then they don't have to take down—"

"*Bao bei*," I interrupt. The crossing signal comes on, and I start to cross, not turning where Pip has requested.

"Syth!" Pip protests, but follows Alis and I across the street.

"Pip," I rejoinder. "We do not need a third playpen between us, any more than we need to keep a spare bag of Alis's diapers and things in their trunk, as you suggested last week."

"I just thought that—"

"That it would be prudent to turn your parents' car into a bug-out-bag on wheels?"

Pip stops walking when we reach the far sidewalk and stares up at me, mouth agape. After a moment where I can see that she is thinking at a rapid pace, analyzing all that we have discussed, she blinks and says, "I didn't know you knew that term."

I level an unimpressed glance at my wife. "Honestly, Pip," I say gently, scoffing a little to keep the conversation light, teasing.

"I... I just..." She shakes her head, hard, and takes my hand again, nudging us back into motion. Pip chews on her thoughts for another block, and I leave her to her silence, answering Alis whenever our daughter pauses in her banter long enough to indicate that she desires my input on her monologue.

Finally, Pip lets out a long sigh. "I guess I *have* been trying to build a bug-out-bag."

"You have," I say. "And what I would like to know is why. Why are we buying doubles of things Alis already possesses? What purpose is it to leave them with Martin and Mei Fan? Pip, you worry me. The training, the running, the long sessions with your therapist, and now this? You wish me to spar and retrain and... Pip, what has you so frightened that you would have us prepare for *war?*"

Pip looks up at my face, her expression morphing from introspective worry to stunned shock. "You mean, you don't *know?*"

"Know what?" I ask, letting my wife choose her words, letting the line on which she dangles play out so that the hook buried in her logic does not tug and harm. If she comes to it on her own, perhaps we can discuss her behavior without any of the shouting I fear might otherwise accompany it.

Because I can well guess where the source of Pip's unease lies. And if she knows that I have been aware of it since the start, and have said nothing, have done nothing about it—at least in her view—she may accuse me of being uncaring. I am not uncaring. I have been vigilant with my scans of the Internet, in assessing the world's news, in playing out the scenarios in my mind.

But there is no *proof* that anything is going awry in

the Overrealm, and as much as I respect my wife's very understandable paranoia, I also do not want to feed it without irrefutable evidence. I had hoped that perhaps she would work herself through this period of frenzied activity and frenetic worry on her own, before we had to confront it head-on, but it seems I had hoped in vain.

"Well... that these things come in threes." She does not clarify what she means by "these things." She does not need to.

"I am not unaware," I say slowly. "But I also refuse to live my life looking over my shoulder. I will admit that I am usually the first to believe in the worst, to prepare for it, to fear it. But... Pip, my darling, this is not a book. We are in the Overrealm, where endings do not tie up neatly and the story goes on beyond Happily Ever After."

"But the—"

"I know," I say, and kiss her knuckles again. "I know, and do not think that I am not preparing on my end. I have laid contingencies into every computer program I write. But it could also be nothing."

"I just get this *feeling* that the... the thread holding up the sword is going to snap."

"I understand. But shall we live all our lives in the shadow of a cramped shield?"

"And the *trilogies*," Pip says, and there is a bit of desperation in her tone. She seizes my gloved hand tightly.

I don't want to tell my wife that I worry she is over-thinking things. After all, only a few months ago, it was I who was paranoid, and worried, and afraid that my spouse thought I was turning mad. I will not dismiss her fears lightly.

Instead, I kiss her hand a third time. "If I promise to resume my exercises with the sword, will that appease you?"

Pip nods tightly.

"Very well. I shall. And you must promise me that, until we are certain something big and awful is actually coming for us, that we will fill Alis's life with joy and comfort, and try to keep a happiness between us?"

Pip puffs out another sigh, and nods again. But I am not appeased. She is agreeing too easily.

I am about to say as much when Pip stops dead on the street, eyes going wide and shoulders locking up. Hastily, I pull us off to the side, next to a large concrete planter box topped with gray slush. Pip stumbles, head rolling back on her neck, and I have just enough time to snap the locks on the wheels of Alis's stroller before Pip falls and I catch her, keep her from striking her head on the concrete planter.

"Hey, man, is she having a seizure?" someone behind us asks. "Do you want some help?"

"I... I d-d-don't..." I reply, sudden terror gripping the root of my tongue, fisting in my throat, making it hard to breathe. The suddenness of Pip's fit has blindsided me, and I am frozen with shocked indecision.

"Hey, it's okay," the someone says, and a young black man, perhaps the age of Pip's students, appears in my line of sight. "Here, lay her down here. You can use my hoodie." He shoulders out of his down jacket, strips off the garment in question, slips his jacket back on, then bundles his hoodie up under Pip's head. My wife gasps and jerks when he touches the middle of her back, cringing away from him, and I manage to croak:

"On h-her s-si-side."

We bracket Pip between us on the dirty, puddly sidewalk, keeping her safe but—the young man advises me as he checks his watch—not holding her down. Melting snow seeps into the knees of my trousers, crawling chilly across my calves. "If this goes on for more than five minutes, we should call 911."

"I... I d-d-don't—" I manage to say again. Alis makes a sort of distressed noise and shouts, "*Bu, da, bu!*" An Asian woman, perhaps Mei Fan's age, is standing by Alis's stroller, keeping her body between it and the street. Guarding my baby, I realize.

"*Nǐ hái hǎo,*" the woman murmurs to Alis over and over again. My Mandarin is still new, but it sounds as if the woman is trying to soothe.

"No!" Alis shouts, having none of it, reaching out with grasping fingers toward her mother. She only uses the English word for no when she is really insistent. "Ma!"

"All w-wuh-will bewuh-well, swe-sweeting," I reassure her, reaching up to grasp Alis's hand in mine, keeping my other on Pip's shoulder as she jerks and twitches on the sidewalk. I hope desperately that I am not lying.

All at once, Pip goes lax, a puppet whose strings have been cut suddenly. The young man sits back on his heels, nodding to himself as he checks his watch again.

"Two minutes forty seconds," he says. "Average for a grand mal."

"I... I b-beg par-pardon, I don't kno-know what th-that—" I cut myself off when the young man looks up at me, eyebrows furrowed.

"Was this her first seizure?" he asks, deeply concerned. "You should take her to the hospital, or at least your family doctor, as soon as you can."

"I... I wi-will do s-so, ye-yes," I tell the man, shaken to the core by the thought that while Pip and I have spent the last two years fighting off magic and monsters and terrible archvillains, something like *this*, some secret horror, something I cannot *fight*, may have been lurking inside of her.

Between us, Pip groans and grabs my shoulder hard to lever herself up to sitting. Her whole side is wet with sandy snow, and it breaks my heart to have to release Alis's hand to help Pip. Our daughter howls. Pip blinks around, clearly wondering how she got on the ground, her eyes hollow-looking and her lips pinched.

"Slowly, now," the young man says. He wipes grit off his palms. "You've had a seizure. But you're safe. You're fine."

"Alis?" Pip asks.

"Safe also," I promise, glancing up at the woman pulling faces at Alis in a futile effort to distract her.

"Listen, let me get you guys a cab," the young man says as he helps us to stand. Pip perches on the edge of the planter box, and curls down over the stroller so Alis can hug her head and babble reassurance in her English-Mandarin mash-up baby talk. "You should let her rest."

"That isn't necessary—" I begin, not because I am offended by his charity, but because I am wrong-footed by his gallantry. It is *my* duty to take care of my family, not a stranger on the street's. The lad retrieves his hoodie and shakes it out. It's sopping and filthy, but he just drapes it over his shoulder, unconcerned.

My mind is whirling, connections coming together, clues niggling at me. My head seems to be spinning as I grasp for the answer to a question I didn't even realize I would have to puzzle out when I stepped out of the house an hour ago.

What has just happened? *Why?* And how could I let it? Is it something I could have prevented? Was there some sign I had missed?

Oh, stupid, foolish Forsyth. Blind and never enough.

"My brother gets seizures. It's fine," the young man offers. His dark eyes are wide and sincere, and I am struck with an intense, longing homesickness for my nephew, Wyndam. "It's scary, I get it, but you're okay now. I know she's going to want to be somewhere alone and quiet for a while. Where are you headed?"

"Up by Beacon Hill Park," I confess, brain whirling.

The young man nods and types something into his smartphone. "All right, the car will be here in about ten minutes."

"Allow me to-to—" I try, fumbling for my pocket, and my wallet, but the young man shakes his head and pats my arm, brotherly, reassuring.

"Naw man, on me," he says. "Just get home safe, okay?"

"I, yes. Thank you," I mutter. And then the young man is on his way down the street, a gallant knight with an urban swagger.

"Do you want me to wait with you?" the woman by the stroller offers. She's now standing to the side, just watching as Alis and Pip reassure one another.

Pip peeks up at me over her arm and shakes her head subtly.

"No," I say, trusting her lead. "But thank you."

"All right. Be safe," the woman says, and then she too disappears into the foot traffic of the street around us.

I place my hand gently on the small of Pip's back, meaning to reassure, and she gasps and jerks again. I remove it immediately, concern swirling up.

"Pip?" I ask, but say nothing further, giving her space to decide when and how to answer me. What I can see of her face is ashen, pinched, and creased with the aftermath of pain.

"It wasn't a seizure," Pip eventually whispers.

"How do you know?" I ask, just as softly.

Pip turns wet eyes to me, and tries to grin, but she can't. "I... I just... I just know," she says with a finality that makes it clear that further prying into that particular topic would not be welcome just now.

"Pip," I ask. "What are you not telling me? Now you're having fits on the street alongside your preparations for war?"

"I..." Pip says, and then hesitates. I look down at her, and am surprised to see that her face is buried in her scarf, her lashes fanned against her cheeks. "I've been... I've been having dreams." She says it softly, like a confession, like a fear.

"Dreams of what?" I slide my fingers between hers.

"Indistinct things. At first, I thought it was, you know, memories of... of then."

Ah, things begin to make sense. "Hence the increased sessions with your therapist."

"Yeah."

"Yah, yah, yah!" Alis says, clearly determined to be a part of the conversation. Her head is thrown to the side, her little Sheil-purple toque scrunched against the back of the pushchair, her gray eyes watching us with careful intelligence.

"What are the dreams like?"

"Pain," Pip says bluntly. "At first, the... you know, the cutting and the carving, but then the itch and pull of the healing, and now they're... I don't know. Not tingling. Not scratching. It's under my skin, and in it, and on it, and... I can't seem to get any relief from it. I wake up and want to go roll in a bath of ice. I work myself to death at the gym so I'm exhausted enough to sleep through it."

I tug my wife close against my side, careful to keep my arm up on her shoulders, and she presses the side of her face into my coat to hear my heartbeat.

"I have not noticed."

Pip peers up at me, suspicious. "You never 'not notice' anything."

"What else?" I croak, my joints stiffening with the chill of the cement under us, the breeze around us, and the fear crawling up my spine.

"Green," Pip says softly. "Green flame, or... or acid... or maybe... magic?"

I suck in a surprised breath, and Alis stills, watching us with fearful, wide eyes, sensing the unsettled feelings that have dropped over her parents like a cloak of morning fog.

"But it's occurred to me," Pip presses on. "What if they're not memories?"

"What else would they be?" I ask, and this time, it is a real question instead of a leading one, because if they are not memories, I do not know what her dreams of blood and pain and green flame might otherwise be.

"Magic doesn't exist in the Overrealm," Pip says, but it is like a mantra.

"Correct," I say. "We tried it all when I first arrived. Every Word in my mind, every spell I know, every rune and potion. Nothing worked."

Pip twists our joined fingers, fidgeting. "I've been thinking... what would happen to creatures of magic, though?" she says. "What if, I don't know, let's say Capplederry or Bradri came into the Overrealm?"

"'derry!" Alis shouts, looking around her in delight. "'derry!"

The Library Lion does not appear, however, and Alis kicks her feet and howls, angry at us for bringing up her companion if the creature is not here. She shoves her plush lion toy into her mouth defiantly, mulishly. Her glare reminds me of Wyndam's, dark and betrayed.

"Would they die?" Pip asks. "Would they fall apart, or crumble, or...?"

"Or would they live?"

"Could a creature of magic bring magic to the Overrealm?" Pip asks, voice tremulous.

"*Bao bei*," I say softly. "Reader though you may be, I

do not think that you qualify as magical."

"But there is magic carved on my bones."

"They are just pictures now," I say. "No more potent than the herb soups my spells become, or the Words that cannot be Spoken here. They are meaningless."

"Are they? Are you sure?" Pip asks, pleading, folding my hands between hers.

I am not sure. How can I be? It is not as if my Writer knows for sure. He may be the inventor of our systems of magic, but its evolution has clearly outstripped even his knowledge of its workings.

"We have tested everything—" I repeat, meaning to reassure her. To reassure us both.

"How recently?" Pip interrupts. Her dark eyes are wide, pleading.

"Shall I try now?"

"Yes!"

I take a moment to think, and then decide to attempt a Word. Not wanting to cause any kind of commotion on a busy Saturday evening sidewalk in downtown Victoria if it is successful—and I have my doubts that it will be—I decide upon a Word of Sleeping. Alis is over-stimulated, and would benefit from a nap, anyway.

I take a deep, calming breath, and Speak.

Though the fog of my breath rises in the evening air, the Word strangles in the open, as do all Words in this realm. It is dead before the breath used to form it has truly left me.

Except...

I gasp, a hand flying to my lips. For just before it puffed out of existence, the Word spluttered and sparked, and left a very mild tingling against my flesh.

Pip freezes. Below me, Alis yawns dramatically, show-ing off her few pearly teeth. She rubs her hands against her eyes. Then she blinks, and frowns up at me, as if she is entirely aware that her newfound sleepiness is my fault and that she does not approve of it in the least.

"No," I breathe, and say the Word again, staring hard at Alis. My child just blinks back up at me, annoyed now.

"Da," she says reproachfully, and then looks away, back down to Library to babble to the stuffie about how exasperating her parents are.

"That had to be a coincidence," I say. "A coincidence and static shock."

"The universe is rarely so lazy," Pip says cautiously. She reaches out and touches my bottom lip, but no electricity arcs between our flesh.

When the cab arrives, we bundle Alis and ourselves into it slowly. We move like creaking, gouty old warriors who are in no fit condition for yet another war. Warriors who know that, despite that, we may very well be called upon again, very soon.

THREE

ELGAR

lgar sleeps poorly, his stomach empty and his ears open for any creaks or thumps that don't belong in the normal nighttime symphony of his house. When he finally drifts off, Linux wakes him almost immediately with a pitiful request for the breakfast Elgar doesn't usually feed him for another few hours. The cat is so insistent that Elgar gives up and gets out of bed. He feels silly for fearing his own cupboards and appliances, but fear them he does. So he creeps into the kitchen slowly, eyes wide, watching every shadow and corner for motion.

The only living creatures seem to be him and his cat, though. So Linux gets his breakfast, but Elgar can't bring himself to open his fridge. Breakfast out it will be, then. He hasn't been to the diner up the street in months, and it's about time he popped back in for those incredible eggs Benny, anyway. On his way past his office, he grabs a notepad and pen, just in case he's struck with an idea to...

Oh. No.

He places them back on the desk slowly, carefully.

No. No writing. He isn't... it isn't a good idea. Not... yet. Not now.

It's drizzling when he steps outside, the sort of cold, gray stuff that isn't completely snow, but isn't completely rain, either. He scrunches into his coat, chin buried in his beard to ward against the chill. The grocery store is between his house and the diner, and it isn't until he's just passing the empty bench outside the entrance that he vividly recalls the stranger in black. The man's glare could have rivaled a basilisk.

And yet, beyond that, Elgar can barely remember what he looks like.

Elgar's head whips around as he searches the sparse early-morning commuter crowd shuffling for the bus stop, his heart hammering suddenly against the back of his ribs. But the man in black is nowhere in sight.

Elgar swallows hard, feeling like a big fat fool, and shuffles along with the rest of the sleep-deprived zombies to the diner. He scopes the place out from the entryway, trying to be as casual about it as possible. Clear. He takes a seat at a table that gives him a good view of both the room and the door. It isn't his usual booth—he prefers the one nearest the warmth and genial noise of the kitchen, with the outlet under the table—but he feels safer here, less exposed.

Maddie, the morning waitress, gives him a funny look, but bustles over with a fresh cup and the pot of coffee all the same.

"You're up early," she says, pouring out the liquid heaven. Elgar flashes her his most winning, most flirtatious smile, the one that all the young readers like Maddie love, and the corners of her lips tighten back in response. "No laptop today?"

"No," he says, taking a gulp of the steaming coffee to keep from having to say more.

He's lucky that he has Lucy and Forsyth, because now he has someone to discuss his news with who isn't just Juan. He isn't as tempted to drop as many hints to Maddie as he used to, when she was the only other person who saw him writing.

He wonders if she misses those hints. Obviously, she's

read his books—he's never met anyone who hasn't—and perhaps she even has one of those websites where she shares everything he's said to her. Another author told him about that; that there were fans who would eavesdrop and try to recreate conversations from their favorite authors on message boards so they could get the scoop on new projects or leak spoilers. It's both weirdly stalkery and, at the same time, actually kind of flattering.

"Same order?" Maddie asks, already half-turned away.

Elgar just nods, his mouth scorched from the coffee. He swallows again to try to get some saliva running over the burns.

Maddie leaves him to his solitude, and he realizes he hasn't brought a magazine, or a book, or newspaper, or anything with him. Usually, he has either his laptop or his notepad, but now, with nothing to read, all he can do, all he is doing, is *think*.

And possibly, just maybe, that's a bad thing.

Although, it's also possible that it could be a good thing.

Because... because maybe Juan was right.

Maybe Elgar isn't getting enough sleep. Maybe he's stressed out. Maybe he's feeling really guilty for not writing anything new. Maybe he's feeling bad about freaking out his agent. Maybe he's too involved and worried about the TV show. Maybe he's focusing too much on being on his best behavior around Forsyth and Lucy. Maybe he's... maybe it was all in his head.

He's a creator. He has a powerful imagination.

So... so maybe his powerful imagination had gotten away from him?

It's possible.

The man in black could be anybody. His glare of hatred didn't have to be aimed at Elgar. It could have been for someone behind Elgar. It could have been resting bitch-face. And a story is just a story in his head.

Except when it isn't.

Elgar scrubs his face and sighs, trying to get his brain to quiet the hell down. He takes his last gulp of coffee. The caffeine isn't helping his out-of-control brain, but the soothing warmth is something. Maddie is right there again with the pot, and he sends her another smile, this one more genuine, and perhaps just a bit watery.

"I hope you don't mind me saying so," she says, slipping onto the bench opposite him, "but you kinda look like hell."

Elgar snorts. "I kinda feel like it."

"How's the writing coming?" she asks, folding her arms over the table. She's in her mid-twenties, and Elgar can't remember if she'd told him she was studying psychology or physiotherapy, but with the way she's encouraging him to talk, he's starting to think it's the head-shrinking.

"Ah, all done," he says, not really in the mood to have this conversation again so soon. "Just some line edits left, I think. But I, you know... it's not that."

"It's just that you don't have your laptop. Or your notebook."

"Yeah."

"So, where are they?"

Elgar sits back, eyes narrowed, a nibble of worry starting to make itself known. "Why do you want to know...?"

Maddie blinks, shakes her head, and blinks again. Her grin gets wider, more natural, which startles him into realizing that her earlier smiles had been tight, and false, her gaze a bit unfocused and faraway. "Oh, no reason. They just seem to make you happy, is all. And you look miserable."

"I think they'd just make me more miserable right

now, to be honest," Elgar says.

"Fair enough," Maddie replies, chipper. She takes a breath to say more, clearly intends to do so, but the chime of the bell on the kitchen windowsill cuts her off. She grimaces and straightens. She's the only waitress right now. "Be right back."

She has his eggs Benedict in front of him in a jiffy, refills his coffee for the third time, and is then called into the back by the line cook. Just before she goes through the double doors, she looks back at him over her shoulder.

Maybe it's his overactive imagination again, or maybe it's the crappy lighting, but for a split second, it looks like Maddie's normally blue eyes are bright green.

FORSYTH

That night, I roll over and ask, into the quiet darkness of our bedroom: "Pip? Do you sleep?"

"'M awake," she mumbles, and it is not entirely convincing. She turns her face into the pillow, an endearing trait that she doesn't know she has. It means that she is just asleep enough that she wants to remain that way, and is pretending that she does not hear me.

Good. I want her to be asleep.

She shuffles and shifts until her arms are beneath the pillows, and she is fully belly down, head craned to the side in a way that she assures me is actually quite comfortable. She looks, in short, as vulnerable as she had been when I first met her, laid out like this in my mother's bed in Turn Hall.

A wave of tenderness stirs and sweeps across me. I love this woman fiercely. I am so happy to be able to call her mine, and to have a daughter that is proof of our love for one another, moreover. I should like to keep them. Forever.

And I shall do whatever it takes.

Slowly, gently, I slide my hand underneath the t-shirt Pip has worn to bed. My fingers skim over the now familiar network of thin, raised scars on her back. The original circumstances of the injury are now slightly more than three years past, and Pip is not unaware of the exotic attractiveness of the artistically swirling pattern that was carved into her flesh, though she does not flaunt it, either. She has ceased to wear tank tops in public, and has purchased a high-backed swimsuit, but is comfortable wearing low-backed dresses when they show the raised ivy to good effect. Many people mistake the scars for an elaborate tattoo. Pip does not correct them.

Under my hand, her flesh is sleep-warm, but not hot to the touch, or feverish. I slide her shirt up, ducking under the covers so that the cool air of our room will not wake her. Beneath the duvet, everything is dark. The scars do not glow green as they do in the presence of the Viceroy's malicious influence, nor are they moving and shifting. All looks normal.

Normal. Frustratingly, infuriatingly normal.

I speak a Word of Light, but nothing sparks against my lips. The room stays dark, and quiet, and cool. Nothing happens.

I cannot tell if my annoyance is rooted in the fact that nothing is out of order. Would I have been more relieved or more scared if the vines were glowing, if Wordlight had filled the room? It would have at least been a clue.

Pip would not tell me what she felt during her fit on the sidewalk, save for repeating that she was fine and that it was something different from a seizure. I looked up symptoms for exhaustion and hypertension, and while some of Pip's experience fits, it is not perfect.

Pip fears, and so she prepares. But for what? Does she keep something from me? No, she wouldn't do so without good reason. We do not have secrets, not of those sort. So then, what is it?

Huffing a frustrated sigh, I wriggle back up the bed, smooth Pip's t-shirt back down, and cuddle up behind my wife. Pip turns onto her side in her sleep, shifting back into my embrace. The tension lines around her eyes smooth out, and she takes a deep breath, releases it, takes another. Whatever ill dreams had begun, hopefully my touch has banished them.

"Sweet dreams," I murmur into her hair, and it is more of a wish than usual. I kiss the leaf-shaped scar on the nape of her neck, and close my eyes, hoping for sweet dreams of my own.

I will not bet on them, however.

I am a character Written to be physically uncomfortable and mentally troubled until I have all the answers, and right now, I have none. There is literally no worse feeling in the world for me, emotionally, intellectually, physically, than being *useless*.

Alis has a better morning than the ones previous. Two of her three new teeth have finally erupted, and while the third still hurts, the degree of the pain is clearly tolerable enough that she is merely sitting listlessly in her highchair, frowning powerfully at her da as he struggles with the coffee maker in his pre-caffeinated state. She has a foil pouch of fruit mush, and her expression makes it clear that she is accepting this as breakfast on sufferance.

I try not to stare at the carafe with the single-minded hunger of a troll lusting after goat flesh. It's a challenge. For reasons that I don't understand, Fridays are always the hardest on me. Perhaps it is because I have already had five days of being unable to sleep in, and am looking forward to the weekend. We did not have work-weeks and weekends in Hain, and even after two years here, I am unused to this sleep- and work-schedule. The fluctuation always flummoxes me.

Upstairs, I hear my wife shut the bedroom door, and make her way to the stairs. Her briefcase is already hanging by its strap off the hook on the back of our front door. She has gotten into the habit of repacking it every night before bed and placing it there so that, in her own pre-caffeinated state, she does not forget to take it with her when she leaves. Which has happened. More than once.

When she comes down, however, her gym bag is slung over her shoulder. Pip doesn't work out on Fridays. She never has. And yet, there is the bag. Worry creeps up my skin, resting like an itch I cannot scratch between my shoulder blades. She drops her gym bag by the door and joins us.

"Mmmm, nectar of the gods," Pip whispers into my ear and cranes up to kiss my neck as she wraps her arms around my waist from behind. "Morning, Freckles."

Because I love Lucy Turn Piper, I pour the first mug of coffee and hand it to her. But only because I love her. I resume watching the carafe hungrily, waiting for enough coffee to drip into it to justify taking another cup as she pads away to sit beside Alis.

"Morning, baby girl," Pip says.

"Ma," Alis says, holding out her foil packet to demonstrate just how dissatisfied she is with this morning's offering.

"Tragic," Pip agrees, and sips her coffee again.

When I have coffee of my own, I sit at the other chair, on the other side of Alis. Pip reaches across the tabletop and squeezes my arm gently.

"I'm going to be home a bit later than usual to-night," she says.

"I see that," I reply, unsure what sort of opening this gives me. Do I ask her why? Do I try to allay her fears? Do I tell her that her paranoia is starting to affect me, as well? "You look as if you got some real sleep last night," I say instead. Coward.

"I do feel better than yesterday," Pip admits. "With the party tonight, I'm glad I got some real rest. I should."

Ah, right, yes. Tonight is the celebration that Martin, Mei Fan, and *wai po* are holding to celebrate Alis's first birthday. In my morning fog, I had forgotten. "We should leave for their house no later than four," I remind Pip. "Will that give you enough time to work out?"

"My last class is at noon. I'm good." She kisses me on the cheek, pulls an apple from the basket on the counter, and puts her empty cup in the sink. She kisses Alis's forehead on her way to the door, and leaves, walking as if she's in a trance.

"Ma?" Alis asks, watching the door close behind Pip. Her brow is furrowed, fruit mush on her cheek that Pip didn't even try to wipe away.

"I agree, sweeting," I tell Alis. "I don't like it, either."

Several hours later finds both of us in my office. Alis has long since gotten bored of sitting on her da's lap banging away at her own toy keyboard and has fallen asleep in the playpen in the corner. How blessed are morning naps. They allow me to focus.

Today, I am focusing on my coding. Like Mandarin, the language of hacking and instructing computers is new to me. "Scarily clever sponge" though I may be, as my wife insists, even I must pay attention when I am working in a language that is new to me. Well, new-ish.

I'm not entirely certain what I'm looking for yet. I

create a program that will scan through the millions of news stories and social media posts on the Internet and flag anything that seems, well, *magical*. Or unexplainable. Or miraculous. Or just downright weird. I set the starting date for the day that Elgar's typewriter vanished—which aligns with the date, a week after Sosticetide, when Pip, Alis, and I were sucked back into the world of *The Tales of Kintyre Turn*, and then spat back out again eight Overrealm hours later. I make a point of flagging yesterday evening as a potential time to compare triggers, highlighting the moment of Pip's not-a-seizure.

From there, I should be able to scan the returned stories and see if there is any sort of pattern, any sort of... well, *anything*. I hate being passive and waiting for the information to come to me when I itch so for the truth. But I am well practiced in it. It always took weeks for my Shadow's Men to return information to me. This program, at least, will do so in a matter of hours.

As I set it into motion, I wonder if I should give it a clever name, the way they do in the movies. Perhaps Finnar, who was my chief leg-work man when I still wore the mask.

Apt, I muse.

With Finnar running all over the web, I push back from my desk. The squeak of my chair wheels wakes Alis, who snuffles and pulls herself upright by the side of the playpen. Though she is advanced in the realm of communication for one her age—her handful of words tops out at about twelve now, in both English and Mandarin—she has yet to master "hungry." Instead, she scowls miserably at me, red-cheeked and flushed, and sucks at the air with her pursed lips.

"Yes, of course, sweeting," I say, and fetch her up. She rolls her forehead against my shoulder and heaves a put-upon sigh. "What do you think? Hard-boiled eggs, perhaps some of that purple applesauce?"

"*Năi*," Alis says.

"*Niúnăi*," I correct. "Yes, you can have some milk, too, if you like."

We have just reached the kitchen when my pocket begins to vibrate.

Alis knows what it means when my smartphone plays a fife-and-fiddle tune. It is a piece that Elgar Reed sent to me. He told me that I was not allowed to share it with anyone, asked my opinion of the arrangement and how accurate it was to the songs I knew from my youth, and then promptly made it my ringtone for his number the next time we got together.

So much for secrecy. *Ridiculous man*, I had thought at the time. But I do appreciate knowing it is him before I answer the phone. Though this time, Elgar's call worries me. Perhaps it is disingenuous of me to pretend that all is right, and that his fears are for naught, but until I know more, I do not see the point in inciting a panic in my creator. More than once, I've wished I had a surveillance camera installed inside his home.

Alis, overjoyed by the sound of the phone, shouts, "Gar Gar!"

"Hello?" I answer.

ELGAR

His stomach aches from bolting his breakfast, so he nearly doesn't see the stranger in black until he's practically standing beside him. The sinkhole of unmoving shadow registers in the corner of his eye at the last second, and Elgar feels the sidewalk drop away as soon as the man is fully in his sight line. The sun has come out, working hard at evaporating the last of the slushy rain on the pavement, but somehow, the man seems to suck even that light up, like a black hole.

Elgar debates stopping, or turning on his heel and going home another way, or maybe even crossing the street to avoid this sinkhole of shadow. In the end, he tucks his chin under his scarf, pulls his cap down on his forehead, and stares at the ground as he scuttles by like a nervous crab. The intense feeling of being watched, of being *stared through*, surges up. With his eyes down, he notices, somewhat distantly and with no little bit of hysteria, that the stranger in black is wearing women's boots. They're knee-high, leather, with a low wedge heel and a lot of Gothy hardware and zippers. It's an incongruent detail. It almost makes him freeze and stare.

Almost.

He takes the long route home, looking back over his shoulder—for what, he isn't sure. He adds a bunch of extra turns before coming in through his back gate and into the kitchen from the garden. He feels so damn foolish for doing it, but it makes something in him feel safer, more relaxed... more... yeah, okay, crazy is what it actually is. Totally bonkers. Mental. Insane.

A strange man in black with women's boots and a waitress whose eyes are maybe supposed to be blue. An assistant who thinks he's been doing drugs. A fear of his own damn job. A worry that his own cleverness is starting to bite him in the ass. And a fictional character he calls his cousin, but thinks of as a son.

His life is mad.

Or *he* is.

"Forsyth," he says aloud. "I gotta talk to Forsyth." He sheds his outerwear and checks on Linux, who's napping peacefully in front of the cold fireplace in his living room. Elgar gets out his phone, turns on the fire, and settles on the sofa. He rubs his stomach to get rid of the cramps as the phone rings, and then Linux's back when the cat crawls onto his lap and stretches his head up to tuck it against the side of Elgar's beard.

The soft rumble of the cat's purrs is soothing. It helps to ground him.

"Hello?" Forsyth says on the other end of the line. "Well, this is a surprise. You don't usually call so early. To what do we owe the honor?"

Elgar looks at the clock on the mantel. It reads five after eleven. That is early for him. Usually, he's just making his first pot of coffee at this time. He's a night-writer, so he generally doesn't go to sleep until the wee smalls, or wake until ten in the morning at the earliest.

"I... I don't know. A friendly voice?" Elgar says, feeling small and slightly silly when he realizes he has no way of explaining what, exactly, it is that's unnerving him. He doesn't want to admit that it might just be his own imagination working against him.

"No," Forsyth says kindly. Right. Elgar had written Forsyth Turn to be a regular Sherlock Holmes of the fantasy realm. "Elgar. The truth, please."

"Were you the only ones who came through?" Elgar blurts.

"I beg pardon, I don't... ah," Forsyth says, after figuring out which track Elgar's train of thought is traveling. "I see. Something has happened that makes you question if we were lying to you when we said it was just the three of us."

"Not lying," Elgar says hastily. "Just... I don't know. There's been some freaky stuff happening, and I can't explain it. There's the typewriter—"

"Yes."

"And there was... god, now that I'm saying it out loud, it sounds stupid."

"Tell me, anyway."

Elgar regales him with the horror of the salad, Linux's strange reaction to it, the man in black, and the odd behavior of Maddie. He tries not to embellish too much, the way his writerly brain likes; he struggles to just stick to the facts, the way Forsyth prefers.

"Hmm," Forsyth replies when Elgar has reached the end of the tale. Silence filters down from Canada for a moment, pregnant with thought. Elgar imagines Forsyth with his index finger on his chin, nail pressed into his bottom lip, the way he holds himself when he's thinking hard. He doesn't seem to realize it's a habit, either, and is always confused when Lucy mimics his thinking pose to tease.

"So, am I crazy?"

"I hesitate to say yes..." Forsyth says slowly. "But you must understand that we left those who would wish to do you harm powerless, and back in my realm. If there is a plot here, it is an entirely mundane one. And since what you have described to me seems to include the hallmarks of magic—"

"You think it's all in my head." Elgar deflates, rubbing down Linux's back, dejected.

"I did not say that."

"But you implied it heavily."

"Elgar—"

"Okay, maybe I am stressed out. And maybe I'm paranoid about my missing typewriter. I'm paranoid that somebody is going to try leaking the scripts, and *Shuttleborn* is out in like six months. And the marketing is just starting to go into drive, and I'm already bonkers, and I don't know how I did this when I was younger, except clearly, I was younger, and maybe I'm not sleeping as much as I should be?"

"Perhaps."

Elgar sighs. "Okay. Thanks for listening, anyway."

"Both my duty, and my pleasure," Forsyth says, and then, "Hmm? What's that sweeting? Hold on a moment, let your da... Alis!"

There's a bit of a thump and shuffle, which sounds like a phone being dropped, and then a sweet, high voice says, "Gar?"

"Hello, darling," Elgar says, trying to infuse his voice with warmth, disguise his fatigue and worry with false smiles. "How are you today, Alis?"

"Gar Gar, hi-hi!" Alis babbles, sounding natural and bright. She had five teeth when Elgar saw her last, and he can imagine how they look as she grins at the phone. "Frog 'issess 'ook Bev 'ook Dah Bev!"

"Is that so?" Elgar replies.

There's a click, and her voice goes hollow in the way that means Forsyth turned on the speakerphone. "Yah, yah, yah!"

"Yes, sweeting," Elgar hears Forsyth correct her. "We absolutely did watch *The Princess and the Frog* yesterday, but against your firm insistence, your Uncle Bevel did not, in fact, write every story that you enjoy."

"Yah!" Alis says back, stubborn in her refusal to change the way she says the first word Bevel taught her.

"Oh dear," Forsyth says with a theatrical sigh. "Such a battle."

Elgar laughs at his dramatic despair, and it feels good. The laughter dissolves some of the worry, makes him feel lighter, more alert. Linux grumbles and butts Elgar's chin with his head, disapproving of the way his chuckles bounce the generous stomach on which he's perched.

"Sounds like she's getting to be more of a handful."

"And I am delighted daily," Forsyth says over more of Alis's thoughtful, introspective babble.

"Frog 'isses! Rib, rib, iiiib!" Alis calls from beside

the phone, and there is a smooching sound. "You, you!" she says next, which is followed by a bigger smooching sound.

"What was that?"

"Apparently, we were both frogs that needed kissing to turn us into princes."

Elgar snorts, and more of the frustration and fear floats away in the wake of the warmth the sweet, domestic image paints for him. "I can't imagine you as a prince."

"Absolutely not," Forsyth agrees. "I haven't the ego for it, nor the legs for the stockings. And I am terrible at flattering the stupid."

"And you'd never—" Elgar begins, but cuts himself off.

"I never?"

Even after a year, Elgar's reflex is still to say something disparaging about Forsyth not being charming or handsome enough. He snaps his teeth down on the insult just in time. Sometimes, it's hard to remember that Forsyth is real, and not the man he could make cutting remarks about with Kintyre and Bevel for fun. Elgar has gotten a lot of comic relief at Forsyth's expense over the last three decades, which leaves him feeling faintly ashamed when he banters with the man now. And he certainly isn't going to be cruel to his face.

"I was going to say you'd nail the politics, but you'd be too honest with the ambassadors," Elgar lies. And Forsyth laughs like he knows, anyway, that that wasn't what Elgar was going to say, which makes Elgar feel about six inches high. "Sorry."

Elgar can practically hear Forsyth rolling his eyes. It's a very young gesture for a new father and a Shadow Hand, Elgar thinks. But he'd written the character to be bratty and insolent when he was first introduced, and it seems some of those character traits had held on as he matured.

"Be nice, or I'll make the elite status of your travel points mysteriously disappear," Forsyth warns, but there's a glimmer of humor in his tone. "Really beleaguer me, and I'll put you on the no-fly list for the summer."

"You wouldn't!" Elgar gasps. "I have four cons! There's no way I'm doing that by train!"

Forsyth chuckles darkly, and it's a surprisingly evil laugh for such a good man.

"So, um... frog princes?" Elgar says lamely, when the silence between them has gotten a little too telling. Alis has moved on to banging something soft against the floor, punctuated by a plastic click. It must be Library, being used like a drumstick, the plushie's eyes snapping on the floor.

"Ah, we are at the 'pretending' stage of development, my app tells me," Forsyth says. "Alis is remarkably advanced when it comes to her language skills, but she has just now begun the important task of equating objects with their uses and playing make-believe. Ladyling Alis styled her mama's hair yesterday with the soft paddle brush. Didn't she? Yes, she did."

"Ma!" Alis says, imperious.

"Mama is at work, sweeting," Forsyth replies. "It's Da and Alis time right now."

"Gar Gar!"

"Yes, and Elgar as well. I suppose we're going to have to pick an honorific for you soon. Uncle?"

Elgar chuckles. "As long as Gar Gar doesn't become Jar Jar, I'm cool," he says. Secretly, he's hoping for "Grandpa." He tries to coach Alis into it whenever her parents leave them alone together, but that isn't often. And so far, Alis has gotten stalled on the G of the word, because it sounds like the second syllable of his name.

But, as Forsyth said, Alis is terribly clever when it comes to speech. Elgar's sure she'll get it soon.

"We'll work on it the next time you are able to—sweeting!" Forsyth calls, his voice suddenly across the room. "Please do not attempt to scale the stove. Writer, my heart." Elgar's own heart skips a beat, the way it does every time Forsyth utters that particular oath. Footsteps come closer to the phone. "I'm afraid this small monkey and I must bid you adieu, Elgar. Time for the park, I think, my dearest, where there are things to climb safely. She grows more like her Uncle Kintyre every day. I am certain I will expire of a stroke before her second birthday."

"Please don't," Elgar says, trying for lightness, but the desperate fear he feels at the thought of a world without Forsyth in it creeps into his tone. He gulps hard, swallowing back the honesty of the knee-jerk reaction a second time.

"Oh. Elgar. Please. Have no fear. I'm not going anywhere."

"You better not," Elgar grumbles, aiming for theatrical and perhaps coming across as more pouty than he wants. "If you go back into the books again, I'm going with you. You can't leave me here alone."

A soft gasp on the other side of the line makes it clear that he's hit maybe too close to the center of both of their secret fears.

"It is a promise," Forsyth says softly.

"Okay."

"Okay. Ah, wiggly glow-worm, hold still. Da will put you in your boots, and we shall go look for frogs before your birthday party. What do you say?"

"'Isses 'isses!" Alis demands.

"Perhaps not these particular frogs, sweeting," Forsyth cajoles.

"Birthday party?" Elgar asks, trying not to be hurt when he realizes that he hasn't been invited.

"It's all Pip's family and her parents' friends," Forsyth says. "Something big and Chinese. I'm not entirely certain. Ah. No worries. We have plans for cake and whatnot the next time you are up. We will not be excluding you from the celebrations."

"No, no. I know that," Elgar says, maybe more to remind himself than to reassure Forsyth.

"*Wai po* has some very specific ideas of how today is meant to go," Forsyth huffs, and it's the first time Elgar's ever heard him even hint at being impatient with the cross-cultural strain in their family. "But when you are next here, we will be celebrating Ladyling Alis's first birthday in true Hainish fashion."

"Oh!" Elgar says, suddenly delighted by the thought. "The stars thing?"

"The stars thing," Forsyth agrees smugly.

Elgar takes a deep breath and lets the excitement of that promised day overwrite his anxiety. "All right, I'll let you go. Thanks for, uh, you know... talking me down," Elgar says. "For being there, you know?"

"Any time," Forsyth says, and it's clear he's distracted by boots and a baby.

"Right, bye. Bye, Alis!"

"Bye, bye, bye!" Alis shouts back, and then Elgar ends the call.

"Well," Elgar says, setting down his phone, and stretching out along the sofa. Linux digs his claws in lightly as his pillow readjusts, then curls into a kitty-spiral on Elgar's chest. "Maybe everyone's right, and all I need is some sleep. What do you say, bud? Nap time, Linux?"

Linux purrs his agreement.

FORSYTH

Standing in the park later, hands in my pockets and face turned up to the watery sun, I sigh and rub my forehead. I can hear my own mother's voice in my memories, telling me not to wrinkle my face so, for it may remain that way should the wind change direction.

I cannot help the chuckle that escapes at the memory. Alis splashes gamely in a small mud puddle formed in the divot under the teeter-totter, utterly unconcerned with her da's clear distress.

"Liar," I call myself. "Nothing to worry about, indeed."

While Alis busies herself with toddling in circles around the play sets, I poke at my phone, and take a moment to update Finnar with expanded parameters: *Magically spoiled salads. Men in black. Diner waitresses with the wrong color eyes.*

FOUR

ELGAR

The rest of the day is dedicated firmly to the sin of sloth. Elgar naps, orders in Chinese, marathons a few episodes of a sci-fi show he's been neglecting, gets caught up on his geek news, and plays with Linux. That evening, he even lets Juan badger him into letting him make Elgar some kind of super healthy stew with kale in it, while his assistant narrates the Tale of the Interrupted Date and the Man Who Didn't Like Books.

Elgar sits on a kitchen stool as Juan moves deftly around him. He takes a moment to reflect on how his life has gotten to the surreal point where his assistant knows his kitchen better than he does.

"So, you did go back to the bar after?" Elgar asks as Juan chops almonds (almonds?) for the stew.

"I did. It would have been totes rude to do a runner, boss. Ghosting is *tres passe*."

"O-kay," Elgar says, not certain he knows what "ghosting" is outside of what he does to dead characters who still need to communicate vital information to his leads.

"And I'm glad I did," Juan continues, tilting his head just so, a sort of self-conscious little smirk rising against the corners of his lips, and... oh, he's smitten. Elgar thinks it's adorable, though he has no idea if that's the sort of thing he's allowed to say to a gay guy. "He told me later that he didn't realize I was way into reading, and he hadn't wanted to admit that he was a big fantasy nerd and put me off, and bam! There we go. Dream Man city. Of course, I didn't tell him who my boss was—NDA, natch—but he's super into the fact that I know a real live writer in the flesh."

Elgar chuckles. "Well, that's not creepy."

Juan laughs. "I'll keep home and work separated. No worries."

"Thanks." Elgar yawns and paws at his eyes. Naps always make him groggier. He doesn't know why he bothers with them. "I'm making coffee."

"Boss..."

Elgar levers himself off the stool and lumbers toward the pantry. "I know. It's after four. But I'm gonna fall asleep in your stew otherwise. And then how will we review the merchandising contracts after?"

"Fine," Juan grumbles. "But no sugar."

"Fine," Elgar says back. He pulls open the pantry door.

Something wet and warm plops onto his foot, and he jerks back, startled. For a second, he assumes it's cat vomit, but it's too red, and Linux had grown out of puking in fun places for Elgar to find a few years ago. "Eugh!"

He shakes the slimy glob off his toes, and it splatters against the open door.

"What's wrong—oh god!" Juan yelps.

Juan seizes his shoulders, and hauls Elgar backward. Elgar is too shocked to do anything but let him. Not that he wanted to stay next to... to... whatever that is in front of him.

The pantry, the whole inside of the pantry, is absolutely dripping with wet, red globs of flesh. Whip-thin, humid green vines weave between the slats of the shelves, the brown and green branches twisted around the wire as if the plant has grown there. There's too much foliage near the floor for Elgar to catch a glimpse of whether or not it had—which, of course, it can't have done, because there's no way any vine could have grown this big, this fast, without water and sunlight, in the five or six hours it's been since he'd last gone into his pantry for a package of microwave popcorn.

And that doesn't explain the... the... *reek*.

The whole kitchen stinks like a slaughterhouse, offal and blood mixed in a barnyard odor that clings like oil to the back of his throat. He coughs, trying to dislodge it, and covers his mouth and nose with the cuff of his cardigan.

The meat hangs from the branches in glistening strips, like rotten, hellish fruit. The flesh is red, globbed with the whitish-yellow honeycomb of fat and organs, and the skin on the underside is pale, and nearly hairless.

It looks... human. Panic squeezes Elgar's lungs, and for some absurd reason, all he can think of is Maddie—the waitress with the eyes that shouldn't be green; Lucy Piper, filleted by Bootknife; a world that he had created, whose magic systems are too perfect, and a villain who wanted his Author dead. The world around Elgar's head spins sharply and dips to the left, and he stumbles back, grips the counter hard. He can't breathe.

"What the actual fuck?" Juan hisses, his cell phone already in his hand. "Hello? Yes, I'd like to—Jesus, boss, don't get closer!—sorry, I'd like to report a... a break-in? I don't know, a violent crime? A threat? It looks like some serious black magic shit, okay? Someone jammed the closet full of dead stuff! I don't know, the skin is pink-ish, there's blood everywhere... yeah!" Juan gives Elgar's address, and then says, "Ten minutes, thank you." He disconnects the call, shoves his phone into his back pock-et, and comes over to where Elgar still stands, propped against the counter. "Come on, boss. Let's go into the living room."

Juan tugs on Elgar's shoulder, and Elgar lets his assistant back him out into the living room, eyes still glued to the mess in the pantry, dull horror creeping up his spine. The smell of raw meat and curdling blood is strong, stuck to the inside of his nose like paint fumes and pennies. He's torn between the twin urges to scream and puke, and clamps his teeth down hard on the tip of his tongue to keep from doing either.

"Where's Linux?" It's the first thing Elgar can manage to grind out around the bile lumping in the hollow of his throat. Juan shoves him down into the sofa and swears.

"I'll look for him, boss."

"Do you think—?"

"I'll look for him," Juan repeats with a bit more force, clearly trying to reassure himself as much as his employer.

Juan rushes upstairs, and Elgar pretends not to hear it when Juan slams the bathroom door and turns on the water to cover the sound of his own puking. Elgar's stomach cramps in sympathy and he burps, acrid and vile, and chews hard on his bottom lip to keep the rest down. He covers his face with shaking hands and resists the urge to call Forsyth and yell "I told you so!" down the line.

But the police are on their way, and Elgar doesn't want to be on the phone when they arrive. Especially to someone who prides himself on his anonymity, and whose livelihood and happiness depends on him *remaining* anonymous, unlooked at, secret. Forsyth has to appear to be bland, an overly intellectual house-husband and stay-at-home-dad who likes his books just a little too much, and stereotypically "manly" pursuits just a bit too little. His whole gig is built on people assuming that crumpled, cardigan-clad Syth Piper is the furthest thing from dangerous.

No. Elgar's seen enough police procedural TV shows to know that if he's on the phone with someone when the cops show up, they'll want to talk to that someone. He can't do that to Forsyth. Instead, Elgar plugs his nose, heaves himself to his feet, passes the kitchen, and goes down the hall to his office.

"*Black magic shit,*" Juan had said.

His laptop is where Elgar left it, and he immediately moves it to the filing cabinet, locking it in the same drawer as the fire-safe filled with external hard drives and papers. A small, fuzzy orange head pokes out of the end of the under-desk tunnel, and mrows pitifully at him.

"I found him!" Elgar calls, and reaches out to gently rub a finger up the bridge of Linux's wrinkled nose. The cat's ears are back, whiskers spread wide and pupils massive, the skin around his mouth pulled tight. He looks terrified.

Whatever it was that had come into their house and done... *that*, has scared the daylights out of the poor cat. Elgar is tempted to try to coax Linux out, to shower him with affection in order to soothe the cat and himself. But he's too relieved that Linux is fine, and too worried that he might get underfoot once the police arrive, that instead, he rubs the cringing cat's head once, then closes the office door to keep him trapped in there. Linux doesn't like being shut up. Elgar expects him to yowl indignantly and bat at Elgar's toes through the gap at the bottom of the door like he usually does. That Linux stays still and silent says more about his fear, and perhaps the danger of the situation, than Elgar likes.

Elgar shuffles back into the living room, where Juan is now sitting as close to the fire as he can get, shivering. There's a quilt over the back of the sofa—Elgar's late aunt Lilah had sewn it back in the forties out of the rags of clothing that were rationed in England—and he drapes it around his assistant's shoulders. He feels, strangely, like he's the world-wise and weary one this time around. Perhaps it's the shock keeping him calm—actually, it's definitely the shock keeping him calm—but with Linux accounted for and Juan to look after, the fear caused by the violation of his home isn't as intense.

"Okay," Juan says softly. "Okay. I guess it wasn't stress after all. Or drugs."

"You think?" Elgar snarls. But it is soft. Not cruel, not accusatory.

Juan cringes all the same. "Yeah, boss. Sorry, boss."

"It's okay. Are you all right?" Elgar sort of wants to do something to comfort him, but... a back slap is too jockish, and he doesn't think his relationship with Juan is on the level where he can offer a hug, so instead, he just twists his fingers around themselves uselessly and squirms.

"I won't be eating meat for... like, the rest of my life," Juan whines.

"Shame," Elgar says, trying to lighten the mood, to distract them from the horror of their situation. "What will your writer-worshipping boyfriend say to that?"

Juan gasps, some of the color that shock had drained from his face bubbling back up to the surface of his skin in two pink splotches on his cheeks. "Boss! Did you just make a blowjob joke?"

"Yes?"

"To a man?"

"...yes?" Elgar says, wondering if this is a trick question.

"Good for you, boss," Juan says, and punches his arm gently.

Elgar grew up in a very conservative household, his parents having passed away when he was young and his Aunty Lilah the kind of god-fearing Christian who had firm ideas of what was right and wrong. She hadn't even been that keen on fiction, believed it was a waste of time and thought, and that a serious young man like Elgar Reed should be studying instead of reading comic books. She hadn't minded so much when his first advance had gotten them both out of the co-op welfare housing, or when the subsequent royalty checks had gotten them into a house of their very own. A house that Aunty Lilah had lived in until she'd died in '91. Elgar had sold that house because he couldn't bear to see her in every wall and carpet, and bought the house he and Juan were sitting in now.

A lot of that god-fearing righteousness had crept into Elgar's work, though he hadn't really realized it until he'd read Lucy Piper's PhD dissertation. It had also colored his perception of the people around him. So much so that he nearly hadn't hired Juan when his previous assistant, Janet, had told him to go screw himself.

It was Lucy who'd encouraged him to give Juan a try. They'd been reviewing the resumes the temp agency had forwarded to Elgar at the Piper's home in Victoria. Elgar had always thought that assistants should be women. Secretaries, receptionists, clerical aides... that was women's work, right? Lucy had smacked him upside the head and told him to stop being so sexist, and to hire the right fit, not the right plumbing.

It wasn't until a month into working with Juan that Elgar realized Juan was gay, and this time, it was Forsyth who smacked him, albeit verbally and via the phone, and told him that Juan wasn't going to try to flirt with him or stick his manhood in places Elgar wouldn't want just because he was into blokes. That gay men did not treat heterosexual men the same way that heterosexual men treated women. It was an eye-opener, and ever since then, Elgar has been doing his best to not be a dickhead about it.

If he can have conversations with fictional characters; if his hero can be married to his sidekick; if the hero's son can be mixed-race, and his spymaster's wife can be Asian and very much not a damsel in need of rescuing; if dragons can be misunderstood victims; if everything Elgar thought he knew about the world he had created had been tipped on its ear; well, then... Elgar Reed can make jokes about blowjobs with gay guys, right?

Right.

The sound of the doorbell startles both of them.

Juan stands to answer, but Elgar pushes him back down. "I got it."

Two officers stand in the space outside his door: a tall black man built like a linebacker, and a petite woman with a straight blonde ponytail and a look on her face that just dared you to call her, "Barbie."

"This way," Elgar says, before they can try to make awkward conversation. "Leave your shoes on."

"Sir, we—" the woman begins, but Elgar cuts her off.

"Trust me. I can't explain. You just have to see it."

He stops at the threshold to the kitchen and waves them inside. The smell is stronger right beside the pantry, and he gags again, trying to hold it together. He claps his hand over his mouth, and backs away. Seeing it again, experiencing it again, shatters the false calm he'd been luxuriating in.

Yup. Definitely shock.

Both of the officers suck in surprised gasps, and then both begin coughing immediately after as the stench hits them.

"Lord!" the woman says, pulling plastic gloves out of her belt and snapping them on. Her partner copies her.

"How long has it been here?"

"It can't be more than a few hours," Elgar says between gritted teeth. "It wasn't there when I last opened the door, around noon."

"But the smell," her partner says, his face pulled into a grimace. "It's like it's been rotting there for days."

"I don't get it, either," Elgar says. "I... I have to go..."

"Go, sit, we'll come find you soon," the male officer says, and then he's speaking into his radio, calling for a forensic team while his partner inspects the windows and the patio door. She already has a fingerprint kit in her hand. Elgar has a swooping fear that the only sets of prints they'll find belong to him, Juan, and the smudges from Linux's nose.

Elgar realizes belatedly that he hadn't let them introduce themselves. He hadn't read their name badges, either. Surely this has to be some sort of catastrophic breach of protocol. The gripping, freezing fear crawls back up his spine. Because what if... what if...

"S-sorry," he calls, without turning around. "I didn't... I didn't catch your names."

"Oh!" the woman says. "I'm Lieutenant Riletti, this is Sergeant Jackson. And you're Elgar Reed, correct? The wri—the homeowner," she corrects herself quickly.

Through his fear, a little surge of writerly pride wells up, the smug satisfaction of being known a sweet balm, even with everything that's happening in the kitchen. Happy to be dismissed, Elgar opens his living room window to try to encourage some fresh evening air into the place, then slumps down next to Juan. His assistant flings a corner of Aunty Lilah's quilt over his shoulder.

He misses her suddenly, intensely and fiercely. She had been firm, but expansive and generous in her love, and he feels keenly alone right now. He'd give anything for one of her strong hugs right now.

It takes longer for the officers to investigate the pile of... that... than Elgar expects. He can hear them chatting softly to each other, and calling to others on their radios. Eventually, a whole wagonful of other people arrive—a forensic team, a photographer, and some paramedics who shine annoying penlights in his eyes, take his pulse, and make him drink water he doesn't want.

And then the detectives are there, pulling Juan upstairs and Elgar into his office. Linux makes a fuss at them until Elgar sits in his desk chair, and the cat is able to scale his legs and tuck himself under Elgar's beard. The detective is accompanied by Lieutenant Riletti, who seems to be squashing down her fannish glee at being in his inner sanctum well. Her expression has grown gray and grim.

After a quick look around the room, her ranking officer introduces himself as Detective Khouri and takes a seat on the tatty old sofa that Elgar keeps in the office for when he's feeling lazy or needs to lay down while reading. The sofa is the last remaining piece of furniture from Aunty Lilah's original apartment. Riletti tries to perch on the arm beside Khouri. When it wobbles under her, she stands back up, quickly.

Normally, Elgar would laugh at that—usually, it's Juan who forgets the arm of the sofa is slowly disintegrating— but instead, he winces at the sinister groan the furniture produces. Okay, yes, he is officially out of the shock phase, and into the fear and worry.

"Mr. Reed?" Khouri says, and when Elgar blinks and turns his attention to the detective, it's obvious that this isn't the first time he's said it.

"Yeah?"

"I said, we're going to jump right into the questions. Is that okay?"

"Yeah."

Linux meows pitifully and snuggles deeper. Elgar runs his hands down the fragile little creature's back.

Khouri asks about Elgar's friends, his family, if any other incidents have occurred, and Elgar, shaken and uncertain, answers with one-word phrases and very little elaboration. He doesn't know if that makes him look guilty, or like he's being cagey or hiding something, but eventually, Riletti is sent for Jackson and Juan, and the five of them crowd into Elgar's office to continue the rest of the questioning together.

Elgar is reminded that, in those procedural shows, they always question witnesses separately, to ensure the stories check out. He doesn't mean to be difficult, it's just that he... he can't help thinking about the strange man on the bench.

"Mr. Reed!" Khouri repeats, yanking Elgar back into the present. "Would it be best if we continued this to-morrow? I'd like you to get checked out by the paramed-ics again. You're having trouble focusing. Did you take a fall earlier that you didn't tell us about?"

"No, I didn't fall. I'm fine," Elgar lies, and he doesn't like the way his voice trembles.

"Are you sure?"

"I'm tired, suddenly. I'm... what was the question?"

"Has there been anything else, besides the salad and this?"

"No," Elgar says, but Juan immediately jumps in with: "The Smithsonian."

Elgar turns to stare at his assistant. "They told you?"

"They told me *first*," Juan says. "You know the call wouldn't have gotten through to you if I hadn't let it."

Khouri shifts closer to Juan. "What are you talking about?"

"In December, someone stole the typewriter Mr. Reed donated to the Smithsonian."

"They stole an artifact from the Smithsonian," Khouri repeats, to verify.

Riletti stiffens. "How come that wasn't in the news? A theft like that, I would have thought it would have been international headlines."

Elgar's flattered that she thinks his missing typewriter is important enough to be international news, but just shakes his head. "Ah, I'm not that important." The admission costs him a little something, a bit of what Lucy calls his Narcissist Beta Male Shield, and as painful as it is to break off that small piece of it, he realizes immediately that he doesn't really miss it. Admitting to one person that he is not, in fact, the alpha and omega of the writing world hasn't harmed anyone. His ego is bruised... but bruises heal. And he has other things to focus on.

"Besides," Juan chimes in. "Jamie, the curator—oh, um, Jamie Denver, with an *IE*, yeah—she said that the Smithsonian doesn't report robberies unless they're really huge deals, because they don't want to encourage copycats, like, uh, like how transit officials don't call it suicide when people jump on the tracks."

"Morbid," Jackson says.

Khouri rubs his forehead and sighs. "Okay, look. I'm going to get in contact with this Jamie Denver, see what's going on, on her end. Obviously, we've got a pattern now, and this person is escalating. I'd like to put a watch on the house, and I'd feel more comfortable if you stayed in a safe house for the next few nights, Mr. Reed. We'll get you put up so an officer can stay with you. Is that acceptable? Riletti and Jackson can drive you out."

"A *safe house?*" Elgar repeats, agog. "Is that really necessary?"

The detective shifts and shrugs one shoulder. "I'd like you to be somewhere we can keep an eye on you, and somewhere whoever did this *can't*. We've got a place, nice and comfy, and it means you can be safe and out of the way, just in case."

"In case he strikes again?" Elgar asks.

Khouri's eyes narrow. "What makes you think it's a 'he'?"

"Oh," Elgar says, caught on the back foot. "Well. It's just... all my fans are male, aren't they?" Riletti coughs. "Well, most of 'em, anyway. I'd assume it was one of them, right?"

"Right," Khouri agrees, though he doesn't quite seem to take what Elgar says at face value. As if he knows that Elgar knows something, or some other equally circular cliche from the detective thriller his life seems to have turned into.

"What about Linux?" Elgar asks. "Can I bring him?"

"I'll take him, boss," Juan says softly, and stands to do just that. Linux is reluctant to let go of Elgar's shirt collar. They have to prise his claws loose. The cat snarls a bit, but goes limp again when Juan tucks him close to his own heartbeat.

That damn cat really does love Juan. More than it's loved any of his other assistants. Elgar muses that he can't ever fire Juan now—not that he has any plans to, of course—because Linux will kick up such a fuss over it that he wouldn't be able to stand it. Juan spoils the little monster.

Free of the cat, Elgar leads Sergeant Jackson upstairs, where the cop watches him pack for a few days away, eyes on the room's shadows. Jackson explains how they'll pull the car up, block the view of the front door from the street with the ambulance, and try to get Elgar and Juan into the cars at the same time so nobody will know that they have left. Just in case someone is watching the house right now.

That doesn't really make Elgar feel any safer, but he

chooses not to say anything about it. If... if someone is watching the house, or watching him... he has a feeling they'll know, anyway.

Some black magic shit, indeed.

"You're quick," Khouri says when they return to the office.

"I travel a lot," Elgar replies, with an attempt at self-deprecating humor. "Hazard of the job, I'm afraid." Then he crosses to his filing cabinet, retrieves his laptop, and drops it into his travel bag. He hesitates a moment, and then also pulls out the big fire-safe case and hands it to Jackson. It has a handle, and is about the size of a large briefcase, so it isn't too cumbersome. Though, by the look on the officer's face, he hadn't expected it to be so heavy.

Nobody asks Elgar why he's taking a fire-safe with him to the safe house, but the look on Juan's face makes it clear that he hasn't before considered that someone might come after the source of Elgar's stories once they've stolen the tools.

"I'll text you when I'm in," Elgar says to Juan, and for a moment, he's struck with a sort of clinging, molasses déjà vu. Elgar has stood in this office a hundred times before, bag in hand, Linux in his assistant's arms, and said the exact same thing. And then the warm, sweet comfort of the moment's familiarity freezes and shatters.

Because this isn't a convention trip.

"Be safe, boss," Juan says. His arms are full of cat, so he can't shake Elgar's hand. And yet, the solemnity of the moment begs for some sort of physical acknowledgment. So Elgar pats Juan's shoulder and rubs Linux's ears, and then lets the officers lead him out to their squad car.

"This is sort of like something in your stories," Riletti says, casually, as Jackson drives. The fannish glint is back in her eyes.

"A little," Elgar concedes, reminding himself that

he's only in the back of the squad car because he's being chauffeured, not because he's under arrest.

"Like something Bootknife would do."

"Bootknife's dead," Elgar blurts, more firmly than he thought he would, and then immediately slaps his palm over his mouth.

Riletti's eyes grow round. "Is he?" she breathes, turning around in her seat to read his face.

Elgar doesn't know how to reply. Of course, to a reader, the sadistic half Night Elf with a love of fine blades and creating wood-block carvings in the skin of prisoners' backs is still alive. He had lived through the final battle that had wiped out so many of the other named characters of *The Tales of Kintyre Turn*, simply because Elgar had had a vague thought of spinning him into the series' main protagonist if he was ever asked to write more. He knew that if that were to be the case, he would need to kill the Viceroy to up the stakes, and Bootknife had seemed like the perfect villain to fill the void the Viceroy's removal would have made.

But Lucy had told him that Forsyth Turn hadn't only bested Bootknife in a duel, but had decided to offer no quarter. He'd stabbed the rogue through the heart rather than let him live to come back and harm them another day. And, narratively, that made sense. Elgar probably would have come to the conclusion that Bootknife wasn't strong enough without the Viceroy protecting him, or clever enough without the Viceroy puppeteering him, to be a villain in his own right. He would have developed a new Big Bad. But to know that the decision had been wholly taken from his hands...

If he had never met Forsyth and Lucy, would he have ever thought of the Shadow Hand slaying Bootknife outright?

Well, actually, yes, he probably would have made that

exact plot choice. Which creeps him out even more. That his characters had acted independently of his writing, but still perfectly within the bounds of what he would have conceived is... eerie.

Instead of telling her all that, though, Elgar says: "I mean... just, that, you know, he's not real."

"Shame," Riletti says. "I mean, not a shame he's not real, but a shame that it's not as easy to solve as that. It would fall into his MO perfectly."

Elgar feels his stomach sink through the seat. "Why... why do you say that?"

"Who else would put fillets of dead pigs and ivy in your pantry, Mr. Reed?" the officer asks.

"Ivy?" Elgar repeats. The dread falls over him so quickly that he actually gets cold. He has to suck on the air to get it into his lungs. "Are you sure it was ivy?"

Jackson and Riletti exchange a look, concern passing between them like a tennis ball.

"I thought you'd be more worried about the dead pigs, honestly," Riletti says. "Why are you worried about the ivy?"

"The symbolism of it," Elgar chokes. "The last victim he had, Bootknife carved ivy on her. Not a landscape."

Riletti frowned. "I don't remember that."

"I never wrote it," Elgar whispers, and the confession falls, hot and molten, from behind his teeth.

The threats, the maggots, the theft, the ivy... they aren't meant to kill him. They're meant to *scare* him.

And it's working.

FORSYTH

We arrive at the Piper household a little after four o'clock, as planned. Mei Fan barely spares a hello for us as she swoops down to scoop her granddaughter out of the stroller and hie her away toward the kitchen, where, by the sound and smells wafting out into the living room and entryway, *wai po* is cooking something delicious.

Martin and I shake hands and wrestle the stroller into the front hall, half-obscuring a pile of his other guests' boots and winter coats. Pip trails after her mother. The four women often congregate in the kitchen, teasing and sniping at each other in a jumbled raucous of Mandarin and English, poking with chopsticks at each other's work and pausing to buzz Alis with kisses. They cover her hands in cool sauces and sticky jams to encourage her to experiment with solid foods, or put her on the floor with a wooden spoon and as many plastic containers to beat and crash as she likes.

Martin continually expresses his surprise at how clever Alis is growing, and Mei Fan often just beams at him and laughs. "What else is he to expect from our granddaughter?" she teases. "Geniuses beget geniuses."

Martin has moved *wai po*'s little family shrine onto a side table in the living room, so the guests don't have to traipse into her bedroom for the celebration, and it is into this room that I follow him. My father-in-law and I sit together on the sofa, where we have a clear view of the shrine, and the open floor in front of it. Martin said a friend of his is an amateur photographer and will be recording the event, so Pip and I are content to sit back and watch the ceremony around our daughter's first birthday unmitigated by screens and phones.

Pip is unceremoniously booted from the kitchen mere moments later, and comes to sit on the floor by my feet, so she can lean her head on my knee. When we are settled, we are handed glasses of wine by one of Martin's work colleagues from the high school. She is an older woman whose name I don't think I have ever learned, though we have met before at other such events. Friends of the family fill the room already—some of Pip's colleagues mingle amid Martin and Mei Fan's, all of them educators of one level of schooling or another, so they have much in common.

"Congrats," the woman says to us, settling in a nearby kitchen chair which has been pulled into the living room so there is enough seating for all. "One year. You must be ecstatic."

"We are," Pip says, and to anyone who doesn't know her as well as I do, she would seem perfectly at ease. Outwardly, she appears to be enjoying herself. But I can see the tightness around her eyes, the way her faint smattering of freckles stands out against worry-paled skin; I can feel where her fingernails dig in next to my inseam, just a little, where she has her free hand resting on my ankle.

"Oh, I'm Nancy," the woman says, belatedly offering me her hand. "I don't think we've had the chance to meet yet."

"Syth," I say. "I don't think we have."

Nancy winks at Pip. "Well, if you'd had a monster wedding like you were supposed to, I probably would have met you there. But you kids just snuck off and did it on your own, eh?"

I don't think Nancy means this as a slight, and Pip certainly doesn't take it as one, but it does seem unnecessarily pointed. We hadn't been entirely secure in our relationship when we'd wed—I had been new to this world, and we were still slowly trading in dragon's tears for cash at various gold-buyers in order to secure our wealth, and I had yet to completely exist in the government's eyes. So we had decided to keep the celebration small so as not to attract attention.

"The point of the ceremony was to bind our lives," I say, trying for a lightness of tone that I'm not entirely certain I manage, if the way Pip glances at me out of the corner of her eyes means what I think it means. "Not to show off. We were very happy with how it was conducted."

"Oh, of course," Nancy says, and she sips her wine, blinking. "Right. But, ah, this is something else, isn't it?" she adds, desperate to regain her footing. She gestures to the room.

"*Wai po*'s only gonna get the one grandchild," Pip says, shrugging. "So we don't mind her going as overboard or traditional as she wants. It makes her happy, and that makes us happy."

"Oh, you'll have another," Nancy says, leaning in conspiratorially. "People always say they only want one, but the urge will be there again. And it's good for kids to have siblings, you know? To grow up with someone?"

"Not always," I counter, and while Nancy blinks and sips again to cover up that she is digesting what I could possibly mean by that statement, Pip pinches the top of my foot, hard. I jerk and squirm, and grin at my wife, who has mischief in her eyes, the teasing minx.

"We're sure," she says. "Just the one. I'm the only child of only children, and I turned out just fine. Besides, it's too expensive to have more than one kid anymore. Curse of the millennials."

I chuckle at that, for while Pip is certainly a millennial, I am most assuredly not. Though my preference toward Hainish waistcoats, neat grooming, formal shirts, and tailored trousers has led me to resemble a hipster, I cannot possibly be one, as I love nothing ironically and have no cultural experiences here to use as social cache.

Just then, Alis is paraded into the living room in her new birthday clothes—an adorable shirt-and-trousers suit called a *tangzhuang*. It is made of red silk embroidered with chrysanthemums for luck. Her wispy black curls have been pulled up into adorable twin puffs at the top of her head, which make her look like a chubby kitten. The crowd around us seems to agree that Alis is cute, for a chorus of "aaawwwws!" greet her arrival to the party on her great-grandmother's hip.

Cameras click and flash. Nancy, apparently, hasn't had enough of her own foot and opens her mouth to swallow down more.

"And where's your family?" she asks me, filled with genuine curiosity and a complete lack of knowledge about my complicated relationship with my blood.

"Ah," I say, and take a sip of wine to wash down the lump that has built in my throat. Normally, I am quite comfortable in repeating the old lie that Pip is my only living family besides an American cousin. But today, on the one year anniversary—by the Overrealm calendar, at least—of my daughter, the Ladyling Alis Mei Fan Turn Piper, it seems... bad luck to deny the existence of my loved ones and friends back in Hain.

Taking pity on me, Pip leans across my body and shakes her head a little. The woman sits back, and says, "I'm sorry."

"I would have liked them to be here," I say. "But wishes summon djinn, and no one ever gets what they really want when that happens."

The woman squints at me, and Pip laughs. "I adore your esoteric and obscure idioms, husband-mine," Pip says. I search for somewhere else to sit amid the crowd in the living room, but every seat is taken. We are stuck.

Pip catches me looking. She smiles comfortingly and pats my much-abused foot. I turn my attention back to *wai po* and Alis, who are now both kneeling before *wai po*'s shrine. The Chinese members of the gathering join in the traditional prayer, and Alis, engaged and fascinated, seems entranced by the curl of incense smoke as it drifts upward from the ember cones.

"What about the traditions of your culture?" Nancy asks after the prayer is concluded. Well, I suppose she must have some sense, at least, if she had enough to remain silent during that.

"Mine?"

"I can't place your accent, exactly..." she fishes, leaving me a space in which to enlighten her as to the origins of it. But I do not answer. Perhaps that is cruel of me, but I am not feeling particularly warm toward this woman. I never feel particularly warm toward anyone who dares tell my wife that she has lived her life incorrectly, no matter how well-meaning their intentions may be. "But, uh, surely there's something you want to do for your daughter today?"

"Many things," I agree.

I want to hold a ball in Turn Hall. I want to summon the Chipping to marvel at the beauty and cleverness of my child. I want to dress her in a Turn-russet frock with thread-of-gold stitching, and dance with her and Pip to the accompaniment of the Turnshire minstrels. I want to invite hedge witches to bestow protective charms upon her, and centaurs to read her destiny in the stars, to feast on Cook's rabbit pie and Dorthi Pointe's unparalleled seed cakes. I want to laugh at Bevel Dom trying to teach my toddler the steps to a Bynnebakker jig, and feel nothing but pride as my brother Kintyre gives her a horrifically inappropriate gift, like a sword with a live edge; for while it would have been impractical, I know it would have come from a place of love and a desire to protect Alis. I want to watch Alis smear cake all over her cousin Wyndam's doublet, and play with Lewko Pointe the Younger, and frolic with Capplederry and Bradri.

But these are things I cannot have. Things that I have said goodbye to twice over. Things that I am learning to yearn for less and less. Oh, I will never cease to wish that my family were with me, but I have also been in this realm long enough that I have learned to hold my memories of them with love in my heart, and to not let the bitterness of missing them poison me against this place and its people and customs. I made my choice. I do not regret it.

"Such as?" Nancy probes, and Pip snorts into her wine glass.

I shrug. "Things that can wait until it is just the three of us at home. We are very keen to have Alis steeped in the culture of her mother's family, so that she may be a proficient bilingual, and today is all about the Chinese way of celebrating. I am happy to be patient. Oh, look, they are going to step on the turtle now."

It's probably the least subtle subject change I have engineered in my whole career as a spymaster, but it is effective, at least.

Nancy turns in her seat to watch as *wai po* and Mei Fan urge Alis up onto her feet. Mei Fan puts a paper plate by Alis's bare foot. On the plate is a *gong gui hao*, a small red cake shaped like a turtle. There is some luck around turtles and longevity, I know, and a correlation between the written word "step." So, it is tradition, I am told, for a child to "step" into life by stepping on a turtle—but as no one cares to harm a real one, a cake is substituted.

Alis—blood kin to Kintyre Turn that she is—stomps on the cake with mad glee in her eyes. Then she promptly lands herself on her well-padded rear, lifts her foot to her mouth, and pulls off a glob of cake with the few teeth she possesses.

"*Bie chi, zang!*" *wai po* laughs, and pulls Alis's leg away from her face.

"Okay, time to swoop in," Pip says, jumping to her feet and setting down her wine glass. "Alis, baby, don't eat the cake off your feet. Yucky."

"No!" Alis opines, and shoves her fingers into her mouth. There is some smashed cake on them, too. Pip scoops Alis up, and tosses her gently into the air. Around her fingers, Alis squeals with joy and adds: "*Bu!*"

"No?" Pip says, grinning, and rubs her nose against Alis's miniature replica when she catches our daughter. "Who are you to tell me no, little girl?"

"Bu!" Alis giggles again, dimpling with delight.

"Ah, clever girl," I tell her as I sit forward on the sofa. Alis turns to me and beams at the praise.

"No *bu buu bu yao* nooo!" she chants as the assembled guests laugh and applaud her for defying us all in two languages. She applauds with them, clearly pleased to be the center of attention—again, showing that she is very well related to my brother—before Pip and Mei Fan sweep her off to the kitchen to clean up.

Mei Fan comes back out with a platter of small red turtle cakes for the rest of us.

"For eating, though," she warns her adult guests as she sets it down on the coffee table. "Ruin my carpets, and I will end you."

Chuckling, I snag up one of the cakes and indulge. As I promised Pip, I have returned to fencing, so I can allow myself this treat. Mei Fan's baking is a wonder, anyway. Nobody will be Dorthi Pointe, it's true, but then, Mei Fan was not Written to be only the plump, cookie-baking housewife. Dorthi has an unfair advantage on all other cooks in the Overrealm when it comes to the wellspring of her talent in the kitchen.

"Now what?" Nancy asks me when Pip and a cleaned-up Alis return with a bowl.

"Oh, the *cháng shòu miàn,*" I answer, doing my very best to mimic *wai po*'s accent. She beams at me from her chair across the open floor and winks. I feel myself flush under her silent praise.

"The what?"

"Long noodles for a long life," I say. "I hope Alis isn't terribly put out that she has noodles and we have sweets."

"She ate another whole cake in there," Pip says, dropping a kiss on the crown of my head as she settles Alis between my legs. Our daughter props herself up against my shins. She shoves her hands into the bowl of cold noodles, grinning manically, and lifts them to her face to gum and slurp.

I keep a careful eye on her to ensure she doesn't choke herself, and dutifully slurp up one of the noodles when she holds it up to me. Alis giggles and claps her sticky hands together as I cross my eyes and theatrically suck the noodle up between my lips. I hear the click and whir, see the flash of a camera, but I ignore them in favor of entertaining my daughter. I am lordling no more, so may cavort and be as silly as I like, with no fear of how I will look to those around me.

As the adults refill their drinks, chat amongst themselves, and circulate, Pip settles onto the floor beside us both, watching Alis with hungry, happy eyes.

"I wish I remembered this," Pip says quietly, privately. "I have Dad's pictures of me, but I don't actually remember it."

"No one remembers much from this age," I say. "Not even folks like, ah, me."

"And what are you like?" Nancy asks, moving her chair closer to involve herself in our conversation once more.

Pip and I exchange an exasperated glance.

"Eidetic memory," I lie. "Or very close to one."

Of course, I cannot say, "*people Written to be clever, who have had the privilege to wear the Shadow's Mask and so can sometimes access the memories of their predecessors of themselves at a young age.*" Not that I could do so now, without the mask to store the memories and provide me access. My external hard drive is missing, as it were, and all I remember now are the files I had accessed so often that I had moved copies of them to my desktop: lists of Words and spells, of names and faces. But little of the personal life of the Shadow Hands that had come before me, of their preferences and memories.

Their knowledge, deep and vast as it is, is lost to me.

Nancy squints at me, then at my empty wine glass, where I have left it on the coffee table, well out of Alis's reach.

"I'll pour you another," she offers, and stands.

"No, I am content. Thank you," I reply. "One was enough for this afternoon."

She makes a sound rather like frustration, and walks away—finally. I cannot blame people for their own social awkwardness, but sometimes, people ought to learn how to read the situation.

A shiver of concern trickles down my spine. Why was she so determined to interrogate me? It could be idle curiosity. She has watched Pip grow, I assume, so of course she would be invested in Pip's relationships and happiness, and as such, only wants to connect with me. In which case, I am being rude.

But there is something... something else here. And I don't know if it's my own paranoia, born of Pip's and Elgar's own, or if it is really something to concern myself with.

When Alis finishes her bowl of noodles, she lifts it between chubby hands.

"Yah!" she shouts in triumph, and I have just enough time to say, "Ah, ah, sweeting," and snatch the bowl out of her grip before she can spill the remaining sauce all over herself and the floor.

"*Bu!*" Alis protests at my intervention, looking mutinous.

"You missed your grandmother's dire threats regarding her carpets, but I did not," I say, grinning. "Now, up, up, let's stand sweeting, and let's wipe your hands clean. One last game for you, my dearest heart, and then we will put out the toys and you may maraud and raid to your heart's content."

Mollified by my promise to let her be as Turnish as she likes, Alis agrees to play along. "Yah!"

"*Yes*, sweeting," I correct, hoping to trade on her current amiableness.

Alis squints and gives me a skeptical look. "Yah," she insists, in a tone much like a Bynnebakker blacksmith. She looks at her mother, and then opens her hand near my face, as if to say, *Can you believe this idiot? Do you see what he's trying to do?*

"I know, sweet pea," Pip says. "Your da is an insufferable snob."

Alis nods, as if she has any idea what a snob is, or if I am one or not.

Martin moves from where he's standing beside Mei Fan, near the shrine, to a bundled blanket in the corner of the room. Martin brings the bundle into the middle of the open floor, and Alis turns her body to face him, standing on wobbly legs to watch what her grandfather is up to.

"*Zhua zhou*, baby girl," Martin says to Alis in a far better Mandarin accent than the one I possess.

Pip moves back to stand beside me, and I rise to my feet so we both can watch unimpeded. She threads her fingers between mine and leans against my shoulder, and all is right and good in the Overrealm.

Martin unfolds the blanket across the carpet and spreads out all the small toys and trinkets contained inside it so that they are evenly spaced. Alis sticks one finger in her mouth, gray eyes watching this process curiously. On the blanket are a variety of objects that are meant to represent Alis's future calling. There is a silver pen, which represents a scholarly life, a wooden abacus, which traditionally represents life as a businessperson, a toy car, a child's stethoscope, a seal-stamp, a plastic spade, a measuring tape, a toy microphone, a small stuffed sheep, and a few other items that I cannot clearly make out from here.

"Go on, sweeting," I say to Alis, urging her to uncurl her other hand from my trousers. "Take whichever toy you want. Pick whatever you like best."

Of course, no game of "pick the toy" will really predict or determine my daughter's future. It is fun, but no more real magic than the made-up Words children use in play, or "spells" cast by young men in taverns looking to trick maidens out of their virtue. Still, I mentally urge my daughter toward the seal-stamp, which represents a life in government office. It would be pleasant if she found her calling in serving others, as I did.

Before Alis has made her choice, Pip's fingers tighten on my hand. The pain of it is intense and sudden, but the concern that flares up in me is worse.

Another seizure that is not? I wonder as Pip leans more heavily against my side, sucking in a deep breath between her teeth, eyes screwing shut. I shake my hand free of her rigor mortis grip and wrap my arms around her waist and shoulders to keep her upright, tucking in behind her like a big spoon and trying to make it look casually affectionate.

Pip is hiding this fit. Why? What could make her want to conceal the pain? She shifts away from my hand at the small of her back and I move it off the scars, holding her hip instead.

"Pip," I whisper.

She shakes her head against a clear message to stay silent on the matter. I look up and around. Everyone is focused on our child, not us. Pip fists her hands in my shirtsleeves and bites down hard on the noises I can feel vibrating in her chest.

A cheer goes up in the room at the same time that Pip exhales a low, deep breath and goes limp. I am able to hold her up for the moment it takes her to get her own feet under her again. She smiles up at me, and whispers: "Hurt more, but didn't take me so much by surprise this time."

"What happened?"

She doesn't have the time to answer, though, for Alis has finished reveling in the cheers of those around her and is looking for the approval of her parents. She toddles over, fists her free hand in my jeans, and holds the other up to me, beaming. Her plump cheeks are pink with joy, gray eyes slitted with sparkling pleasure.

What she has picked is not the stamp. It's also none of the other shiny, plastic toys.

"Show us, sweeting," I say, projecting a calmness I do not feel.

"Da!" she cheers, as she holds up a tendril of ivy.

"I... I didn't put that in there," Pip says, face going gray, her pulse fluttering hard enough in her throat that I can see it jumping. She stumbles, torn between batting the branch out of Alis's hand or backing out of the room. She covers her mouth with her palm, puffing hard.

"Honey?" Martin says, voice dropping into the "concerned father" tone that I occasionally hear in my own words. Martin scoops up Alis, but this brings the ivy closer to my wife.

Pip flinches. Martin pauses. I reach out and pluck the foliage away from my daughter. She snivels at me and says, "*bu!*" One of the other guests, trying to break the tension they don't understand, declares, "Gardener!"

The room cheers again, and if they do so too loudly, and with the bright falseness of desperation, then no one cares to comment on it. The ivy clenched in my fist, I grab Pip by the wrist and head straight through the kitchen, out into the backyard.

"Syth?" Martin calls after us.

Pip calls back: "Be right back! Stay inside." Martin pauses halfway to the door, confused. In his arms, Alis jerks and whines, fist opening and clenching, reaching for us.

For us? Or for *it?*

I pull Pip swiftly around the corner of the house, where I know none of the windows offer a view of us, and raise the ivy between us.

"I didn't put that in the bundle," Pip insists, hands shaking where she grips my free one between us. "You have to—I would never be that cruel. Why would I—I would have remembered—"

"I believe you," I interrupt her.

Pip looks up at me with wide, dark eyes that are white all-around with fear.

"And I am so profusely sorry that I doubted you, or gainsaid you, for even a moment," I say. "You're right. There is magic here. Though I do not understand how, or why."

"Did I do this?" Pip asks, staring at the tendril. "Is this my fault? God, Forsyth, what if I brought it with me? What if, just by existing here, I..." She breaks off miserably. "We should have stayed in Hain. You said so, but I wanted to go home, and I... we, we should have stayed."

"No," I say. "No, this was the correct choice. This is where I want Alis to grow and live. Do not second-guess yourself in that. I chose this just as much as you did. I chose it twice."

Pip nods, and rolls up on her toes to press a swift kiss to my mouth, but otherwise does not look any more relieved. We both look to the ivy in my hand. It is freshly torn from its vine, that much is clear. The leaves are still vibrant green, the end of the thin branch still sticky with sap.

"What do we do now?" she asks. "I could ask Mom if she put it in. I mean, maybe we're freaking out for no reason?"

"Do you really believe that she did?" I ask her, arching an eyebrow.

She licks her lips. "I want to."

"As do I."

"But?"

"Yes. But."

Pip peers back into the kitchen, and I follow her line of sight, craning around the corner of the house. Through the patio door, I can see Martin juggling Alis in his grasp while she sniffles and sobs great crocodile tears for being denied her treasure. Mei Fan and *wai po* are speaking with him, their gestures indicating that their concern is growing larger the longer we're absent from the party.

"Here," Pip says, lunging for the barbecue grill sitting on the patio under a thick black cover. She roots around the cabinet underneath and comes up with a lighter.

Understanding what she means to do, I hold out the sprig, and we both watch with grim determination as it burns. Maybe this achieves nothing, but it makes me feel better.

"Now what?" I ask. In my hand, the twig withers and crumbles in on itself, turning to ashes in the breeze.

"We'll go back inside. Finish the day. Keep our eyes peeled," Pip suggests.

"Yes," I agree. "No need to alarm anyone else."

"Because whatever this is..." Pip says slowly. "It won't bother with them, will it?"

"I sincerely hope not," I agree.

I wipe away the smudges of soot on my fingertips. And then, together, we go back into the house.

"Everything okay?" Mei Fan asks immediately.

"Yes," I say. "We were... just startled. I feared it was poison ivy, you see, and the leaves did not match my, ah, app. Alis seems to have developed no rash, but we will watch her."

The other three adults in the kitchen relax visibly at this explanation. The human mind will always seek and accept the easiest answer. It is something I have long learned to take advantage of.

Pip crosses the room and pulls Alis into her embrace. Our daughter clings to her mother, staring up at Pip with a look that pains me to admit that I know all too well. Alis knows something is wrong, that there is some reason to be frightened, and she has accordingly gone silent and still.

This is a thing she learned on the road in Hain, and it guts me that, even now, she remembers.

"Shall we wash your hands, sweeting?" Pip asks Alis, and takes her over to the sink, where both of them are able to hide their expressions from the others. After this, Pip sets Alis back down on the blanket, and the rest of the partygoers turn their eyes back to the center of the room.

"Sorry for the scare, everyone," Pip says. "You know new parents. I flipped out, thought it was poison ivy!"

The room laughs.

"What's that old joke?" one of the more elderly fellows asks the woman next to him, who is clearly his wife. "About the dime?"

"The first time my kid swallowed a dime, I took him to Emergency," she supplies. "The first time my second kid swallowed a dime, I took it out of his allowance!"

The room howls with laughter, relieved that everything is fine, and pretending that they weren't worried. More wine is poured, a few more cakes are passed around, and Martin crouches at the edge of the blanket with a marvelously large grin.

"Okay, baby girl," he says, clapping his hands to get Alis's attention. She turns to him, startled, and then dimples adorably at her beloved grandfather. "Shall we try this again?"

FIVE

ELGAR

The safe house isn't anything cool. Not like in the spy movies, with steel-shuttered windows and a locked armory in the pantry. It's just a little farmhouse whose decor is stuck somewhere around 1973, located about forty minutes outside of Seattle, on the eastern side of Fall City. The house does, however, have movie-spy grade surveillance, a camera-and-security room where the back mudroom ought to be, and an IP scrambler that will keep people from pinpointing his location when he uses his laptop. Riletti and Jackson have explained that they'll take shifts sleeping, so that one of them will always be on duty. What the goon in the mudroom will be doing instead of sleeping, Elgar decides not to ask.

All the same, the only security Elgar really wants right now is the sound of Forsyth's voice and a promise from his penultimate spymaster that this is a problem he can solve. But with the police around, Elgar doesn't feel comfortable calling Forsyth.

Firstly, the cops might object to him sharing details of the case over the phone with an unknown stranger (no matter that Elgar would explain that the Pipers were family). Secondly, he doesn't want to have to use subterfuge and nicknames, and he's afraid he's too upset to remember to do so. He might slip-up and call Forsyth by his real name, and with a fan in the other room, listening in...

No. It's not a good idea. Not yet. Maybe if the situation gets dire enough, but not now.

Instead, he sits in the small living room, opens his laptop, and considers sending Forsyth an email—wait, is it possible that someone's watching his emails, too? Deciding that it's safer to forego the email to the former spymaster, just in case, he spends the rest of the evening answering fan mail and updating his website to clear his mind.

Jackson is asleep in a room upstairs, and Riletti has just finished sticking a frozen pizza in the oven when Elgar finally clears his inbox. The zero count, in and of itself, is a feat to be celebrated, and with no Juan nearby to scold Elgar for his dinner choices, he and Riletti spend the rest of the evening watching ridiculous cooking shows, eating pizza, and talking around the two elephants in the room: the Incident, as Elgar has started referring to it in his mind, pleased by his own melodrama, and the Work.

Riletti is fan enough that she's read the books, but she's no Lucy Piper. And frankly, Elgar's a little surprised she likes the series as much as she does, being a... well, being a woman. Elgar has always thought his main audience consisted of young, nerdy men. Or maybe not so young anymore, seeing as much of his fan base has aged with him.

Oh, god, is Riletti young enough that her father introduced her to the books? He does a little mental math and realizes that... yes, if she's relatively new to the force, as her bright-eyed eagerness suggests, then Lieutenant Riletti is literally young enough to be Elgar's own daughter, and that... well, he's trying really hard not to find that weirdly hot.

Partway through dinner, Gil, the producer at Flageolet Entertainment, calls to say he's emailing over some head shots and would like Elgar's opinion. Trying not to look as if he has anything to hide, and yet also hiding, Elgar takes his laptop into a corner, along with a cup of coffee (which Juan also isn't here to scold him about), and peruses the options.

Along with the head shots, Gil sent video files labeled "self-tape," which turn out to be the actors speaking into a camera with lines the producers wrote up specifically for their auditions. They're no more than a few minutes each, but he doesn't have his headphones with him, so he starts with just the photos.

They're looking for relative unknowns on purpose—the production company wants to cast actors for their ability to play the characters rather than the star-magnetism someone known would bring to the project (though that doesn't mean they don't intend to use big stars for one-offs and cameos)—so Elgar doesn't know any of the faces. He has to flick back and forth between some of them to be certain that they are, in fact, two different people. He's being awfully particular about how each character has to look, and the groups of actors do, he's pleased to note, actually resemble his characters. And therefore, one another.

He searches online databases for some of the names, flipping through their credits and screenshots of their other work to get a sense of what the actors look like in motion. Of course, he knows it's probably a bit too in-depth for what Gil wants; Gil probably just wants his opinion on how they look. It's even possible that this is just busywork meant to keep him pacified and feeling like he's a part of the production. He's never heard of any of his colleagues being asked to participate in the casting process, and he wonders if maybe he'd been too pushy at the beginning, too eager to meet his characters before he, well, met his characters.

A shiver passes over his shoulders, and after a moment of looking around for a throw blanket, or considering getting up to go put on another pair of socks, Elgar realizes that he isn't actually cold. It's just that it's so... not *quiet*, that isn't the word he's searching for. Because Jackson is snoring upstairs, and Riletti has the television on. But... Linux isn't here, fighting for space on his shoulders, and Juan isn't in the other room pretending not to be mother-henning, and it's... wrong.

Quiet, but not in noise level. In people. In the *right* people.

In... in attention, if he's going to be honest with himself. Which he's been trying to do a lot more. It made finishing the *Shuttleborn* trilogy harder, because he kept second-guessing his choices, asking why the things that felt natural to him did, and were they actually natural, and could they be harmful, and... all that. He tries in his daily life, too. Because Juan would look at him all disappointed-like. And Lucy would smack him. And Forsyth would tut.

And... and he has a granddaughter now. Sort of. He owes it to Alis to... try to do better.

He doesn't really need the help, but he's curious about her opinion and, to be honest, he's... feeling a little lonely. He's used to being the focus of the room. Wherever he goes—conventions, meetings, networking events—all eyes turn to him when he walks in, and it's always for *his* attention that people are vying. To be in the same room with someone else and to be so thoroughly ignored in favor of the television is... frustrating.

It's a calculated risk, inviting her help, and okay, maybe he is showing off a little, but he wants her to like him. He doesn't want her pity, because she has to protect him; he wants her interest because he's *interesting*. If his mere presence isn't enough, then the sneak peeks and tidbits he can entice her with will have to do. He wants to fall into the personality of Convention-Elgar, where everything rolls off his back and he is charming and gregarious. Convention-Elgar wouldn't be scared of men on benches and bloody threats in his pantry. Convention-Elgar wouldn't be concerned about a room full of the wrong kind of silence.

How's that for insight? he huffs at himself.

So he licks his lips, screws up his courage, and says: "Hey, Riletti."

"Yeah?" she asks, immediately sitting up and turning off the TV. Her free hand hovers at her hip, and Elgar realizes that she's waiting for him to say that he saw something, or that something's bothering him. She isn't ignoring him, she's bored.

"I... I wanted to say thank you, you know, to you. And to your partner. For being here."

"It's what we do, sir," she says with a smile.

"I know that, but all the same. The detective is right, I wouldn't have wanted to stay at home alone tonight."

"I get that."

"Do you have someone I'm keeping you from?" Elgar asks, and then catches sight of her ring. "A husband?"

Riletti cuts him a side-eye. "A wife, actually."

"Oh," Elgar mumbles, feeling his face go red. "Sorry."

"Hey, it's fine. I don't have a dyke haircut, so everyone assumes I'm straight. Stereotypes; am I right?"

"Right," he says, then clamps down on the ridiculous urge to tell her that he knows other gay people, like Juan. Why would she care? Lots of people all over the world know more than one queer person. It's not like they're rare or anything. "Look, uh, you look bored. If I swear you to secrecy, will you help me with something?"

Riletti's glare softens. "Sure."

Elgar heaves himself to his feet and trundles over

to the sofa with his laptop. He sets it on the coffee table and, with a wave of his hand, invites Riletti to sit beside him and look at the screen.

"What's this?" she asks, eyes darting back and forth between the two windows Elgar's set up on the desktop side by side: one filled with the head shots, the other a browser with thirty different IMDB tabs open.

Elgar points at the head shot of a very muscley hunk, with bright blue eyes and an infectious puppy-dog smile, but dark hair. "If he was blond, do you think he could play Kintyre?"

"Maybe. He might be too old, though. He would need—wait. Wait!" Riletti hisses. "Are you... are you telling me tha ... ? Oh my god!"

"Shhh," Elgar laughs. "This is supposed to be a secret. Don't wake your partner."

"Oh my god!" Riletti says again. "The rumors are true!"

They spend the next few hours going over the head shots and watching the self-tapes, compiling a careful email to the casting team, and by the time they're finished, Elgar is yawning.

"That is so cool," Riletti says, falling back against the sofa. Her hair, which she had loosened during their argument over why Elgar was taking so long to choose the perfect Forsyth Turn ("It doesn't matter this much, does it? Why are you tying yourself up in knots? We only see Forsyth for like, a chapter in the first book, right? Oh, and I guess in book four? Three? Which is it?"), puffs around her shoulders like a capelet.

"It is cool," Elgar agrees, though he feels a little empty and selfish for doing so. He realizes he has just successfully manipulated this woman into spending hours with him to keep him company, to keep him entertained. Though, he supposes that's what real friendships and dating are like, not that he's had much experience with either. Only, he wouldn't have had to use the bait of forbidden knowledge to tempt them into spending time with him.

"Thanks for asking me to help."

"Thanks for helping," Elgar says. "I think I'm going to turn in."

"Sure," Riletti says. "I'll be out here if you need me, and I'll be waking Jackson to swap in an hour."

"Okay." Elgar packs up his laptop, and then brandishes a teasing finger at her. "Now, no texting your, uh, wife about what just happened. No leaks allowed."

"Cross my heart," Riletti promises. And she really seems to mean it.

FORSYTH

Several days pass in research for me, and in a sort of holding-pattern stasis for Pip. She is scared, but she will not admit to being so. She cuddles Alis, goes to work, attends the gym and her martial arts classes, and comes home. We eat, we watch television, we talk, but neither of us really says *anything*. Because we are unsure. We are *waiting*. And in the meantime, because our misfortunes must always come in groups, Alis has not one but three new teeth coming in. She spends much time clutching her cheeks and muttering to Library about how stupid and ineffective her parents are, while I corral my Turnish temper. Between my intensive focus, Pip's fear, and Alis's misery, nobody is getting as much sleep as they ought to, and everyone is weary and listless and cranky.

A full week after Alis's birthday party, she wakes us just an hour or so after dawn with her shrieks. Pip rolls over into my shoulder and mutters: "If you make a joke about her being my daughter after the sun is up, I will punch you in the nose."

"Wouldn't dream of it," I return, heaving myself up. Pip pats my rear end as I shuffle out the door toward the nursery, and I can't help but snort. Ah, yes, the loving affection of the sleep-deprived.

Alis is standing, holding the edge of her crib, and sobbing miserably. She is flushed and angry at her inability to communicate and her parents' obvious deficiency. I scoop her up and bring her to my office, where, in my haze last night, I for some reason left the little tube of pain-numbing gel that we rub on Alis's gums. I distinctly recall Sheriff Pointe using whiskey for this task, but Pip tells me that getting children drunk enough to pass out and forget their pain is frowned upon in the Overrealm.

It doesn't mean that it isn't an appealing alternative.

Alis quiets down after a few moments, sniffling miserably and burrowing into my shoulder as I spin us in slow circles in my office chair. On the fifth or sixth revolution, I am finally awake enough to realize that there is a small red icon flashing in the middle of my main monitor. After a frustrating span where diving into the deep files and illegal monitoring software that the law-abiding citizens of the Internet don't believe exist yielded nothing but ill-defined results, Finnar has at last *found* something.

Frowning, I flick my mouse with my elbow on my way by, waking up the screens. Then I put down my foot, hard, and jerk us to a stop.

"That unbelievable, selfish bastard," I hiss, forcing myself to reread the title of the report Finnar has turned up.

Alis whines once in my grasp.

"Sorry, sweeting," I say, standing and walking her into our bedroom. "Cuddle with your mama for a bit. Your da needs to call your Uncle Gar Gar and scream at him."

Pip struggles upright, eyes bleary as she leans back against the headboard and lets Alis climb into her lap.

"What'd he do this time?"

"The fool man has been in protective custody for a *week*. And he has told neither of us."

"A week?" Pip repeats, suddenly coming awake. "Why?"

"Apparently, he is being threatened. I have not read the whole report yet, but I assure you that I will be calling him immediately after I have. I only know because Finnar—my program, that is—caught his name in a document stating that he is to be released back into his home later this morning."

"Why didn't he tell us?" Pip asks.

"That is something I am looking forward to asking *him*," I mutter. "Please excuse me."

"Yeah, none of us are getting any sleep now, are we, kiddo?" Pip asks Alis as she slides them both out of bed. "Might as well put on some coffee."

"Thank you," I say. "I'd appreciate that very much."

Pip leans up to kiss my cheek. "Who says I'm making it for you?"

"Tease," I say to her, smacking her own arse lightly as she walks by.

"Always. Come on, baby girl. Breakfast."

"Bah bah Mama *bu*," Alis comments.

"Bah-rec-fast," I encourage, and Alis scowls at me over her mother's shoulder as they descend the stairs. "Oh, very well, I give up. Speak like a backwater Bynne-bakker blacksmith for the rest of your life, see if I care, my sweeting."

I return to my office and set about the task of discovering who is threatening Elgar, and why, and what has happened to make the authorities believe he is safer in protective custody than in his own home. A secondary problem begins to tickle at the back of my mind as I delve into the deep dark recesses of the Internet, bypassing the security barriers surrounding sensitive information, and it is this: how do I confront Elgar for failing to confide in me?

The very *first* person he should have told he was being threatened is *me*, and I—

Oh.

Oh, foolish Forsyth. Sometimes you really are abysmally slow.

Elgar had, in his way, already told me. "*Were you the only ones who came through?*" he had asked, and in my overconfidence, I assumed he was being paranoid. But Pip's strange fits had already begun, even then, and I should have pieced this clue in amid the others his call offered.

Instead, I had rebuffed him.

As our familiarity grows, Elgar has begun to treat me more like a human being and less like an exotic creature to interrogate and study, and I have begun to see him as less a fickle, cruel god and more as the desperately lonely man he is. All the same, it would please us all if his next work was less... well, *less.*

Though, Pip and I are unconvinced that Elgar actually is working on something new. He completed the first drafts of his debut science fiction trilogy well before he met me. But since shaking my hand that first time, Elgar seems, well... *terrified* to put pen to paper. Or fingers to keys, as the case may be. A small, vicious, vindictive part of myself is pleased to hear it. I would not wish the backstory-building pain that seems to be a requirement for fictional characters in the Overrealm to be visited upon anyone else, no matter if they are aware of it or not.

However, there's also no evidence to suggest that any of the other fictional characters Elgar has created—for he wrote a goodly amount of short fiction before his career ignited with *The Tales of Kintyre Turn*—are alive and aware in the way that I, and those from my realm, are. As best as we can guess, magic exists in my realm only because Elgar Reed accidentally and completely unknowingly wrote a system of magic into being that was so perfect, so *literary*, that it began to exist. No other author's works deals in Words and Deal-Makers, and that, it seems, has made the difference between awareness and simply remaining fiction for my fellow creations.

I am unique in the universe.

And if I am not, I have found no evidence that any other characters have slipped their pages to live amongst their creators in the Overrealm. As much as it is a popular narrative trope, especially in children's literature, it simply is not true. So, if the problem is not magical, then it must be mundane. It must be a *person*.

And a person, I can track.

Several frustrating hours, and two trips downstairs for coffee later, I must admit to myself that what I thought was my first real lead was in fact nothing at all. Finnar reports too many instances to comb through when I leave the parameters broad, and too few when I make them more specific. Finnar, it seems, has found nothing. I begin to think that this is less because there is nothing to find, however, and more because whoever has done it has found a way to do so completely unseen. Not for the first time do I wish Elgar had let me install security cameras inside his home, as I have done in ours.

The problem, of course, with being a hacker is that if a thing does not exist in the realm of the digital, then I cannot access it. I cannot overhear conversations that happen in rooms that are not bugged, or where a laptop is not already open with the web-camera exposed.

I can turn on the camera and microphone without anyone knowing, but Elgar has, it seems, elected to keep his laptop shut and off for now. Elgar has a habit of leaving his smartphone in his pocket, prefers not to use it at all if he can help it, and like many men of his generation in the Overrealm, he simply does not turn it on if he doesn't intend to use it. Which means I cannot use its camera to track what is happening around him, only its GPS.

And his assistant Juan does not seem to be doing anything untoward, from what I've observed of his digital life. He has no photos of roommates or romantic partners on his phone, no one who could easily access his files or technology, and nothing telling in any of his chat and text logs. His texts speak briefly of a new boyfriend, but nothing more than that. No spats, no overheard vengeful plots. If he is facilitating this stalker, it is not on any of the devices I know to be his. The most questionable of his activities is an absurd amount of time spent in fan fiction archives and online RPG forums, but who am I to judge a man who enjoys spending his free time in fictional worlds?

And of course, I cannot track the flow of information if one is simply verbally passing it on. It's possible that someone close to Elgar might be... but I vetted Juan myself, and according to what I've been able to find in the Seattle Police Department records, the people assigned to work on his case and protect him are all equally reliable and honest.

So how is whoever doing this, well, *doing this*?

Unless it's not a person at all.

Another fearful thought adds to the ball of consideration at the back of my mind, the pieces twisting, reforming, slotting together and breaking apart again. The clues aren't all there yet, though, and like the fictional Sherlock Holmes, whom I've come to admire (if I were to wish to meet any other fictional creation, it would be him or Spock), I do not like to theorize before I have all the facts.

When I extract and open the crime scene photos of a break-in at Elgar's house, I expect nasty slurs painted on a wall, or shattered crockery, or stolen goods. I am so unprepared for what meets me that it takes me an embarrassingly long time to parse what I am seeing.

Blood, that is certain. Blood, splattered and splashed on a white wall. Sprayed over canned goods, and unopened jars, and foodstuff boxes, and white wire shelving. *Ah, his pantry closet*, my brain tells me, even as the rest of it is trying to understand the other bright splotches of color in the frame. It doesn't help that the series of photographs were harshly lit, the whites too white, the shadows too deep. And then I *see* it.

I feel my gorge rise and swallow hastily. I resume parsing the pictures, all the air suddenly rushing out of my lungs, leaving me gasping.

The photographs of what has happened in Elgar's home are *horrifying*. I consider not showing Pip. But I know she would rather be in the loop than out of it, and it makes no sense to keep this secret from my wife when, historically, doing so has not proven to be the wise choice. It is always better to have her mind on the case alongside mine—and she will not be angry with me for keeping yet another thing from her again. We have, the both of us, had enough of Turnish tempers and betrayed feelings.

I come downstairs in a rage and hand Pip my tablet, onto which I've transferred the photos.

"Freckles?" Pip asks, looking up from where she is grading papers on the kitchen table.

"This was left in his house," I say. "I warn you, those photographs are revolting."

"More disturbing than a Red Cap slaughter?" Pip asks.

"Possibly," I allow. "Will you look?"

She nods silently and flicks on the tablet. Then she

drops it on the table top in shock. Alis, seated in her high chair, building some sort of tower out of building blocks on the tray, knocks it over when she is startled by Pip's outburst.

"Mama!" she scolds Pip, and then utterly ignores us in favor of recreating the structure.

"Holy fuck," Pip whispers, eyes wide and caught on the image of a tangle of flesh, and gore, and vegetation. "That's ivy."

"It is."

She taps the screen hesitantly with one plum-colored nail. "Is that... human...?"

"No," I say, and it is a relief to be able to report this at least. "Porcine, according to the laboratory reports attached to the photos."

She wraps her arms around her stomach and shudders all over. "Jesus. Who did this?"

"I don't know," I admit, and it feels like acid on the tongue. I cannot keep the sneer out of my voice. "I have done my best to trace the stalker's digital footprint. Whoever they are, their hacking skills far exceed mine."

Pip goggles. "They what?"

"I have found no evidence of emails, of texts, or even of photographs or CCTV stills of someone planning to do my creator harm. Outside, of course, the usual entitled fanboys whose self-loathing has become so vitriolic that they project it outward onto Elgar." I run my hands through my hair, flustered and upset by my failure.

Pip pulls my hands down, kisses the back of each of them once. "You think it's that?"

"I don't know. Usually, this sort of cruel narcissism is a crippling paralytic, but sometimes, in directing it outward... possibly?"

"These sorts of revolting threats are completely different than bringing an assault rifle to school," Pip says.

"This is a different MO."

"My only lead turned out to be as substantial as Wisp-light," I admit. "One of the obsessive fans I keep tabs on—the one from Detroit?—seems to be acting outside of their usual pattern. But a look into their new habits reveals only that they are perhaps starting to drift away from the vitriol of their former web-forum colleagues. They've initiated a friendship with a new online gaming partner, and are spending more time in video-chats that are streamed, and which I therefore cannot access."

"Well, good for them, I guess," Pip says, bitter.

"Yes." I dismiss my disappointment at not having an easy villain to roust with a huff. "Any move away from their usual horrible online rants is a good one."

"So, what do you want to do now?" Pip asks.

"Honestly, *bao bei*, beyond calling Elgar and scream-ing in his ear, there is little I *can* do. Whoever did this, however it was done, the Seattle Police Department seems to have it well in hand. I have set a few new alerts to cer-tain keywords that may be used in their reports, but I am not yet prepared to meddle with another district's opera-tions for fear of making something worse. And from the tone of the reports, Elgar doesn't seem too affected. It is a shame to say, but... he's been threatened before. He knows how to protect himself."

Pip rests her head against my clavicle and sighs. "And he'd call us if he needed us."

"I should hope so," I say, the rage rushing back in. "Though the fool did not tell us. So make of that what you will."

Pip snorts. "He's being a dramatic martyr."

"All the same," I admit, "I shall be strengthening the digital protections around our home."

"Shame you can't set wards," Pip says, and I don't think she's teasing.

"Perhaps if magic really is here, I may be able to—*Pip!*"

I have just enough time to keep her from pitching sideways against Alis's high chair when Pip freezes up and her eyes roll up in her head. She sways with greater force than I've seen in one of her fits thus far, as if she has been flung from her chair by a mighty, invisible blow. I manage to get us onto the tiles safely, Pip piled in my lap. Her arms jump up, as if to ward off something coming at her face, and the suddenness of the movement and the blow of her wrist to my forehead drives me back against the side of the table. I crack my head hard.

Alis screams.

I manage to stay upright, shaking away the stars that spark in the edges of my vision.

Alis wriggles and writhes, and I am grateful that her high chair is both sturdy enough not to tip and comes with a little seatbelt that she has not yet learned to undo on her own.

Pip slides from my lap down onto the tile, and I just manage to keep my hands under her head, keep her from bouncing it off the hard surface. Pip cries out once, a long, high keen, arms still raised to protect against something I cannot see, cannot fend off for her.

Dear Writer, my poor love. What is *happening* to us? To her?

When she finally slumps, chest jumping as she struggles to catch her breath, I take the time to gently set her down and go see to Alis. My daughter is sobbing nonsense, a string of words in English and Mandarin punctuated with, "*Bu yao, bu bu!*"

"'S all right, sweeting," I mumble, and lift her from her high chair. Alis tips herself forward in my arms, trying to get at Pip on the floor. "No, no, let your mother rest for a moment." Alis screams louder as I walk us into the living room, twisting and jumping in my arms like a live wire.

For a moment, I fear that, as Pip's daughter, whatever is affecting my wife is torturing Alis as well, but a careful examination of Alis shows no pain in her back, no reaction to my light touches on her skull. She seems only to be upset by Pip's fit.

Another few puzzle pieces floating at the back of my mind slot into place. When Pip is well enough, she staggers into the living room and joins Alis and I on the sofa. This time, I let Alis crawl over to Pip, who seems content to hold her daughter close and whisper nothings into her ear. She pets Alis gingerly, though, and holds herself stiffly.

"Pip," I say, acting on my concern and closing my fingers around Pip's wrist gently. Pip lets me pull her hand away from Alis's back, and I am startled to find her palm an angry red, already blistering a little, as if she'd burned it badly. Pip offers up her second palm without saying a word, proving that it has happened to both hands.

The burns go part of the way past her wrists.

"Cloth Cage of Neglect time for you, sweeting," I tell Alis, trying to lighten the mood. It doesn't work. I pluck Alis away from her mother and drop her into her playpen. She grumbles unhappily, but luckily, her rage seems to have worn her out, and she lays down and cuddles some of her board books crankily.

"And upstairs to the bathroom and the first aid kit for you, wife," I tell Pip. She nods wearily, and lets me help her lever herself upright. She minces as she walks, cradling her rib cage.

She sits down on the edge of the tub, and then gasps as I turn around to fetch the first aid kit from under the sink. "Forsyth, your head."

"Hmm?" I touch the place from which my headache

seems to radiate, and my fingers come away slightly tacky with blood. "A small hurt," I say. "Let's see to you first."

I run the sink as cold as I can make it, and Pip rinses her hands while I peel up her shirt to get a look at her side. Her torso is bruised with deep purple marks, the kind of bruises Kintyre used to get when he took a fall from Stormbearer. But these ones look days old already. Even before my eyes, some of the smaller bruises are beginning to lighten to the sickly green-and-yellow of healing. It is unnatural and alarming.

If I didn't know any better, I'd say someone was Speaking Words of Healing over Pip right now. Working on a theory, I pull Pip's cold, wet hands up to my face and Speak my own Words of Healing. The Word crackles and sparks in the air, an actual puff of watery glitter, but nothing happens.

Still, it is more than a Word has ever done in the Overrealm before.

"It's getting stronger," Pip says, face ashen.

"But not nearly strong enough for what we need right now," I say.

None of the blisters on her palms have grown large enough to require lancing, so I set about swabbing her hands with antiseptic wipes and covering them with a generous helping of burn cream. Pip gestures wearily at my head.

"I can't help you clean that when I'm covered in goo."

"No need, my love," I say, kissing her forehead gently.

I rip open a fresh swab and search the back of my skull until I find the part that stings. It doesn't start bleeding again, so that's a blessing, I suppose.

When I am done, I help Pip back downstairs and to the sofa, where she can lay down within easy reach of Alis.

"I'll call the school and have your TA teach your

classes today," I say, and this final act of thoughtfulness seems to be what undoes my wife. Pip rolls over, buries her face in the sofa cushions, and begins to weep. "Pip."

"I don't understand what's happening," she says. "I don't *understand.*"

"Shhh, rest for now," I say, sitting on the arm of the sofa and petting her hair.

"You know what it is. You're thinking something," Pip accuses, looking up at me with tears forming along her lashes. "Come on."

"I have my theories," I admit reluctantly.

"Spill."

I sigh, and shake my head gently to avoid any residual dizziness from my knock. "When you a-a-are re-reh-rest-ed."

"*Now,*" Pip insists, gaze hardening.

"It se-seems th-th-that th-the d-d-dates and t-tah-times of your f-fits ma-tch the day-dates and t-tuh-times of the inci-ci-ci-dents happening arou-nd Elgar-r," I say softly. I watch, tense and waiting, as Pip digests this.

"It's me," she gasps, and then the waterworks begin in earnest. She twists around and lays her head on my knees, sobbing fit to shake apart. "I knew it. I knew something had to be wrong. I knew it—I just... *fucking trilogies.*"

"We d-d-don't know th-that," I remind her. "We ha-have no p-pro-proof."

"Oh, god, the light, the burns," Pip gasps, staring up at me. "Elgar. You need to—"

"In a mo-ment," I say. "Whatever has ha-happened has h-happened, and nothing yet has happened to him p-personally. I will see to you, and then I will check on hi-him."

"I'm fine," Pip lies. "Call him."

"Pip, you are my first priority. If he was still with the p-puh-police, he will already have received the best first res-ponder care. Perhaps they have caught the person th-threatening him and—"

"What if it's not a person?" Pip asks tremulously, chin wobbling. "What if you... you can't find anyone? What if there's nothing to find because there's no one behind it?"

A frisson of fear crawls over my flesh. "*Bao bei*, what are you implying? That it's—"

"I don't know. I don't *know*," Pip sobs. "Is it me? Oh my god, is it me? Am I doing...?"

"You can't possibly. N-Not con-consciously, a-at least—"

"Maybe it's really the magic? What if it's tearing out of me? Going after him?" Pip looks at Alis, asleep in her playpen. "What if I—? What if it *gets out* and hurts—?"

"I wo-won't l-l-let it," I vow, as firmly as I am able.

"You can't promise—"

"If there is enou-enough m-ma-magic in the air to harm m-me or A-Alis, then th-th-thu-there is en-nough to st-st-stop it fuh-first."

"I hope you're right," Pip whispers into my thigh, pressing her forehead against my hip. I cradle her head gently. "God, *bao bei*, I hope you're right."

ELGAR

Come the following Saturday, Elgar is desperate to leave. Not because it's scary, but because he has *nothing to do*. Elgar has slept, watched television with a rotating cast of various stony-faced agents, kept abreast of the casting news with Riletti, let Jackson bully him into long and rambling walks around the walled-in garden, an-swered the panicked phone calls from his agent when she learned he was in a goddamn safe house, and tried very hard not to miss writing.

In this week alone, surrounded by neat spy stuff and

with only his own thoughts to occupy him, he's had a dozen ideas for a magical cop-procedural mystery series, and he's jotted them down in his notebook, carefully keeping from envisioning his main protagonist too clearly, just in case... in case... *aw, hell.*

Elgar doesn't think it's possible to be so scared for such a sustained amount of time. He wonders if this is what it must feel like to be a peasant living in a castle under a siege you can do nothing about. Or, possibly, what living in the Middle East right now might be like. The constant and complete awareness of everything around you at all times, being constantly prepped and primed for fight or flight, is exhausting. He's tired, but can't sleep. Every creak and crack of the strange house startles him. He's too tense to really be bored, but too bored for time to pass quickly.

He calls Juan every day, via secure satellite phone, to stay abreast of what's going on with Flageolet and the TV series, as well as the house. Juan's also managing his social media feeds, pretending to be Elgar and making no reference to the stalker, or the horror that has been following him, in order to keep everyone calm and not tip-off the crazies. Elgar's been amused to note that Juan has him taking "long walks" through the park a lot recently. The dig isn't as subtle as his assistant thinks it is.

Linux chirrups and meows in the background sometimes, which makes Elgar homesick in a way that has nothing to do with places.

Four days into Elgar's exile, the stress of it all makes him slip up in exactly the way he feared he would. Juan asks him if he's been in contact with his Canadian cousins, and Elgar uses Forsyth's full name when he replies.

"Forsyth?" Juan asks. "Okay, yeah, no, that makes sense. Did you name Forsyth in the book for him? Is it his real name?"

"What? I... " Elgar says, caught out and wishing he could see Juan's face, could parse his expression so he can figure out what his assistant is getting at. Tomorrow, he's going to insist on a video-call. "Yeah, I guess you could say so. Why are you stuck on this?"

"It's a bit funny, is all..." Juan says slowly. "It's just that, the other day, my boyfriend was asking about him. Forsyth, I mean. The character. He wanted to know what I knew about him."

The familiar icy chill crawls up Elgar's spine. "Why?" he asks, trying not to sound paranoid.

"I dunno—for smutty fan fiction or something? You know fans like slashing the side characters. He's probably one of those Three Pointe Turn writers."

"The what?"

"It's a ship name. You know? Three Pointe... the sheriff, his wife, and Forsyth?"

"What about them?"

"They're stories about a threesome with...? Never mind," Juan says quickly when Elgar makes a garbled, sort of disbelieving sound.

"Rupin and Dorthi and... right, no. No," Elgar says quickly.

Juan chuckles. "I dunno, boss. Wouldn't be the first polycule you'd written."

Elgar rubs his eyes hard enough to make the darkness spark in his head. "No."

"All right, I'll lay off. Did you get the email about the table read in LA?"

"Yeah."

"Do you... want to go?"

Elgar looks back over his shoulder at the man in the impeccable suit and large headphones listening in on his conversation. The man gives a nod.

"I guess," Elgar says at length. "I... I mean, I can't stay

here forever."

"Right, and maybe jetting off to LA for a few weeks is a good idea. Clear your head."

Elgar snorts. "Clearly you've never been to LA. The air there is many things, but clear will never be one of them."

Juan makes a sort of wistful sound.

"Oh," Elgar says slowly. "Do you... want to come to LA with me?"

Juan makes another sound, this one a bit strangled. "Linux, boss..."

"I hate to say it, but maybe Linux will be, ah... better—"

"Safer?" Juan interrupts tentatively.

"Yeah. In a, you know, a kitty hotel."

Juan sighs, and Elgar can envision him nodding. "If someone is still watching your place, they may now be watching mine, you mean?"

"Come to LA," Elgar blurts. "We'll stay two weeks. You can go clubbing somewhere appropriately gay—"

"Boss," Juan chuckles.

"We'll do everything face-to-face for a while. I haven't seen Kim in the flesh in a dog's age, anyway. Come on."

"Boss, you sound really—"

"*Please*, Juan." Elgar is aware that it's needy and begging, but he can't seem to keep the desperation out of his tone.

The silence on the other end of the connection makes it more than clear that Juan has heard it, too. Heard it, and is moved by it.

"Yeah. Okay. I'll book the tickets. Out of SeaTac?"

Another look over his shoulder and another subtle nod from Impeccable Suit has Elgar saying, "Yes, SeaTac's fine. Book it for two days from now."

"Okay, I'll pack a bag for you—"

"No, I... I want to go back to the house myself. I can pack."

Impeccable Suit has no opinion on this desire, apparently, as he neither nods nor shakes his head.

"Are you sure, boss?"

"I've got some stuff I need to take with me to LA. Papers and things, and a gift for Kim. It'll be faster if I do it."

"If you're sure..."

"I'm sure," Elgar says, and he's proud of how his voice doesn't *quite* quaver when he says it.

"So, we're not telling anyone we're going, right?"

"No," Elgar says.

"Not even your cousin?"

"Maybe," Elgar hedges. Impeccable Suit has no opinion on this, either. Elgar hasn't had enough privacy to call Forsyth yet, but his worry that his email and texts are being watched is waning with each passing day. He's determined to call them tonight, safe house or no. It's time he brought Forsyth in. Maybe he can even take a minute while he's packing—nip into his en suite and do it then.

Whoever it is that seems to be trying to scare him hasn't threatened him in any new ways. The cops that were casing his place for clues said nothing out of the ordinary had happened, and nothing about the TV series—which is all he'd been emailing his agent about for the last three days—has appeared online. If someone was watching his email in order to scare him or find ways to ruin his life, then wouldn't they have leaked the TV series casting all over the place by now?

Perhaps it's a bit arrogant to conflate leaking optioning news with grievous bodily harm, but for Elgar, they're analogous. He wants this TV series to go well so badly. He needs to know if the things he created can have happy endings. He wants to get to the end of the TV series, nine seasons down the line, so he can canonize Kintyre and Bevel's relationship, the joy of Kintyre's son Wyndam, and to make sure that no one else can ever write something into his world that will hurt the people that Forsyth and Lucy love. Or take away the happily ever afters they created for themselves after he stopped writing them.

He needs to know that Tristin and Vanna from the *Shuttleborn* trilogy are going to be able to find happiness after everything he's done to them.

"How's Linux?" Elgar asks, because the silence has grown a bit strained over the line.

"Bit of a terror," Juan says. "He didn't like the new environment at first, but once he had a good sniff around, he was fine. But, boss, I can tell you, he really doesn't like my new beau."

"The book nerd?"

"Yeah. Some people just really don't like cats, I guess. And Linux can tell."

"Poor little buddy," Elgar says.

"Yeah. How you holding up, boss?"

Elgar shrugs. "I've never been so on top of my admin. Riletti's been good help— Jackson's reading *Hand of the Foesmiter* now. They're okay company." Elgar pointedly doesn't say anything about the rotating cast of men in suits.

"So, when will you head out?"

"I assume I'll be going back to pack... tomorrow?" Impeccable Suit nods. "Yeah, tomorrow. Probably the morning, after rush hour."

"Tomorrow, after rush hour," Juan repeats. "Okay. Oh! Also, I had Carmen come in, give it all a scrub after forensics left. I hope you don't mind the extra bill."

"God, no!" Elgar says. "No, I hadn't thought of that. Thanks."

"No worries, boss. You pay me to think about these things."

"That poor woman."

"The cops took most of it away as evidence. She said there wasn't much left but, uh... stains."

Elgar bites his tongue hard to keep his gorge from rising. "Thanks for that. I don't think I... I could have—"

"Do you want me to come to the house with you, boss? I can change my plans. Let me call—"

"No, no, it's okay," Elgar says. "I think I need some time with the house to myself. You know... get used to it again. But when this is over, as a thank you, I'd like to... I don't know, cook? And the boyfriend? He can come—"

Juan makes a noise. "No, I don't think so. I'm figuring out that he's kinda weird about authors. I'm not going to inflict that on you until I'm sure he's a keeper."

"Okay."

"Okay."

Quiet descends between them again, and as he always does when that happens, Juan feels compelled to fill it. Which, in the end, turns out to be worse for Elgar than sitting in the safe house alone, his mind spinning. Because, at least in the safety of his own head, Elgar can consider that magic and the world he created might have something to do with it all.

With no reason to assume magic is involved, Juan's imagination keeps running toward obsessive fans, or angry authors who're jealous of Elgar's success, or, god forbid, that myopic rabid faction of spec-fic fandom that tried to hijack the Hugo Awards. And while they might be good guesses, Elgar fears, deep down in his not-inconsiderable amount of gut, that they are dead wrong.

What the real answer is, he still can't admit to himself. He's edging closer to it, mind circling like a vulture patiently coasting on updrafts, waiting for the wounded gazelle of thought to finally go still. It makes his head light—or maybe that's the excess of coffee he's been indulging in without Juan around to scold him. The rest of him is well-rested, as there isn't much to do in this place but sleep and sit around, but his mind hasn't stopped chugging the whole time. Like a perpetual motion machine, he can't seem to find the brakes.

The drive to his house the next morning is quicker than he remembers the drive to the safe house being, and Jackson parks the unmarked car in the alleyway behind Elgar's home. Elgar leads them in through the backyard, and up to the kitchen patio door. Jackson insists on being the first to enter the house. Once he's swept through each room, checking them for anything amiss, he returns to the kitchen to wave Elgar and Riletti inside. His face, however, is grim.

"What did you find?" Riletti asks, as Elgar sets his bag down on the kitchen table.

"You found something?" Elgar yelps, unable to hold in his surprise. "But I thought... what happened?"

Jackson only waves down the hall, toward his—oh god, his office.

Panic strikes like a fist to his solar plexus, punching all the air out of Elgar's lungs. A jittering kind of energy seizes his limbs, and he jerks down the hall, filled with horrified anticipation that makes his gait disjointed and wobbly. He braces himself with one hand on the wall, leaning hard, pressing his palm into the textured wallpaper as he slides across it.

What is it going to be this time? A jungle of threatening greenery? An ocean of blood? A body?

"Watch where you step," Jackson says, trailing after him. The door, which Elgar knows he left closed when he left, is now hanging open. Elgar doesn't know what Jackson means by the admonishment until he looks at his office floor. Glass fragments litter the carpet, from where the big bay window that looks out onto his side garden has been broken in. No, not "broken," that word isn't forceful enough. It's smashed. Shattered. Exploded. *Fragmentalized.* Shards are sprayed all the way to the far wall.

The rest of the office is in a similar state. His precious cat-tunnel desk is in splinters so small, Elgar wouldn't have been able to guess they used to be the desk if it wasn't for the distinctive honey color of the wood. The paintings on his walls have been slashed and shredded with either parallel strokes from a knife, or some very sharp claws from a very large beast. His filing cabinet has been upended, the drawers pulled out and crumpled against the floor. Papers lie in ashy, smoldering drifts all over the floor. And the carpet is scorched; a section of fibers by the window is actually still smoking.

It looks as if a bomb, an *actual bomb*, has gone off in here.

And it must have happened when they were just blocks away, heading in this direction.

"Oh god," Elgar chokes as Jackson crosses the room to stomp out the last of the embers on the carpet. "Did my neighbors not call 911? I mean, look at how hard someone must have hit that glass! It looks like someone put a sledgehammer through it! Look at the scorch marks! There had to have been noise."

The only part of his office that is untouched is the bookshelf. The novels, comics, and reference books are all eerily, perfectly pristine, untouched by the blast that seems to have shredded the rest of the room, almost as if they had been shielded.

Something about them looks wrong, though, but he can't place what. The shelf just looks... funny.

Jackson steps back out into the hallway, pulling his radio off his belt. Riletti, who'd followed them, steps around him and into the room to stand beside Elgar. Elgar moans, clutching at his hair like a distressed Regency suitor. It's ridiculous. Laughable. *Gelastic*. But he doesn't care what kind of picture he makes. God, he can't breathe.

"How did this happen?" Jackson is shouting down the line. "When did this happen? There were eyes on the house twenty-four-seven!"

Elgar stumbles back, out of the office, hand over his eyes as if blocking out the sight of the wreckage can undo it. He gropes his way to his living room, folding onto the sofa with a miserable, terrified sense of déjà vu.

Riletti follows him, making sure he doesn't trip over anything, and sits on the coffee table. She grabs his chin, forces him to look up at her, checking his eyes and taking his pulse. She pulls Aunty Lilah's throw off the back of the sofa and over his shoulders.

Shock, Elgar thinks. Again. It's funny, in a way. Twice in one week. And I put Kintyre through worse than this, over and over again, in every book... Never once did I think that he would... would react. Like this. Like me. Oh god. What's happening?

"Good thing you brought your laptop and fire-safe with you," Riletti says, tucking the blanket around him. "Or this could have been much, much worse. Stay here, I'll get you some water."

"Yeah," Elgar says, his whole body numb. Because at that exact moment, he realizes why the bookshelf looked wrong, lopsided and strangely gap-toothed. "Yeah. You're right. It can be much, much worse."

Because the books, his leather-bound, special-edition books, are missing.

The Tales of Kintyre Turn are gone.

SIX

Elgar texts me the next morning, and all it says is: **GOIN 2 LA 4 2wks.**

I wonder that a man so dedicated to the English language would choose to slaughter it so brutally when smartphones allow for people to text in full sentences now. Then I wonder if it is wise to travel when one is being stalked and threatened with bodily harm. And then I realize that being elsewhere, especially when one has the support of the police force to help them vanish, is probably the best course of action one could take. It gives the stalker no satisfaction to watch an empty house, and perhaps, if we are lucky enough, it will bore them into giving up the chase.

I can only hope that that will be the case here.

As for why Elgar is headed to LA, that much is obvious.

I'm not entirely certain how I feel about this adaptation of my brother's life for the small screen. Though I do think it makes me feel better to know that this version of Forsyth Turn will be a peripheral character. Pip tells me that I only appear in the first, fourth, and eighth books of the series, and I do not even speak in the last of these. Whomever they cast to play me is therefore destined for a bit part.

Unless, by some meddling on Elgar's part, the role of

this fictional Forsyth is expanded. That possibility, I don't mind admitting, has me even more emotionally wibbly.

I reply to my creator's text, confirming that I got it, and then roll over in bed to watch my wife sleep. Though "sleep" might be a generous word for it. She is twitching, and mumbling, and I wonder if I ought to wake her, or if startling her would be unwise.

I slide out from between the covers and stand by her side, observing—the burns and bruises from the day before have all but vanished. Either the magic that made them appear is withdrawing, taking the evidence along with it, or the person to whom the original injury occurred—which we are seeing mirrored in Pip—is using Words of Healing so steadily that he or she must be utterly drained of energy this morning.

I have not yet told Pip about this second theory. I have no proof for it, and I do not wish to worry her with it when she has so much worry already. Deciding that waking Pip is the better option, especially with Alis's own soft breaths coming through the baby monitor as proof that this round of horrible teething, at least, is finally over for her, I say, gently: "Pip?"

She snuffles and flops, and when I repeat her name, a little louder, her eyes snap open. "Morning," I say. "I think you were having a nightmare."

"I think I was," she agrees, and sits up, groaning and wincing. She studies her palms, and then lifts her t-shirt to do the same to her ribs. "Nearly gone."

"Yes," I agree.

"Creepy."

"Yes," I agree again.

She holds out her arms to me, and I obligingly return to bed. She slides onto her side, pulling my arm across her so that she may be the "little spoon," and I wonder at this gesture. I have never known my wife to be so desperate for consolation and comfort as she is this morning. She is a very sexual creature, yes, but cuddling for no reason but to cuddle hasn't always been her preference.

I feel my insides twist, my heart sink, and I press my forehead against the nape of my wife's neck, because I cannot, I do not want to ask this next question out loud, let alone while looking her in the face. "Pip, I have something to ask you, and I... I wish I did not have to."

"Yeah?" Pip folds her arms across mine, and I squeeze her waist tight, screwing my eyes shut. I can feel her shaking. Or maybe it is she who can feel me shaking. I'm not certain which of us is the source. "Ask."

"Do you recall the exact wording you used when you bound the Viceroy's magic?"

Pip jerks in my grip, rolling down, curling herself over my arm as if clinging to the edge of a cliff. "Oh my god," she chokes, and her voice is tight and terrible. "Did I get it wrong?"

"I can't recall the exact wording..."

"Neither can I. I could have... did I leave a loophole?"

"Perhaps?" I say, softly, quietly, every syllable an agony.

"What have I done?"

"It could be a copycat," I say hastily. "It could be someone who knows us and is using this as ammunition against Elgar."

Pip frowns and turns into my chest. "I should have let Wyndam kill him," she mutters. "Just to be sure. I should have... I should have done the smart thing, instead of the right thing. Why didn't I do the *smart* thing?"

"Because you are good, and kind, and compassionate," I say, tucking my knuckles under my wife's chin and lifting her head so that I may kiss her, comfort her. "Because you felt pity for the Deal-Maker."

"Bilbo's pity got half the armies of Middle Earth

killed," Pip says, disdainfully. "I should know better. Why did I do it? I've never been... been *affected* by the tropes in your world before. I thought I was immune to them."

"You were never immune," I correct. "Just *aware*."

Pip pauses, digesting this. "And I missed this one."

We are both thinking it, but neither of us is prepared to say it. Not out loud. Not yet.

But if we had left the Viceroy even the smallest ability to retain his magic... then, with the blood of a Deal-Maker, the blood of his mother, even the great archvillain may have been able to open a way to the Overrealm.

We do not speak on it further. Pip, I think, needs time to adjust to the idea that the Viceroy may be here. May *have* followed us here. She leaves for work subdued, and returns, grim, after her morning classes, determined to do her grading at home rather than in her office. That she skipped her daily workout at the school gym is cause for only mild concern. She is, I assume, still too sore to contemplate exercise.

I am glad she is here when she suddenly jerks back from the counter, where she'd been making a fresh pot of coffee, to stare at her hands in horror. Blood drips and pools around her feet, splashing against the tiles.

"Dear Writer!" I gasp when I see what has happened. I jump up from where Alis and I have been reading to Library in the living room and rush into the kitchen. Pip seems too numb from the shock to know what to do about the gore running in small rivulets down her fingers, so I push her toward the sink. "Pip, are you hurt? How did this happen? What broke?"

She makes no answer, and that's when I realize that her eyes have rolled back in her head and she is having another fit. This one is smaller, more subdued, like the person wielding the magic on the other end of the tether can only cast small charms; a tether that seems to be connecting them more and more. I tuck myself behind my wife in case she faints on the spot, and turn on the taps.

When I rinse away the worst of the blood, I can see that the cuts are shallow, deliberate strokes, weaving and curling up her forearms. They are not quite of Boot-knife's handiwork, not so clean or artistic as he would have done, but are very similar all the same.

The cuts flare open and closed almost as soon as they've been made. Like flowers blossoming on her skin, the red gaps widen and shrivel into pink scars, which then flake away before ripping open again like hungry mouths, gasping for air, moist with crimson. The wounds are about the size of a quarter at their most distended, and they open in twos and threes, trailing up toward her elbow before snapping shut and a new wave begins. It is ghoulish and disgusting, and I cannot tell if Pip is in pain from them or not.

Alis clings to the little pillar that divides the kitchen and living room and watches with wide gray eyes, bottom lip trembling.

"Mama?"

"Mama's going to be fine, sweeting," I tell her.

"Help?"

"Absolutely. Can you go to the bookshelf and fetch your da *The Wizard of Oz*?"

"Yah!" Alis says, and trundles away to pick the book out of the pile her shelf on the bookcase always becomes.

With her safely out of the kitchen and away from us for a moment, I give Pip a hard shake, rocking her back against my chest. She blinks, convulsing a little, and a second shake has her lifting her head and looking around. She looks down at her arms.

"Fucking fuck," she groans.

The gaps are all closed now, with none opening anew, but red lines run up and down her forearms. They look like nothing so much as scratches from a pet cat who got too playful. But the amount of blood on the floor, the counter, and still clinging to the sides of the sink, belays the idea that the cuts were ever inconsequential.

"Sit," I tell Pip, and she staggers to a chair by the table. I wipe down her arms with a damp dishtowel, and then start mopping up the blood on the floor.

"'Ook, Mama," Alis tells Pip from the doorway, holding up *The Wizard of Oz*.

"Sure is, babycakes," Pip says lightly, but her voice is tight and raspy. "Come on up here and read it to me?"

Alis bounds over, flashing her dimples, and scrambles up onto Pip's lap with her mother's assistance. Pip winces and groans, but gets Alis settled, and together, they start to read the story. The cadence of the tale is familiar and soothing, and soon, my heart is back to its regular, staid rhythm. Alis loses interest in Oz and Munchkins as soon as I am finished cleaning the floor, and demands milk in both Mandarin and English, doubling, she thinks, her chances of getting it.

As I scrub my hands clean, and then prepare Alis her bottle, Pip dozes in her seat.

"It could be someone else," I say after Alis is equally dozy in my arms, head resting on my shoulder as she sucks at her bottle. "It might not be him."

"Come on," Pip says, stirring and raising an eyebrow at me. She offers a disdainful, skeptical look. "Freckles, you're smarter than that."

"I'll find him," I vow. "I'll work on Finnar tonight, and I will *find him*."

ELGAR

With only enough time to pack a suitcase of fresh clothing, Elgar is immediately packed into a nondescript town car and driven straight to the airport, a day early, their ticket changes expedited. They stop over briefly to secure his fire-safe in the Seattle PD's labyrinthine evidence locker for safekeeping. Plans are made over the radio unit in the car, and by the time they're at SeaTac, Elgar knows that he's going to have to go and check-in alone. Or at least, it will look like he's alone. Jackson and Riletti are already there, waiting for him in plainclothes so they can accompany him through the airport, and take the flight to LA with him and Juan. There, he'll be handed off to counterparts within the LAPD who'll monitor him and the people around him for the duration of his stay.

Everything is secretive and hush-hush, and if it wasn't for his fear of the mysterious man in black, Elgar would be reveling in how important and cool he feels knowing he has an undercover police detail.

They'd decided that Juan would meet him on the other side of security, where someone without a ticket can't follow, just in case someone might decide to follow his assistant in order to get to him. But as the flight time gets nearer and nearer, Elgar feels sweat starting to bead under his beard and cap. Juan isn't here yet. He isn't *here*. The longer Juan's arrival takes, the more fidgety he gets. Riletti and Jackson don't seem disturbed, but Elgar can't help staring at his phone, his knuckles white around the casing, willing it to chime with a message from Juan saying that he'd arrived safely. He's so intent on the screen, in fact, that when someone flops down into the seat beside him, Elgar jumps and makes a noise that he will never, in a million years, admit to being a yelp.

"Chill, boss!" Juan says, struggling to pull the smile off his face. "Just me." He's laughing, the jerk.

"I was worried... I thought you'd be here by now," Elgar says.

"I don't look at my phone or text while I drive," Juan

counters. "Bad for your health."

Elgar narrows his eyes and sizes up his assistant. "Speaking of—you look like ass."

Juan snorts, but doesn't contradict him. "Up all night."

Elgar decides now is a good time for some more of those gay-sex jokes. "In a good way?"

Juan's strained smile collapses. "In the exact opposite way. Boyfriend lost the entirety of his chill when he learned I was taking this trip with you."

Elgar sits back, concerned. He's never cared about the love lives of any of his other assistants, but Juan is rapidly becoming a friend, too, and, well, Elgar isn't a complete narcissistic asshole. He hopes. "Is he not cool with you going for two weeks? Or is it that it's me? Or...?"

Juan grimaces. "He figured out who you are, and he's been seething to have me introduce you. He started to get really creepy about it, and honestly, I just..." Juan rubs the inside of his elbow, shifting and wincing. "He got, ah... he's into some kinky shit that I'm not... he didn't even *ask* first and..." He rolls up his sleeve to show Elgar a messily taped square of gauze about the size of his palm. "I ended it. Kicked him out."

Elgar wants to reach out, to see the wound under the bandage, but he thinks that would be invasive. Juan will show him if he wants to. Instead, Elgar seizes on the one phrase that stands out. "Kicked him out?" he asks, thinking that Forsyth would be proud of him for catching it.

Juan rolls his sleeve back down and shakes his head, rueful. "I didn't realize it until I snatched the keys out of his hand and booted his ass to the curb, my old duffle stuffed full of his shit, but the crazy bastard was living with me. He left the house every day, but he was there every night—or near enough. He'd taken one of my bags and was... I don't know, stealing laundry from the neighbors' lines, or something? Christ, I don't know. And I don't care now. He's out. He's gone."

"But where did you meet him?" Elgar asks, and that icy prickle down his spine is back. "How could you not know he was... homeless, I guess?"

Juan swallows hard, his eyes getting wet, a faraway glaze stealing over his face. "I... I met him in... in a bar," he says, his voice dropping down into a thin, reedy breath that concerns Elgar instantly. "He was... end of the bar... asked me to... buy him a drink."

"Juan!" Elgar snaps, the shaking horror seeping into his own skin making him feel chill and clammy.

"Boss," Juan says, voice small and sounding very much like a child expecting to be chastened. "I think my... I think he..."

"Shhh," Elgar says softly. "You don't have to say it."

"I'm sorry. I should have—"

"No, you couldn't have known," Elgar says gently, forgivingly. He doesn't say: *and there is nothing you could have done, I suspect, if you had.* "Juan, I need to ask you something. I need you to tell me: what is his name?"

Sitting in the seats behind him, dressed like a married couple on their way to California for some sightseeing, Jackson nods once. He's preoccupied with his smartphone, while his "wife" looks at a map of wine tours in Sonoma Valley, and from his position, Elgar can see that Jackson's making notes on their conversation.

"I don't..." Juan says, voice crackling and eyes suddenly shining, a desperate frown pulling furrows between his eyebrows and along his chin. "I don't know. I don't remember his... oh god, boss, why don't I... why don't I remember?"

"It's fine. It's probably just stress," Elgar lies, trying to be soothing. Juan buries his face in his hands, struggling hard to keep it together as his shoulders shake. Elgar has a pack of tissues in his carry-on, and he hands these to his assistant when Juan next looks up, red-eyed and white-cheeked.

"Yeah," Juan says thickly. "Stress. God, I cannot wait to get on this plane."

FORSYTH

Several hours later, Alis is finally asleep and drooling on my shoulder. I have been typing away at Finnar all afternoon while Pip rested, searching for any clue that what happened to Pip earlier had happened in some way to Elgar as well. But according to all my sources—including the CCTV of the SeaTac waiting lounge—Elgar has simply been sitting in the security lounge of the airport, waiting to board his plane all afternoon.

Pip and I are both wretchedly exhausted, so dinner is order-in pizza, which Pip brings upstairs to my office when it arrives so we needn't dislodge Alis. She is feeling a little flushed again, and spent a good few hours poking at her mouth with her hands, drooling all over my desk. I don't doubt we're in for another few nights of teething, so am determined to let her sleep now while she can.

Pip and I eat in silence for a few moments before she says, with the air of someone who has come to a hard decision: "We need to tell Elgar."

My eyes snap open. "I agree. But I hesitate to do so, only because he—"

"You think his imagination will run away from him."

"Perhaps? Pip, he is being sta-stalked," I say, and then swallow hard, trying to helm my tongue long enough to explain my worry. Of course I would be stuttering now—I always do when I have something heartfelt or important to say, when I am heavily emotional. It's hateful. "And w-w-we ha-have no def-def-in-initive proo-of that it is by a ma-ma-ah-dman of his own creation. If we put th-the idea in his he-hea-ad that his attacker-er-er is ma-magical, he may miss a ve-ver-very r-r-real non-magical th-threat."

Pip kisses my tripping tongue calm. "None of that, *bao bei*."

"I am fruh-frus-frustrated," I complain.

"I know." Another soft kiss. "We have to at least tell him we suspect it, though."

I am torn. I agree that he should be fully armed, but I also don't want to scare him with an unproven hypothesis. Finnar has yet to actually *find* Elgar's stalker. "But if the attacks are magical, there is little he or the police can do to stop them."

Pip rubs her face. "And is there anything we can do?"

"At the moment?" I say. "I doubt it very much. These fits have you too weak to travel, let alone fight whatever or whomever we may find, and I am without both magic and Shadow's Men, or an army. Finnar is my best bet now, and I cannot take this rig with me to Seattle. For now, we must wait."

"Wait for *what?*" Pip groans. "For something worse to happen? To me? To Elgar? Jesus, how do you know we're doing the right thing?"

"Elgar seems safe enough in Los Angeles," I say softly. "Let him stay there, ignorant, until I find something concrete in Seattle."

Pip nods, but I can tell that she is chewing on a thought. I wait, quiet and still, until she is ready to share it.

"Are we committing the cardinal sin of psychodrama novels?" she asks in a small voice. "Should we be communicating more? Should we be sharing information? I mean, is this...?" She trails off and scrubs her hands through her hair. "I don't know this genre. I don't know spy thrillers. Are we making the right choices? Are we just talking ourselves around in circles? I don't know."

I stand, careful not to jostle Alis back into wakefulness, and walk over to Pip. She takes my extended hand and lets me pull her up into a hug. Pip slides her arms around my waist, and rests her cheek softly against Alis's side.

"You needn't be the expert at everything, *bao bei*," I whisper into her ear.

Pip huffs a laugh. "But that's my role in all this, right?" The way she says it recalls that morning in Gwillfifeshire, the smell of the fresh reeds on the floor and the trailing smoke from the embers in the hearth-grate of our room in the *Pern*.

"Perhaps you and Alis should go help sow a field and you will find your eureka moment," I suggest, standing again

Pip pinches my rear in retaliation. "Cheeky," she murmurs.

I stiffen up to avoid jumping and yelping and waking our child.

Eventually, when the pizza is eaten and Alis clearly out for the night, we make our way to bed. Finnar does not need me to babysit it. Neither of us have really attempted sleep, but as Alis has been put in her crib already, it felt strange not to curl into our own bed as well. We neither of us, I think, wanted to be as far away from her as the sofa downstairs. Pip sits up against the headboard with her PhD thesis open on her lap, muttering about having missed something, about having forgotten something important.

"Are these Stations?" Pip finally says. "Are we missing something? Is this a quest?"

Above our dresser, opposite the end of our bed, the Excel Sheet from our first quest in Hain is framed and hung upon the wall. Pip had it in her travel bag when we crossed into the Overrealm. And like the precious few items I still have left from my previous life, I treasure the large, creased, shakily written-upon piece of parchment. It is obvious that Pip's new line of questioning, her new worries, have come of staring at it in the half-dark of our bedroom.

"It is nothing like Elgar's plots, if it is," I offer into the darkness.

"I don't know where it would have started, what the First Station would have been, or the call to action, or... I mean, we're at home, but it feels like we've already started the adventure, so how can we have left home if we haven't 'left home'? What the hell kind of bullshit quest is this?"

I roll onto my side, enjoying the quiet whisper of the duvet sliding against my pajamas as I do so, and take Pip's face between my hands. My wife is beautiful in the orange gloaming of the streetlights outside our bedroom window. I kiss her softly, gently, taking the time to linger, to communicate that I wish her to be at ease, to feel safe, to know that she is loved. Pip folds up her thesis and lets it drop to the floor. On my bedside table, the baby monitor pushes the steady, sure white noise of Alis's deep, undisturbed breaths as she sleeps.

"Do not get caught up in the Hero's Journey," I say, when our kiss has wound down to its natural conclusion. "It is entirely possible that this is no adventure at all, and it is only our natural worry coloring our perspective. Terrible things happen in the Overrealm all the time, after all, and none of *that* is connected by narrative."

"That's not what I—"

"I know. These fits, the horrible threats, of course they're connected to one another. But we will not solve how if we do not sleep. And we neither of us can do anything more tonight toward finding... the stalker. Elgar is out of Seattle, and presumably safe and sound. Tonight, let us just sleep."

"That's not exactly a comfort," Pip sighs, and snuggles against my chest, pulling my arm over her waist and holding on to my admittedly thin bicep as if she were Alis and I, Library.

"Well, I am sorry that your realm is not clever enough to operate on the same predictive narrative rules as mine," I sniff theatrically. Pip giggles and buries her cold nose against my neck in revenge, giggling harder when I yelp.

ELGAR

The flight down is uneventful, and by the time they've been collected by their shiny new California security shadow, and set up in a three-bedroom suite in a Beverly Hills hotel happy to bend over backwards to accommodate their early arrival, Juan is feeling calmer. A shower, a good sit-down with a tea, and a walk around the block energizes him, and they spend the evening eating weird California sushi and compiling everything Juan remembers about his nameless ex-boyfriend with the author fetish into an email for the Seattle police. That is the most they can do to help from LA, and they get a reply a few minutes later, thanking them for the extra information and assuring them that they should enjoy their time away and not let this mar their trip.

Despite the frenzied schedule of flesh-pressing, brunch catch-ups with his agent, long lunch meetings, and the indeterminable hours always gluttonously gobbled up by having to drive through the incessant LA traffic, the first two days Elgar and Juan spend in the city are akin to an actual vacation. Knowing that their troubles are stuck in Seattle (*hopefully*, Elgar's mind whispers traitorously), and that there are two LAPD officers shadowing them at every turn, helps Juan enjoy his first trip to La-La Land and reminds Elgar of just how damn cool it is that someone is turning his books into a TV series. He'd lost perspective on that with all the fear and worry.

It turns out that having his cheery, optimistic, stylish assistant along is a great way to pull him out of his funk and help him get excited about the storytelling process again.

In fact, Elgar is in such a good mood that he even concedes to Juan dragging him clothes shopping, letting his assistant treat him like some sort of runway dummy. Though, he has to admit that the red velvet smoking jacket really does make him look suave. Elgar's almost sad that Forsyth isn't here. Juan's endless nattering about color would have been the perfect compliment for Forsyth's never-ending nagging about the importance of tailoring.

Juan is also an interesting eye to have along when they tour the production design house—Flageolet is going with a more shabby-Victorian-chic mishmash than Elgar had really envisioned when he'd written the books (he'd been thinking more Errol Flynn and less Neil Gaiman, if he were honest). But with Juan along, Elgar can see the appeal of a consistent, stand-out visual style that will, god willing, be easy and fun for cosplayers to emulate.

The casting agents had been busy during Elgar's safe-house exile, and the two-day marathon table read of all ten episodes of the first season is scheduled for the third day of their stay. On the morning of, Juan and Elgar shake hands with the principal cast—who all look uncannily similar to what Elgar's had in his head this whole time, save for Forsyth.

They had gone with an eleven-year-old boy who was

gawkier and weedier than any son of Algar Turn really should be. Elgar can forgive that, though. It's not like the showrunner knows the boy is meant to grow into the Shadow Hand of Hain, and an excellent swordsman. The books never *explicitly* say that.

The actors are all keen to meet Elgar, and he shares a breakfast in the studio canteen with the principals before the first episode's reading is scheduled to begin. (And yeah, okay, he might have whispered into that skinny ginger kid's ear that he might want to consider picking up a sword-training regime. What of it?)

It's surreal to listen to dialogue he'd written two decades ago re-purposed into lines spoken by real people, with real emotion. But the joy of sitting at the giant square conference table, sipping coffee and listening to his story come to life sweeps the weirdness away. His only real moment of grimacing disconnect comes when the Forsyth actor speaks—it's all wrong; his cadence, his emphasis... he sounds sneering and squirrelly instead of calm, collected, and well-spoken like the real Forsyth. Never has Bevel's biased point of view as the narrator been so evident.

The readings go on for the full two days, and with lunch breaks, each day tops out at about twelve hours. Following the final day's last reading, when everyone in the room is emotionally exhausted from the ups and downs of the narrative and the long hours sitting and listening alike, Flageolet's lead executive producer pulls Elgar aside. Gil crowds Elgar into a shadowed corner of the hallway as people are filing out with their confidential boxes of scripts, empty water bottles, bags of partially used notebooks and complimentary pens, satchels of scarves and sweaters and cough drops, and all the other detritus of being a working actor.

"Listen," Gil says. He's a vibrant man with chicklet

teeth and artfully graying hair, but the beginnings of the kind of pooch that comes from not enough time in the gym and too many cocktails at Hollywood parties. "If you're free, I'd like to take you out for dinner tonight. You and your assistant; we'll need him on board with this."

"With what?" Elgar asks, trying not to take the secrecy the wrong way. A quick glance at Gil's eyes confirms that they are brown, not green.

But Gil only grins, wide and gleeful, and says, "Come on, man. Eight tonight, Chateau Marmont. I've got us a booth."

"Who's us?" Elgar asks, and again, Gil doesn't answer. He winks instead, cheeky and sure of himself, and moves to leave. Elgar shoots out a hand and grabs a fistful of Gil's sleeve, the creepy chill back and climbing up his spine once more. "Gil. Who's *us*?"

"Jesus, Reed," Gil says, startled. He reaches up and lays a gentle hand over Elgar's. "Are you okay?"

"No," Elgar grits out. "I'm... there's someone..."

"Stalker?" Gil asks kindly, and the concern on his face makes Elgar feel ashamed enough to release the man's shirt. But Gil doesn't let go of his hand. Instead, he claps it between both of his in a gesture of friendly solidarity. "All right. No, it's fine. I get it. It's the biz, man. We all have to be careful. It's just me, you, your guy, Olivia from marketing, and Stan and Andy."

"Stan and... the showrunner and the director? What for?"

"We've got an idea to pitch you. But tonight. For now, go back to the hotel. Unrumple. Have a drink. We'll send a driver for you guys, okay? No worries. We'll take care of all of it."

Elgar considers this for a moment. "I'd rather have my own driver, if that's cool," he says, not adding that their driver is a cop.

"That's cool, I get it," Gil says. With another firm handshake, he releases Elgar and is out the door, trailed by his own PA.

On the ride back to their hotel, Elgar tells Juan the name of the place they're eating. Juan's mouth drops open, and he makes a pleased little gasp. As soon as they are in the suite, Juan bustles over to the shopping bags and unearths Elgar's new red velvet jacket. He shoves the blazer at Elgar with a stern look that brooks no argument.

They each shower, Juan shaves, they indulge in a drink of the disgustingly lavish whiskey that had been in the welcome basket from Flageolet, and soon enough, they're sliding into the navy-blue leather seats of their corner booth reservation. The Chateau Marmont is made for deal-making, it seems. The backs of the banquettes are tall enough to block out the sight of the people at the table over; the lights are tastefully dim, but bright enough over the tables to read the menus (and potentially any contracts or plans); and the music is just loud enough to create a muffled din of calm white noise, but not so loud that voices are drowned out, or secrets have to be shouted.

Gil is already at their table when they arrive, a sweating bottle of something that is no doubt expensive sitting in a silver bucket stand beside it. Juan admires the wine when Gil pours it out, and while they wait for the other three people, Juan and Gil get into a discussion about vineyards, which leads to wine pairings, and the revelation that both men have an absolutely embarrassing crush on a celebrity chef with a reportedly dishy Australian accent.

Olivia from marketing arrives next, a confident, attractive African-American woman with a waterfall of gorgeous twists done in her naturally black hair and wefts of an unapologetic purple. As Elgar has never met her face-to-face before, he swaps his bench seat for the chair closest to hers so they can chat about the re-release of all the *Kintyre Turn* books with screencap images on the covers.

Andy and Stan show up within minutes of each other, Stan bidding what turns out to be his son goodnight on the phone as he approaches, and Andy still stripping off his motorcycle gear. He shoves his gloves in his helmet, and hands both that and his jacket to a waiter to take away to the coat check. Stan the showrunner looks so much like a "dad" that he is practically a parody. Andy is a skinny guy with an infectious grin, which he turns immediately on Elgar as he plops down into the seat beside him.

It isn't until Andy is beside him in the booth that Elgar has a chance to get a good look at his face. They've met before, of course, over contract negotiations and for drinks events, but this is the first time Elgar is close enough to catch the color of Andy's eyes.

They're green.

The familiar knot of exhausting terror forms behind his ribs so quickly, and so unexpectedly, that Elgar is suddenly afraid he's going to vomit, right there on the table. Gulping at the air, he shoots to his feet and, in the quickest wobble he can manage, makes for the gent's.

In the washroom, Elgar rushes by the wall of urinals and locks himself in the accessibility cubicle. Then he fumbles his phone out of his pocket, and searches for Andrew Sammet. He pushes the toilet seat down and sits heavily while the browser searches, switches to the images page, and clicks on the first picture. It loads infuriatingly slowly, the image resolving pixel by agonizing pixel.

And then, finally, Elgar is able to zoom in and get

a good look at Andy's face. His eyes are green. Elgar closes the photo, noting that it had been taken six months ago, and loads another, from last year. Then another, then another. Two years ago, before Elgar had ever met Forsyth, before he had known that he had accidentally created a magic system so perfect it actually worked. Three years ago, back before the TV deal had even begun. Four, and seven, and twelve years ago, when Andy was doing crappy commercials for instant rice, and dreaming of his first feature film. In all the photographs, Andy's eyes are the same: a hazel that tended toward green, with flecks of dark brown around the outer edge of the iris.

Relief rushes through Elgar like someone has opened the top of his skull and poured vodka straight in. The tingle of it splashes down his limbs, and he feels suddenly lightheaded with giddy relief.

Oh, thank god.

He's even relieved enough that the slight embarrassment that comes from the realization that he had shot off without even excusing himself isn't enough to dull the sensation. He exits the stall, washes his hands, and returns to the table with a mumbled excuse about too much water at the reading today. Everyone accepts it with a little nod, and then resumes the habitual complaining about how hellish the traffic had been on the way to the restaurant—a perennial LA favorite for small talk.

A quick glance at Andy sweeps away the last lingering cobweb of doubt—his eyes, while green, have the hazel undertones and the brown flecks he'd seen in the man's photos. They're not the bright, burning emerald that Forsyth's described.

As the adrenaline begins to seep away, Elgar finds his hands trembling. Juan shoots him more than one concerned glance, but Elgar just shakes his head, and listens to the small talk happening around him. He sips his wine until dinner has been ordered, eaten, and the dishes cleared away. That's when the real conversation begins.

"So, here's the thing," Gil says, once the last plate has been removed. He sits forward to pour more wine out for everyone, finishing their second bottle. "Olivia and I have been back and forth a lot about audience demographics, and the reality is that the majority of your fan base is white dudes over the age of forty."

Juan makes a confused noise, and looks as if he wants to raise his hand for permission to cut in. Gil smiles at him, and Elgar is struck with the impression that Gil might have developed a bit of a crush on his assistant. If he isn't careful, Juan might be pinched out from under him and swept off into a fantasy romance of Hollywood parties and all-you-can-shop trips to Rodeo Drive.

Elgar hadn't known that Gil was gay when he'd signed the contracts with Flageolet. But if he actually *is*, then all the concern he's had with having to convince the producers of the series to add in the Kintyre and Bevel romance in the later seasons would evaporate. If they'd fought it, he'd planned on throwing Lucy at them, but now, maybe all he'd have to do to get it to happen is "accidentally" let it slip at their next story meeting.

Excellent. Fortuitous. Useful.

"I thought that was good, though?" Juan asks. "I mean, dudes over forty? That's the exact demographic that still engages in wall-of-eyes appointment viewing."

Olivia raises her eyebrows at Elgar, impressed by his choice of help. "True, Juan. But they're not brand ambassadors, not the way the Tumblr generation is. And it's the engaged, convention-going cosplayers who pulled *Lord of the Rings* and *The Hobbit* into the mainstream, far more than fans of the books ever did. The creative engagement of fans between fifteen and twenty-five, primarily but not necessarily all female, is a demographic that we need to encourage to really get a groundswell going. It's the cosplayers, the gif-makers, the fanficcers, you know?"

Juan laughs, delighted. "Oh, yeah, I know. Count me among that crowd."

"Half the writing staff on the show, too," Gil says. "It's nice having people so invested in the story on our team."

Elgar blinks, startled. "You fic?"

Juan grins cheekily at his boss. "I read 'em. And, to be honest, I've always wanted to cosplay."

"Then you're gonna love this," Gil says. He reaches out and presses his hand over Juan's arm. It's right over where his assistant's bandage is, and Juan winces and shifts just enough for Gil's touch to move off the wound, but not enough that his hand drops away completely. Gil's smile grows softer, a little sweeter, and Elgar has to look away.

Not because it's gross, or uncomfortable, but because it reminds him sharply of how alone he is. He hasn't had a real girlfriend since 1998, when Tiffany had told him she was sick of his condescending douchebaggery and slammed off in a huff. She'd moved to Indiana, last he'd heard, and was married, running a hobby ranch, and had three boys. Since then, it'd only been one-night stands at cons, nothing more than a bit of fun for him and a notch on a star-fuckers bedpost for the girls. But even those were growing fewer and further between. He isn't a hot name anymore, the kind that a certain kind of young woman likes to add to their tally books. He's aged out. He's been coasting on the popularity of *The Tales of Kintyre Turn* for too long. Wanting to be important, wanting to be recognized and relevant again, that was half the reason he'd begun the *Shuttleborn* series at all, to be honest.

"Love what?" Juan asks. "You guys are laying the mystery on thick."

"Listen." Olivia leans into the middle of the table, and grins with mischievous joy. "We know some people who know some people, and if you're willing to go along with us on this, Elgar, we can pull some strings and get you invited to ConClusion as a last-minute guest of honor."

"Okay," Elgar says, sitting back, and trying not to frown. "Which one is that? I don't think I... have I been to that one?"

Juan's already shaking his head, staring down at his phone, where he's diligently reviewing what Elgar assumes is some sort of spreadsheet or something. "No," he says musingly. "It's the new one in Toronto. I've got the website up, 'Con-Inclusion, because fandom is for everyone. This con is in a state-of-the-art, accessible facility, with braille signage, extra large elevators, audio announcements', blah, blah, blah, every panel has an ASL interpreter, strict harassment policies, cosplay is not consent, etcetera... huh. Looks really good, boss." He looks up, grinning, and turns the phone around so Elgar can see a beautifully framed crowd shot filled with faces of every ethnicity.

"It's the ideal market," Gil says. "The engaged fans who are using their geekery to change the world."

"And here's the thing, right?" Olivia says, holding up a finger. "We'd put it out that you have a special announcement to make at the con."

"Oh, that's how you want to break the show news?" Elgar asks, still not seeing what's so special about this. The original plans for a splashy, full-color spread in Variety seemed like enough to him.

"Yes! But!" Olivia says before he can interrupt further. "Hear us out."

"Yeah, instead of just announcing the news in the middle of your Q&A, you would have them lower a screen, dim the lights, and show them the clip," Andy says, so fast that it's nearly incomprehensible.

"What clip?" Juan asks, looking just as confused as Elgar feels, which is nice. It's good to know he isn't alone in this. "A bit of the show?"

"There's no way you can pull together a trailer in three weeks, is there?" Elgar asks. "I mean, you won't have even finished filming the first block by then."

Stan sits forward then, adding his voice to the excitement: "We thought, if we do this, we'd push the first filming block back a month. We'd be... Reed, we'd be filming something entirely self-sustained. The actors have already agreed, if you do."

Elgar scowls. "Explain."

"We want to film a short!" Gil blurts. "Something with just Kintyre and Bevel. Something that's not in the books!"

Elgar slumps back in his seat, wide-eyed with thought. "You... really? That... might be good."

"More than that," Olivia says, reaching out to lay her hand on his forearm, a mirror of Gil and Juan. "We want you to write it."

Elgar feels his face go cold, and suddenly, he's sliding sideways. Juan lunges across the table to grab his arms.

"Whoa, boss!" Juan says, even as Andy wraps an arm around Elgar's shoulders and pulls him against the back of his chair. "Breathe, boss."

"I... I..." Elgar says, and realizes that his lungs are burning. He sucks in some air, coughs, and accepts the glass of water Andy pushes on him.

"Sip slowly, man," Gil says, also standing, concern scribbled across his face. "If we knew you'd react like this, we'd have tried to soften the blow."

"Is this good fainting, or bad fainting?" Olivia asks Juan. "Like, hypoglycemia?"

"We just ate," Juan points out as she shuffles aside so he can get out of the banquette. "Boss?"

"I..." Elgar tries again, but the rest of what he wants to say is caught in a sharp, scraping lump at the base of his throat. He swallows, and swallows, and coughs, and can't seem to dislodge it. He sucks down another deep breath, through his nose, and covers his face with his hands.

"Is he okay?" he hears Stan ask.

"It's..." Juan begins, makes a helpless sound, and tries again: "He hasn't been writing. At all."

"At all?" Gil asks.

"Not since he finished the *Shuttleborn* books six months ago," Juan says softly. "He says it's not writer's block, but—"

"It's not!" Elgar protests, dropping his hands to his lap. "I'm just... I can't!" The urge to explain why, exactly, is like a sudden and unexpected shove against his lungs. He gasps again.

He could tell them. Right here. All of them. He could explain why he'd pulled out of writing a script, why he'd retreated to the back of the series' digital writing room, why he'd been reluctant to start a new book series. He could confess it all.

And then watch his career go down the drain as they realize he's a nut job, pull out of the project, and probably help him get committed as soon as Juan could arrange for his care.

No.

Everyone is looking at him. Staring. Patient, but expectant. And the worst of them is Juan, eyebrows raised in surprise, a small smile nearly there, hope shining in his eyes. Shit.

"I... I can do it," Elgar says, resigned and terrified at the same time, and still so damned flattered that they've asked him. "I'll do it."

The victorious hollers are like a firecracker going off in their corner of the restaurant. Gil punches the air, then looks at Juan like he's bummed the younger man is on the far side of the table now and out of range for an "I was just so swept up in the moment" celebratory kiss.

Andy pumps Elgar's hand, Stan slaps his back, and Olivia, strangely, pinches his cheek. Gil waves over the waiter, orders a bottle of bubbly, and makes Olivia shove over so Juan can sit beside him again.

"So! Let's brainstorm stories!" Gil says as they wait for the waiter to return. "I had some thoughts about—"

"No," Elgar says, sitting up and interrupting with maybe more panic in his voice than he would have liked. "I... I need to talk to someone first. I have an idea, but I need to... vet it."

Gil looks to Juan, who shrugs, clearly having no idea who Elgar means.

Good. That is... that is good.

Elgar's a little drunk when they get back to the hotel. Juan stops at the concierge desk to make arrangements to extend their stay by a few days, while Elgar makes his tipsy way up to their suite with his cop-chauffeur shadow. The shadow heads for the vending machines as soon as Elgar is settled. Knowing that he won't have the place to himself for long, he shuffles into the bathroom with his phone, sits on the edge of the tub, and calls Forsyth.

"Forsyth's phone, his super hot wife speaking!" Lucy

Piper says as soon as the call is picked up.

"Lucy," Elgar says, and he is proud at how sober he sounds. "I have to... can you guys video-call? Do you have the time right now?"

A crash and a baby howl in the background answers the question better than anything Lucy could have said.

"Ah," Elgar says softly, instead of waiting. "Guess not?"

"Hold on," Lucy says, and the sound of the phone being set down is unmistakable. There's an unintelligible conversation further away, and Alis is sobbing unhappily, and then the phone is picked up again.

"Elgar?" Forsyth says. "Pip says you want to talk?"

"I'd like to talk to both of you, if I can. But if it's a bad time..."

"No, no, it's just... more teeth. You understand. She hurts, and she can't express herself well enough, and we can do nothing, really, to help and... everyone here is at their wit's end. But perhaps a bit of face time with her Uncle Gar Gar will help soothe her. Give us a moment to set up?"

"Sure," Elgar says, and hangs up. He nips out into his bedroom for his computer, then heads back into the bathroom. He hasn't heard Juan come back yet, nor his shadow, but the bathroom is the furthest from the suite's front door, just in case.

He sets the computer on the counter, and nearly as soon as he's opened the program, Forsyth is calling. The video opens on Forsyth seated at his desk in his upstairs office, Alis on his lap, swollen-eyed and miserable, and chewing on what looks to be a small frozen plushie. Both of them are a little swollen-eyed and miserable, actually. Forsyth knuckles his eyes and grins weakly.

"We look a fright, I know," Forsyth says, sardonic and exhausted. "It's been a... a long few weeks. What can I help you with? You sounded slightly desperate."

Elgar nods again, and then swallows hard, considering his next words carefully. He can feel his pleasant wine buzz evaporating with each moment that passes in silence. "I'd like your... your permission, I guess?"

Forsyth sits up, intrigued. Alis jams her plushie further into her mouth, gagging a little, and without taking his eyes from the screen, Forsyth pulls it back out. Alis whimpers and kicks.

"Permission for... ah." His eyes go a little rounder. "You've been asked to write something."

"Yeah."

Forsyth ponders for a moment, gray eyes skipping over Elgar's face, down to his clothes to root out whatever clues he seems to read there, then back up to meet his creator's eyes. "You don't want to."

"I don't... I don't know," Elgar admits. "I don't know if I should, and if I do say yes, I don't know what I should write, story-wise. I don't... I don't want to change things. I mean, I don't want to make things worse, you know? I don't have any power here, no way to write something and make it happen in the real world—the Overrealm—" *More's the pity,* he thinks, *or else I could write this stalker away.* "But whatever I write about there might... I don't know, it can... you see where I'm coming from, right? I'm... it's a legitimate worry?"

"Certainly," Forsyth says, petting Alis's sweaty curls away from her forehead as he thinks. "But consider, Elgar, that you are a Writer. In the same way that I was created to be clever, and learn quickly, and to be addicted to spying and bettering the world, so too you are created to be a teller of tales. Do you follow?"

Elgar nods dumbly, uncertain of what his heart is doing right now, or why his eyes are burning.

Forsyth sits forward, as if he can arrest Elgar's fidgeting with his gaze through the computer screen, his gray eyes pinning him in place. "Elgar, you cannot spend your whole life living in fear of your pen. Write respectfully, and thoughtfully, and there should be nothing to be afraid of."

"I... I don't want to hurt people," Elgar admits softly, and the confession costs him more than he thought it would. It tastes like ash and bile. "I don't know how to write without hurting people. Conflict causes pain, but how do I make a story without conflict?"

"I see." Forsyth says. "Elgar, let me put your mind at ease. I have been watching you slide deeper and deeper into your misery. And I have been pondering. And it seems to me that it is only Hain and its denizens that are, well, 'real.' Your *Shuttleborn* trilogy contains no magic at all, and it is the magic of the Deal-Maker Spirits that has birthed our realm into reality, yes?"

"...yes," Elgar says, feeling the knot in his chest starting to loosen.

"Then it is conceivable that, without the magic of the Deal-Makers, any other realm you invent will be just as dormant, just as imaginary as those of any other Writer."

"Maybe," Elgar says.

On screen, Alis seems to have calmed down enough to realize who her da is speaking to. She drops the plushie and reaches out her chubby hands to the monitor, chanting, "Gar, Gar, Gar, Gar, Gar."

"Hello, sweet girl," Elgar says back, waving and pulling faces at her while he considers what Forsyth has said. Alis giggles, pain momentarily forgotten.

"I think..." Elgar says softly, "I think it'll take me a bit to get over the... I don't know, the anxiety of it all, I guess. But... thank you, Forsyth. For, you know... just thanks."

Forsyth nods gravely, in that way that makes it look like it should have been a courtly bow. For all Elgar knows, maybe it is, of a sort. Forsyth had often given counsel to King Carvel Tarvers. It is possible that this is a gesture left over from that.

"And now, the reason behind the permission you sought from me?"

"Ah, yeah, see, there's the problem..." Elgar says, and then recounts the evening to his creation. "I'm right back where I was. How can I say yes, knowing that I might change things there?"

"Do they wish you to alter the story or the characters?" Forsyth asks, and his expression grows tight with what Elgar realizes, after a few seconds, is probably the closest thing to fear he's ever seen on Forsyth's face.
"I... I wonder if changing the way the story is told in the television series will have any impact on the people I left behind. On me. Will my memories of events alter? Will I even know if they do? Will Pip one day tell me that I am misremembering something, for she will know the difference between the novel and the adaptation?"

"That's a terrifying thought," Elgar mumbles, dread creeping up his spine. He wants this series. He wants it *so badly*, but what if Forsyth's right? What if...?

"But no," Forsyth goes on, musing. "If another Writer adapts the script, not my Writer, then surely the story as it is told in the books will remain intact. My memory, my character, my motivations and morals and preferences, my annoyances will remain the same. Adaptation cannot blemish what is originally set down on the page, correct? It cannot change it. Or me. Any more than the existing fan fiction has. I will remain as you Wrote me, and so will my world."

"You're sure of that?" Elgar asks.

"As sure as I can ever be, but..." Forsyth nods firmly, once. "Yes. I am sure."

Relieved, Elgar squirms on his uncomfortable seat.

"So they... they want me to write a short film."

"Do you want to say yes?" Forsyth asks gently, earnestly. "Because you seem to be forgetting that you have the very real option to say no."

Elgar chews on his bottom lip for a moment. "I do," he confesses quietly. "I thought I was done with the series, but this opportunity, the ability to write Kintyre one last time, I want... I want to be able to say goodbye to them. Like this."

"I see."

"It means I get to set the tone of the series, too," he adds, twisting the cuffs of his velvet jacket between his fingers; Juan is going to yell at him for rumpling it. "The first thing the fans will see would be by me, a sort of bridge, you know? Between what I did and what the production team will do, and I... that means something to me."

Forsyth nods along, seriously considering his explanation, as Alis squirms and gets fussy again, now that neither adult is paying attention to her.

"I just..." Elgar adds, after a thoughtful pause of his own. "I just don't know what's safe to write."

Forsyth presses his finger to his lower lip, thinking. "Please elaborate."

"They'll want something that introduces the characters, something that starts *in media res*, you know? But something cool, something... engaging. Something with just Kintyre and Bevel."

Forsyth nods again, eyes narrowing, and then his whole face blossoms into a relaxed, happy smile, and he leans down to kiss his daughter's head. She switches her litany from "Gar Gar" to "Da Da."

"Your solution seems obvious, then," Forsyth says, letting his fingers substitute for the frozen teddy bear as Alis gets toothy again. He winces when she bites down, but doesn't pull away.

"And that is?"

"Write a memory. Write something that has already happened, so it changes nothing in the timeline, only expands upon an event that has already occurred."

"And how will I pick one?" Elgar despairs. "If I make something up, how can I be sure it's not... not something new? I don't remember everything I was thinking when I wrote it all. It was decades ago."

"You can ask me." Forsyth's smile grows more mischievous. "After all, as both younger sibling to the Great Hero of Hain and former Shadow Hand, I do have quite a number of stories about my brother stored up. Many of them embarrassing, if you prefer."

And then, with glee, he starts to tell some.

SEVEN

FORSYTH

In the weeks that Elgar is in Los Angeles, Pip suffers three more fits. These leave her feeling weaker, needing more and more rest after each, more sleep and more recovery time. My fear must show on my face, for she tries to make a joke about how "it's normal, it's all fine, women are always hurt to give the male hero the impetus to act." It falls horribly flat, and has the opposite result of what Pip is aiming for, I think, for it only makes me more upset by her circumstances.

"I am a failure," I respond. And then surprise myself by promptly bursting into exhausted, heartbroken tears that I suspect resemble nothing so much as Alis's own.

Pip's eyes widen, and she pulls me down onto the sofa where I had placed her after her most recent fit—where light began sparking out of her fingertips—moving over so that I may lay beside her. Alis has become quite competent at breaking herself out of her playpen, and she does so now to crawl up onto the sofa, lay herself down upon my chest, and pet my hair.

"Shhhh, Da, shhh," she says, in fantastic approximation of Pip's soothing tone. It is such an accurate impression that Pip and I can't help but laugh, though mine is a bit more blubbery.

"I will figure this out," I tell Pip, whispering it into her ear even as I pull Alis down between us. Our daughter wriggles contentedly, happy to be bracketed by our bodies, and only knees me in the ribs twice. "I promise. I will make it stop."

Pip does not offer a reply to that. I think, I *hope*, it is because she doesn't want to set off another round of unexpected waterworks.

But the truth of the matter is this: I am *frustrated*. I am angry. And I am scared. It has *never* taken me this long to roust a villain, or uncover a plot, or decipher a riddle. And I cannot determine if this lack of clarity is because whatever story we are now in is not, in fact, a fantasy hero's quest, as Pip suggests, or if it is because lazy old Forsyth Turn is getting rusty. Worse, I dread that it is because I have been in the Overrealm so long that all the *specialness* I was imbued with as a fictional character has begun to fade. What is the use of being the know-it-all younger brother who was secretly the spymaster, if it gains me nothing here and now, when those very skills are what is needed most of me? What if I am becoming horrifically, impotently *normal*?

Once Alis and Pip are safely tucked up in bed for the night, I return, as I have for every night this week, to Finnar and my desperate search. Following Elgar around LA has been fruitless—the back rooms and board offices of Flageolet are monitored by cameras, but from what I can see, nothing out of the ordinary has happened. The lobby and hall cameras of his hotel are equally without clue, and as there are no monitoring devices in his rooms, and the man makes a point of keeping his cell phone off and his computer closed when he doesn't intend to use them, I cannot turn on his microphone or camera to catch what is being said and done.

Sleepless, angry with myself as well as with the world, my ears strain for the sound of Finnar pinging a result. I am so desperately awaiting that sound that I nearly miss it when it actually does go off.

I bring up the program immediately—it is an assault report filed by a Mr. Louis Garcia against the boyfriend of his daughter, Madeline. He spotted what is reported to be an electrical burn on her shoulder, hidden by a sweater that had slipped to the side. The time recorded for the incident matches that of Pip's most recent fit, this morning.

Electrical burn. Lightning.

The culprit, it seems, is in Seattle still. And Miss Garcia is a waitress at Elgar's favorite diner. At last, I am one step closer to Elgar's tormentor. But there is no address given for his location, no arrest record, no indication that the police are even aware of the connection between Miss Garcia's abuser and Elgar's stalker. I dash off a hasty note to the police, taking care to make it appear as if it comes from a junior officer who noticed a similarity in the MOs, flagging it for the detective in charge of Elgar's case. While I spin in my chair, fruitlessly, the bastard remains at large.

I can do nothing else from here, and so, flush with this one small, if bittersweet, victory, and confident that Finnar is clever enough to use this incident to branch out and search for more reports that are similar, I retire to bed.

Sometime around midnight, Pip wakes screaming.

I am alert before I realize it, and rolling over to cover her body with mine in an instant. I tense, preparing for a blow to fall upon my back, or the sharp slice of a knife to pierce my skin, but none come. Pip jams her fists against my chest and screeches: "Off, off, oh god!"

I roll away, and Pip sucks in a heaving, choking breath and moans.

Pip's screams echo in my ears when I flick on the

light. She has moved onto all fours, her head buried under her arms as she writhes and groans.

"Pip?" I ask, pitching my voice to carry over her cries. "Pip, what is wrong?"

"Hurts," Pip hisses out, and it is more syllable than vowel.

I sit softly on the side of the bed, hands out and held over my wife, soothing, but not touching until I am certain that I won't harm her further. After a very long moment, she flops onto her face, and then holds absolutely still.

"Pip?"

"It's easing," she sighs, but it is still between clenched teeth. She's panting, her face flushed, her jaw clenched, the tendons and veins of her neck standing out as she fights back the pain.

"May I touch you?"

She grunts what sounds like an affirmative, and so, carefully, I lean over and peel her sweaty t-shirt up her back. I half expect to see the scars torn open anew, blood rolling down her sides to bloom like gunshot wounds against our white sheets. Or, failing that, for the scars to be red, or inflamed. What I do not expect—what I *should* have expected—is the faint, faint tinge of green. It looks like someone has dry-brushed green greasepaint along the very tops of each puffed ridge of hard white scar tissue. The suggestion of the color is so faint that I have to squint and turn my head to be sure of what I'm seeing.

I stand, make my way back over to the door, and turn off the light.

In the gloaming of the street-lamps outside our window, Pip's scars glow, weak and watery.

"By the Writer," I breathe, and, horrified, turn the lights back on.

Pip nods, and reaches out for me, and I go. She sobs

again, tears soaking into my pajama shirt as she curls into my embrace as if I were the only thing in the world worth clinging to, and then suddenly unclenches. A whooshing sigh of relief escapes her lungs as she drops onto the mattress. She turns her head to the side, and regards me with red-rimmed eyes. "'M fine. It's over."

But Pip is covering up the fear that still lingers in the echoing aftermath.

When she lets go of my shirt, a smear of something vibrantly orange is left behind on the white fabric. "What is this?" I ask, touching it.

It is tacky with blood. And in that blood are short, orange fibers, no longer than an inch, a great tuft of them, mixed with small, cream-colored hairs. Fur. By the Writer, it is cat fur.

Pip is back on her knees now, staring at her own hands—smeared with more blood, more fur—like they are foreign, alien things.

"This looks like... this is... oh, no. *Linux*," Pip hiccoughs, and starts wiping the mess off in frantic swipes with the pillowcase.

"Pip, come, we will rinse it off, and you—"

She stands and bolts for the en suite.

"It's me," Pip says, scrubbing her hands frantically in the sink. "It must be me."

"What do you mean?" I ask, squirting soap on her hands when she fumbles with the dispenser.

"What if it's not... what if...? I'm the only magical thing left in this world, aren't I? Didn't I bring a spell on my bones? What if this is the magic trying to get out? What if this is the magic reaching out to Elgar because he made it, and...? What if this is my fault? All of it? What if I have to go back into the books to... what if I have to *stay* in the books—?"

"No," I say firmly. "No. If that is what this is, we will

solve it another way."

Pip looks up at me with big, inky eyes, desperate and brimming with tears. "If it keeps us safe, if it keeps Elgar alive and keeps whatever is happening from lashing out at Alis, I could—I could stand it. I promise. I could—"

"I don't want you to *stand* Hain," I tell her, gently pulling her hands away from the sink before she scrubs them raw. I skim off my filthy shirt and throw it in the tub, then wrap her hands in a towel, tucking them up against my heart. "If we returned to Hain, I would want it to be because we chose to do so. Not because we were chased away from the Overrealm. This is my home now, too, Pip. I shall not give it up."

Pip sniffles and wipes her nose on my shoulder.

"Delightful," I deadpan. "How you fill me with such strident ardor, wife. I simply adore being used as a hand-kerchief."

This makes Pip laugh, as I hoped it would, and eventually her sobs subside.

Curious, half hoping it will work for Pip's sake, and half hoping it does not so that my fears will be allayed, I speak Words of Comfort. The Word leaves my mouth, thin, anemic, nearly breathless, but spreads like dandelion fluff in the air and settles in gossamer threads across Pip's back. What little tension still remains in her posture vanishes and she goes all the way lax, even as her eyes blur and cross slightly, the way they always did when I Spoke Words in Hain.

"Blast," I curse softly to myself.

"It worked," Pip breathes, shaking her head and coming back to herself. "What does it mean?"

"It means that whatever is happening, the magic is accumulating."

Pip shakes out of my grip and throws the wet towel into the tub after my soiled shirt.

"This is ridiculous," Pip says, and clutches the sides of her head. "If it's not me, if you're sure it's not me, then it's... it's *him*. It has to be!"

"There doesn't seem to be any other explanation save for his, ah, following us."

Pip peers up at me, scowling. "Say his name."

"What?" I ask, startled by this sudden and bizarre demand. "Why would—?"

"This is... he's not some boogeyman!" Pip insists. "We're not going to summon him to our doorstep by saying it. We're both thinking it. We've both *been* thinking it. It's the Viceroy. It's the Viceroy. He's here. Forsyth, he's *here*! And he's trying to get back inside my head."

"No," I reassure her, opening my arms again, inviting her to decide whether she wants this comfort right now or not. She wraps her arms around my waist. I kiss the back of her neck, thread my hands through her hair, massage what little unblemished skin she has on her shoulders. "No, he shall never get back inside your head. You cast him out, once and for all."

"But he is here. Admit that."

"I admit it," I say, reluctantly. "I suppose I hoped that if I did not say it aloud, it would not be true. *Could* not be true. Is that not how fairy tales sometimes work? To summon a thing, you must name it?"

"This isn't a fairy tale," Pip says. "If this is a story at all, it's definitely not a fairy tale."

"Fucking trilogies?" I venture, and Pip huffs a laugh against my skin.

I try the Words again, but nothing happens.

"Why didn't it work this time?" Pip asks.

"We have, I think, exhausted what little excess magic lingered here. It will probably work again if more magic accumulates. Or if he is close by. Is he near? Can you tell?" I ask. I assume that the Viceroy is still in Seattle, but his mother had means to travel swiftly by cloud. It is possible that he has modes of transportation, both magical and mundane, that I know nothing about.

"No," Pip says immediately, strongly. "No. No, he's not close. He's far away. But he did something. The spell was strong and... I felt it. The malice. The power. It's taking him time to... get it all together. The pain was... sympathy pain."

The way she says it makes something click in my head. The last puzzle piece slots into place in the back of my mind, and I cannot help but snap my fingers.

"That's it! When strong magics are performed, they need ley lines to siphon off the excess and the blowbacks. In a magical world, the magic dissipates into the air."

"But this *isn't* a magical world," Pip whispers.

"So it just flows, I suppose," I say slowly. "Flows until something else magical can suck it up and disperse it."

"Lucky me," Pip growls, but she does so quietly. Exhaustion pools in her eyes, and she blinks hard, obviously working to stay awake. The ominous premonition in her snide reply daggers into my bones and leaves a chill there. "This is my fault. I messed up. I fucked it all up."

"No, Pip."

"It is. I should have chosen my words better. I could have... I could have *killed him*. I should have."

"After not allowing Wyndam to do the same?" I pet her head gently, soothingly.

"I should have said it better."

"You were rushed," I say, trying to keep Pip from too much self-recrimination.

"I've been trying to remember. I think I said, 'you won't have access to the magic in your blood.' But I didn't say anything about anyone else's blood. What if he found another Deal-Maker? What if she had another phial around? There's hundreds of kinds of magic in Hain. He could have used any of it to get his own back. I should have... I should have—I don't remember exactly what I said, and I wish I—"

I bow forward over my wife, kiss her cap of dark hair, and rock her in my arms.

"Shhhh, shhhh," I say softly. "You could not have known."

"But I *should* have," Pip mutters darkly. "That's the point. I'm the Reader. I should have known better."

"You did what you thought was best at the time."

Pip thumps her forehead into my sternum in self-recrimination.

"Ouch," I murmur, but it is not a real reproach. I cradle the back of her head in my palm and scratch lightly at her scalp, soothing.

"Do you think it was really Linux?" Pip whispers after a long moment.

I flex my bare toes against the chill tile floor, and debate how to answer.

"Your silence means you agree," Pip says.

"I will find out," I reply. "In the meantime, back into bed with you."

"No," Pip says. "There's no way I can go back to sleep now. I'll be... I'll go put on the coffee. If we have any left. We've been drinking a lot lately."

"We have," I murmur, and let her change the subject as she shuffles away.

I emerge from my office about twenty minutes later, filled with chilling horror and regret that Pip's guess was correct.

A black cloud of self-recrimination and shame coalesces in my chest, weighting each of my pathetic, shallow breaths. I should not have watched... I should have fast-forwarded the video, or looked away, or... I should not have watched... that poor cat. I knew the Viceroy could be cruel, but to torture a small, defenseless animal, to flay it alive and literally paint the walls with its blood. To *rip its head off...* while it still *breathed...*

Oh, foolish, over-confident, Forsyth. When will you ever learn?

Pip has Alis with her in the kitchen, gnawing on her frozen stuffie, looking puffy-eyed and as miserable as I feel. Apparently, the Great Writer is determined that none of us are to have any sleep tonight.

"You were right," is all I can say to Pip's questioning look.

ELGAR

Elgar and Juan are down at the concierge desk, working out how much longer he can stay in his suite. He's preparing to spend another week in LA in order to write the script, but there seems to be someone else booked into his rooms for the weekend, and apparently this person is important enough that the hotel is reluctant to shift their reservation.

Juan gets phone calls all the time, so Elgar doesn't really pay attention when he steps away from the desk and fishes his phone out of his pocket. It's his job, after all. The concierge keeps clicking through the computer, and Elgar tries not to tap his fingers impatiently. Then, over the sound of Juan's ringtone, Elgar hears him gasp. He turns just in time to see Juan blanch and nearly drop the thing as he fumbles to answer it.

"Boss, it's the cops," he says, heading for an alcove where he can take the call in private. Elgar's heart shoots into his throat.

"Sir, did you and your, ahem, partner think you could stand to share a single—?"

Elgar holds up his palm, silencing the concierge, who

makes an annoyed sound in the back of her throat and clicks her keyboard in a way that Elgar would have worried meant they wouldn't be getting a room at all if he'd been paying enough attention.

Juan paces up one side of the lobby and back again, shoulders hunched in, hand over first his stomach, then his mouth. The concierge tries to speak to Elgar again, and he interrupts with:

"Wait. Just a second." When she makes another annoyed sound, he adds: "Please." He scrunches his fist in the bottom of his cardigan and waits. Whatever news Juan's getting, it doesn't look good.

Please not Forsyth, Elgar thinks suddenly. *Oh god, please don't be the Victoria police. Please not... please not that.*

Juan comes back a few minutes later, face white.

"Juan?"

"Cancel the reservation," Juan says to the concierge. "And arrange for a car to the airport. Boss, we're going upstairs to pack."

"Why?" Elgar asks, dread filling his gut and curdling whatever is already in there.

"We gotta go home," Juan says softly. "Someone... they think your stalke ... it's..." He takes a deep breath and rubs his eyes, frowning hard, hands shaking. "That asshole... he killed your cat."

The police sent crime scene photos to Juan, who hesitates to show him, but... Elgar wants to see it. He wants to know. If—how—his beloved little buddy suffered. Knowing is better than imagining. Especially since his imagination has already proven to be the source of all his misery.

The photos are shockingly red and white, especially on the small screen of Juan's phone. He's barely able to parse the splash of gore on the otherwise sterile, white tile wall of the kitty hotel. Four little paws are lined up neatly under the bursting splash like shoes in a hallway. But severed. No legs. The little head displaying Linux's last expression of utter terror—pulled back lips and exposed fangs—sits beside them, a white ribbon of spine curled around it all like revolting gift wrap. Tufts of ginger fur stick to the drying blood between the tiles.

Elgar makes a strangled sound and runs for the lobby washroom. Somehow, he makes it in time to hurl up what feels like every meal he's had since he accepted the fragile little marmalade kitten from a neighbor's litter.

The final choking groan gives way to sobs pulled from the depths of his gut. He spits, flushes, wipes his face and beard with toilet paper, and then curls up on the tile between the toilet and the wall. He cries. Cries in a way he hasn't since his Aunty Lilah died. Presses his forehead to his knees and curses himself for ever sitting down to that race-car red typewriter in the first place.

Elgar has been accused of lazy writing before. Usually, he lets the criticism roll right off his back, especially when it comes to the way he chose to portray his arch-villain. He's tortured innocent boys, raped maidens, and flayed horses just to prove how dastardly his bad guys are, to cause the sort of emotional pain required to push the hero into action. And he got letter after letter from people complaining about those scenes, about how unfair to women he was being, about the animal cruelty, about how sensational gore for the sake of sensational gore isn't a substitute for plot. And he's ignored all of it.

Which makes this, in a less roundabout way than he really wants to admit, completely his fault. If he hadn't created a villain who did... *those sorts of things*, then Linux might still be alive.

"Boss?" Juan asks, and he's standing in the open door of the washroom because Elgar hadn't even had the time to lock it. There are tears on his cheeks, too, because he'd loved that wretched little menace just as much as Elgar. "Boss, shhh. C'mon. We should go."

"I—uh—I can't..." Elgar says, and is sick again. He can't stop sniveling.

And then somehow Gil is there, and Elgar can't really remember how long he's been clinging to the toilet, shaking. But Gil is standing in the hall of the cubicle, handing them both paper towels to clean up with, gum, and a small bottle of mouthwash. He's talking on his own phone, voice soft in the ringing echoes of the washroom, barely audible under Elgar's gross, heaving wretches and sobs.

"—change Mr. Reed's flight, please," Gil is saying. "And can you go to their suite and get them all packed? Yes, as soon as possible. They'll be leaving immediately."

"Boss, get up. We'll go. Gil's brought his car; it'll be faster. We're going straight to the airport."

And then somehow they're in a town car, and then the airport, and then the plane, and Elgar is feeling weak, and shaky, and his stomach is roiling. He doesn't want the water Juan keeps pushing at him, and if one more person asks him if he's okay, he's going to scream.

"Boss," Juan says, as the captain announces their descent into SeaTac. "Are you—?"

"I am terrified!" Elgar hisses. "I am furious. I feel so guilty. And I despise that I am terrified, because I don't even know what I'm terrified of! It feels like my heart is going to burst right out of my chest! I can't swallow."

"Breathe, boss," Juan says, rubbing his back.

The plane tilts toward the earth and Elgar swallows, and swallows, and swallows, and feels like he'll never get the lump out of his throat. He barely remembers disembarking. He follows after Juan like a supertanker being towed in the bobbing wake of a determined, self-bronzed, grim-faced tugboat.

A local vet clinic is holding what little remains there are, and Juan explains that he's going to drive Elgar straight there, so they can decide what to do. The owner of the kitty hotel, devastated and so apologetic, has offered to pay for any burial or cremation costs. In the meantime, Juan says, the police think they have a lead on their suspect. Someone has called in a tip.

Elgar's supposed to meet the cops at the precinct first thing tomorrow morning, after he's had a chance to go home and rest, and... and...

Oh, god, Linux isn't going to be there.

Elgar is going home, and his cat isn't going to be there to chirp indignantly, to try to trip him as soon as he comes in the door. No fuzzy orange menace to scratch the back of his hand, or meow indignantly at the cupboard door, or to sit on his face first thing in the morning and demand breakfast when his bowl is already full.

Elgar sucks down hard on the sobs that want to crawl out of his throat, pulling his cap down so no one can see his face, trusting his PA to guide him through the airport to the parking garage.

"Here, boss," Juan says, and Elgar folds himself into the passenger seat of his car while the porters heft their bags into the trunk. Elgar does up his seat belt, then hunches down, unwilling to look at or deal with the world.

A few minutes later, Juan jumps in. "Okay, boss. Vet clinic. Here we go."

They roll out of the parking garage, the traffic light for this time of early afternoon, and Juan eases the car onto the ramp that will merge them into highway traffic and take them back to Elgar's neighborhood. There's a stop light at the bottom of the ramp, but instead of slowing on the approach, Juan starts going faster.

Elgar yanks his head up, startled, as Juan jerks in his seat and slams his foot down hard on the brakes. He lays on the horn.

"Shit!" he yelps, jamming the brakes again. "Shit, shit! Boss, cover your face. I can't stop. We're going to—"

FORSYTH

Several hours later, Finnar pings again, and I pop upstairs to check what the program has found, dread yanking at my heart. It takes a long time for me to come back down again. Each step down into the warm domesticity of my home seems as if bringing this news into it will soil what Pip and I have worked so hard to build.

"I've made a horrific mistake," I say, joining Pip in the living room, where she and Alis are trying, unsuccessfully, to nap. Pip has called in sick to work for the rest of the week, which I feel is wise. Neither of us want her to have a magical fit in front of her class. "I must go to Seattle directly."

"Oh god," Pip breathes. "Why?"

"Elgar is in the hospital."

"What?" Pip screeches.

Alis jerks at the sudden loud sound. "Da!" she says, indignant, as if inviting me to share in her recrimination of her mother for being so uncivilized.

"Sorry, baby," Pip says, and tugs gently on Alis's foot in apology.

"It all happened so fast, I have barely had time to follow the connections. My creator is a pincushion. That was surgery, Pip. *Surgery.* On his *skull.*"

"Okay, first, how about you take some deep breaths for me," Pip says. I realize I need them, and do as she suggests. "Right. Okay. Surgery. On his skull."

"To alleviate the swelling."

"From the... okay, start at the beginning here, spy-master. You're losing me."

Alis squirms to be let down, and goes immediately to her little reading armchair, busying herself with a picture book about the life cycle of penguins. Who tap dance, apparently. As best as I am able, I fill Pip in on what I've found. It fills me with shame to have to admit, aloud, that I have failed him so spectacularly.

"Oh, but I am a terrible spymaster," I confess, miserable, and Pip pulls me down against her chest so that I may listen to her heartbeat, may revel in the close, warm scent of my wife. "This is all my fault. I hesitated when I should not have. I should have warned him, or—"

"Whoa, whoa," Pip says softly, kissing the very center of my ever-widening bald spot. I grumble at her for reminding me that it exists. "You don't actually have powers of prognostication, you know."

"But I should have—"

"No."

"Pip—"

"Nuh-uh."

I sit up, meeting my wife's kind gaze, and she cups my cheeks, keeping my head still as she forces me to meet her eyes. "How could you possibly love such a silly, stupid, useless man as me?"

Pip's brow wrinkles, her eyebrows arching up in the middle, her mouth pulling down. "*Bao bei*," she says softly. "You're not silly, or stupid, or useless."

"My creator is being stalked and threatened. His cat is *dead*. All because I have been unable to definitively track the movements of the singular, most powerful archvillain of his series. This is because of me."

"Say that again," Pip says gently.

"This is all because of me?" I echo, aghast that she wishes me to repeat it.

"No, the bit before that."

"I have been unable to definitively track the movements of the singular, most powerful archvillain of his series?"

"Yeah." Pip leans forward and kisses me again—once on the lips, once on the tip of my overlarge nose. "Even Kintyre Turn couldn't defeat the Viceroy."

"But I should have been able to—"

"Forsyth," Pip interrupts, and there is steel in her voice now. She will not be crossed. "Stop wallowing. Elgar is alive. He's recovering. You said so yourself."

I nod miserably, and remain silent. For some reason, my wife chooses to reward me for this with another slow, lingering kiss.

"Okay, so, you're going to Seattle," she says, and it sounds less like she's repeating the facts I told her, and more like she's trying to convince herself it's a good idea.

We both of us look over to the trio of armchairs around the fireplace and bookshelves. Alis is content, flipping through the book and narrating the pages in rapid babble to Library.

"I can't come," Pip says, and it's both a confession and a complaint. "Alis—" she begins, even as I say:

"The magic."

"The magic?"

"We are aware that you are acting as the Viceroy's pressure valve. But is *he?* And if you move closer to him, may he not feel it? You know he is far from you. What if he feels you getting closer?"

Pip nods tightly, jaw clenched, watching Alis.

"Pip," I begin, but she says:

"No. Fuck. No, you're right. I get it. Doesn't mean I have to like it. But I get it."

"I hate to leave you both," I say. "I'm not even certain if I should. Pip, if I leave you two behind, and someone comes—"

"I'll call the cops."

"I would feel better if you had a gun of your own."

Pip looks startled. "Really?"

"I would feel much better if you were able to cast defensive spells, or use Words, or were proficient in any sort of weaponry. But, failing that, a gun is simple—you point, and shoot."

"I think there's a bit more to it than that."

I knuckle my forehead. "Why, why have I been neglectful in teaching you to defend yourself with a sword? Foolish man."

"Hey," Pip says. "No more of that. And I'm not exactly defenseless. It's not like my extra hours at the gym have been spent at ballet booty camp." She makes a fist and bats my shoulder hard enough to get her point across.

"Splendid, splendid woman," I say, and this time, I am the one initiating the kiss.

"And don't forget, we may not be able to ward the house, but I don't think there's ever been a home security system as thorough as ours in the history of home security systems."

"And while I have been warding the house, you've been preparing for when my work fails," I point out.

"If, not when," Pip says against my mouth, smirking. "I've been kidnapped twice now. That was enough. I'm determined that, next time, I'll hold my own. I refuse to be a damsel in distress."

"There will be no next time," I proclaim grimly.

Pip's smirk grows tremulous. "Trilogies," she reminds me.

"I will book my ticket directly," I say. "I just... excuse me for a moment?"

Pip nods, wearing a look on her face like she already

knows what I'm about to do, as I head for the front door. Shoes on, I step out into the chill morning, and because I am a paranoid bastard, I take a long, lingering walk around my house, searching for... I don't know what. Something. Anything. Clues. Proof that I would not be mad to leave my daughter and wife alone, undefended save for what Pip can do with her own fists and feet, while I scurry off to the side of a man who, a year ago, I didn't even particularly like.

I peer at every passerby, glance into every shrub, check every locked gate. Nothing.

Nothing.

It should be a relief.

Instead, I wish I had found something. Some clue. Something to keep me here, by their side. Some reason to... but no. This is cowardice. Elgar needs help. Needs me.

I must go

And Pip cannot come.

ELGAR

When Elgar next opens his eyes, it's in a pastel-colored room with a white, halo-like curtain around *his* bed. His bed? Yes, he's in a bed. But a bed that is hard, and narrow, and not his bed. The air smells of disinfectant, and the sheets are slightly scratchy. The bit of wall he can see over the steel rail is pale peach, and the overhead light is a harsh fluorescent.

His neck and head ache, and his right forearm burns. His mouth tastes like stale cotton, and he wants to scrub the grit out of his eyes, but as soon as he tries to move, every muscle in his body screams. He groans out loud. The curtain hisses open, and a woman in green scrubs—a *nurse*, his brain tells him, but not without another sharp ache—appears in the gap.

"Hello, Mr. Reed. Good morning." Elgar tries to answer, and she shushes him and holds a cup of water with a bendy straw to his lips. She tuts at him after a few sips and takes it away, the tease. "Now, try again."

"Morning?" he rasps. "How?"

"You were unconscious when they brought you in, Mr. Reed, and with the mild edema, they decided it would be best if you stayed asleep while you were treated. They took you off the anti-inflammatory meds yesterday evening."

"Edema? Unconscious?"

The nurse frowns, looks down at his chart, and then comes back up to the head of the bed. "Mr. Reed, do you know where you are?"

"Hospital?" he guesses.

"Do you know how you got here?"

"Um," Elgar says, casting his mind back to recent events. "Airport, then the car, then... Juan!"

He struggles to sit up, ignoring the nausea the motion causes, the way his neck and head throb and seize. But the nurse pushes him back down, makes soothing noises. "Don't move yet, Mr. Reed. We haven't been able to prescribe you any muscle relaxants, not with the other meds in your system. Just relax, don't make it worse."

"Juan?" he asks again, voice trembling, dreading the answer.

Before the nurse can say anything, a soft voice says from the other side of the curtain: "Here, boss."

Relief is like a gut-punch, and Elgar can't help the groan that escapes him.

The nurse pushes the curtain around his bed all the way open, and Elgar is able to see that he's in a small hospital room with a bright window, a private washroom, and two single beds. Sitting up with a rueful smile on a face that is half bruise is Juan. He tries to grin at Elgar, but ends up grimacing instead, touching the bandage over his nose gingerly with his free hand. His other arm is one long, shoulder-to-knuckles cast.

"Jesus, Juan," Elgar breathes, trying to look without moving his head. He ends up straining his eyes until his vision sparks.

"Don't move," the nurse says. "Just lie still. I'm going to go get you a refill on your IV and some nice, shiny new painkillers, Mr. Reed." She bustles out, and Elgar doesn't even have the heart to check out her ass as she goes.

"Looks worse than it is," Juan lies cheerily. "Gonna get the doc to set my nose nice, get rid of that stupid bump I hate. Gil will have to kiss me if I have a George Clooney nose, right?"

"Right," Elgar says, eyes burning with relief and sorrow. "Juan, I'm so sorry. If you weren't my PA—"

"No, boss," Juan says. "This isn't on you, and you're not allowed to make it on you. I've had plenty of time to think about it. It's all him."

"Maybe," Elgar allows. *But if I hadn't created him...*

"So goddamn cliché," Juan snorts, and then winces again, free hand back on his nose. "Cutting my brake line. What a cunt. I think he got that from one of the movies we watched."

"What happened?"

"Couldn't stop," Juan says, looking guilty and exhausted suddenly. He keeps his eyes on his lap, twisting the sheets in his good hand.

"Not your fault either, if it's not mine," Elgar admonishes quietly.

Juan's eyes flick back up to Elgar's, and his smile, a softer, more tentative one, shines through. "Okay, boss. Well. Uh. We got t-boned when we rolled out into the road. The other guy smashed into the driver's side door, did me up good, and you hit your door pretty hard. Hard enough to..." He stops and swallows. "At first, they couldn't tell me if you were gonna wake up or not, what with the swelling."

"Jesus," Elgar says again, the reality of it starting to settle in his guts. "He's really trying to kill us."

"Yeah, I think he is."

They're silent then, as the nurse comes back with a new drip-bag and a tiny plastic cup with two yellow, house-shaped pills, as well as something Elgar knows for a fact is an antacid. "Swallow these, Mr. Reed, and they'll put you out in a few minutes." Elgar obeys. "Do you need the bedpan while I'm here?"

"No!" he yelps, mortified.

The nurse smirks. "Okay. When you wake up next time, we'll see about getting you sat up and some food into you." She turns to the door, then stops and comes back. "Is there anyone you want us to contact, Mr. Reed?"

Elgar blinks, brain already starting to soften at the edges. "Uh..."

"I'm listed as your emergency contact," Juan says. "And as I was conscious enough to make decisions about your health care, they didn't contact your next of kin. We sort of wanted to..."

"Make sure I woke up at all?" Elgar hears himself slur, but his eyelids feel so heavy, and the room is starting to float away from him.

"Yeah. I called Gil and Kim, though, to let them know that you... hey, boss? Boss? Right. Sleep tight."

FORSYTH

I have a key to Elgar Reed's house. Until now, I have never had occasion to need it. But I am grateful to be able to store my luggage and take a quick shower in his guest bathroom before I head to the hospital. I am also grateful that my connections with the Canadian Security Intelligence Service have set me in good stead, and that not only are Seattle's finest not going to arrest me the moment I trip their motion sensors in Elgar's house, but they have also agreed to go so far as to escort me to Elgar's hospital room themselves.

My escort consists of two police officers in full uniform, respectively named Riletti and Jackson, who are already familiar with the case. Believing in the badge I flash at them, and their orders from on high, they fill me in on what's been happening here while Pip and I have been run ragged surviving her magical attacks. The hospital smells the way they always do in this realm—no calming lemon, and lavender, and menthol from Mother Mouth's poultices and potions, but strong astringents and bleaches. It makes my nose twitch as Riletti and Jackson lead me to the secure ward where Juan and Elgar are convalescing.

Police officers stand outside their door, and I pause there to take a deep breath and prepare myself for what I am about to see. I read the report. Severe cranial edema—swelling of the brain—for which they kept Elgar immobile and unconscious until they were certain the swelling would cease. The updated report I read upon landing in Seattle had mentioned that he had awakened, and was currently undergoing a course of muscle relaxants and painkillers to deal with the traumatic whiplash his injury had caused. In addition to that, the glass of the car window had broken and been driven into his right arm, so his flesh will be a mass of tiny stitches covered over by light gauze.

I bet it itches horribly, and Elgar will be giving the prettiest nurses he can find as much trouble about it as possible in an attempt to be charming. Juan will have more luck with that—his left arm was broken in four places, his nose as well, and one of his ribs. But even though I have never met the man, I know from Elgar's reports that Juan has all the charm and grace my creator aspires to claim for his own.

I flex my own right hand, contemplating what the nerve damage will do to Elgar's ability to write once the injuries have healed. He will be able to type, I am sure, and to dictate to the computer, but will he be able to hold a pen without it shaking? Will he be forever deprived of the ability to sign his own books for his fans?

"Mr. Piper?" Jackson asks me, as I hesitate by the door to Elgar's room.

"Do we know if he is awake?" I ask, stalling. "I wo-would n-n-not l-uh-like to wake either of th-the-them when they are s-so in need of sle-ep."

Jackson gives me a funny look, and I realize I've slipped, in my distress, into my old, formal mode of speaking. Blast and drat.

"I'll check with the nurse," Riletti says, and turns down the hall to double back to a station we passed, set in the junction of several wings.

"Co-could we n-n-not ask the——?" I say, gesturing to a nurse who is standing at the other end of the hall from us. She is speaking to a man in dark jeans, a wash-grayed hoodie pulled up to cover his face. His hands are in his pockets, his posture slumped and miserable, and I wonder what trauma or tragedy he is having to endure. He is nodding slowly, talking elaborately with one long-fingered hand.

The gestures are familiar to me, and I turn for a better look. But as soon as I have made a move in their direction, the man freezes and jams his hands back into his kangaroo pocket, embarrassed. The nurse starts and jerks to face me, a grimace crossing her features.

"Apologies," I say, just loud enough for them to hear.

"I thought I—"

A frisson of fear races over me then. Something in the air is... something crackles against my lips like summer lightning, brief and fresh, and the air, for just a moment, tastes of wonder and *home.*

Something of my joy and horror must have shown on my face, for Riletti puts a hand on my arm and says, "Mr. Piper?"

"*Pip,*" is my only response, as I fumble my phone out of my pocket. The nurse immediately bears down on me with a "sir, you can't use your phone in the hospital; it interferes with—" and I shout my apologies and excuses as I run for the door at the far end of the hall, brushing past the nurse as my fingers shiver and slip on the phone's slick surface.

The man in the hoodie levels a look of loathing at me that I barely register, his light eyes flashing as I rush past, and then I am banging back the heavy fire door and striking the call button probably harder than necessary. The phone rings only once before the call connects.

"I feel it," Pip says, breathless, as if she's been panting. She makes a strangled sound. In the background, I hear peppy, upbeat music. The sounds of many people doing something with metal things in a small space grow muffled and give way to the sterile echo of an empty, tiled room.

Ah, my wife was at the gym, and is now in the dressing room.

"Alis?" I ask, and I needn't say anything further, for Pip already knows what I mean.

"At my parents'," Pip says.

"Pip," I reproach her.

"No, I'm fine. I was crawling out of my skin waiting. I just wanted to... *nunnngh,*" she groans, and there is the heavy thump of her hitting the lockers and sliding down to the ground.

"Pip!"

"I'm okay. I just need... just need a second to... god, I can't *breathe*—" she pants, and, futile and impotent on the other side of the connection, I simply inhale and exhale as loudly as I can, keeping my own head, trying to calm my own heart, trying to trick my wife's body into following along. "The—the *rage*," she stutters around her ragged breaths.

"Rage?"

"He's so *angry*."

"Pip, do you tell me you can feel what he—?"

Pip's voice is growing shallower, fading away, and I do not know if it is because she is suffocating, or if the phone has dropped away from her face. "How... how dare the-the-the S-Shadow Hand inter... interfere..."

"Interfere? How... what are you—?"

"Not supposed... how—*hcccck*—can they travel so... *ung!*... fast in the Overrealm... had *time*—" She chokes and splutters her way through the words, like a prophet drowning, but determined to spit one last verse of dire warning.

"Pip, please, breathe," I plead, my free hand balled into a fist.

"Ma'am?" someone says on the other end of the line. "Hey, lady, are you okay?"

"Help her!" I shout, hoping that my voice will be heard. "Please, it's... a fit of some sort. She can't breathe!" My heart twists and burns in my chest, my throat closing up in fear.

Writer, please, please, do not let my wife die when I am too far away to hold her as she does so.

"Lady, Jesus, hold on. Let me... I'm just going to tip your chin up, okay? Open up your airways," the woman says, and she sounds confident and collected. Perhaps she has first aid training. Whoever she is, I owe her a thousand thanks.

Pip gasps, and then sucks in a hard, shaking breath. I can hear the phone clatter onto the floor. And then Pip screams: "A knife! Forsyth, there's a... oh fuck, *stop him!*"

"A knife?" I take a moment to echo, and then I understand.

The man in the hoodie, I realize suddenly, and the revelation is like a punch to the gut. *The hand gestures. Spell-weaving. His eyes weren't merely light—they were amber.*

"I love you," I shout down the line. "Breathe."

"She's fine. It's over," says the woman.

I take just enough time to shout my thanks, and then hang up, shove the phone back into my pocket, and run. The fire door slams back and cracks against the wall opposite as I burst through it. My dress shoes are slippery against the polished floors, but I run full-out all the same. The same nurse I saw on my way out still stands in the hallway. She looks dazed, green fading from her eyes. She moves to stop me, but her gestures are slow, jerky, puppeteered by a master whose mind is elsewhere.

Outside of Elgar's room, Riletti and the two officers protecting it are staring aimlessly, heads turned only vaguely in my direction, hands on the butts of their guns, eyes turned emerald.

"Mr. Piper," Riletti says, "You can't—"

She and the officers both make a grab for me, but, borrowing a move from my nephew, I roll low under their arms and through the open door into the pitch-back hospital room. No, not pitch-black. There is light—dim and twilit—leaking in around the edges of the curtains.

And against this, a shadow suddenly moves on the

other side of the room. It peels away from the rest of the darkness, as if it has been pared off with a knife: a slow, keen slide that curls into a tall, slender silhouette. It cuts between the window and the far bed, where Elgar's unmistakable bulk lays in oblivious repose. In the moonlight, the blurred edges of the figure resolve into a head, and limbs, and a thin torso.

"Found you," a voice made of honey and poison hisses into the quiet. "I wondered what it would take to lure you out, Shadow Hand."

Choking on the swell of terror that rises up in my throat, I rise to my feet, ready to strike however I may. I am not proficient in unarmed grappling, but the adrenaline coursing through me will, I hope, help. But Elgar is between us, and I am unsure if I can reach the Viceroy before he can swing his upraised knife down.

A brief glance about the room provides me with no weapon of my own, but at the foot of Elgar's bed, a table on wheels arcs over his calves. And on that lays a half-finished meal on a metal tray.

"Do not do this thing," I say, and my voice sounds harsh in the muffled silence of what feels like a secrecy spell. "Harm him, and who knows what will become of the world we left behind."

"I care not," the Viceroy snarls.

"Your mother lives there still—"

"She died so that I may regain my magic! Do you know how I suffered? How it feels to be a magical being who is denied that magic? How it *hurts?* How it *burns!* Incessant! Never-*ending!*"

I realize that Elgar is not quite so oblivious as I thought. His eyes are open, wide and bulbous in his fear, and he is repeatedly jamming the emergency buzzer on the side of his bed.

"If you must take your vengeance on us for what

we took from you, then do so. But leave him alone," I command, sounding far more confident than I feel and cursing myself a fool for leaving Smoke in Victoria. For failing to obtain a gun of my own, as I suggested to Pip.

I have a vague thought of trying to snatch Riletti's out of her holster, but I dare not turn my back on the Viceroy.

"Oh, I will have my revenge on you, and your whore," the Viceroy sneers. "But first, I will have it on the man who is the Author of all my misfortunes and sorrows."

Elgar makes a pained sound, and jerks his head around. "Forsyth!"

"Look at you. So small," the Viceroy says to him, and it is nearly sorrowful, nearly gentle. Nearly. "You are human, after all. And I am *more*."

His knife begins its downward swing, and I leap forward, grabbing the tray and sliding it over Elgar's heart, hoping that it is thick enough to stop the blade. The scattered remains of Elgar's meal—dirty dishes, old rice, cold tea—fly at the Viceroy's face, and he rears back, indignant. His blade skids along the tray, no longer strongly wielded, and I am able to knock my hand hard enough against his wrist to send it flipping end over end into a shadow-laden corner.

Within seconds, the sound of feet running up the corridor and toward this room rings out in the hall.

"Riletti!" I hear Jackson shout. "What the hell is— why are you just standing there?"

The Viceroy turns on the balls of his feet, snarling as he comes back around toward me, and I shout a Word of Protection, just in case the room is saturated with enough magic for it to work.

It does.

The Viceroy rears back again, hands over his face as if the mere sound of the Word is dazzling to his eyes. He hisses again, wordless and infuriated. Then he seems to fold in on himself, shadow curling in upon shadow, and is gone.

Riletti, Jackson, and the two officers fall through the door like spilled water, whatever spell the Viceroy had placed on the entryway to keep them out suddenly vanished. The latter three shake their heads, pushing off the compulsion, while the nurse shoulders her way through them to check first on Juan, who is now bolt upright in his bed, eyes round with terror, and then to the obviously panicking Elgar.

"It's him," Elgar says over the din of doctors arriving and Juan loudly demanding an explanation, the officers speaking into their radios and shouting at one another. But Elgar's words, his desperate, teary gaze, those are for me alone.

"Oh my god, Forsyth," he says again, a tremulous whisper. "That was *him*. He's here. He's really *here*."

EIGHT

ELGAR

"We nearly had him," Jackson says, standing at the foot of Elgar's bed with notepad in hand. Elgar, still shaking, and having just witnessed how very much the police had not almost had him, stays quiet. He's desperate for five minutes alone with Forsyth, but Forsyth's stepped back out into the hall to call Pip, to make sure she is all right.

Forsyth's explanation had been quick, and whispered hard into Elgar's ear while the rest of the room around them was calming down, getting sorted, turning on lights and righting tables. Elgar isn't entirely sure he understands what Forsyth meant about Pip being affected by the Viceroy's magical blowback. He wants, *needs*, to understand. He wants Forsyth to be beside him, to be holding his hand to prove that they're both still okay, dammit; to reassure him that the Viceroy is gone, that Elgar is safe, and that he isn't going totally and completely *bonkers*.

Instead, he has to nod along with Jackson, and do whatever it is the nurse looking him over wants—look here, swallow this, drink that, lift your arm, make a fist, stare into this light—while Detective Khouri has a tête-à-tête with Juan. Who, by the way, looks like he's about ready to crawl right out the window and run away screaming.

"How... where has he been?" Elgar manages to ask,

just as Forsyth returns to the room. His posture is more relaxed now, the lines of worry on his face smoothed away. Pip must be fine.

"He was holed up with the waitress from that diner you frequent—Miss Madeline Garcia," Forsyth says smoothly, stepping into the conversation with all the confidence of a man who knows he has every right to be a part of it.

What a character development, Elgar thinks dazedly. *Forsyth would never have been comfortable doing that without the mask on before.* And then his bruised brain catches up to what Forsyth actually said.

"He what?" Elgar splutters, stunned and horrified and suddenly feeling so very guilty. Here's another person who has suffered simply because they're part of the loose orbit of people Elgar has in his life.

A flash of green eyes over her shoulder, he remembers, as she went back into the kitchen. And the vague thought that her eyes were supposed to be blue. God, he really is an idiot. Ten thousand kinds of idiot. Moron. Imbecile. Witless.

"Yeah," Riletti says. "There was a report from her father. He hadn't heard from her in a few days, was concerned about her, about her new boyfriend. Says that he'd given her a black eye and maybe a burn, and when a duty cop went over to check on her, the guy took off. Apparently, straight here. The CCTV cameras caught him out in the hall, and at one of the stop lights outside Miss Garcia's house. It was a match. I'm sorry, Mr. Reed."

"Was that last night?" Elgar says, risking the pain of the stitches pulling on his right forearm to scrub his hands through his greasy hair, only to be met with another wad of bandage behind his right ear, and another patch of extreme tenderness. Dammit, he'd forgotten about that.

"Indeed. It was lucky that I booked so early a flight," Forsyth says quietly.

"Yeah, it is," Jackson says, equally soft, still looking sideways at Riletti, like he hasn't quite figured out how to feel about her apparent nonaction just hours earlier. Elgar bets that she doesn't even remember she'd just stood in the hall, doing nothing but trying to stop Forsyth when he entered the room. "The detective says that he doesn't think this is the kind of stalker who kills his target—just everyone close to them, so they're the only ones left, you know?"

On the bed beside Elgar, Juan whimpers, covers his face, and looks away.

"Sorry," Jackson says softly as Khouri straightens and glares at the sergeant. "But we'll keep you safe. We don't know how he got in last night, but we've bumped up the security detail on you."

It won't matter, Elgar thinks, but doesn't say. *Put a hundred cops with a hundred guns in this hospital. Magic can get past them all.*

A glance at Forsyth tells him that his creation is thinking the same thing. And, knowing Forsyth, he's also starting to figure out how to stop even that. God, Elgar's glad that Forsyth Turn is here. He wishes Lucy was here, too. Lucy Turn Piper understands his work, and his creations, better than even Elgar himself. She'd know what to do next, where to turn, what trope to use, or spell to invoke, or quest to undertake, or... or *something.* Not that Forsyth won't figure it out, but if Lucy was here, it would just... make Elgar feel better. Okay, all right, he'll admit it. He wants his whole family around him—Lucy, and Alis, as well as Forsyth and, yeah, Juan—because he's scared. He wants their comfort, and to see with his own eyes that they're safe.

Eventually, the nurse chivvies everyone out of the

room so Juan and Elgar can rest. Forsyth, as Elgar knew he would, slips back in with three cups of coffee as soon as the nurse is gone long enough to let her guard down. She's been fierce about protecting Elgar since the incident, and he thinks she's probably feeling guilty about letting the Viceroy slip by her. Elgar has a short, sharp moment of resenting her for it—*Good! She should feel guilty!*—before he beats it back. It's not like she could have helped it.

Juan accepts his cup of black coffee from Forsyth, but says nothing else. Forsyth snags a chair with his foot and pulls it into the space between their beds so he can see, and presumably address, both of them at once. But Juan keeps his face turned away.

Elgar manages only a few sips of the wretched hospital coffee before the nausea robs it of its admittedly meager appeal. He shifts in the bed, waiting for Forsyth to say... something. *Anything*. But Forsyth seems just as lost in thought, going round and round things in his head, as Juan is.

Annoyed by everything that's hanging in the air between them, Elgar finally sets his coffee aside and says, "You know, you're allowed to be angry with me."

Juan gasps, as if Elgar has slapped his face, and whips around to look at him, though he winces and has to shuffle to do so. "Angry with *you*?"

"It's my fault," Elgar says, remembering at the last second not to jerk his head at Juan's arm; he gestures with a weak finger instead. Even that hurts. He lets his finger drop.

"Elgar, of course it's not your fault—" Forsyth begins, even as Juan interrupts with:

"It's not your fault! But I... god, I just..."

Both men trail off, staring at one another, tense and unsure of what should be said next. Or not.

Man up, Elgar chastises himself. *Go on. Admit it.* "I'm scared, too," he eventually whispers.

"What that cop said!" Juan blurts. "About him going after the people close to you. I can't... Boss, I *can't*. I... I mean, I don't want to... to abandon you, but—I can't stay!" The wetness in his eyes spills over, spiking his lashes and leaving wet trails on his cheeks. "I'm sorry. I can't stay." It's clear that the accident has frightened him deeply, and opened his eyes to the reality of working for what amounts to a celebrity, to all the danger that a position like that can sometimes entail, whether he's working directly in security or not.

"No, no, it's fine. I understand," Elgar says softly. He isn't surprised. He's a little disappointed, maybe, because he likes working with Juan, and he thinks their friendship is getting somewhere. But no, no, he can't ask Juan to willingly and knowingly remain a target. No.

Forsyth makes a sort of confirming noise, not quite a grunt, and nods a little. "Where will you go?" he asks, and Elgar can already see the wheels turning behind his eyes, the small ways in which Forsyth will use his powers to ensure that Juan's flight into anonymity remains cloaked.

"Gil's invited me to come stay with him while I recover. Says he's got a great physiotherapist on tap." Juan blushes a little as he says it. Elgar knew that Juan and Gil liked each other, but he hadn't realized how deep the connection had been between the two of them. It reminds him a little of Kintyre and Bevel—he hadn't known the depths of that connection, either, but Lucy says Bevel fell for Kintyre near immediately.

"I'll bet," Elgar says, and feels himself grinning. "But not with family?"

"I can't bring this to their doorstep. Gil's got security at his place; private neighborhood, great CCTV, and all that."

"Admirable," Forsyth says. "And leaving the state can only help. I approve."

Juan blinks owlishly at Forsyth, as if he's not entirely sure why the approval of a man he's literally just met should mean anything. "Okay. Um, thanks?"

"Okay," Elgar says, grabbing Juan's attention back before his former assistant can start to question who Forsyth really is beyond just Elgar's cousin. "Send me a postcard from La-La Land, yeah?"

"Yeah," Juan agrees, tension seeping out of his posture.

FORSYTH

The next morning, Riletti and Jackson escort us back to Elgar's house. I was meant to have left after visiting hours were over at the hospital, but found myself too caught up in working out Juan's safe passage to Los Angeles, as well as checking in with Pip and Alis, to actually leave. No one questions one more sleepless- and harried-looking man sitting in the maternity ward waiting room with a tablet in his hand, his clothing and hair rumpled.

Riletti shows us how to use the new emergency buttons that are hidden in each room of Elgar's house, and then she and Jackson say their goodbyes. I know the place has already been cleared, and that there are guards in discreet places all around the neighborhood with their eyes on us. Yet I cannot help walking from room to room, checking the windows and locks on each door, peering into closets and under beds. I search for spell-bags, and curse runes, and ill wishes. The sorts of things the police would not understand, or may not notice.

Elgar's office has been cleaned up. The window has been replaced. His fire-safe is back in the filing cabinet.

But there is an obscene gap where his desk used to be, matched only by the one on his bookshelf. The pantry is also empty and still smells of bleach. I find nothing that should not be here, and it leaves me slightly hollow and frustrated, and feeling like I've missed something.

When I find Elgar after my search, he is sitting on the floor of the kitchen. One of the lower cabinet doors is open beside him, and in it, I can see cans of cat food, baggies of treats, and an assortment of small furry, feathery toys. Elgar is cuddling one such toy to his chest, tears rolling down his cheeks, apologizing over and over to a marmalade ghost that isn't really here.

"Come," I say, helping him upright when he has finished his cry. "I shall order in some dinner—I shan't make it; Pip says I'm horrific at anything complicated—and we shall discuss our next move."

"Next move?" my creator echoes, mopping at his face with a tissue. "What next move?"

"The Viceroy will come for you again," I say, settling Elgar on one of the stools by his kitchen island. "He wishes revenge on you, and wishes to both lure me out and to hurt me by killing you. We know he will come for you again, wherever you are."

"So, what, I'm supposed to just... wait for it?"

"Of course not," I say. "We know he will come for you. What we must do now is ensure that it is at a time and place of our own choosing, that it is to our advantage."

"Like a trap," Elgar says.

"Exactly so," I agree. A little bit of searching through the cupboards turns up a few take-out menus, and some instant coffee. I can't help the sneer that must show clearly on my face, for Elgar huffs a laugh.

"It's not that bad. When you're out of the good stuff."

"Has the doctor given you permission to walk about?" I ask, dropping the container of crystals right into Elgar's trash bin.

"Yeah?"

"How close is the nearest grocery store?"

"About six blocks," Elgar says, wary.

"Give me your keys," I say. "I will not abide this."

Elgar laughs a little more heartily this time, and I am pleased to hear it.

"A-shopping we shall go," I say, playing up my accent and my imperiousness both for comedic effect. But it has the opposite outcome. Elgar hunches a little, dour. "What is it?"

"Juan always picked up the little things for me. And if he wasn't here, he wanted me to walk."

"Well, I am here to pick up the little things now," I say, opening the fridge. It is barren of all but condiments and bottles of water that are inexplicably all half-drunk. "And it is unsafe to walk."

"I know, but I just..." He trails off, wringing his fingers together. Normally, the physical tic is muffled in the cuffs of his many chunky-knit cardigans, but the doctor has forbidden them until his stitches are removed.

I shut the fridge and walk over to Elgar, placing a comforting hand on his unscathed shoulder. How strange that two of the three people I care most about in the Overrealm bear scars inflicted upon their flesh by the Viceroy. How infuriating.

"Elgar," I say. "He is on his way to safety, and he would not wish you to risk your own. I will check over your car, and we will drive to the shops."

Elgar nods wordlessly, then winces, holding his neck stiffly.

"And then, after you have eaten, you may take your medication and sleep," I add.

"What about planning the trap?" Elgar asks.

"It will keep," I promise him.

ELGAR

After informing the guards via the texting system Riletti explained to him, Elgar grabs his largest cap to hide the little spot on the back of his head where *they'd drilled a small hole in his skull,* and then watches as Forsyth inspects his car for black magic. And, he assumes, cut brake lines.

The drive to the grocery store is short, but paranoia has him glancing over his shoulder every few seconds, anyway. He freezes when they walk out of the parking lot and past the bench outside the entrance, but it's occupied only by an old lady and her dirty little terrier. No man in black.

Everyone in his periphery is an extra burden he has to try to pay attention to, a potential new source of attack, and Elgar's not ashamed to admit that he has a pretty tight grip on Forsyth's elbow by the time they've picked up a plastic shopping basket. Forsyth pulls him around the store at as quick a pace as Elgar's battered body will allow. He tires quickly, head aching from the fluorescent lights.

I should've stayed home, in bed, Elgar thinks. The wish is followed by a flash of memory—the Viceroy looming over his hospital bed, eyes glowing amber and filled with vicious glee, knife shining in the meager light of the monitoring screens. Elgar shudders.

"Elgar?" Forsyth asks, pausing in the middle of the cereal aisle. "Do we need to leave?"

"No, I... I'm fine. I just—" He looks up to try to reassure Forsyth, but all thoughts of what he was going to say next are knocked out of his head when he sees someone he recognizes. "Maddie!" he breathes, when he catches sight of her profile.

She turns to him with a weak smile, until she recognizes who he is. Then her mouth drops into a miserable frown, her shoulders hunch, and... yes, she has the yellowing remains of what must have been a spectacular bruise around her eye. Her blue eye.

"Mr. Reed," she says, inching backward. "I—"

Elgar, who's been coming down the aisle toward her, stops. It occurs to him suddenly that she might not be happy to see him. That she might blame him for what has happened to her.

"I'm happy to see you, Maddie," he says, instead, from halfway up the aisle. He folds his hands and tries to look as harmless as possible. "I'm glad to see you're safe."

She makes a sound like a half-swallowed sob. Behind him, Forsyth steps up, standing just over his shoulder, wary and watching.

"No thanks to me, I know," he allows. "I'm sorry."

Maddie shakes her head, makes a dismissive gesture, but never actually says, "It's fine," or, "I accept your apology." Elgar just stands there, waiting to see if she wants to keep talking to him. If she decides to walk away, he'll let her. He won't blame her for it, either.

But she doesn't walk away. She just stares at him, face inscrutable. "I told the cops this," she says at length, "but you should know, too."

"Know what?"

"The day he left"—Maddie hiccups around another half-sob—"it's when he saw the appearance announcement."

"The what?"

"ConClusion, in Toronto?" Maddie says slowly, as if Elgar's stupid, or slow. Maybe he is. Maybe the meds are stronger than he thinks. He's heard of people not realizing they're hopped up on painkillers and doing dumb stuff like grocery shopping before. "They announced your surprise addition to the line-up. He made me monitor the social media around you, and when they said you'd be there..."

Forsyth makes a considering sound, and Elgar is desperate to ask him what he's thinking. But not here. Not now. Not yet.

"Since the car crash, he..." Maddie says, and then hesitates. "He thought you wouldn't get hurt. I don't know why, but he thought it would only kill Juan. He never explained why he thought you'd be fine, and I... I never asked. I *couldn't* ask."

"I'm sorry. Maddie, I had no idea—"

She holds up her hand, silencing him. "He tried to get me to drive him all the way to Toronto. But after the black eye, my dad took my car keys, to keep him from... a-and I couldn't go, so he left. Thank god, he left without me. He just... let me go." She sobs again, pressing her hand against her mouth, shaking and white-knuckled.

"My dear Miss Garcia, you are overwrought," Forsyth says, coming forward, probably to escort her to a bench or something else gentlemanly, but Maddie jerks back, away from him. Forsyth stops where he is, respecting her choice.

"He said..." Maddie goes on once she's caught her breath. "He said, he never just wanted to kill you. He wanted to do something worse first. Something more terrible. Something that would make you suffer the way you made him suffer."

Elgar feels all his joints seize up with new terror, dread prickling along his scalp, under his beard. "What's worse than killing me?"

"I don't know," Maddie whispers. "Mr. Reed, I really

don't know." Then she sets her shopping basket down and abandons the store.

Elgar's mind begins to churn, but Forsyth only shakes his head, once, when he turns to ask him what he thinks is going on. They're silent for the rest of their short shopping trip. It isn't until they're back at his house that Forsyth says: "Well, he has chosen the place and time, it seems. Now it is up to us to be prepared."

"I have an idea," Forsyth says after Elgar's woken from his post-breakfast-and-meds nap. "But we must include Pip in the conversation." He points to his phone, which is already on the kitchen counter, along with a fresh pad of paper from Elgar's office, and a pen.

"Uh, no," Elgar says, the gummy, fuzzy feeling the meds left in his brain sizzling away at the sight of the tools. "Nuh-uh. Not happening."

But Forsyth isn't listening. He's already calling Lucy, speakerphone on.

"Hey, Freckles," Lucy says when the call connects. "'Sup?"

"I wanted to discuss an option with you. With both of you," Forsyth answers, leaning on the counter and his folded arms. Even this looks noble and poised, the perfect distillation of the lordling in thought. Or maybe the Shadow Hand.

While Elgar watches Forsyth—the way he presses his fingertips to his bottom lip as he listens, the elegant tilt of his head—he is struck all over again with the awe that this is a man he created, this is someone Elgar Reed thought up and who is sitting right in front of him. Forsyth, meanwhile, catches Lucy up on their conversations in the hospital, and the one in the store with Maddie.

"*ConClusion?*" Lucy says. In the background, Elgar

can hear Alis chanting, "Ma, Ma, Ma, Ma!" She obviously wants Lucy to stop paying attention to the phone. "Shush, baby girl, I know. Here, here's your book."

"'Ook!"

"Exactly right. 'Ook."

Forsyth huffs out an exasperated sigh at Alis's word. He must still be trying to correct her baby mumbles, and Lucy is teasing him.

"Yes, ConClusion," Forsyth says, pulling her attention back to the call.

"Interesting choice," she says, and Elgar winces. Maybe the dig was deliberate, but even if it wasn't, he knows why she's surprised. It's not exactly the kind of con he'd have chosen to say yes to before he'd met her. "And what, you want to set a trap there? Around all those people?"

Forsyth winces and rubs his eyes. "The Viceroy is already going to be there. We know that for a fact. If we let this opportunity slip by, then we are once again in the dark. We will have to wait for him to strike. And that may result in us being caught unaware, and you..." He trails off, looking up at Elgar.

"And if he's not at ConClusion?" Lucy asks.

"He *will* be," Forsyth says, and Elgar's not sure who he's trying to convince more—his wife, or himself. "Where else would the Viceroy seek his revenge but during Elgar's moment of glory in front of his adoring fans?"

"At the screening of the film, you mean," Elgar says. "Oh, god."

"But if we are prepared for him," Forsyth insists, "we can stop him. We can contain him."

"We can kill the son of a bitch," Lucy growls.

Elgar would be shocked at her bloodthirstiness, if he didn't understand her fear of the Viceroy so clearly now. "So, all we can do is dangle me like a... like a *cat toy*," he blurts, "and invite the bastard to come after me?"

"Yes," Forsyth says, and then he grins slyly at the paper and pen beside him. "I do have one more thing to try, though. Elgar, you are the Author, yes? You Wrote Pip and I out of the books once before. Maybe you can Write the Viceroy back in. And ensure he stays there."

"No," Lucy says, even as Elgar jerks away from the island with a "no!" of his own.

"No?" Forsyth asks, straightening, bewildered.

"No, kill him. Don't write him back. Write his death," Pip says, pleading now. "He'll go after Kin and Bev and Wyndam if we send him back, you know he will. Or he'll find another way out again. He'll rip apart every realm there is to get back here. Kill him and end it, like I should have done on the top of the Ivory Tower."

"Yes," Elgar agrees. "But no."

"Elgar," Forsyth says. "You must write. We have already spoken—"

"This is different," Elgar confesses, sweat beading on his forehead. "The screenplay, that's only recounting something that's already happened. What you're asking... this is *new*. This is... I could hurt someone."

"That's the *point*," Pip snarls.

"But someone *else*—"

"Then don't write about anyone else!"

"I don't think I—"

"*Enough*," Forsyth booms over them both, and Elgar shrinks away, startled. "Pip, it will do you no good to bully him into this. And Elgar... peace. We must try. Do you see? If we can prevent the Viceroy's plan from coming to fruition, if we are to protect all the people he will be surrounding himself with, the people you know he will be using, like Maddie and Juan, then is it not worth your... discomfort?"

Elgar fists his hands and feels shame turn his face red.

"I... guess so. Yes."

"Very good," Forsyth says. He pushes the paper and pen toward Elgar.

"Make sure to write something else into the passage, to let us know that it worked," Lucy adds hastily. "Like, I don't know, a chime sounding, or a firework going off, or something? I want to know that the bastard is dead."

Elgar takes both implements, and returns to his stool on the island. He uncaps the pen, presses its ball to the page, and then hesitates. "You're... you're not going to stand there and watch me, are you?" It's weird, having Forsyth there, his creation watching him do something so intimate. It's like your kid watching you have sex to make another kid.

Forsyth gives him a searching look, and then says, "No, I suppose not. I shall be upstairs if you need me." He picks up his phone, clicks off the speakerphone, and lifts it to his ear. "Pip? Yes, Elgar is... patience, *bao bei*."

Elgar nods, and waits until the sound of Forsyth's conversation has disappeared into the guest bedroom. Then he turns his attention back to the page. The tauntingly, infuriatingly familiar blank page. Right.

Writing is hard enough when he's in his own office, with only Linux to... with only Linux... with only... He shakes his head and clears his throat, and forces his eyes down.

Writing to specification in front of an expectant and eager audience is a thousand times harder. Elgar sips his coffee and taps his lips with the pen.

Think, he scolds himself. *Come on, think. You can do this. You need to do this. They need you to do this. Think of Alis. Think of Maddie. Think of Juan. Come on.*

Jesus, shut up, don't pressure yourself.

Fuck, Eglar thinks, pressing the nib of the pen into his leg. The pain is sharp, different from the dull ache that still manages to plague his shoulders and neck despite the painkillers. It helps bring his focus back to the blank page. Then, carefully, pen-stroke by pen-stroke, agonizing over every single word, scratching out more than he keeps, he writes:

> Though the Viceroy is a formidable villain, he is no match for the will of the Man Who has Created Him. The Writer, admitting that it was at last time to kill off one of his most powerful, compelling creations, knew that the simplest way is often the best. And so, the Viceroy, who had been so dramatic and so theatrical, clutched at his breast. The breath fled his lungs, and he was unable to speak words, nor cast any spells, nor flick any air-runes. He could do no magic. He collapsed to his knees, his lungs refusing to reinflate as his heart began to beat faster, faster, faster in his chest, fluttering like a furious caged fairy. And then suddenly, all at once—it stopped.
>
> The Viceroy, the archnemesis of Kintyre Turn and the only wielder of magic in the Overrealm, fell over dead. Never to be resurrected, by magic or science. Dead. Finally, and completely, dead.
>
> The End

Sweat beading around his hairline, hands shaking, his own heart fluttering in the hollow of his throat, Elgar sets down his pen. There. Done. Just to be sure, he compiles his notes and scraps and copies the two paragraphs onto a fresh sheet of notepaper in a clear, fair hand. At the last minute, remembering Lucy's directive to make it obvious that the magic has worked, he adds:

Epilogue

Over the city of Seattle, a massive cloud suddenly gathered. A crack of thunder echoed between the buildings, a flash of lightning dazzled everyone who looked up at the sky in stunned awe, and a hard but brief rain began. The Overrealm, overjoyed to be rid of the vermin, wept with joy.

"You can come out," Elgar calls, standing to stretch out his back and work his way carefully through a few of the exercises the hospital physiotherapist had shown him to ease the pain.

"Are you done?" Forsyth asks as he comes back into the kitchen.

"Yeah." He moves to the patio door, presses his hand against the glass, and looks up at the sky. The hatefully clear, sunny sky. Still, he looks, strains to see, thinks maybe over there, is that a dark smudge of...? No. Nothing. *Nothing, goddamn it.*

"Not a fucking cloud in sight," he groans.

"Cloud?" Forsyth asks, and Elgar hands him the paper. Forsyth reads it aloud, and still, nothing happens. "Ah," he adds, a sound caught between disappointment and resignation.

"But how could I write you out of the books, if this didn't work?"

"I cannot say," Forsyth says. "Narrative convenience, I suppose? Or that Pip and I wanted to leave? Or the Viceroy is somehow blocking us?"

"Maybe because it goes against the story," Elgar says. "I never planned on killing the Viceroy, not really. The publisher had talked about a ninth novel, but after I wrote the eighth, we agreed it was a good stopping point. So he just... stayed."

Forsyth nods, lips pursed, and then, slowly, says: "It was worth the try."

"So we're going to ConClusion?" Lucy asks after a long silence, and Elgar jumps, realizing that Forsyth has put the phone back on speaker.

"We?" Forsyth repeats, eyebrow raised.

"I'm coming with you." Her tone brooks no argument.

Forsyth tries, anyway. "Pip," he begins, but she steamrolls over his protests.

"Look," she says. "I hate this whole creeping around the edges of the adventure crap more than ever. My parents can take Alis."

"And if the Viceroy comes after her instead of us?"

"He won't," Lucy insists. "You said so. You're never wrong."

"*Rarely* wrong," Forsyth says. "It is not *always*. I would much rather you—"

"I know you would," Lucy cuts him off. "But I refuse to just *sit* here."

Elgar watches Forsyth working this through in his head.

Forsyth presses his finger to his lips in that comical thinking-pose of his, and cautiously adds: "If something were to happen, I would much prefer that Alis grows up with one parent than none."

"*Forsyth*," she says, like he's being particularly dense. "If I'm not there, if I stay behind with the baby, don't you think the Viceroy is going to notice? Don't you think he's going to *wonder* where I am? If I stay here, we'll be doing the opposite of protecting our daughter. We'll be painting a target on her." Her voice crackles, which startles Elgar. Maybe it's unfair, but he's never thought of her as the kind of woman who cries. "*Bao bei.* He'll *find* me. He always does." She doesn't just sound like she's crying, though. She sounds *shattered*.

"Lucy," Elgar says, at a loss for how to comfort her.

"I don't... I'm sorry."

"It's not your fault. But I can't help thinking... that maybe he already knows where we are," Lucy whispers, struggling to raise her voice above the lump in her throat. "Maybe my fears are for nothing, and it's too late. But he hasn't come here. Not yet. He's too focused on his revenge. But believe me, Forsyth, the microsecond he's done with Elgar and... and y-you, if you're there... he will come for me. You know that. I will be next on the list. And if I'm here with Alis... If I'm there, and we... we lose, then maybe not being here will save her. Maybe he won't be able to find her. Maybe he won't care."

"We won't lose," Elgar says, firmly, loudly. He sounds a lot more confident and resolved than he feels. But he can't stand the sound of Lucy so upset.

"No," Lucy says, her own determination bleeding through. "No. We won't lose. And having me there might tip the odds in our favor just that much more."

Forsyth sighs, and then nods to himself. "Yes, of course. And to be truthful, *bao bei*, if I am to go to war, I would much rather do so with you at my side."

Elgar resists the urge to say something snide. Instead, he rips up the paper with his ineffectual scratchings and jams it down the garbage disposal.

FORSYTH

For the next three weeks, I stay in Seattle with Elgar. Pip returns to school, the fits seeming to have subsided for now—I cannot help but worry over what the Viceroy is preparing during this period of seeming absence—and between Mei Fan, Martin, and *wai po*, Alis is well cared for, if not bounced around and missing her da. I have never been separated from my wife and daughter for so long. Three weeks without them, and I feel as if I have lost a limb.

But in that time, Elgar's script becomes an actual film. It is a curious process, to see one's memories transform into someone else's art. Though we don't go down to LA to watch the filming personally, it takes place over the second week following our return to Elgar's home. I do not feel Readers' eyes on me, or anything so concrete, but there is a sensation of being aware that all eyes are soon to be on my life. Or rather, my brother's. The filming is done in an LA sound studio, on one of the sets constructed for another fantasy television series whose producer, luckily, is a friend of Gil's. It is rushed, according to Andy, and he doesn't have time to finesse it the way he would prefer, but we are on a deadline.

The week following that is dedicated to the post-production process, where effects and dramatic music are added. Luckily, both were already being prepared for the television series itself, so there is a library from which the artisans can draw. I didn't realize how much thought and diligent work goes into writing, and filmmaking. I have much more respect for Bevel and what he's created with his scrolls than ever before, especially since he has no software to help him rearrange and rewrite.

In between all of that, Elgar has many doctor's appointments—physiotherapy, cognitive tests, removal of the stitches, massages to have his lashed neck coerced back into mobility. I sit in the waiting rooms, looking around, watching, waiting for traps that are never sprung, attacks that never come. All in all, it is both one of the most mentally taxing and tense periods of my life.

And in all that time, Finnar is silent. The Viceroy has effectively vanished. The Overrealm is quiet—for a given value of such. The announcement that Reed will be appearing as a last-minute, surprise addition to the guest lineup at ConClusion causes the predictable online outpouring of joy and jubilation from his fans, but nothing out of the ordinary. Even the loathsome troll from Detroit seems to be taking a break from their vitriol.

My influence as a hacker for the Canadian Security Intelligence Service has pull, but not as much as my role as Shadow Hand used to. While I can place the Viceroy on a no-fly list based on his appearance, and try to limit his travel and access to weaponry, the truth is that, if the Viceroy wanted to buy a gun, or hitch a ride, or take a taxi, or buy a bus ticket, none of the law enforcement agencies I could put digital pressure on are impervious. The wily villain has, for the time being, outfoxed me.

And oh, aren't I galled to have to admit to it.

In my free time, I resume my sword-fighting practice in Elgar's backyard, with a broom stick of comparable length and weight to Smoke. I confer with Pip about possible methods of trapping the Viceroy, and how he, in turn, may attempt to trap us.

In Victoria, Pip digs our adventuring clothes out of the back of the closet, the leathers we had both been wearing during our first foray through Hain. Through Elgar, I am able to obtain a permit to travel with Smoke. Pip insures the sword as a prop for Flageolet Entertainment, which makes it permissible in her cabin baggage so long as it is in a case which is locked shut.

She reviews her thesis yet again, and consults the Excel hung in our bedroom for any ideas or revelations they might provide. But this adventure was not Written by Elgar, nor is it occurring within the realm of his imagination. If it is following his typical Seven-Station archetype, neither Pip nor I can decipher what they are, or where in the cycle we stand.

In the evenings, I compose a list of spells and Words that I remember, writing them in a small, cramped hand in a smaller notebook, which I intend to tuck into the knife pouch of my sword belt. I am out of practice with magic, but if the Viceroy is able to use it, then perhaps I will be, too.

Strangely, and against all of my previous desires, I find myself missing my brother fiercely. The Viceroy has always been his enemy, not mine. Not the Shadow Hand's. While I kept tabs on the rascal, it was never my duty, nor within my purview, to take him down. One rogue warlock was never the Shadow Hand's concern.

But now, I wish dearly that Kintyre was here, so that he could tell me if any of my preparations, my concerns, my *predictions* are anywhere near good enough.

"Forsyth!" Pip hisses at us as she crosses the expansive hotel lobby to where we stand, just inside the grand entryway. "This is *not* the side door."

Elgar, clearly travel-fuddled, plane-rumpled, and hazy

from pain medication, stands his wheelie suitcase up to balance on its own in the middle of the crowded hotel lobby, and says, quite eloquently: "What?"

"The side door," Pip says again, crowding up next to him, trying to get her body between him and the open windows of the front wall. Of course, she will never be able to completely block him. Elgar is both taller and wider than my wife. "Remember how you were supposed to come to the exit near the——?"

"It was locked," I interrupt. "We tried."

Pip grimaces, then waves it away.

She tries to hustle us toward the elevator banks, but Elgar's brain clearly hasn't caught up with the rest of him. He tries to twist his head to follow her, but his feet stay planted and he stumbles. I catch his arm, and he winces and bites back a groan. He's holding himself stiffly. He is not as well as he thinks he is, and he is overdoing it because he is vainglorious and ridiculous.

And I will admit, he is not the only one of us who is feeling fuddled and sore. Oh, how I hate airplanes. How Pip looks so energetic is beyond me, and so very unfair. Her plane only landed two hours before ours. She has checked into the hotel on our behalf, but she cannot have had the opportunity for a nap and a shower.

"Christ, you've lost weight," Pip says, staring at where her hand landed on Elgar's chest to keep him from falling.

"Yeah. Living in utter fear for three months does that to you," he says, trying for a light, jocular tone and nearly getting there. Pip allows my creator the hug he is obviously angling for, though it's more like he collapses around her shoulders than hugs her. They are not as awkward as they have been in the past, and that is something, at least. Though Pip does wince when his meaty hand lands between her shoulder blades. Elgar doesn't notice, of course. It seems I am the least injured of the lot of us, which doesn't fill me with confidence for the coming days.

"I'm pretty darn pleased to see you again," he says softly. "Nearly thought I wouldn't."

"How's Juan?" Pip asks, breaking away to grab the handle of his large wheeled suitcase. She is subtly trying to shove him toward the elevator again. He is still not catching the hint. I scan the crowd around us, checking to see how many people noticed him stumbling in through the front door.

Too many for my liking, is the answer.

"Another week in the cast," Elgar says. He mimes a covering from shoulder to fingertips. "But they set his nose real nice."

"Come, we're attracting attention," I point out, and indeed we are. Around us, fans wheeling their own suitcases and carrying their large costume props have paused in filtering toward the check-in counter. Elgar's silhouette is distinctive. Before a gaggle of young ladies standing just to one side of us have managed to screw up their courage and set off a domino-chain of fans approaching us, I thread my arm through Elgar's, as if he were a vaunted magisterial elder, and maneuver us toward the elevator banks. Pip is watching both of us, keeping his bag between us and the rest of the people in this tiny hallway.

Déjà vu settles hard between my eyes as we wait for the elevator to arrive. Two summers ago, when Pip was enormously pregnant, we traveled to this very city to meet Elgar for the very first time. And here Elgar and I now are, staring at each other via the reflective mirrored walls, pretending that we aren't terrified of what's to come.

I take a moment to really study Elgar, for his weight loss was not as startlingly apparent to me, as I have seen it happening bit by bit. Elgar's face is a bit more gaunt than the first time I met him, his double chin turning to sagging jowls. He's covered it well by letting his beard grow in a bit more, but the salt-and-pepper of his hair has given over entirely to salt now. He looks tired. His cheeks are flushed, and his eyes are slightly glazed. He is blinking unevenly, swaying a little on the spot as we wait. His clothes are just slightly too baggy. All in all, he's probably lost about twenty pounds, but I cannot fault him if his appetite has been off since the stalking began, and that he hasn't been eating much at all since the salad incident.

In short, he looks more like my life-worn, alcoholic father than ever, and I must forcibly remind myself that the man beside me is Elgar, not Algar. The dim, inadequate lighting and bronzy hue of the mirror does much to try to fool me of this fact, though, so I must look away to regard my creator's profile instead of the reflection, to *see* the difference. A twist of fear that I had not realized had screwed itself into the place behind my sternum uncoils. The thrum of adrenaline is unexpected, as is the remnant of childhood terror that had kept me small and quiet around my father. In my own reflection, I see that my shoulders have rounded down, my face lowered; I am trying to be small and unobtrusive. In my mouth, my tongue flutters.

Blast and rubbish, and damn all that to all seven of the hells, anyway.

I take a calming breath, force myself to stretch my spine, to raise my eyes to Elgar and smile as reassuringly as I can. He is Elgar Reed, and I am Syth Piper now, and this is not Turn Hall.

"Oh, hey, look! Kintyre and Bevel!" Elgar says suddenly, eyes pinned on something back in the hotel foyer.

"What? Where?" Pip asks, head whipping around to follow his line of sight. My heart squeezes in my chest, and I stumble after him, juggling the luggage and scanning the crowd for my brother. He is tall; he should stand out. Or above, at any rate.

"How did he get here?" I ask, unable to see what Elgar is pointing to. Kintyre is nowhere in sight.

"Cosplayers!" Elgar turns back to us, face filled with childish delight. "They look perfect!"

Pip and I look at each other, disappointed and self-conscious, and follow his pointing finger. We both realize at the same time that we have been hoping my brother and his trothed had somehow found a way to traverse the realms and join us here, found a way to help us with this fight.

Elgar's delight shrivels, however, when the two women dressed as Kintyre and Bevel kiss at the urging of a crowd of fans with their cameras out. The crowd crows and squeals with delight, flashes snapping, as the Kintyre dips her companion.

"Wrong way around," Pip mutters, grinning.

Elgar scoffs and turns away. Then he stares up at the numbers above the elevator doors, as if willing the car to come faster. It appears to be stopping at every single floor on its way down to us, however.

"What, it's not like they're wrong or anything," Pip says. "This is Con-Inclusion, don't forget. Kin and Bevel are a thing. Hashtag Binky lives."

"Yeah, but, it's not that it's... it's the way they've *always* done it," Elgar mutters, pouting in his exhaustion. "Fans and the fetishization of male homoromantic and homo-sexual identities, and all that other stuff."

Pip's eyebrows jump. Pip, the woman I fell in love with, resurfaces from behind the mask of Lucy Piper, concerned and overstressed warrior-heroine. "I didn't know you knew those terms," Pip says, grinning at Elgar in parental approval. "Nice use of the ten-dollar jargon."

"I *did* read your thesis, didn't I?" Elgar says. "It's up on the web and everything. I even understood it. Well, most of it."

"Aw, you do care, Uncle Gar," Pip says, grinning and perhaps even blushing a little. It is easy to forget that my wife once admired my creator, quite genuinely. Seeing her change in demeanor and energy is like a sharp slap to the face, and I realize all at once how very *shut down* Pip has been since our return to the Overrealm. How much her concern about the Damoclean sword, the proverbial other shoe, the hurricane outside of this artificial eye, has thrown a muffler over her naturally bright, energetic attitude.

"Yeah, just... not so much for that," Elgar says with a huff. "It just feels like they're... devaluing what I wrote."

"I suppose it is fetishization in a way," Pip admits. A small crowd of people are starting to appear around us, waiting for the elevator. More than one of them has their ears tuned into Elgar and Pip's conversation. I wonder if I should put a stop to it. "But don't forget that if fans want to make something with a romantic theme, then the audience-favorite characters are going to be overwhelmingly male, simply because a significant percentage of main characters in mainstream media texts are also male. The characters the audience identifies with or loves are mostly dudes, because overwhelmingly, the main characters *are just* dudes."

"But my characters—"

"Elgar," Pip interrupts gently, and around me, more than one eavesdroppers' eyes pop wide. "Fan fiction has nothing to do with *you*. Sure, it's about using your characters and worlds as building blocks, but it's... Fan fiction is a place where a lot of women of all ages learn about and experiment with their own sexuality, and using male characters not only gives them a sort of anonymizing distance, but frankly, it's a bigger reflection of what it is women *want* in a relationship, rather than what they think a relationship between two dudes is actually like."

"Okay, yeah, but—" Elgar grunts, and flings his good arm at the cosplayers, who are beginning to move on. "I mean, like, is that fair, to do that to someone? To just pretend they're gay for *fun*? To impose on their identities like that?"

"But Bevel is *gay*," I remind him. "And Kintyre is bi."

Elgar makes a frustrated sound in the back of his throat. "There's a difference between knowing it and... I mean, knowing that they're together, and Paired, and there's a *kid* and everything, and... and, you know... *seeing* it."

Pip's eyebrows turn down. "Careful, Elgar. You're skirting awfully close to sounding like a homophobe."

"I don't hate the gay stuff!" Elgar protests. "I just hate when people make stuff that isn't gay into gay stuff because... because... I don't know, like, what's wrong with friendship, right? Why does every intense and close relationship have to be romantic and sexual? Why do people devalue male friendships so much? Why do *fans*? I mean, if I meant them to be gay together, I would have written it that way!"

"But you *did*," Pip says. "They *are*."

"Well, I know that now, but I just... I don't know how to... my head hurts," he complains. "I can't... think right."

"Sorry," Pip says gently, patting his hand. "Sorry. I know you're scared and just looking for something to lash out at. I get it, okay? It's fine."

We fall into silence then, everyone side-eyeing us, wondering if that's the end of the dispute. I appreciate this bizarre respect for privacy that celebrities seem to engender in Canada—everyone *looks*, but nobody *bothers*. And when the elevator doors open, and all the other passengers are disgorged, only one man stops to stare.

This man is wearing an electric blue t-shirt, and a

badge lanyard that marks him as staff.

"Mr. Reed?" the man says, his voice strangled with surprise. "What are you doing here?"

Elgar turns to look at him. The young man doesn't move on, and ends up blocking the entrance for those around us. I would prefer if we were not the center of a crowd, so I pull us back against the opposite wall to allow the other people waiting their chance to board the elevator, and to try to block Elgar from view of the lobby.

"Uh, I'm Ichiro Eiji," the young man says suddenly, when he realizes that Elgar has no good reason to answer him. He shoves his hand at Elgar so abruptly he nearly punches him in the gut.

"Ah, the guest coordinator," Elgar says, brightening, accepting the handshake. I can tell that it's all forced charm and smiles, but Ichiro can't, apparently. He doesn't seem to see that Elgar's too wrung thin to want to do this now.

"You're here early, Mr. Reed," Ichiro says, and he's thumbing the walkie-talkie clipped to his belt absently. He wants to tell someone that he's seen Reed, inform his higher-ups, possibly. That would throw all our plans to keep Elgar under wraps straight into a pool of kelpies.

"Wanted an extra night to spend time with family," Elgar says. It's an elegant half-lie, and just true enough that it comes out as sincere. It's the one we decided on, secretly, so that if someone had swindled the secret of his travel dates and itinerary out of the convention committee, they would be misinformed.

"Syth Piper," I say, reaching out to shake Ichiro's hand, as well. "Elgar's cousin. And this is my wife, Lucy."

"Oh," Ichiro says, looking back and forth between us.

"It's fine," Elgar says.

Ichiro, on the other hand, looks like he's trying to swallow a tack. "Mr. Reed—"

"It's not a big deal. So I came a day early," Elgar repeats, as if repetition could make Ichiro Eiji less anxious. He flops his hand in dismissal.

"But your room isn't—"

"Don't worry," Pip jumps in, tamping down her ire. "We have a suite. We thought he could just stay with us? You know, save the con some money." She smirks at that. If there is one thing ConClusion has, it's an abundance of money. The attendees number in the hundreds of thousands—that is a lot of badge fees.

"But the insurance..." Ichiro says, dithering. "And you need to meet your handler for the weekend."

"I got an email already," Elgar says, dismissively. "We've talked."

Pip smiles at Ichiro—her steamroller smile, the one she uses when she's about to intellectually bludgeon acquiescence out of someone. She slings a friendly arm across his shoulders, and pulls him to the side, speaking softly enough that I cannot actually make out all that she is saying. It seems to work, though, for Ichiro nods miserably, and unclips his radio. He walks away, chattering into it, heading down the hallway partially blocked off from the lobby by a large easel with a sign that reads: "Convention Staff Only."

"Lucy Piper, the miracle worker," Elgar says, grinning. He puts a hand on the mirrored wall in a way he probably thinks is subtle.

"Not that big a miracle," Pip says. "He's still informing his boss."

"At least they do not have the room number," I say. "We hold that secret yet, do we not, *bao bei*?"

"As long as the concierge doesn't give it to them," Pip says in answer.

The elevator dings again, and this time, we manage to make it aboard.

A few others join us, and we are squeezed between the wall and a large luggage cart overflowing with suitcases, plastic grocery bags of chips and sodas and a tray of pre-cut vegetables, and a massive pile of board games in battered, well-loved boxes. There are four other occupants on this ride with us—two men, two women—and the tall, thin man on a cane elbows his shorter, larger companion in the ribs and jerks his chin toward Elgar. The car goes quiet as all four try, and fail, to not stare at my creator.

Elgar offers them a cheeky wave and a little lopsided smirk, and the youngest woman—dark skin, dyed red hair, glasses, clad in a fannish t-shirt—has nearly worked up enough gusto to say something when the elevator chimes and the door opens onto their floor. Bravery aborted, they trundle out, lugging the cart, all four pairs of eyes fused to Elgar's face until the door closes again and cuts them off from view. Just before it snaps shut, Elgar waggles his fingers at them, grinning.

"That's never not going to be funny," Elgar says, chuckling drunkenly to himself.

Pip rolls her eyes, and then we are on the top floor of the hotel, where a bit of judicious juggling from within the hotel's booking system allowed me to ensure we had a two-bedroom suite with kitchenette reserved for our needs. Elgar seems pleased with it when we leave him in his bedroom to get settled. Pip goes immediately into the kitchenette for the bottle of wine she's left on the counter.

"A bit early in the day," I chide.

Pip grimaces, but applies the point of the corkscrew to the foil all the same. "If I'm going to put up with his 'sense of humor' for the next four days, I need it."

"Just a small one," I allow. "We must remain on our guard."

Pip groans at my nobility. Having just worked the cork out, she jams it back into the mouth of the bottle. "Spoilsport," she complains.

"Here," I say, leaning back against the counter and opening my arms, spreading my legs. "Let your husband soothe your ruffled feathers another way."

Pip accepts the invitation and steps in between my feet, throws her arms around my waist, and cradles her cheek on my sternum. I take advantage of our closeness and slide my hands under the back of her belt to hold her close. We remain locked together, just listening to one another breathe, for several long minutes.

"I missed you," Pip says, and if her voice is wobbly, then it is not my place to tease her for it. For my voice is just as wobbly when I reply: "And I you."

We only break apart when a deliberate cough echoes from the threshold of the kitchenette.

"Yeah, yeah," Pip says, and turns away from me to smirk at Elgar. "I know, we're so gross."

"I wouldn't say that," Elgar protests, shifting uneasily from foot to foot. "Kinda romantic, actually."

The uncharacteristic compliment startles me, and I cannot help but study Elgar's face. He has his eyes turned away, his hands folded behind his back. He looks more like a contrite little boy than an adult. But he is leaning heavily on the doorframe, clearly still affected by his medications.

"Coffee?" Pip asks, and breaks away to try to dissolve the awkward moment with caffeine.

"Yeah," Elgar groans. "Yeah, that'd be great." He lowers himself into the office chair beside what can be tentatively called 'the living room,' and tips his head back, closing his eyes with a hard sigh.

The suite door opens into an open space with a sofa, a large chair and ottoman, and a sleek entertainment center right beside the floor-to-ceiling patio doors that lead to a balcony too windy to really enjoy. To the left are the bedrooms, with matching en suite washrooms, and to the right, against the wall, is the kitchenette, which is directly abutted by an office nook with a desk that looks out through the windows over downtown Toronto.

As Pip putters with the hotel-room coffee machine, complaining when she realizes she failed to pack the good coffee sachets, I join my creator in looking out over the skyline. He sits up, wincing, and stares out the window.

The coffee machine beeps, and I rise and fetch us three mug-fulls, each doctored to our preferred strength. Pip likes her coffee dark as night and sweet as sin. I prefer mine creamy, but sugarless. And Elgar drinks what Canadians call a "double-double"; two creams, two sugars. Juan had been trying to wean him onto black coffee to cut out some of the excess sweets, but now that he has left, Elgar has returned to all his bad nutritional habits. Perhaps I ought not to be enabling him.

"Thanks," he mumbles, but he presses the mug to the skin between his eyes instead of taking a sip. The heat helps to soothe away some of the worry lines that have etched themselves around his eyes, though it does nothing for the dark smudges under them.

"So, are you guys cosplaying?" Elgar asks at length, when our silent communication has clearly become too unnerving for him.

"Hmmm?" Pip asks, looking down at her attire. She is already dressed in her adventuring gear. My own is laid carefully along the back of the sofa, waiting for me to don it. "Oh. Yeah, I guess."

"As?"

"Lordling Forsyth Turn and his Ladyling Wife," I answer with a knowing grin. "We figured it was best to attire ourselves as if we were going into an adventure, just in case we are. Padded jerkins to absorb blows, you see here? And tough leather leggings that will not tear. Boots with sturdy soles that do not slip, and which lace up and give support to the ankle when running."

"Where'd you get the stuff?" Elgar asks, reaching out to touch the fabric of Pip's sleeve. The sash laying on the arm of the sofa is the one I wear under my sword belt. I'd had it on when I returned to the Overrealm from our second adventure. Elgar picks up the end, examining the locks and keys picked out in gold thread in the fabric.

"My mother embroidered that," I offer.

"Real Hainish embroidery," he repeats, breathless with awe. "From the hand of Lady Alis Sheil Turn."

"That it is," I say gently. Elgar carefully sets it back down, and I take the opportunity to head into our room and change. As I step back out, properly clad in clothing that now feels like it fits too tightly, my question about how I look is interrupted by Elgar's smartphone ringing, blaring out that same fiddle-and-fife tune he told me was meant to be secret.

For all his desire to be covert, Elgar is woefully bad at it. Setting the song as his ringtone; walking in the front door of the hotel; engaging in conversations with people he knows full well will go repeat them elsewhere. He would not have made a suitable candidate for Shadow Hand at all. But he does not desire to be stealthy, to be spy-like. He wishes to be *loved*. To the point of recklessness, sometimes.

When he answers the phone, Pip and I listen, equally intently, to one side of it as Elgar has a conversation with someone who is obviously the convention organizer, based on the sorts of questions he's answering. Elgar, as a guest of honor and a major financial draw in terms of star power, certainly has the ability to dictate his own terms and create his own leeways and rules that I assume the lesser guests do not have. All the same, his arriving early seems to have caused a tizzy which I wish we could have avoided. In the end, he soothes the organizer—though I must mime urgently that he not provide the number of the room we are staying in—by agreeing to meet with him tonight.

"Why not?" he asks after he's hung up.

"What color are the organizer's eyes?" Pip asks, and Elgar blanches so quickly that I jump up from the sofa to guide him back down into his seat.

"I... I don't know."

"What color were Ichiro's?" Pip presses him.

"I didn't check," he confesses in a small voice, hand pressed against his chest.

"Exactly. We must be cautious," I remind him.

"Yeah," he says shakily. He swallows hard, head clearly still a bit muzzy. "Yeah. I, uh... they usually do this thing before the con where all the guests get together in a suite with the organizers and have a few beers. They give us our honorarium, we stick around and talk for a bit, they usually feed us. I've been asked to go down this evening."

"I'm not sure I am comfortable with you going to—"

"I wrangled invitations for you, too," Elgar interrupts.

Pip and I exchange another glance, but this time, her eyebrows are raised. She is thinking it over. "It may give us a chance to scope out everyone in positions of authority," she says eventually. "And if no one besides the convention committee knows Elgar's here yet, it might give us an advantage."

"What advantage?" Elgar asks.

"Warning them," Pip says, but she does so with that sideways, one-shouldered shrug that means she's not certain that what she's saying is really worth considering.

Elgar snorts. "What, we're going to waltz up to the

ConComm and tell them that one of my own characters has slipped his pages and intends to kill me?"

"That you have a maniacal fan who is stalking you," I correct.

"Yeah. Yeah, they can warn security and... I don't know. I usually have someone from convention security escort me everywhere. Maybe they can get a real cop?"

"Possibly," I allow. "But I doubt that even Toronto's finest will be utterly immune to the Viceroy's influence should he choose to exert it. I would rather it be just us two—more people added to your honor guard means more opportunity for treachery."

"I hadn't thought of that," Elgar says on a whimper.

"That is what I am here for, Elgar," I reassure. "When must you go down to the room?"

"Now, if we can," he says. "Does that work?"

"Yes," I say. "Just let me fetch Smoke."

Elgar's eyes bulge out. "You're going to just walk around with a real sword?"

Pip grins at him and punches his shoulder gently. "We're cosplaying, remember?"

"They'll cable-tie it into the sheath. They're serious about security."

"It is a risk I am willing to take," I say. "I can break the tie with magic later."

"There's no guarantee there'll *be* magic," Elgar protests.

"If I need to draw my weapon," I say gravely. "There will be."

"This is Abby," Elgar says, about twenty minutes later. He is smiling too widely, and his eyes are too bright—he is in what he calls "Convention Mode": gregarious, energetic, his jokes flat and desperate, his smile false. As a fellow natural introvert, I can see how exhausting the performance is. He is trying too hard, and he is too over-the-top as a result.

He slings his arm around a young woman with large dark eyes, and long dark hair. She is dressed in a great deal of bubblegum pink and misty mint, from her sneakers to her leggings, to her knee-length skirt, which is patterned with ice-cream cones, and the matching scarf over her long-sleeved shirt. She is terrifically pretty, too, very carefully made up with false lashes and the careful sort of artistically intense makeup that Pip has called "contouring," and "a massive pain in the ass," and "a waste of a perfectly good hour of my life." Bless my wife, but she does reject the traditionally feminine with a vigor that nearly borders on insult to those that embrace it.

However, the young lady before me seems to be the exact opposite of a simpering femme, wearing her pastels and makeup with a sort of warrior-like pride which I admire. She is clearly of Indian descent, not African, but I am reminded so intensely of Captain Isobin for a moment that the déjà vu fills my breast with a brief, intense stab of homesickness. Though, of course, this young woman is neither pirate, nor captain, and unlike Isobin, is not filled with the raucous self-confidence required to push my creator back on his arse for his presumption. She is clearly not comfortable with the way he has taken liberties with her personal space without asking, and he has just as clearly gotten her name wrong. Her badge, which marks her as a guest liaison, says, "Ahbni."

"Hi," Pip says, holding her hand out for a shake, and Ahbni uses the excuse to duck out from under Elgar's arm.

"I'll be able to tell her apart from the rest of the brown girls because she's the hot one," Elgar goes on, sticking his foot further down his throat.

Pip pinches the bridge of her nose and groans. "I honestly can't tell if it's the meds talking, or the stress."

"Actually, I—" Ahbni begins, but Elgar talks over her.

"You can get my friend a coffee or something, right, Abby?"

"I'm the assistant guest liaison, Mr. Reed, and I need to talk to you about—"

Elgar laughs. "Cute. No, no, grab your boss and send him my way, okay, sweetie?" And then he gives her a little shove. She steps away, off-balance, and Elgar's eyes drop to... oh. They drop with the full intention of watching her walk away.

Beside me, my wife makes a noise like a strangling cat.

"Lucy?" Elgar asks, having heard the sound as well, bushy eyebrows knitted with confusion. "Are you okay? Abby, can you—?"

"It's *Ahbni*," the liaison corrects.

"Ahbni," Elgar repeats, not entirely sure where he misstepped. "That's a cute fantasy handle."

"Nope. It's my name," she corrects.

"Oh!" Elgar laughs. "Were your parents fantasy fans, then?"

"They're Telugu," Ahbni says, and I get the distinct impression that she is considering using her badge lanyard to garrote my creator. I am doing my best to control the urge to laugh.

"I might use it, though, you know? It's a good name. The beautiful Princess Ahbni, with skin like fresh-roasted cafe latte—"

"No," Pip snaps, smacking Elgar's good arm like an errant puppy. "Bad writer. Women of color are not dessert products."

Elgar jams his hands into his pockets and scowls. "It's supposed to be a compliment—"

"I swear to fuck, one of these days, I'm going to

throttle you myself," Pip says, deadpan and staring straight at Elgar. She's got her index finger stretched out and is tapping him right in the chest, fingernail clicking against his plastic button. "You know that being terrified out of your mind is no excuse to fall back into old habits, right?"

Elgar immediately looks ashamed. "I... you're right. I didn't think—"

"Try to," Pip says. Then she blows out an annoyed breath, forces herself to flex her fist, runs her fingers through her hair, and pointedly turns away from him. "Ahbni, if you'd like to tell us where the coffee is, I can make sure that my husband fetches it for his own damn self. And then you and I can review where Mr. Neanderthal over there needs to be, and by when."

Chastened, Elgar scowls and jams his hands further into his pockets. "Sorry," he mutters.

"Are you his security, then?" Ahbni asks, clearly not convinced, even as she waves me toward the table at the back of the small conference room the ConComm has commandeered for this small shindig. I don't blame her. Pip, in her leathers, looks nothing like a professional.

"Close enough," Pip says. "Believe me when I say that I'm mostly here for his own good."

Ahbni snorts and offers Pip a crooked smirk. "That must be a hell of a job," she says.

"You're telling me," my wife agrees. It seems as if she's made a new friend.

I take this opportunity to slink over to the aforementioned table, accepting the out that Pip and Elgar have proffered. Though only the former was, I think, aware that I had a desire to divide and conquer the crowd. Or, no, not conquer. *Assess.*

While Pip charms Ahbni and corrals Elgar, I spend a few hours practicing my Canadian accent so as not to stand out too much in the memory of the people around me. I sip coffee that I have fetched for my own damn self, and drop subtle phrases and suggestions in the ears of a large black man who is the head of security; the skinny, overworked and underslept white man who is the convention organizer; and Ichiro. Though I have no Words to compel with, I am able to murmur, and plant suggestions, and pry in ways so subtle that the subjects of my machinations do not realize they are being manipulated at all. It is nice to don the persona of the Shadow Hand once more; it is a little like a homecoming, and I find my hand drifting to cradle the pommel of Smoke so often that I must fold my hands behind my back to keep from making the security-seeking gesture appear as if it is meant to be a threat.

We leave the party shortly thereafter. Pip is assured that Ahbni will personally oversee Elgar's schedule and safety, no matter that she is annoyed with his personality, and I am pleased with my progress with the rest of the staff.

And no one, as far as I could see, has green eyes.

A tension that I had only barely registered in Pip's posture is more relaxed as we "batman" out of the party (Pip calls it this when we leave without calling attention to ourselves or announcing it), and head back to our suite. Pip and Elgar take the first elevator up, and I linger, pretending to read the newspaper left on the tall, thin table by the elevators, to take the next one. No one seems to be following us from the event, though I linger once again when I reach the penthouse floor before heading to our rooms.

When I get there, Pip and Elgar are already a few sips into their plastic cups of wine, and, satisfied for now, I indulge in one myself before we bid each other goodnight and make for our separate bedrooms.

"Should we sleep in shifts?" Pip asks me as I prop Smoke between the bed and the side table.

"I have considered that," I admit. "And far be it for me to say that I think we are fine for now—"

"Don't," Pip says with laughing sternness. "You'll call down trouble."

"I think we ought to indulge in sleeping as much as we are able. I'm not certain we'll have the chance for the rest of the weekend."

ELGAR

Elgar wakes to a screech. For a second, sitting bolt upright on his bed with sweat on his face and his heart thundering in his throat, he mistakes it for the fire alarm. He blinks rapidly and swallows a few times, the noise ringing shrill and... penetratingly *discordant* between his ears.

It's not an alarm of any kind. It's a scream.

He scrambles out of bed, yanking on a pair of lounge pants to cover his crumpled boxers, and searches his room for a weapon. Lucy is *screaming*, and he can't hear Forsyth, so he might be dead already, and *oh god*, that means the Viceroy is going to come in here next, and Elgar is armed with *literally nothing*, and what can he do anyway, with a sword or a gun or a dagger, against *magic*?

Determined to not just stand in this room, a lone target, a stupid goose just *waiting* for the slaughter, Elgar grabs the bedside lamp, chucks the shade off it, and yanks the cord from the wall. The lamp is skinny enough that he can get his whole hand around it, and has enough heft that he can swing it like a baseball bat. If he's lucky, the bulb might even shatter in the Viceroy's face.

Oh, god, I'm contemplating smashing one of my own

fictional creations in the face with a lamp, Elgar thinks a little wildly. His hands start to shake, and he redoubles his grip. And then, while his courage is up, he throws back his door, thunders down the hall, and kicks open Lucy and Forsyth's with a roar of rage. He hefts the lamp over his head, ready to swing at their attacker and... freezes.

Lucy is on the bed, arched on her shoulders and heels, howling in agony. Forsyth is beside her on his knees, hands reaching out to press on Lucy's arms. There is no one else in the room. Just Forsyth, and Lucy, and... and a room filled with a sinister green glow. The source of which is—

"Jesus fucking Christ," Elgar hisses, sleep-muddled and still thrumming with adrenaline.

"Fetch a glass of water," Forsyth shouts over Pip's wails, and even knowing that it's make-work, that it isn't actually important, Elgar is eager for the excuse to get out of there. To not have to watch. To not be forced to *witness*.

More than that, Elgar doesn't know Lucy as well as he knows Forsyth, or even Juan. She plays it close to her vest, doesn't like to be emotional in public, and is almost ridiculously desperate to distance herself from anything feminine or "weak" looking. Elgar has a feeling that she won't appreciate her deepest and most personal pain being goggled at. He drops the lamp, spins on his bare heel, and goes.

"Pip, *bao bei*," Elgar hears Forsyth shout as he stumbles over to the galley kitchen.

His feet are unsteady. His vision swims, and he leans down over the counter, rests his forehead on the cool rim of the stainless-steel sink for a minute, squeezing his eyes shut and willing his head to stop spinning.

The screams peter out, replaced by a mewling whimper.

"Wake now. It's just a nightmare, my darling. Wake up," Forsyth commands from the other room, his voice a soothing cadence. Elgar feels his heart rate settling, the flush draining from his cheeks, his whole body trembling from the unspent adrenaline.

There's a choking gasp, another small yelp, and then the sound of what is probably soft sobs muffled by the presence of clothing, or a pillow. Mortified by the thought of Lucy—strong Lucy; no-nonsense Lucy—weeping against her husband's chest, Elgar straightens and turns the tap on full-blast. He pulls down a cup, clattering the cupboard door, and fills it.

By the time he goes back to the room, Elgar is feeling a bit calmer. The sounds of crying have faded. He peeks around the threshold. Forsyth is still crouched over Lucy, sitting upright, her hands fisted into his pajama top. Lucy sucks in air through her teeth, hard, hissing inhales that make her nostrils flare and suck closed, sweat painting her hair along her forehead like ink-strokes. Her exhale is reedy and mumbled.

"Lucy?" Elgar gasps. Her head jerks to the side. She blinks hard, eyes coming into focus.

"E'gar?" she mumbles, and all at once, her body goes lax. Instead of tensing upon waking, this seems more like wakefulness-induced freedom.

"Is it-t-t... is h-he...?" Forsyth tries to ask, hands shaking, teeth clattering and blocking whatever it is he actually wants to say, and Elgar realizes that his soothing and commanding act was just that—an act.

Lucy turns her head a little further and kisses one of Forsyth's palms. "No," she says. "No, I promise. He can't get back in."

"B-uh-but he's tra-try-trying?"

"I don't think so," she whispers, and her voice crackles. She licks her lips, and Elgar's glad Forsyth sent him on his silly errand. Lucy must be parched after all that screaming. "Don't even think he knows we're here. I don't know where he is. It's just... thanks," she says as Elgar steps around the lamp on the floor to hand her the glass of water, careful not to let go until he is sure she won't drop it.

"Ma-ma-magic r-ru-runoff," Forsyth finishes for her, when she seems more concerned about draining the glass than completing her thought. She sets the empty glass down on the side table, and Forsyth leans down, scrunching unattractively to press a reassuring kiss against her mouth.

"Is that what that was?" Elgar asks.

"Yeah," Pip croaks, and struggles to sit up properly. Forsyth helps her prop herself against the headboard. She scrubs her forehead, making her fringe stand askew, and Forsyth pets it back and away from her face.

"So, that's what magic looks like," Elgar hears himself say, echoey and hollow and feeling a bit like the words haven't really come from himself. He assumes his expression must have some sort of stunned, smashed-in-the-back-of-the-head-by-a-branch look to it. 'Cause that's definitely how he feels.

Lucy lets out an exhausted huff of laughter. Her eyes crinkle, and her mouth quirks up. Elgar's not sure why she's feeling so warmly toward him right this moment. Hysterical fatigue, maybe? "Yeah. Is it what you imagined?"

"Of course it is," Elgar says, blinking and trying to get his head back into the present, to stop floating along on a current of shock, of... traumatism and consternance. "Exactly like it. Even with the... the watercolor brushstroke swirls around the outside of the aura that—" Forsyth flashes a glare over Lucy's head at him, and Elgar stumbles to a halt mid-sentence. "Right, sorry. I should maybe be less excited about this than I am."

Lucy huffs again, then plants her head in her husband's lap. "Can I get you an-anything?" Forsyth asks, voice tremulous and small.

"Not yet," Lucy whispers, fingernails digging into his thigh as if she fears he'll jump up and run out the door. "Just... not yet."

"Very well," Forsyth says. Elgar is not entirely sure what he's doing, but Forsyth makes a show of breathing in tandem with Lucy, slowing his own cycle of in-and-out imperceptibly, so that she follows along. Elgar, desperate to get his heart jammed back down where it belongs, copies them. Eventually, Lucy's pained panting evens out to a light wheeze.

Lucy turns her head just enough to grin wearily up at Forsyth. "You think you're so subtle."

"I *am* subtle," he protests.

"Are not."

"It worked, didn't it?"

Lucy grumbles and resumes her careful breathing. But Elgar isn't following this time. He stares unashamedly at her back, hungrily fascinated and intrigued, all wrapped up in awe and wonder and... trepidation. Alarm. *Dread.*

The green in the deepest part of her scars is still fading, slowly, just visible through her thin tank top. And on her exposed shoulders, the filigree webwork of her scarring forms a delicate, realistic, artistic interpretation of ivy leaves, the result of days of agony under the knife of a talented but psychotic sadist, magical healing, and a vicious spell.

And Elgar is seeing them for the first time.

He's entranced. He can't look away. He can barely *blink.* And at the same time, horror roils in his gut. Horror of what was done to Lucy. Horror that it was done by someone spawned from *his* imagination. Horror that the next person tortured by the Viceroy might possibly be *himself*.

"So, what do we... do now?" Elgar asks. "With the, you know, the trap and the bait and stuff?" He gestures vaguely to himself.

"We wait until tomorrow," Forsyth says.

"That's it? Just wait?" Elgar asks, aghast. "But this has to change something, right?"

Lucy closes her eyes and shakes her head a little.

"No," Forsyth says. "This is, unfortunately, meaningless."

"But the *Stations*. What about that plot map you told me about?" Elgar asks. "The one you made for the other two adventures?"

"I'm not sure there's a point this time," Lucy says quietly, opening her pain-deep eyes to meet his. "Stories in the real world, do they follow your pattern? Not usually. Will this one? I think relying on the Excel to tell us what to expect will do us a disservice. We can... miss things. Like with Lanae..." she finishes softly.

Lanaea. A woman Elgar has never known, has never written, and yet had lived in the land of Hain, had been born in Milliway Chipping, and raised in Sherwilde, and been murdered in the Lost Library. She had been loved, and mourned, and Elgar'd had no idea she'd even existed. Like so many people who populate his world, she had just been there for the convenience of plot, one in a crowd he would have killed to make the bad guy look badder, someone he would have thrown at Kintyre as a reward, would have endangered and threatened, or dismissed, just for the sake of conflict, of narrative tension.

It's not like you knew, Elgar tells himself. *It's not like you were aware that these people were, well, people.*

"Still not your fault," Forsyth tells Lucy gently, wrapping an arm over her shoulders.

No, Elgar thinks grimly. *It's mine.* But what he says out loud is: "So we just wait. Go back to bed, sweet dreams, all that bullshit?"

"All that bullshit," Forsyth agrees lightly.

"I have to say, I'm not feeling all that confident here," Elgar confesses. "Maybe I should have stayed in the safe house."

"With personnel who have no idea what the Viceroy is capable of and no way of guarding against him?" Forsyth asks archly.

"Well, do you? Really?" Elgar challenges.

Lucy looks up at him, eyes wide, and a bit hurt, but mostly resigned.

"We all agree that the plan is limpid and relies too much on hoping that whatever the Viceroy does, we'll be able to spot it coming and stop it," Forsyth says slowly, trying to make this conversation cease to be anything but an acknowledgment of an utter losing situation. "I will be honest myself and admit that I highly dislike being on the back foot, as we are. But this is not like a quest, Elgar. We cannot formulate a plan, nor mark a map. This is a siege. The best we can do is eat well, sleep while we can, and prepare ourselves for whatever we think might come our way."

Elgar's mouth twists sourly. "While parading me around with a target on my back. He has *magic*," Elgar blurts, all patience with this attempt at reason lost. "He's the son of a Deal-Maker, you say. Maybe he doesn't have *all* his magic, but he got here somehow! He can compel people! He put illusions or *things* in my house, and he... he killed..." Elgar chokes on the name of his cat, eyes welling.

Elgar turns his body away, angling so Forsyth and Lucy can't see his face as he mops at his cheeks with the back of his hand, desperate to be a man in front of them.

"He has magic," Elgar repeats at length, when he's gotten himself back under control. "And we've got nothing."

Forsyth sits straight upright, as if he's been hit by lightning all of a sudden. "Maybe... maybe not. Pip, you bound the magic of his blood within him with your Deal, correct?"

"Yeah," Lucy says. "But that left out the magic that he'd learned, the magic that doesn't have anything to do with his heritage. And that's where I made my mistake."

Forsyth snaps his fingers and points straight at her nose, like Elgar's seen Lucy do when she has a revelation. "The Viceroy punched a hole through the veil of the skies, and those magics he has learned came with him. Magic, I believe, sits upon him like a mantel. Perhaps even leaks through from the other world."

Something inside Elgar, some half-remembered concept of world-building that he has filed away in the back of his brain, flares to life. *Leaking, yes, leaking and flowing and—*

"And magic is a fluid!" Elgar says suddenly, jolting up and turning so swiftly to face the bed that he forgets for a second that he's still recovering from a neck injury. There's a hot pop, a sear of pain crackles up his back, and the air punches out of him in a wincing gasp.

"It's a what?" Lucy asks, startled. "That isn't in your books."

"No," Elgar agrees, massaging his neck to try to get his body to relax and the seized muscles to cooperate. "Only in my head. I could never find a good place to put it. But the way I conceptualized it, it's like... it *flows*, right? It lives in your cells and in your breath. Magic glows because it's *steam* rising from a hand. Words are born in moisture, formed in damp mouths, are exhaled like fog on a cold day. So it can pool, too. It can *rush*. It can follow a riverbed, the path of least resistance."

"So it's flowing around the Viceroy right now," Lucy says, shifting closer to Elgar. "So what? That doesn't help us much."

"But... okay, but hear me out here," Elgar says, brain ticking over like a stalled engine just about to catch. "What if... I mean, you think it's magical runoff, right? The reason your back is... and your nightmares? The magic is flowing into previously dampened channels, or trying to."

"If we're going with this analogy, then the dam is closed," Lucy replies slowly. "I slammed it shut. To keep him out of my head."

"But you can always open another, er... tap?" Elgar asks, then frowns. "No, listen, so the Viceroy is doing magic. He's doing magic, just now. We don't know what, or why, but he is, and that's why you're... glowing. The, uh, the waste-water of the sorcery nuclear plant."

"Yeah?"

"Okay, I'm no hard science fiction writer, so correct me if I'm wrong, but... that water is still radioactive, isn't it? Isn't the by-product of nuclear fusion still nuclear, in and of itself? Isn't that water still... wet? God, this analogy is really being stretched here. But can't it... pool? Around you? *In you?* Can't the evaporated atoms of it still... re-coalesce?"

Pip frowns at Elgar, working through what he's trying to say.

"I wonder," Forsyth adds, following along probably only marginally better than Lucy. He jumps up and crosses to the small table by the armchair. Forsyth tears one of the leaves off the pad of hotel stationery, and turns to face his rapt audience, the paper pinned between two fingers like a magician.

Then he takes a deep breath, and says a Word.

Elgar's never heard Word magic before. He's imagined what it might sound like—a gong in the deep, or high whistle on the wind. And that's what he hears: a deep, resonating sound that vibrates in his bones. He gasps—he can't help it. He's moved near to tears almost immediately. The Word has no syllables, not really. No vowels; no consonants. No form. But he can hear it. Clear and easy. He feels like if he just purses his lips right, he could even repeat it. Close. It's so close. It's sitting there, just on the tip of his tongue.

He closes his eyes, inhales, sways, but he cannot echo what Forsyth has Said.

Because it's not a word, not really.

Well, of course not. You never wrote down what the Words are. That's the point of them. They aren't silly spells in pseudo-Latin. They are Words of Power that you never tried to transcribe.

Silence rings heavy in the room. Elgar opens his eyes and looks at the paper expectantly. Nothing's happened.

"Forsyth?" Lucy asks, but he shushes her gently, and then, carefully, reaches out and places a hand on her shoulder. Quietly, in the breathless, anticipatory hush, Forsyth says the Word again.

Elgar sucks down a sob, covering his mouth with his hand, stunned by the beauty of it, the deep buzz and whistle, the bells and the tinkle and the rushing roar that vibrates between his ears.

And then a small curl of smoke wafts in the gentle breeze of the air-conditioning. One edge of the page glows coal-red for a brief second, before curling in on itself, black and brittle. Forsyth's startled gasp puts out the ember before it's really caught, but it's enough.

"Magic is leaking into the Overrealm around the Viceroy," Forsyth says, setting the burnt paper carefully inside the otherwise empty wastebasket. "But it's pooling around Pip, as well; a familiar, once-flowing river. And while Pip may never have learned any spells, cannot wield the magic that is beginning to pool within her, it appears that, as long as I am in contact with her, I can."

"That's beautiful," Elgar whispers, reverent and feeling like he has just had, for the first time in his life, a religious experience.

Lucy jerks her head around, narrowing her eyes at him. "What?"

"The Word. It's gorgeous. I never... I mean, I *imag-ined*, but... the magic looks just the way it should, but the *Words*—"

"You can *hear* them?" Lucy challenges, sounding hurt and envious.

"Well, yes?" Elgar says, scratching his palm. "Can't you?"

TEN

Once showered, caffeinated, and dressed, we eschew room service in favor of the hotel's breakfast buffet, where—I hope—a villain might be less inclined to poison the food meant to be consumed by several hundred people. Once more, Elgar is difficult to disguise, but we find a table in the corner, where he can have two walls at his back, and I fetch a plate for him rather than sending him out into the masses.

"Juan would be pleased with you," he complains when he sees said plate piled with fruit, avocado, scrambled egg-whites, and brown toast. To be fair, I've fetched the same for myself. Pip's plate, when she takes her turn at the buffet (neither of us wanting to leave Elgar alone, a tempting target for either the Viceroy or Elgar's fans), looks very similar, but includes bacon. I snatch away a slice and Elgar sighs wistfully.

"This is the worst," Elgar says, as he picks at the avocado, mashing it with the tines of his fork like my toddler daughter. "Waiting sucks."

"What do you mean?" I ask, my own toast partway to my mouth.

"I just wish the... wish *he*... son of a bitch, I am not treating my own damn villain like I'm too scared to even speak his name—I wish *the Viceroy* would stop fucking around and just show himself."

Pip snorts. "Your fault for writing the Viceroy as a

Trickster Figure Gone Wrong."

"Well," Elgar says, straightening, "the next time I think up a villain who might slip his pages to try to assassinate me, I promise to make him more predictable."

The joke isn't quite as funny as he hoped. We let it lie, anyway.

With breakfast concluded, we make our way to the foyer. We still have an hour before Ahbni is to meet us, and after Elgar's attempt to brain Pip's nonexistent attacker with a lamp, it has occurred to me that perhaps my creator ought also to be armed for the coming confrontation. A trip to Artist's Alley to find a replica or prop to use is high on my list of priorities.

The hotel stands on top of a large conference center that is two stories high and stretches the length of a city block. The second level consists of floor-to-ceiling glass—an unfathomable expense in my world, but standard urban architecture in the Overrealm—but the ground floor is clad in white blocks and tiles that create an interesting mixture of glossy and matte textures. The main entrance of the center opens into a large, paved courtyard bordered by a park filled with grassy knolls and potted trees. Alternately, one may enter the conference center through the hotel lobby. The center's foyer is circular, a small glass dome perched above allowing a flood of morning light to filter down through the curved banks of escalators that curl up to the balcony-floor above, and down into the windowless underground storey below. A small fountain with a single jet of water that spurts upward like a playful kelpie's spout on a timed interval lends the otherwise glass, chrome, and concrete space a grandiose air.

"According to the map, the upper level is going to be the dealers' room and vendors' tables, the space on the ground floor is for ticket line-ups and photo sessions, and the basement will have the food court, gaming tables, the signings, and the ballroom for the Q&As and dance," Pip says, staring up at the poster hanging from the ceiling next to the main entrance.

Through the glass doors to the outside world, I can see that the convention is already setting up the long, snaking entry queues with black retractable barriers. A small handful of dedicated geeks sit or stand patiently a few meters back, some already in costume; others mill about, chatting, or playing card games, or chasing augmented reality monsters on their smartphones across the parkland.

"Great," Elgar grumbles. "Another weekend spent in a lightless, airless hole in the ground. Looks like the Green Room for guests is downstairs, too."

"I would much rather we were downstairs, to be honest," I say. "Easier to defend."

"But harder to escape," Pip points out.

"Oh, don't be a complete ball of sunshine or anything," Elgar grouses. Pip chuckles and pats his arm. "Come on, I have to meet Abby in an hour, so if we're going to go snooping, we have to do it now."

"It's *Ahbni*," Pip corrects as we head for the escalators.

"That's what I said."

Pip groans and pinches the bridge of her nose as we step onto the moving stairs. "You explain," she says to me. I try as we ascend, saying that it is impolite to deliberately mispronounce someone's name, or worse, to "whiten" it without being invited to do so. Elgar looks chastened and promises to do better.

The security volunteers at the top of the escalator are happy to let Elgar browse before the crowds arrive, and we make a tour of the room, stopping to chat with artisans and merchants, checking eye colors and looking for signs of the Viceroy's influence. I scan the high corners of the booth spaces for runes and spell bags, peek as unobtrusively under tables and within merchandise as I can. Our walk through the Artist's Alley is woefully brief, and I take a moment to feel sorry for myself that we probably won't have the opportunity to peruse it properly this year. Last time we attended a convention like this, I found a lovely, hand-embroidered bunting to hang over Alis's crib, the artist's rendition of my family's emblem picked out in gold thread on Turn-russet brocade.

"I don't actually know what I'm looking for," Pip says eventually, hands planted on the small of her back, frustration twisting at her mouth. "If there are spells here, lying in wait, I can't feel them. Everything looks *fine*. But I know it's not, and it's driving me *bananas*."

"Here, then," I say, pulling Pip over to where a vendor is laying out a selection of swords and daggers. The man is twitterpated by Elgar, reaches out to shake his hand, and shows him a sword he says he patterned on Elgar's description of Foesmiter.

"And this!" the young man says eagerly, fumbling a sheathed dagger out of its leather casing and brandishing it proudly in the sunlight.

Pip sucks in a deep, horrified breath and backs up so quickly that she crashes right into my chest.

"It's not sharp," the young man scoffs at her. "I'm not planning on stabbing you."

But it's not the blade that has Pip flummoxed; it's the hilt. It's the *recognition*. "Chailin's dagger," Pip breathes, eyes wide and glazed with painful memories.

"Actually, it's Kintyre Turn's dagger," the young man sneers, then turns back to simper at Elgar, showing off the glass gems set into the hilt, the intricate floral designs on the cross guard. "Fake geek girl."

"God grant me the self-confidence of a mediocre

white man," Pip grumbles, but straightens herself and screws up her courage to approach the table and take a closer look at the dagger. The young man doesn't like it, but he doesn't protest when Elgar hands it to Pip. My fingers twined casually with my wife's free hand, I whisper a Word of Revelation, but the dagger is only what it appears to be—a collection of glass, and steel, and wood, and leather. There is no danger here.

It feels good to be *certain*, to have access to my arsenal as a spymaster and, yes, adventuring hero. It's not quite like having a limb once thought forever lost suddenly regrow on a stump, but it does make me feel whole and confident in a way that I had not expected to experience again.

"Do you like that dagger, Elgar?" I ask my creator. "Does it fit well in your hand?"

"Uh, yeah, I guess. Why?" he asks, taking it back from Pip to test the heft and weight.

"We need to get you both armed," I say, low enough that the young man—now trying to take a stealthy selfie with Elgar in the background, instead of just *asking* one of us to take a photo for him—cannot hear us. "With more than lamps."

Elgar chuckles, allowing the gentle tease to cover the nerves we're all suffering under.

"These are props," Pip points out.

"My whetstone is here," I whisper, patting the small pouch on my sword belt where I keep the items needed to maintain Smoke. "Though they will not be strong, they will at least be sharp."

Pip nods thoughtfully, eyes skimming the wares, and selects a sword not unlike mine. It's too long for her, though, and she keeps testing the swords until she finds something that I'm certain is meant to be a replica of a weapon used by one of the hobbits or the children who traveled to Narnia.

"We have katanas," the young man says as he watches Pip. "Or a ninja star? Something more anime."

Pip's mouth twists and her eyebrows come together in a dark V, and I can see her biting back the tirade about Asian stereotypes. As much as I enjoyed watching her take to task the Schrödinger's Rapists in the tavern, we both know that now is not the time and place to do the same with this lad.

"No, I think this sword will do," she says, raising it to point the tip at his ear. The man takes a startled step back, suddenly realizing that perhaps condescending to an armed woman, even one armed with a blunted length of steel, is a bad idea.

Elgar distracts the man from his foolishness by waving his credit card under his nose.

"I wish you hadn't picked that one," Pip says to him as the young man wraps their purchases in bubble wrap, cardboard boxes, and mountains of packing tape to make them acceptable to carry in public. Little does he know his work is wasted.

"But it's Kin's knife," Elgar says, eyes dancing with glee. "Seems appropriate!"

"And it was Bootknife's before it was Kintyre's," I remind him gently, and Elgar's face does something complicated when it's clear he's not certain how to feel about this reminder. "And it was at King Chailin's tomb that—"

"I remember," Elgar says sharply, the joy drained from his posture. He accepts the boxes from the young man, signs a battered copy of *The Serpent of the Sleeping Vale* that the vendor had under his table, and then we make our way down to the lower levels of the convention center. This area is easier to investigate, as there are fewer people setting up the various rooms for panel discussions. In the grand ballroom, technicians are running the final sound and light checks on the stage, while volunteers set out what, by my rough estimate, appears to be about five thousand chairs.

It is here that Ahbni catches up to us.

"Mr. Reed," she says. "I thought I was meeting you in the hotel lobby?"

"Yeah," he replies casually. "But I wanted to get a little shopping in first."

Ahbni frowns at the boxes in his hands. "I wish you'd waited for me to escort you."

"I had Syth and Lucy here."

Ahbni turns to face us, her people-pleasing expression firmly back in place. "Morning."

"Good morning," I say. "Elgar, let me take those up to the room for you. Pip, you'll be fine tagging along without me for a while?"

"'Course," Pip says, grinning at how I make it sound like she's only sticking with him to keep from being bored.

Ahbni frowns again, but doesn't say that she can't go with them. "There's a hospitality suite on the second floor of the hotel," Ahbni says. "I was thinking we could head up there, grab you some breakfast, and review your schedule for today?"

"We've eaten," Elgar says. "But I could always do with more coffee."

"Okay. Okay," Ahbni says, mentally realigning her plans. "Coffee we can do."

The four of us head toward the escalators, and Ahbni, I notice, falls into step with Pip.

"I like your outfit, by the way. I wanted to say it last night, but, well, you know," Ahbni says.

"Oh, thanks," Pip says, happy to take the offered conversation, and the leisure to get Ahbni warmed up to her. Any ally we can cultivate is worth the work of it.

"Is it homemade?"

"In a sense," Pip allows. "I like your outfit, too."

Ahbni grins, and it's like a sunrise. We step onto the moving stairs, giving Ahbni the opportunity to turn a little circle and show off. Today, she is wearing a knee-length skirt patterned with glittery pink-and-lilac cherries, skulls, and tubes of lipstick. Her blouse is another long-sleeved, flowing one made of a creamy gauzy material, and topped with a violently pink muslin scarf whose tails hang gracefully to the hem of her skirt. She wears leggings in the same shade of pink, and sneakers in the same lilac that is on her skirt. And, like yesterday, her makeup is impeccable and intricate, and her long dark hair is pulled back into the most complicated braid I have ever seen.

"I'm in fashion design. I made this all myself."

"Color me impressed," Pip says.

"I really like your shirt. Did you sew it yourself?" Ahbni asks, touching Pip's sleeve to investigate the fine stitching around her cuff. "This was done by hand. It's excellent work."

"Nah, not me. I don't do that useless girly stuff," Pip says, clearly thinking back to that afternoon in my mother's rooms when she kicked the basket of sewing and embroidery supplies onto the floor, rejecting all the symbols and trappings of what it meant to be a woman in Elgar Reed's world.

She levels a mischievous grin at me as we share the memory, but between us, Ahbni's mouth twists into a bitter smirk.

"Oh, I see. You're not like other girls, then?" Ahbni asks, but there's a note of mocking in her tone.

"What?" Pip asks, turning to look at Ahbni full in the face, startled.

Ahbni shoves her hands into her skirt pockets and radiates ire.

Pip looks down at her own feet, her brain chugging along to follow what just happened in that conversation, where the wrong turn occurred.

"Um," Pip says at last, and looks up to me. I'm afraid I am no help, however, for I am too amused. We step off the escalator, and Pip is so befuddled that she just stops in the middle of the marble floor. Pip smacks her forehead with her palm and groans. "Oh my god. I did it. I fell into a trope again. It's just like you said, Syth. Aware, but not immune. Fuck me."

Elgar looks her up and down, and frowns. "What trope?"

"Strong Female Character Who Disdains Femininity and is Not Like Other Girls," Pip says, running her free hand through her hair. She looks *mortified.* "Ahbni, I'm sorry. I don't mean to—"

"'S okay," Ahbni says. "I just... I can't stand that kind of crap. I call it out when I encounter it."

"As well you should," Pip says, nodding firmly.

"What my wife meant to say is that she doesn't enjoy many of the traditionally feminine pastimes naturally," I explain, dropping a kiss onto her cheek. "Which I think is best for us, all told. I can't imagine what a disaster our wardrobe would be if I left you to do the laundry."

"*Hey,*" Pip protests, affronted. "I cook!"

"And beautifully, *bao bei.* But what I am saying, dearest, is that the average Chipping Estate would utterly fall apart without 'women's work.' It is not worthless."

"I'm not denying that," Pip says with a frown. "I'm just... I don't *do* that stuff."

"And that's fine," Ahbni says. "Just don't call it 'useless' because it's female coded when we all know it isn't *actually* useless."

Pip groans and runs her hands through her hair again. "No, you're right. I'm not—never mind, I'm an asshole.

I'm sorry. Can I take it all back?"

"Yes," Ahbni says, with another one of those sunrise grins. "As long as you admit that you're a bad feminist who needs to work on her intersectionality."

Pip laughs, and slings her arm over Ahbni's shoulder, grinning blindingly at the young woman. "That's it. It's official. I'm keeping you forever," Pip says. Ahbni tries to protest, but she's smiling too much to get the words out properly. "No, nope, nope. I'm adopting you. You're coming to live in Victoria and you're going to be my new TA and I'm going to supervise your PhD and you're part of the family now. No point in resisting."

"Okay," Ahbni says, head ducked, scuffing the toes of her shoes together, blushing madly. I don't think Pip's obvious glowing approval and proximity are doing any-thing for what appears to be Ahbni's budding crush on her. Poor dear.

"Now," I say. "Off with you all. I'll meet you in the hospitality room once I've rendered these, ah, props to be safe for the convention hall." Ahbni probably thinks I intend to zip-tie the blades into their sheaths, as other cosplayers must do if they want their props to pass a weapon's check. I have no intention of disabusing her of that notion.

ELGAR

As the former Shadow Hand of Hain, Elgar figures Forsyth can appreciate the need to protect information. But what Forsyth actually says when he sees the briefcase with the combination lock *handcuffed* to a nervous-look-ing techie is: "There's *protection*, and there is excess. It's just a *film*."

Elgar knows what Forsyth means—in the grand scheme of things, someone getting the short film out into the world a few hours ahead of Flageolet doing it at the con is a relatively minor disaster. It would announce the series too early, but the series is still going to be announced today, one way or another. Because Flageolet Entertainment fears this very kind of leak, they'd even arranged for the teaser short to be among the first block of the con's programming.

But compared to getting horribly murdered by the Viceroy? Yeah, it seems excessive.

"Come into the washroom with me, Elgar," Forsyth says, rolling his eyes. "I wish to fix your hair before your panel."

"You do?" Elgar asks, startled. Forsyth fixes him with a telling stare, and Elgar scrambles to his feet and follows Forsyth into the hospitality suite's large washroom.

"Honestly," Forsyth says, closing the door behind them and locking it. "You would never have survived in the court of King Carvel. *Subtlety*, Elgar."

"I can never really figure that out," Elgar says with a shrug.

"Yes, and my brother is proof of that," Forsyth replies, but it's with a smile, at least. "Here, turn to face the mirror so I may attach this."

He pulls the replica of Kintyre's dagger out of the back of his leather jerkin. When Elgar turns, he can feel Forsyth tugging on his belt and tucking in his shirt, but he can't actually see what he's doing. The press of the sheathed knife against the small of his back is strange and alien, and at the same time, a huge comfort.

"Try to grab the knife," Forsyth says, and Elgar reaches back. He can get his fingers around the hilt well enough, though he got some of his shirt with it, too. "Ah, you'll have to be wary of that. Lucky for us you have lost as much weight as you have, and have not yet replaced your shirts. This will cover the hilt. Try again."

Elgar does, and then again, and again, until Forsyth is content that he can grab and unsheathe the dagger quickly, easily, and without cutting himself. Elgar has to keep wiping his palms on his pants to keep the handle from getting too sweat-slicked.

"Now, when you stab," Forsyth says, reaching across his shoulder to position Elgar's grip behind the guard, "do so like this. Up, from under, not over like a horror-movie villain. If you must stab, attempt to position your arm like so, or like so." He tugs Elgar's arm through the motions a few times, then steps back to watch in the bathroom mirror as Elgar copies him.

"I wish we had more time," Forsyth says. "But I think you are as prepared as I can make you. Now, allow me to *actually* fix your hair."

Elgar turns to Forsyth and lets him fuss with water and a bit of the product someone's left on the bathroom counter that smells strongly of verbena and coconuts. In a way, Elgar is reminded of Juan—fussy, fastidious, and picky about projecting the correct image. But Forsyth has grown up in Hain, in Lysse Chipping, in Turn Hall, where power and strength and virility are more prized than intelligence and manners. Forsyth has learned to wear his clothes as a weapon, to make a shield of a perfectly knotted neckcloth; to behave so appropriately and so correctly that Algar Turn wouldn't be able to find any fault in him to exploit or harm; to be so good to the people under his care that the citizens of Lysse had no reason to rebel or oust him. Fear fueled his every action, his every practice, his every stride toward perfection. And still he was never valued above Kintyre—brash, rakish, windblown and road-soiled and bad-mannered. Save for by the Pointes, and Pip, and now, after a long time, Elgar.

It breaks his heart, just a little.

When Forsyth is done, Elgar reaches up, grabs his

creation's hand, and squeezes it gently. "Thank you," he says, meaning a lot more than just the hair gel, and the fussing, and the dagger. "I'm glad I met you."

Forsyth scowls. "Don't talk as if your death is ensured," he says, shaking his fingers out of Elgar's. Every time they touch, flesh-to-flesh, there's a sort of low-buzzing electrical current that runs between them. Elgar pretends that this is what Forsyth's trying to escape when he steps back.

"I just mean..." Elgar gestures at the small of his back.

"Of course," Forsyth says, and unlocks the door. He goes through first, and it occurs to Elgar that he's doing it so he can scope out the room before Elgar reenters. "One must take advantage of those few things that Algar Turn taught that are useful. There are a vanishingly small amount of them."

FORSYTH

Once Elgar is armed, Ahbni hustles us all to the door of the suite, snagging a bottle of water and pressing it into Elgar's hands as we file out the door and toward the elevators. Elgar is busy chatting with Kashif the Handcuffed Techie, a poor attempt at a companionable smile stretched across his face to mask his terror. Pip is concerned with checking the lay of her sword, tightening her belt, verifying that her boots are double-knotted. I do as I always do before a fight: I breathe deep, try to center myself, eyes and ears open and heart trembling.

For make no mistake, we are on the eve of battle now.

If the Viceroy plans to strike, he will do it now. No time is better than when Elgar is the least protected and the most visible. This panel is being viewed by five thousand fans in attendance and millions more on the video livestreaming service. And the Viceroy has always loved an audience.

I just wish I had more access to my magics. I am not, however, entirely without my own tricks. I have had the opportunity to watch many television shows and fantasy films about magics and monsters since my arrival in the Overrealm. I have picked up a few ideas.

I reach out and grasp Pip's hand as we exit the elevator and cross the foyer to the escalators that will take us down to the main convention space and thence the ballroom. She looks at me, startled, as under my breath I begin to Speak Words of Protection, of Shielding, and every other charm I can think of. I hold my hand over my mouth, breathing the Words into my palm, feeling them condense and ball against my skin.

When we reach the escalators, Ahbni steps on first, followed by Kashif, Elgar, me, and then Pip. I hold the ball of Words tight in my fist, and then swiftly, gently, press them into the bare skin on the back of Elgar's neck.

"Ah! That's cold!" Elgar says, jumping and turning around to look at me. "What did you—?"

"Don't touch it," I say. "And let us hope that the Words remain while I am not in contact with you. Pip, don't let go of my hand."

"Right, okay," she says. My wife is clever. She understands why.

I look up from our small tête-à-tête to find Ahbni watching us with slitted eyes, thoughtful and curious. She says nothing, keeping her own council for now. It occurs to me that we are going to have to be straight with her eventually. If things get dangerous, she deserves to know why. She deserves to know what we will be fighting, what *she* will be running from, if I have any say in the matter.

Unlike the rest of the crowd that files forward when they step off the escalator toward the large set of doors marked "Grand Ballroom" on the far side of a long, table-scattered hall, Ahbni doubles back and leads us to a small room underneath and behind the escalator. This door is marked with ConClusion signage that tells me that it is the "Green Room," and when we enter, there are a half-dozen round tables with chairs already populated by three other guests and their three matching handlers. I recognize one as a famous actress from a major comic book film, but have no clue who the other two are. Pip does know them, though, for her eyes narrow at them both, and I can see her fighting the urge to go over to speak to one of them. By the set of her shoulders, I assume it will be an unpleasant conversation. But we haven't time.

"Last chance for a visit to the potty, or to grab a nibble?" Ahbni asks as we pass a long table strewn with pre-wrapped sandwiches, cans of soda, and snack bars.

Elgar shakes his head, and, as if him declining were the flag at the start of a car race, Ahbni spins on her heel and heads directly for a door at the rear of the room. "This will take us the back way to the ballroom," she explains, ushering us through.

It is narrow, filled with piles of unused chairs and the scent of concrete dust. The walls are windowless, and the corridor is lit with harsh, buzzing fluorescent lights that make Pip wince. We shuffle along single file. I severely dislike the way this limits my visibility, for I cannot see around the corners. Pip doesn't like it, either; I can tell by the way her palm starts to grow damp and clammy with fear-sweat in mine. At the head of the line, I can see Ahbni texting, most likely announcing our arrival to volunteers on the other end.

We hit a roadblock in the form of a small mountain of piled cardboard boxes. They are clustered around a doorway, half-piled up a slight ramp that probably heads to a loading dock.

"Oh, yeah," Pip sighs, rolling her eyes as we all squeeze past this obstacle. "'Cause that's both fire safe and accessible."

The corridor eventually opens into a small staging room, carpeted with something hideous and orange, and boxed in with walls of what appears, to my inexpert eye, to be technical equipment for a theater. The computers are similar to those I have at home, but beyond that, all the other wires and baubles and devices are completely incomprehensible. I feel a pull toward them, my natural curiosity piqued, but I do not have time to pursue it.

If we get out of this—when we get out of this—I may consider volunteering with my local community theater group. I've seen the posters for auditions on the wall of the coffee shop; perhaps they could use a hacker to run their microphones and lights?

Ah, but I am getting ahead of myself, I decide.

Kashif sets down the case and unlocks himself from it, then waves Elgar over to wire him up with a personal microphone. I watch carefully to ensure that the nervous young man doesn't slip anything else into Elgar's pocket, like a spell-pouch, or a rune-scroll.

By my side, Pip is occupied with talking to a young man in a wheelchair, who is coming down the ramp that leads up to, I assume, the wing of the stage. When he reaches the bottom, Pip introduces us all, and Ahbni stands back, eyes on Elgar and her phone, equally.

Then we are leaving Kashif and his case behind to begin the setup, and follow the lad in the wheelchair up to the stage. I see no monsters laying wait, no summoning circles scratched into the hardwood or painted with blood. The Viceroy is not skulking amid the black curtains at the back of it. But the space is filled with many places to hide weapons and bombs. It is high. It soars above us by at least two stories, and the catwalks above are corseted with ropes, and lights, and nooks that I do not have any good excuse to explore. I could bully my way onto them, behave as Kintyre does and simply walk over to the ladder, ignore anyone who tells me that I cannot climb it.

But I dare not release Pip's hand and break the spell of protection I've cast over Elgar. Pip looks up at me in knowing pity, and I feel a sudden swell of affection for my wife. She understands how torn I am, without me ever needing to say it.

Is this what Kintyre thought when he looked at Bevel, out there on the road, in the midst of their adventures? This surge of affection, this sure and steady knowledge that his life was safe cupped in Bevel's hands? Possibly— though Kintyre is startlingly unaware of himself. Had he known all along that what Bevel looked at him with was love? Had he felt it himself, lodged behind his heart as my love for my wife is lodged behind mine, and mistook it for something else? Indigestion, perhaps?

Kashif calls out: "House is open!"

The murmur of a crowd entering the room fills my ears, and I find Kashif at my side, suddenly, hustling Pip and I back into the staging room and from there, through another narrow doorway and into the auditorium.

"Well," Pip says, when we find ourselves blinking in the bright fluorescent light of the ballroom. She flexes her fingers in my grip. Behind us, the stage is silent and still, the curtains open, a single spotlight on one black leather club chair. "He's certainly efficient."

"That he is."

She points to two chairs right at the front of the room, beside the center aisle. "Let's sit?"

We are quick enough to snag the seats, and the VIP status of our badges allows us to keep them. This is a good position from which to have a full view of the stage, and Elgar, as well as the auditorium.

"How you holding up?" Pip asks me, and I am pulled out of my contemplation of the people taking their seats around us.

"I think I am the one who should be asking you," I say. "How is your back? Your head?"

"Sore, and aching," she allows. "I feel like I could sleep for a week."

"Soon," I tell her.

She smirks morbidly, eyes droopy with exhaustion. "One way or another, eh?"

I kiss her temple reverently. "No need to be such a Debbie Downer."

Pip snorts a laugh against my chest, chuckling at my use of the Overrealm colloquialism, and pets my thigh with her free hand.

"That's my man," she says softly. "I've trained you up good."

"That you have."

"But you're dodging my question. How are you holding up?" She cranes her head up to meet my eyes.

"I am frustrated, and on edge, and wish I could do more," I admit. "I wish I had more power. Wish I could drag the bastard out into the light and slit his throat."

Pip swallows hard. I can't tell if it's fear, or anger, or arousal that makes her pupils expand. But she leans up and places a chaste kiss on my mouth, more a reassurance than a gesture of lust.

"Soon," she echoes back to me.

I am about to chide her in return, but the lights around us suddenly dim, and music is piped over the sound system. Ah, that same fiddle-and-fife tune from my ringtone. I cannot help but roll my eyes at Elgar's vanity. Even when he is scared for his life, and knows he is the target of a madman of his own invention, he cannot help but brag.

My wife shivers as the music begins, her whole body shaking for a brief second. Pip sucks a startled breath in through her teeth.

"Pip?" I ask softly, squeezing her fingers.

"Oh, but there is magic here," Pip says. "I feel it in my *bones*."

"Then be prepared," I whisper. "We are about to get our wish."

ELGAR

Whatever it is that Forsyth did to the back of his neck sits like a cold ball on the knob of Elgar's spine. And yet, the cool chill of the... *the spell? Yeah, a spell*, he decides, is actually comforting. He's sweating, nervous, the fingers of his right hand flexing as he reminds himself, over and over, not to reach for the knife. Not now. Not yet. And especially not while Kashif is getting him outfitted with a lav mic.

It takes a bit of quick talking to get them to thread the wire up the front of his shirt, and put the battery transmission pack in his front pocket instead of clipping it to the back of his belt, like folks normally do. Kashif vanishes behind a bank of computer monitors, and returns without the briefcase, looking much more relaxed. He checks the lav mic, and lets Elgar know the order of the presentation—introduction by a moderator, walk out onto the stage, sit in the free chair, chat with the mod for a moment, and then the screen will start to descend on the verbal cue word. Both he and the mod are supposed to act surprised and confused, and then the lights will suddenly cut out, and the short film will start playing.

It's all a clever and dramatic ploy, of course—Elgar

knows it's coming, and so does everyone else on this side of the curtain—and when they'd first come up with it, he'd been delighted with the little show of dramatics. Now, the idea of being up on that stage in the dark, for even a second, out of Forsyth and Pip's line of sight, is terrifying.

But the moderator is already pushing his way across the stage, smiling and waving to the screaming crowd once he reaches the center. Elgar can't change the plan now. It's too late.

Too late.

He swallows hard as he hears the young man shout his name. The crowd roars. Nothing else happens. Nothing blows up; no one screams in horror. They just chant his name like he's some sort of sports hero: "El-gar, El-gar, El-gar!"

Envisioning himself as a professional storyteller when he was a teenager, receiving his New York Times Best Sellers congratulatory phone call, accepting his first award, deciding what to do with his first six-figure check—none of that was as fluster-inducing and sweat-evoking as this. It's everything Elgar has ever wanted out of his writing career, and simultaneously abominable.

He wants to step out on that stage so badly. He wants to hear them cheer, see them shoot to their feet and clap, watch their faces glow in the reflection of the stage lights and his own star-shine.

But he doesn't want to die. He doesn't want to be bait. And yet, if he doesn't... if he doesn't...

Maddie, he tells himself. *Juan. Linux. Forsyth and Lucy and Alis. Think of them. Think of what he'll do, what he has done, what he could do, if he isn't stopped. This is it. This is the moment.*

"You've written about heroes your whole life," he

whispers to himself. "Go on. Go be one."

With that push, he lifts his left foot, takes a deep breath, swallows hard against the bitter fear pooling on the back of his tongue, and steps out onto the stage. The crowd hoots and hollers with glee, and he just barely manages to turn the flinch away from the wall of sound and the wave of aggressive motion toward him into an awkward pat along his hair and a waggle of his fingers toward the crowd.

"And there he is!" the moderator—Randy? Ryan?—says, wheeling gracefully back and diagonal in a way that Elgar thought wheelchairs couldn't move. He looks like a cross between Vana White and a Vegas showgirl, and next to him, Elgar feels like a turkey that's been plucked and set on its hind legs to shuffle on a marionette's string.

"Hi," Elgar chokes, and waits as the crowd screams some more before he takes a seat in the black leather club chair that's been set up on the far side of the stage.

The moderator—Russ? Dammit, why didn't Elgar listen when they told him this guy's name?—shakes his hand and gestures for the audience to simmer down. As they take their seats, Elgar scans the crowd for anything... well, anything unusual. But there are no golden eyes piercing him, no ominous green watercolor glow, nobody staring at him in stillness while surrounded by the fidgeting crowd, nobody wearing a telltale bad-guy hood.

He does catch Lucy and Forsyth in the front row, though. Lucy looks up at him, her free hand crossed over her lap and on her sword. Beside her, Forsyth scans the crowd, gray eyes darting around the room, up to the catwalk, across the stage, and everywhere but at Elgar himself. Their hands are still gripped tight between them. On the back of his neck, the Words sit, reassuring and waiting.

"Welcome, Elgar Reed!" the moderator crows, and

the crowd shouts and claps and stamps their feet again. "How lucky are we to have you at the last minute, eh?"

"Th-thanks, y-yeah," Elgar manages, and takes a sip from the bottle of water he realizes is still clutched in his left hand. He clears his throat and pastes on his "performing monkey" smile and says, "Thanks for having me."

"Always a pleasure. So, we're kicking off this con with a nice juicy Q&A panel," the moderator plows on. "But before we get people lined up at the microphones on either side of the stage, let's talk a bit about what you've been up to. I hear tell that there's a new trilogy in the works?"

"Done, actually," Elgar says, letting the smugness he's feeling show on his face. He doesn't add: "*Has been done for years, but I've been stalled in the editing process by the terror I've felt about writing anything new. Oh, why, you ask? Because I learned that my characters are real and actually feel all the pain I put them through. Don't believe me? Ask that guy sitting right there in the front row.*"

"And what's the series called? Actually, forget that, what we all really want to know is when can we expect to see it hit the shelves?"

"Book one of the *Shuttleborn* trilogy will drop next summer, and—" He is nominally prepared for the mechanical whine, but he can't help the way he jumps and looks upward, wild-eyed and heart leaping up into his throat, when he hears it ring out from above him.

It's only the sound of the mechanics in the fly lowering the massive projection screen, though, and Jesus fucking Christ, Elgar is almost starting to wish the Viceroy would just hurry up already. The *waiting* is going to give him a heart attack and kill him before his archvillain ever gets the chance.

"Hey, speaking of dropping..." the moderator says,

looking up with faux-nervousness and playing along. "Guys? Hey, techies! What's going on?"

No answer comes from the wings, though, except for the lights snapping off.

Elgar knows that this is part of the game, but he can't help it. He is freaking *frightened*. He reaches behind himself in the semi-darkness of the hall and wraps his hand around the hilt of his dagger. Small blue lights flare to life among the crowd—phone screens, he realizes. None are green. Beyond that, only the red glow of the exit signs interrupt the miles of darkness he struggles to peer through.

And then, in the blackness, music. The crowd hushes instantly as the first plaintive notes of a wavering penny whistle warble like a sorrowful loon over the sound system. Elgar hasn't seen the completed film yet. He'd wanted to be surprised, wanted to be genuinely affected by it when he spoke to the moderator and his fans after viewing it. He wanted to *share* the awe of seeing it for the first time with everyone else in this room.

And listening to the song now, feeling the way this particular gentle orchestration seems to reach out and snag on his heart, he's glad he did.

All at once, the gentle music swings into the fiddle-and-fife tune that's going to be the show's opening theme song. But it's been made brighter, brasher, more confident, bullying the tempo into keeping up with it.

With no title card or credits as a warning, the darkness on the screen surges bright and focuses on the image of a grand, three-storied manor house made of sandy-gold marble at the end of a long, wide, impeccably manicured white gravel drive. The trees on either side of it are landscaped within an inch of their lives. Then, all at once, with a dramatic flutter, two massive Turn-russet banners are unfurled from the roof. They're easily as wide as a man's outstretched arms, and long enough to brush the top of the house's grand portico. Bordered in gold fringe and tassels, they're embroidered with the massive image of a key lancing a lock, the sigil of House Turn.

The crowd goes *bananas*. People start screaming, "Oh my god!" and, "No way!" and, "I knew it!" and, "The rumors are true!" and all manner of expletives.

Elgar feels a surge of pride and excitement and, strangely, a bit of paternal affection. He knew that keeping the series a secret would be worth it.

"Oh," he hears Lucy gasp from the front row, and Elgar can see just enough in the glow of the screen to catch the way she turns her head to watch her husband and nothing else. Between them, their hands are white-knuckled. Forsyth flexes his fingers, and brings the basket woven of their fingers to his lips to cover his expression.

The film isn't long—ten minutes, give or take—and follows Kintyre Turn as he walks around the estate, overseeing and approving of the work being done on it in advance of his eighteenth birthday celebration. The exterior set of Turn Hall was already mostly completed when Elgar had been asked to write this, so it was nice to be able to show it off. Kintyre swiftly thereafter sneaks out of the stables dressed in Shiel-purple, with a horse, a full set of saddlebags, and enough food to get him to the Urlish border, where he can volunteer for the foot-soldiers brigade fighting in the war. Everyone knows that what happens next is his first meeting with Bevel Dom, seventh son of a seventh son, then just an illiterate blacksmith-in-training. It's the first actual scene of the first book, that fateful meeting.

But this story doesn't go that far. Instead, it focuses on the few hours after Kintyre escaped, when he stopped in a glade to water his horse and realized that his bratty younger brother had followed him. He and Forsyth fight, and scrap, and tussle, and Forsyth falls through a bit of rotten sandstone into a wide, deep cave. When the young boy playing Forsyth drops out of sight on the screen, Pip makes a sound of horror that is echoed by a few other people in the audience.

In the film, the young Kintyre races back along the road to fetch help from Turn Hall, but stops when he finds an abandoned farm. Stealing rope from the ruins of the tilting barn, he returns to the chasm and rappels down to rescue his unconscious and bleeding brother in his first act of heroism. But before hauling them both back into the daylight, he spots something glittering on the bottom of a still, deep pool.

It's Foesmiter. The crowd whoops and applauds hard when, after his third dive, Kintyre breaks the surface of the pool with the sword held aloft, glittering in the lone shaft of syrupy-golden sunlight. The music surges, the room cheers, and Elgar can see tears running down Forsyth's cheeks in the reflected light of the film.

Homesickness? Elgar wonders.

The rest of the film is taken up with Kintyre getting Forsyth home and being scolded by his father for trying to run away on the eve of his own birthday party and the opportunity to choose a wife from all the pretty, stupid girls tittering at him from behind their fans. But Elgar isn't watching anymore.

All he can see is the way Forsyth pants and shakes, the way he flinches at every movement on the screen, clenches his jaw at every word. The way Lucy presses her forehead against his shoulder, squeezes his thigh with her free hand, as if she has to hold him down, hold him still as Forsyth, who has always been intensely private and buttoned-down, is forced to experience one of the most profoundly emotional ten minutes of his life—in *public*.

Just for the sake of catching the Viceroy. Just for the

sake of protecting Elgar.

He suddenly feels very small, and profoundly guilty. He wishes, suddenly, that he'd thought to offer Forsyth a private viewing first. But then the lights snap back on, and Elgar is caught staring. Heads swivel and murmurs rise as people try to figure out what he is looking at. Mortified, Forsyth mops at his face and ducks into Lucy's embrace.

"So, what the heck was that?" the moderator asks, wrenching Elgar's attention back to the stage, and the conversation he's supposed to be having. The moderator says it with wide eyes and a grin he can't quite conceal.

"What do you think?" Elgar replies, and then barrels on, too excited to actually let him answer. "It's a teaser for the new... wait for it... *Tales of Kintyre Turn* television series!"

As he knew they would, the crowd surges to its feet again, screaming and hollering, stamping and applauding in joy. When the noise has died down again, the moderator says: "So, this series is about the Great Hero of Hain himself?"

"Yeah, it'll follow the path of the books, tracing the story from when Kintyre leaves home at the end of this snippet and meets Bevel at the start of book one, right through to the defeat of the Viceroy."

Elgar stops. Waits. Listens as the crowd cheers and thunders their feet against the carpet. He squints against the stage lights, searching. Now, the moment is now, it has to be... He holds his breath, scanning the rafters, muscles clenched, ready.

Nothing happens. Nothing changes. Nothing jumps out of the shadows.

God dammit, Elgar thinks. *I thought that would be his cue. Where the hell is he?*

"Wow!" the moderator says, filling the awkward silence. "How awesome."

Elgar jolts his attention back to the stage, where the moderator is making a "go on" face at him.

"Oh, uh, there'll be more, too," Elgar says slowly, drawing it out. Waiting, *waiting*. "Uh, it will follow some of the life of the people Kintyre left behind in Turnshire. Um. Like, uh… like his little brother, who, I am happy to report, has a whole storyline of his own now."

Forsyth starts in his seat, eyes wrenched back to the stage by this pronouncement. His eyes are red-rimmed, his nose puffy, and he looks shocked. Shocked, and pleased.

The hall quiets. There is no crackle of fire, no evil laugh, no shouted oath. Nothing.

"That's exciting!" the moderator says. "So we'll be seeing everything, all eight books?"

"Absolutely, including how the Viceroy is finally defeated." Elgar waits again, watches, braces himself.

Nothing.

Nothing.

Goddamn fucking nothing, Elgar snarls mentally. *What's taking so long?*

He slips his downstage hand back to the hilt of the knife, unable to stop himself. His hand is shaking. His chest burns. The bottoms of his feet itch.

"That's right, we don't get that in the novels, do we?"

What? Elgar thinks stupidly, and yanks his gaze back to the man on stage with him, who's starting to look annoyed.

"No. I've always had an idea of what happened to the villain, how he got his comeuppance," Elgar says, feeling daring. Feeling invincible after the overwhelming positivity of the reception of this short, feeling *reckless*. Feeling like the kind of bait that's getting sick of dangling. "He was always a bastard."

In the front row, Lucy tenses, the corner of her

mouth turning down.

"True enough!" the moderator laughs. Then he claps his hands, a sharp burst of sound that makes Elgar jump in his seat, wild-eyed and heart racing. "Right, we've got some folks lined up for the microphones, so let's have at it, people! Who do we have first?"

"Hi!" a young woman says over the sound system, and the lights in the auditorium come up enough for Elgar to see her standing to the far left of the room, wearing a shirt with the map of Hain printed on it. "I'm Adrienne. I wanted to ask, can you talk a little about your writing process?"

Elgar takes another swallow of water, then a deep breath, and reapplies his performing-monkey smile. A quick glance at Forsyth and Lucy shows that they are as confused and on edge as he is.

"Sure, Adrienne," Elgar says, and answers. And answers. And answers.

Elgar talks for two hours, his ears pricked, eyes straining, mouth dry with anticipation, his heart thudding against his ribs the whole time.

And nothing happens.

ELEVEN

As soon as the moderator has thanked the crowd for coming, and the lights have come on to signal the audience to trickle out through the large double doors at the back of the ballroom, Ahbni pokes her head out of the small, curtained-off area beside the stage and gestures for Pip and I to come in.

Pip and I rise with the rest of the crowd, hands still laced together, prepared to draw our blades if need be. We share a look of a confused anger, and I know that I am grinding my teeth in my frustration, a disgusting habit. I take a deep breath and shake out my shoulders, which startles Pip.

"Where *is* he?" my wife asks.

But I have no answer to give her. Instead, I tug her hand gently, hopefully reassuring, and we follow after Ahbni. Elgar stands in the middle of the overcrowded curtained-off area, bumping the computer banks behind him as Kashif removes his microphone. Elgar's eyes are wide, his face sheened with sweat, and he is scrumpling the cuffs of his cardigan.

"That went well," Ahbni says conversationally, tapping away at her smartphone. Pip snorts, and I resist the urge to growl. "Good crowd?"

"Uh, yeah," Elgar murmurs, subdued. His tone makes Ahbni's eyes snap up to him.

"Hey, you okay? You hungry, or...?"

"I could... coffee?" Elgar asks, clearly remembering her annoyance at the request last night.

Ahbni just nods and says, "We'll get you set up in the con suite upstairs for a bit, okay? There's a few hours until your signing session."

"Sounds great." Elgar raises his eyebrows meaningfully at me. "It's all going so *smoothly*."

As ever, my creator thinks he is more subtle than he really is. Ahbni shoots me a confused look of her own at his theatrical emphasis, and I shake my head minutely, dismissing it. She doesn't seem placated, but at this point, I frankly do not care.

The beginnings of fury itch the underside of my skin. And beyond that, the place in the back of my mind, the place where the puzzle pieces usually float, is a throbbing agony. Elgar Reed Wrote me to *need* to understand. And right now, I do not. And I *despise it*.

"Okay," Pip says, attempting to hasten us along. "Someone's feeling a bit hangry. Let's go."

"I am not—"

Pip kicks my shin, and I gape at her.

Fuming, though now my ire is directed at Pip's audacity, I let her pull me along in her wake, through the back hallways again, to the Green Room, then out to the escalators. A few steps above us, Elgar turns to me and blurts: "You said he'd—" Pip kicks his shin, too. Affronted, and agitated, Elgar snaps his mouth shut and glowers.

Once in the con suite, I push both of them into the spare bedroom with a quick, "Excuse us for a moment," and lock the door behind us.

"Your coffee...?" Ahbni starts.

"In a moment!" I snap back through the door.

Pip tugs me hard through our joined hands and grinds out: "Quit it."

"I don't get it," Elgar starts again. "You said that he'd—"

"There was always a chance—" I begin, but Elgar barrels over me with:

"If he wasn't there, then where the hell is he? Can't you feel him, Lucy? Where is he?"

"I'm not a magic compass! How do you expect me to—?" Pip protests.

"*Enough*," I snarl, and both Pip and Elgar turn mulish expressions toward me. "We cannot change what happened, and we cannot force the Viceroy to show his hand, clearly."

"So what now?" Elgar asks.

"Now, we fetch coffee, and eat something to cure our *hangriness*," I say. Pip rolls her eyes at my childish tone, but I will not lie, I am feeling very close to an Alis-style tantrum. I would very much like to scream and break something, but of course, I will not. It would only cause more problems I do not need, and solve none of the ones I already have. "And then we sit down and *figure this out*."

"You can't just think through every problem," Elgar says.

"It is what I do!" I reply. "I am no Kintyre Turn, to bash at things he cannot see! Though I wish he *was* here. Maybe that would draw out—"

"Forsyth, hey now," Pip begins, but Elgar interrupts with: "If we keep waiting, then—"

"There is no foe before me to slay," I counter. "So what else do you suggest I do?"

"Okay, let's all just..." Pip takes a deep breath and lets it out slowly. "Let's all just chill for a second and stop sniping at each other, okay?"

"But what if—?" Elgar protests.

"Deep breath!" Pip interrupts, pointing at his face. He

obeys, albeit grudgingly, and she swings her finger toward me. "You, too." I obey, as well.

Once we've all taken a moment to *breathe and chill*, Pip lifts our twined hands between us with a question in her face. I nod. Slowly, finger by finger, we release one another. My joints ache, and my skin is damp with sweat when we finally let go. Elgar gasps and straightens, as if someone has dropped snow down the back of his shirt. I wipe my hand dry on my shirtsleeve as best I can.

Elgar sits in a chair beside this room's desk, slumped over and morose now that our mutual impotent anger has dissipated and the tension in the room has been dispersed. He takes another deep breath, and holds on to it for a moment, clearly chewing on his thoughts. Finally, in a small, quiet voice, he says: "He's not here, is he?"

Pip and I share a look that lets me know that my wife isn't entirely certain what her answer ought to be. She walks over to the window, flexing out her hand, and opens the door to the narrow balcony that looks down onto an interior courtyard that appears to be connected to the foyer with the fountain. She leans her elbows on the rail and hangs her head. I am reminded of how little we all slept last night, how exhaustion pulls at our eyelids.

"It didn't *work*, and he's still *out there*, and I..." Elgar's gaze is broken, glassy, the skin around his eyes pinched. His mouth trembles. "We have no *idea*, and I just—I can't!" He hunches over the desk, back to me, I assume, so I cannot see him crying. His shoulders are moving, though. The blade of his dagger is sticking up from the sheath clipped awkwardly to his belt. I must remember to adjust it in case it slips loose.

"The Viceroy doesn't usually appear until the third act," Pip reminds him, as if he was not the one who Wrote it that way.

"Except I saw him in the hospital," I remind her.

"Well, then, I don't have any fucking clue, do I!" Pip snaps, whirling back around to face us. "I can't just deconstruct the plot and—Elgar, what are you doing?"

She straightens and sweeps down to grab something out of Elgar's lap. Before I can see what it is, Elgar reaches up and clasps the part of Pip's neck where it joins her shoulder, where her shirt gapes just enough for his palm to touch skin. Pip grunts, staggers slightly to the side, as if she's been pushed. Light flashes in my peripheral vision, but it is not the green glow I expect, that I fear. It is white. It is colorless. It is *familiar*.

There is a sound like a world shattering. I know this noise intimately. It makes every hair I possess stand straight up, goose bumps flashing across my flesh and fear splashing ice-cold up my spine.

I turn back to blink at Elgar through the haze, but he's not sitting at the table anymore. He's standing beside Pip, his palm cupping the back of her neck. Pip's body is tensed upward in one long line of agony, her eyes wide open, her head thrown back, her arms a rictus, fists balled so tight I fear she will cut her hands with her fingernails. And her eyes, her *eyes*, they glow. They glow green. Pupil-less, iris-less, whites-less. Solid, verdant, acidic, dangerous green.

"Writer, no!" I shout, my heart jerking so hard in my chest that I feel my whole body lurch.

Elgar, thinking I am speaking directly to him rather than swearing, jerks his hand away from Pip, stumbling up onto his feet and back into the desk. Pip sucks in a great gout of air, and collapses downward. For once, Elgar is quicker than I, for he catches Pip in his arms before she hits the garish carpet.

"I'm sorry. I'm sorry," Elgar babbles, cradling Pip against him, lowering them both to the floor. "I couldn't think of any other way. Lucy? Lucy!"

The white light is slowly, slowly fading, and I turn my back to it, swooping down over Elgar like a harpy. A touch to the side of my wife's neck tells me that her pulse is rapid, but not dangerously so. She's panting, smacking her lips together as if parched, and she shakes, a fine earthquake of tremors that wrack her whole body.

It is *terrifying*, but more so because I can do nothing to either help her or stop it.

There is something white in my creator's hand, and I focus on that, instead. It is paper. Yes, the desk had a little pad of notepaper on it—I remember seeing it as we came in, but I didn't think I would have to take it away from Elgar like an errant toddler. I am stunned, *stunned* that he would... that he has... I snatch the piece of paper out of Elgar's hand, horrified to see his thick, familiar scrawl all over it.

The Reader had the magic of the Viceroy inscribed on her bones, in her muscles, in her flesh. And while only the power of the Deal-Maker Spirits could rip a portal through the veil of the skies, the Viceroy was descended of one of the strongest; the weather witch who was his mother. His magic was Deal-Maker strong, and so were all the spells he had ever woven. He was a warlock in full possession of all the magic afforded to him by study and blood alike. That strength, that power, lived on in the corporeal essence of the Reader. Her husband could draw upon it—and so, too, could his maker, when he touched the Reader.

And so it was that the Writer placed his hand on the bare flesh of the Reader, cupping his palm over her scars and leeching the magic still held dormant there, releasing it, tapping it. And with that magic, that power, the Writer did what only a

Deal-Maker had been able, in the past, to do.

He reached through the veil of the skies and pulled

Through the rip stepped Kintyre Turn and Bevel Dom. They were attired for battle, armed with all their best and most treasured weapons and armor, and in the pocket of Kintyre's jerkin, he carried a flask of the best dragon whiskey Drebbin had to offer. They came, ready to fight, ready to protect, ready to finish the final battle between good and evil. Ready to win.

"You complete, self-absorbed, narcissistic *bastard*," I spit at him, shoving my fist and the crumpled paper under his nose. "What have you *done*?"

Elgar heaves Pip onto the bed, and she curls into a ball, clutching her head and moaning.

"How *could you*? How could you do that to her? How could you have promised to leave them be, to never Write of them again, and then—this!" There is a part of me—perhaps a Turnish part of me—that wants to throttle him. Instead, I fist my hands in his lapels and shake him, hard, as a compromise. "You *fool!*"

"You said!" Elgar gulps, hands up and around my wrists as if he fears I will move them onto his throat. "You *just* said that you wished that he was here! That you didn't think you could... you could... I just can't stand the *waiting* anymore."

"Better than this!" I shout, my skin buzzing and my brain static and my ears half-stuffed with cotton. *Betrayed!* my mind screams. If Elgar had been one of my Shadow's Men, I would have had him in the stocks in a trice.

"How dare you *weaken* us so! How dare you go behind—how dare!"

"*I don't want to die!*" Elgar sobs, fingernails scratching at my wrists.

"You utter *fool!*" I repeat. "'His magic was Deal-Maker strong'! Do you realize what you've done? What you've given *back* to him?"

"I didn't—"

"You Wrote it, and you touched Pip, and you *made it true*. You called him strong! You called him *powerful!* You gave him everything that Pip took. If he had any binds left on his power, if he was constrained in any way before, you have removed those bindings!" I screech.

Behind us, the door to the main suite rattles, and Ahbni calls through the wood: "Is everything okay?"

"I never said—"

I release one hand and uncrumple the page. "'A warlock in full possession of all the magic afforded to him by study and blood alike,'" I read. "*Idiot!*"

The knob clicks, and the door swings open. She must have a key.

"Holy crap!" Ahbni says, as soon as she sees Pip on the bed.

"You're hurting me..." my creator whines.

"Good!" I snarl, and shake him again. "Our *only hope*, Elgar, our only hope was that Pip's Deal had held, and the magics in his blood had been locked away. That his powers would be *limited*. But you have put paid to it with this... *this*... ill thought-out, selfish *drivel!*"

"Whose drivel?" a voice asks, and I realize that, in my fury, I have utterly ignored the spot of light. It is a voice I know well. Have known for over two decades. Have missed desperately. "And why in all the seven hells am I wearing this Shadow Hand nonsense?"

"Bev?" a second voice calls out. Another voice I never thought I would ever hear again. There is the sound of a shocked gasp being choked back, a deep gasp, and then my brother's deep baritone saying my name: "For-syth?"

I release Elgar, ball up the paper still in my hand and shove it into the pocket over my heart. Then I turn, slowly, to face Kintyre Turn and Bevel Dom.

Just as Elgar Wrote, they are attired for war. Kintyre is in his battle leathers, a chain mail kirtle under his customary Sheil-purple jerkin, Foesmiter at his hip, and seemingly every knife he's ever owned strapped to his chest. Bevel, as he complained, is dressed in the full Shadow Hand attire—silver mask on his face framing his unhappy scowl, the cloak wrapped tightly around his shoulders. He is in the process of jerking it off, revealing his own battle leathers, short-sword belted to his waist, bow slung over his chest, and quiver strapped to his back. They are both flopped on the carpeting, struggling to sit up, grasping at the bed and the dresser and whatever other furniture they can lay hands on for stability.

"Slowly," I caution them both. "You will be a bit woozy."

"Woozy?" Kintyre asks, and I can see the moment the crossing catches up with them both.

My brother staggers, reaching out for the television stand and missing. He crashes forward to his knees, and I dart forward to keep him from falling flat on his nose. Bevel has a better go of it, managing to sink himself onto the bed, sprawling backwards with a nauseous groan.

I set Kintyre carefully on his side, in case he vomits, and jump up to check on Bevel. I pull the Shadow's Mask off his face, tuck it in next to the crumpled evidence of Elgar's selfish betrayal. Bevel is panting harshly, but his eyelids are already starting to flutter open. He is coming back around.

Satisfied that my brother and brother-in-law are well,

I turn back to my wife. Pip's eyes are open, and she is sitting up, thank goodness. Some color has returned to her cheeks in ugly pink splotches, though the rest of her skin is still papery and strained. She has her hands jammed between her knees, trying to stop her shaking. Her eyes are wide, and dark, and trained on Kintyre and Bevel. Behind her, Ahbni is propping her up. Though the other young lady looks about ready to take her turn keeling over.

My fury surges back to the fore now that my protective concern has been satisfied. Elgar has curled himself into as small a ball as possible, shame radiating from him in near palpable waves.

"What just ha—? *Who is tha*—?" Ahbni chokes, but can't seem to sort out all the questions crowding up behind her teeth.

Pip turns questioning eyes to me, and I fetch out the balled paper and hand it to her. Her eyes, already strained round, grow even wider as she reads what Elgar's Written into being.

"Dear lord," Pip breathes. "Elgar Erasmus Reed... what the *fuck* have you done?"

"Forssy?" Bevel asks, baffled and staring around him, still reeling. At least he's sitting up now. "What's...?"

"You are at an inn," I say, bringing the heroes up to speed as quickly as I can. "Our Writer, the fool, has drained Pip of what little magic has pooled in her and brought you here to help us defeat the Viceroy, who has crossed the veil of the skies to enact his revenge."

Invoking the name of my brother's archnemesis is as effective as I had hoped. Kintyre rolls onto his hands and knees, and between them, Kintyre and Bevel get themselves to their feet relatively quickly. Bevel shucks the Shadow's Cloak finally, balling it into his quiver for the time being. Ahbni gets Pip up, and it is left to me to yank my traitorous creator upright.

"Where is he now?" Kintryre asks, cupping my shoulder in an earnest, manly way.

"I do not know," I admit, frustrated. "Pip is tied to him, though. When he does magic, she suffers the blowback."

Bevel shakes his head, and pinches the bridge of his nose, clearing his fuzzy brain. "So, does that mean the Viceroy felt Pip yank us here?"

"Oh, Jesus, probably," Pip husks, and then coughs, sucking on the air. Ahbni curls an arm around her shoulders protectively.

"Forsyth, I'm so sorry. I—" Elgar jabbers, going paler.

"Shut up," I say, too livid to add anything more eloquent. I wriggle his dagger holster out of the back of his trousers and clip it instead within easy reach on the front of his hip. "And keep a hold of that. I don't doubt that you'll need it, now."

"Hey, that's my dagger," Kintyre says, squinting at it. He wavers forward, and Bevel tugs him back.

"It is not," I say. "Only a replica."

"Is there time to get our bearings, or must we be on the move?" Kintyre asks me.

"We have a moment," I say. "I don't know what the Viceroy may be planning next, but if he felt the spell as strongly as Pip has felt his, he will need time to regain his strength."

"Pity we don't know where he is, so we could just go stab the bastard while he's recovering," Bevel says, but his tone is hopeful.

"We do not," I admit again.

"Shame," Bevel says with a shrug.

Elgar's eyes keep cutting back and forth between Bevel and Kintyre, his mouth noiselessly flapping. Bevel and Kintyre ignore him utterly, and I don't know if it's because they are peevish about being summoned out of our realm without so much as a by-your-leave, or if it's because they're terrified to look their Writer in the face. I am not ashamed to admit that I was frightened when I first met Elgar, as well. I would not blame them if this was the case.

"Well, if we've the time, then," Kintyre says. Then he comes straight to me and engulfs me in one of his habitual rough and hard bear-hugs. "Hello, brother!"

"Oof! Hello, Kintyre," I say, chuckling despite the way he is making my ribs ache. I pat his massive shoulder. "Well met and well come."

"Well come to *where?*" Bevel adds, wrapping his arms around me and pounding my back as Kintyre drops me back to my feet to treat Pip to the same enthusiastic greeting.

"The Overrealm, brother-in-law-of-mine," Pip says, accepting Bevel's gentler hug and offering him a kiss on the cheek.

Bevel snorts and looks around, hands on his hips. "Oh yes. Very impressive."

Pip pinches his arm, and Bevel grins at her.

Bevel then turns to Elgar, and I can see that already, Kintyre and Elgar are engaged in a tense staring contest. Elgar looks desperate, wrecked, his eyes wide and his fingers twitching, his weight rolled up onto the balls of his feet as if he is about to fling himself at his greatest creation. For his part, Kintyre looks just as ready to leap out of the way should Elgar do so.

Bevel moves to stand beside Kintyre, shoulder pressed to his trothed's bicep. Not impeding him, not holding him, but offering his support all the same. Bevel's free arm comes around Kintyre's back. He grips hard, hand fisted on the back of Kintyre's jerkin. I don't know if it's the transition that has them off-kilter and seeking each other for grounding comfort, or if it's the sudden danger, or the new environment, but I would wager that they wish they had more time than I can, unfortunately, allot them.

"So you're him," Kintyre says, and his voice is gruff with an emotion I am having trouble naming. I do know, however, that it is not joy. He turns away then, I assume, to disguise the look on his face, which is oscillating between fear, and disgust, and awe.

"Look at me, please," Elgar begs, reaching out to snag Kintyre's wrist. My brother jerks away from him as if he were a hydra attempting to coil one of its necks around his arm and drag him into its lair. "Please! I've waited your whole life for this moment."

"Don't!" Kintyre shouts. "Don't! I'm not... not yet."

Elgar swallows hard and nods, though it must be killing him. He turns his attention to Bevel. "Sir Dom," he says respectfully, with a head bob.

"Lord Consort Turn, actually," Bevel corrects him, crossing his arms defiantly, as if daring his creator to deny the evolution of his story arc since the book's ending.

Elgar's eyes get impossibly wide, and he darts a look between his two lead characters before he looks to me, pleading.

"Elgar, you cannot be *surprised*," I say. "I told you. *Pip* said just yesterday—"

"Yeah, but like I said, there's a difference between knowing it here," he touches his forehead, and then his chest, "and knowing it here, and then *seeing* it."

In a fit of pique, as if Elgar's statement was a dare, Kintyre swoops in and lands a possessive, biting kiss on Bevel's mouth. Bevel, unprepared for his trothed's display, grunts and splutters, arms flailing to keep his balance for a moment before he grabs Kintyre's arms and sinks into the kiss.

Pip whistles and applauds. Ahbni looks like she's been smacked between the eyes with a mackerel. Elgar flushes red and moans, "Christ, I need a drink."

"I have this flask in my pocket that I don't remember putting there," Kintyre offers when he finally lets Bevel up for air. "I don't know what's in it, but you're welcome to it."

"Oh! Dragon whiskey!" Elgar says, and takes a greedy sip when Kintyre tugs the flask out and hands it to our creator. Elgar's eyes start watering immediately, and he coughs into the back of his hand as soon as he's swallowed. "Holy shit, that burns."

"That's what dragon whiskey does," Bevel says with a frown. Then he turns to my wife. "Pip?"

"Yeah-huh?" she asks.

"What's that fantastic bit of blasphemy that you enjoy so much?"

Pip beams up at him. "Fuck."

Bevel beams back. "Yes."

"Why?"

"Because I also think I need a *fucking* drink."

"This way, bro," Pip says, slinging her arm over Bevel's shoulder, mostly so she can lean on him, and leads him into the main room of the suite.

ELGAR

Elgar knows Kintyre Turn better than anyone alive. It doesn't matter that Lucy was the one pulled into the world of the books instead of him because she knows more, by whatever metric the Deal-Maker Neris had employed. Nobody knows Kintyre *better.*

Elgar studies Kintyre's every gesture as he follows Lucy and Bevel out to the main room. Everyone—except for one security guy—has cleared out, probably uncomfortable or embarrassed by the shouting. Lucy helps Bevel to a glass of wine with a word of warning: "Careful, the wine isn't watered here." Bevel winks at her, and Lucy rolls her eyes before offering one to Kin, too. Forsyth demures, Ahbni says she doesn't partake, and Lucy clearly doesn't want one right now, though she's looking at the bottle longingly. She doesn't offer any to Elgar.

Ahbni insists that Lucy sit on the sofa, and Lucy agrees. Forsyth goes with them, pulling a computer tablet out of its leather pouch on his belt, and tapping through the data he sees there. He's muttering about Finnar, and traces, and "the Detroit bastard did a live rundown of Elgar's Q&A, and was revoltingly vitriolic. So why can't I find the wretch on the internal security feeds?" Ahbni narrows her eyes at him, and pulls out her phone, sneering a little as she sends a message of her own.

Elgar remains in the doorway, clinging to the doorjamb, unsure of what to do. Unsure of what would be *welcome*. After their cups are empty, Bevel steps up to Kintyre's chest, pushes him gently to the other side of the room, and tips his head up as they converse quietly. Are they planning? Commiserating? Elgar isn't sure. He can't help the small gasp that escapes him, though, when Bevel rocks up on his toes to plant a gentle, chaste kiss on Kintyre's bottom lip.

Oh yes, Elgar knows Kintyre better than anyone alive. And right now, watching Kintyre and Bevel cling to one another in a small, silent, private moment that is nonetheless happening in public, in the main room of the con suite right beside the drinks table, he knows that Kintyre is sad. So *sad* that Elgar can barely stand it.

Lucy is leaning on Forsyth, eyes drooping and every line of her body curved in miserable pain. Elgar feels guilty about that. He does. Maybe he should have asked first. But better to beg forgiveness than plead permission, right?

And they would have said "no." They'd been saying goddamned "no" for two days, and for what? Because they were afraid that bringing Kintyre Turn into the Overrealm might break something? Might make something worse? Except that, yeah, okay, it *has*. But how was Elgar supposed to know that it would work that way?

The thing is, he's the Writer, right? He knows Kintyre Turn, and he knows the Viceroy, too. And he knows that he has created a dynamic where only Kintyre can kill the Viceroy. It's poetic justice. That's what Kintyre is for. And if Forsyth and Lucy want to save everyone trapped in this building, then they *need* Kintyre. And where Kintyre goes, so too has to go Bevel, and...

Ungrateful, Elgar thinks to himself, face flushing with anger. *That's what they are. I did the right thing. I did.*

When Elgar looks back up again, frustrated at his own introspective pity, Bevel and Kintyre have broken apart. They're talking in low tones, gesturing and clearly making plans. Another step closer, and Kintyre looks up at him.

Kintyre. Staring him in the face, his glacier-blue eyes narrowed, his look thoughtful. His normal blond queue is a windblown mess around his face. He's gotten older. His hair is going elegantly silver, and the lines around his eyes make him look charming in a movie-star kind of way. *But Bevel looks old. Bevel looks tired*, Elgar thinks. There are deep pouches under his eyes, and his wrinkles aren't charming, and his hair is shaggy and thinning on the top. He's got a little *belly*.

Elgar has never really thought about what Kintyre and Bevel would look like when they were in their later years. In his mind, they were always the brash, perfect eighteen-year-old hero and the plucky, bull-doggish sixteen-year-old sidekick, no matter how many titles he heaped on them or adventures they went on. Sure, they grew more mature—old enough to drink and swear and... and *fuck* by the end of the first book, which spanned nearly two years. But never *old.*

And never *settled.*

Yet here they are, leaning into each other's warmth, Kintyre's hand on Bevel's shoulder, comfortable and sweet like an old married couple. It strikes Elgar that they *are* an old married couple now, and the realization churns in his gut. Kintyre is looking at Elgar expectantly, waiting for him to decide whether or not to join them. Elgar nuts up and walks closer.

"Hi," he says, low.

"Hello," Kintyre replies.

Bevel says nothing. He just narrows his eyes at Elgar, and Elgar is struck, *again,* by how something he'd written as a throwaway has had so much impact on someone else. Bevel's eyes are a deep sapphire, and just below his left one, there is a thin white scar.

I did that, Elgar thinks. *I did that to him. That's where Bootknife nearly cut his eyes out to give them to the Viceroy as a gift.*

Kintyre finally turns to Elgar. "Have you quenched your thirst enough?" Elgar nods, eyes wide and watering, not expecting to be caught out the way he is. "Good. Because I have a question for you. Why do you look like my father?"

"I'm, uh... I'm not sure how to answer that one," Elgar admits. "I mean, Forsyth told me I looked like him, too, but I can't honestly say that I did it intentionally. I guess that it's just that... well, as the father of the hero, I guess I always just sort of conflated myself with him? And, um, my world had just... run with that. That assumption. This is so confusing."

"Very much," Kintyre agrees. Beside him, Bevel scoffs.

"You don't approve of us," Bevel blurts, suddenly.

"*What?*" Elgar splutters.

"You keep *staring.*"

"No, I mean ... I created you, and you came out of the books, and... it's not—"

"You don't stare at Forssy like that," Kintyre says, reasonably.

Elgar bristles. "Well, I'm used to him. Besides, Forsyth's not... I mean, he's not like I predicted, there's a bunch about him that I never fleshed out, but you guys... I know you so well, and I didn't, I never knew that you..."

Bevel jerks back, his expression open and wounded. Oh, how Bevel's expressions were always easy to read, easy to *write,* but Elgar never wanted to see this look on his face.

"You didn't do it on purpose," Bevel breathes.

"Do what?" Kintyre asks, hand tightening on Bevel's shoulder.

"Make me love Kin," Bevel says, and Elgar feels shame, strangely, curl around his lungs.

"No, I... I didn't. I—"

Kintyre scowls. "I almost see why the Viceroy is so vengeful."

Elgar chokes on his own teeth. "You can't mean that you want me to—"

"I mean, he's a madman. A complete nutter," Kintyre dismisses. "I don't want to kill you. But Bevel is the most important person in my life and you never thought so. You didn't even *know.*"

Wrongfooted, Elgar blusters. "It never occurred to me!"

"That we would fall in love?" Bevel asks, aghast.

"That it's something you would want!" Elgar blurts back. "That... that domesticity, a house, a family, a *kid* is what you—" Bevel takes a step back, abruptly. He stalks away, and prowls directly into one of the shadowed corners of the suite.

Bevel makes a slow circuit of the massive suite, making a show of searching for... *oh, for booby traps, maybe?* Elgar thinks. "What's he—?"

"He's *angry*," Kintyre says. "He does this now, goes for long walks instead of shouting. For Wyndam's sake. And Bradri doesn't know better—she's so young. You can't yell at a dragonet."

"Why would he be angry?" Elgar asks. "I'm only being honest."

"Being honest is not the same as being deliberately cruel," Kintyre corrects, and Elgar goggles at him.

Is he being *talked down to* by his own creation? If anyone should agree with him on every opinion he holds, it ought to be Kintyre Turn. Right? "Was I wrong, then? Is that something he wants?"

"He's a bit baby-hungry, if I can be forgiven for spilling his darkest secrets," Kintyre says. He is answering Elgar, but watching Bevel pace from corner to corner of the room, peering up and around, disguising his fury by making it look like he's searching the unknown spaces for unseen dangers. "It's a bit womanish," Kintyre adds. "But it's what he wants, and I wouldn't say no, if we were able. Are two human men of the Overrealm able to have children together?"

"No," Elgar answers, stunned.

Kintyre sniffs and shrugs. "Shame."

"But he... *really?*"

"He is Written with a massive family. A whole gaggle of nieces and nephews. Are you surprised that he misses children? That he wants a large family of his own?"

"Not when you put it like that, I guess. I just... I never imagined domesticity for you because it's not... it's not something I have."

Now it's Kintyre who goggles at Elgar. "What, no wife?"

"None."

Kintyre looks baffled, his dimples drawing down. "But you're a Writer."

Elgar chuckles, and rubs the back of his neck, feeling self-depreciative and anxious. "Surprisingly, that isn't much of a draw here."

Kintyre snorts and crosses his arms over his chest. "You must be doing something wrong, then."

"I do everything wrong," Elgar agrees, sadly. "I see what you have, and I... I'm not jealous. I don't want to take it from you, and hoard it for myself. I just... I'm loved," Elgar says, thinking of the fans who always look at him with quiet adoration. "But not... not like you. Not like you have. I wish I could have... the difference between us is that someone thinks that you're worth loving. You came from me—if you're worthy, shouldn't I be, too? What am I doing wrong?"

"Perhaps refrain from saying things like that," Kintyre says, and gestures to where Bevel is returning, his face a study in deliberate blankness.

Elgar chuckles, hollow and angry at himself. "'S funny. That's exactly what your brother says."

"Listen to Forssy," Kintyre says, but it's kind. He pats Elgar's back, and the strength behind the affectionate gesture makes Elgar rock on his feet. "He's the smart one, after all."

Elgar means to say something more to that, maybe something pithy, but before he can decide *what it* will be, there's a resounding, hissing *crack*.

TWELVE

FORSYTH

The room around us shakes.

"Earthquake!" Ahbni shouts as she jumps to her feet.

"No," I correct, for beside me, Pip's eyes are glowing faintly green. *Blast and damn it.* I move to help her, but Pip bats me away, already seeming to find her focus again. Why so quick a recovery this time? Was the magic only minor? Or is it because the Viceroy is closer?

"How much time was that bastard going to need to recover?" Kintyre sneers at me, an accusation, and I shout back: "Well, I am no master warlock myself, am I, brother mine? I couldn't possibly know—"

Another crunching *boom* makes the building rock. The floor, where Pip's feet touch it, begins to crumble away. So, too, the sofa under her hands. She jumps up, takes a step away, but each step leaves a flaking crater in its wake.

"Get her up!" Bevel shouts. "Get her off the ground!"

"Don't touch me!" Pip says, even as Kintyre lunges for her and scoops her up like a sack of flour, his wide shoulder under her stomach, her feet by his face.

"You don't touch *me*," Kintyre says, and I can see the logic in his choice of carry, even if it is undignified.

"Elgar, move!" I shout at our creator, and the man lurches into motion, following along beside Ahbni as we all make for the door. Bevel swings it open, and then halts so abruptly on the threshold that Kintyre has to twist to keep Pip's knees from hitting the back of his head.

"What's—?" I begin, as I cannot see around the height of my brother and the width of our creator.

"The hall's gone!" Bevel says.

"What do you mean, *gone?*" Ahbni asks, straining to see around everyone. "You can't just make a hall not exist!"

Bevel and Kintyre both move out of the way, and around Elgar and Ahbni, I see what they mean. There's just a blank, black void beyond the jamb. A sucking wind screeches in my ears now that they are not blocking it. It is cold, and endless, and frightening. Ahbni reaches out and slams the door shut on the horrifying, howling nothingness.

"Right, the window, then," Kintyre says. "Bev, rope."

Bevel nods and pulls a coil of rope from the bottom of his quiver. I didn't know Bevel carried rope there, but Elgar *had* Written it so that they were both fully outfitted for war.

"Wait, the window?" Pip wails, as Kintyre carries her over to it. "You've been in the Overrealm for five god-damn minutes and you're making me crawl out a *window?*"

Kintyre laughs and pinches Pip's bottom. Pip boots him in the rib, but it is quick and sharp to keep from dissolving any part of him.

"You deserved that," Ahbni says when Kintyre makes a small, pained noise.

In revenge, my brother grabs Pip's ankle and presses the sole of her boot against the glass. It begins to crumble and dissolve at once, and I must commend Kintyre for thinking of it. The glass in these rooms is always double-glazed, and thick enough to prevent all but the most deliberate destruction. The crumbling, while effective, stops spreading almost immediately, however, and the resulting hole is only big enough for one to put an arm through, not a whole person.

"Wait, let me try my hands," Pip says, craning over Kintyre's head to see. He obligingly turns her around. Placing her hands on either side of the hole widens it, but only barely. "Shit, outta juice," she says, and Kintyre drops her back to her feet. The carpet remains intact. Her eyes are no longer glowing.

"Stand back," Bevel says, and everyone jumps out of the way when he hefts one of the chairs over his head.

"Okay, then," Elgar says, looking bemused as Bevel knocks out the loose glass around the crumbled edges, until the hole is big enough for even him. "And now what?"

Bevel drops the chair, and with a quick and practiced motion, he ties one end of the rope coil to the shaft of an arrow. Wordlessly, like the well-practiced team they are, Kintyre grabs the buckle of Bevel's belt, steadies him as his trothed leans backward out of the hole and chooses a target above him. Bevel looses the arrow, and it catches.

On what, I'm not sure, but I decide that when trading on the narrative convenience of being "rescued" by a Main Character, one ought not question the logistics.

Kintyre pulls Bevel back inside and to his feet, and then my brother-in-law grins cheekily at me and gestures grandly for me to go first. "After you, my lord Shadow Hand," he says, and I shoot him a dirty glower as I wrap a hand in the rope.

"Wait, what?" Ahbni asks. "Shadow Hand?"

Pip jerks her thumb at me, smirk widening into a high-wattage grin.

Ahbni blinks, looking back and forth between us, and then sits back, mouth a perfect O.

"No," she gasps.

"Yes," I say.

"I put it in the books!" Elgar grumbles. "I don't know why everyone's so *surprised*. I put in the clues!"

"But *Forsyth* Turn." Ahbni frowns.

I wonder when she realized that I was not, in fact, merely Syth Piper. Probably right around when she saw Kintyre Turn and Bevel Dom appear in a flash of light in a hotel bedroom.

"Forsyth is so much more than his tropes," Elgar defends, a bit shamefaced. "He was supposed to be— you'll forgive me, my boy, for being brutally honest—the craven, envious sibling. The, ah, the one who might betray the hero out of greed or guilt. The Edmunds and Worm-tongues. I even thought, for a time, that you might secret-ly be Bootknife," he says with an introspective chuckle, while I grab the rope and wrap it around my foot the way Rupin Pointe the Elder taught me.

"*Bootknife?*" I echo with horror, and touch the thin scar on my left cheek, covering it with my fingertips as if afraid that it will suddenly sprout limbs and give birth to the villain if I say his name too loudly.

"Turns out, you're a Hufflepuff hero instead," El-gar chuckles. "You talk people down instead of hurting them."

"Oh goody. Lucky us," Ahbni says, and sends a glare out toward the rope, where it's clear she wishes I had been more a man of action.

"Stop stalling, Forssy," Kintyre says, and slaps my back hard enough to send me swinging out into the open air.

"Elfcock!" I yelp back at him over my shoulder as I scramble to grip the rope tight.

Luckily, the con suite was only three floors up, and it is not so far a drop. All the same, I hand myself down the rope as swiftly and surely as I may. When I reach the cobbled inner courtyard and drop free, my palms are burning and my fingers stiff, my shoulders aching. This was not something I learned to do from either of the Pointes I used to duel with.

I check the building, but the rest of it seems intact. Our destruction was localized, then. *Focused.* That means the Viceroy must know exactly where we are. We are now targets. Blast.

Above me, Bevel has Ahbni on his back, and is scaling down swiftly and expertly. Pip must be doing some rope climbing in her gym sessions, for she is quick and efficient in scaling down on her own after him. Next, Kintyre wraps Elgar in the rope, then mounts it directly after him, clinging with only one hand. Together, they inch downward in small jerks as Kintyre presses his feet against the glass wall of the building, and rappels down one-handed, the other wrapped in Elgar's cardigan. Elgar's hand never leaves his ankle, and Bevel reaches up to let Elgar stand on his shoulders when he gets close to the ground, before Elgar stumbles down and onto his feet and Kintyre hops lightly down after him.

"Holy shit," Elgar pants, chest heaving as he wipes his forehead on his sleeve. "Oh my god. I've never done anything like that before. That was crazy."

"It was three floors," Bevel says, eyebrow raised skeptically.

"Yeah, dangling *outside a building*," Elgar answers. "Oh my god."

"This is our Writer?" Kintyre asks me, hands on his hips and head cocked.

I wish to say something glib, like, "*unfortunately,*" or "*if you can believe it.*" But Elgar is looking up at me with big, scared eyes, and I know too well the danger of an ill-thought word or a playful insult taken the wrong way.

Instead, I say: "Come, let's head back inside."

"Why?" Ahbni asks, but she's already following us as we all make for the entrance to the convention center foyer.

"Because the Viceroy is here," Pip says, "and clearly, he's hiding in plain sight."

I tap the pouch with my tablet in it. "Most of the men matching the Viceroy's physical description are down in the gaming area. We shall start there. I have a feeling that the Viceroy will not be able to resist flying at us if he were to spot his archnemesis among the throng."

"Oh, well, doesn't *that* make me feel loved," Kintyre snorts.

I cannot help throwing a cheeky grin over my shoulder at him as I lead our party toward the escalators. "Well, brother mine, you are good for *something*, you know."

When we reach the bottom—after much wonderment and vocal amazement at the magic of moving stairs from Kintyre and Bevel—I say to Elgar: "Pull down your cap and hunch your posture. Pretend that you are... not you. We do not have time for you to be mobbed right now."

Thankfully, my creator does as he's told. He puts his head down, and bulls through the crowd in my wake. I have no real plan, which irks me to no end, save to parade Kintyre through the convention and hope that the Viceroy takes the bait. We cannot fight what we cannot see, and if Elgar and I are not temptation enough for the mad villain, then I hope Kintyre and Bevel may tip the scales in our favor.

For our part, I hold Pip's hand in one of my own, muttering Words of Invisibility, and Slipping, and everything that I have learned as Shadow Hand that may help us pass unseen, and in the other, I grip Elgar's, so that the slipping spell might include him, too, and spare us the possibility of being impeded or delayed by eager fans. I hope this allows the Viceroy to see Kintyre and Bevel, and miss us.

Of course, I must also hope that the Viceroy doesn't have the ability to sense where the magic is being siphoned off to, that he cannot pinpoint us *because* I am leeching power from Pip. I wish I had a third hand, so I could have Smoke freed, and bared, if need be.

We emerge into the gaming area, a wide swath of round tables surrounded by seated folks of every possible description. Fortunately, most of the people are too focused on the cards in their hands, or the elaborate dioramas of battle on their tables, or colorful board games, to note our passage. Kintyre and Bevel weave around the massive clusters of gamers, walking back and forth, back and forth like inane, meandering shuttles amid the loom of people, spooling out their path temptingly.

Pip, Elgar, and I follow more slowly behind them, in a more or less straight line, dodging around the folding chairs, hopping lightly over satchels and the glossy plastic bags of purchases littering the walkway, trying to keep our presence as minimal as possible. Elgar follows as best he can, less agile, but motivated by urgency and the pull of my grip to move quickly. The feel of someone's intense, hateful gaze prickles on the back of my neck, but the only other person behind me is Ahbni. For everyone else, the Words seem to be working. Damn Elgar Reed for Writing me to be so *paranoid*.

It's not paranoia if they're really out to get you, I think, recalling the clever poster I had once seen hanging in Pip's office back in Vancouver. At the time, I'd thought it a terrifying warning, before I understood that it was intended to be humorous. Now, I find it wryly appropriate.

When Kintyre and Bevel have finished wandering the warp of the area, they slowly, looking utterly natural, begin to walk the weft. They stick out, literally head and shoulders above the crowd, easily seen. The rest of us pause on the edge of the floor, where the gaming gives way to the open space of a food court populated with snack trolleys. I cannot help but imagine that we look like a troop of meerkats, waiting for any indication that our bait has proved to be temptation enough. Elgar, at least, welcomes the chance to catch his breath.

Beside me, a young man with a cane hung off the back of his chair cranes his head up and, in a deeply French accent, asks: "Can you move, please? You're blocking my light."

"Huh?" Elgar asks, and then starts. "Oh, hey, it's you. From the elevator."

And sure enough, there is the foursome we met on the elevator yesterday—the Frenchman with the cane; the shorter, rounder fellow wearing another pithy t-shirt; the young black woman with the funky glasses; and the older woman who had blinked so owlishly.

"Uh, hi, Mr. Reed," the older woman says, her attention stuck to my creator like day-old bubblegum.

"Turtle, it's your turn," the younger woman scolds her.

"Kora, it's—"

"I see that," her friend replies. "Play!"

The older woman lays down a card amid the complicated pattern of previously dealt cards between them and says, "I cast Darkness."

Pip tugs on my hand, ready to start moving again, but then skids to a stop after just one step. I crash into her back, Elgar likewise crashing into mine, and we stagger forward a few steps, blind.

Blind, because as soon as the woman named Turtle lays down her card, the entire facility plunges into a deep blackness. A shiver of sound trembles upward as thousands of people gasp in unison, chairs scrape back, and items are dropped to the cement floor. And then the first shout goes up; a child wails, someone screams. Someone near the food court shouts: "Calm down. Stay still! The emergency lights will come on in a second!"

His prediction rings true as the baleful red glare of the emergency exit signs blink on, and a bank of buttery yellow floodlights splutter and surge, as if the electrical feed is fighting against the power of the spell cast upon it. There is no point trying to cast Words of Hiding in the dark, and I release Elgar to fetch out my tablet. Blast and damn, my live feed has gone dead. It is useless. With an oath, I jam it back into its pouch.

When my eyes finally adjust, a quick glance tells me that both Elgar and Ahbni are staring down at the card game beside us, eyes and mouths dropped wide in shock. Kintyre and Bevel have circled to the other side of the table, regarding the cards thoughtfully, and with no little amount of trepidation and awe. Turtle still holds the corner of the card she played pinched between her fingers, the rest of it flattened to the bare table, but she is staring straight upward in a sort of giddy awe.

"Did... did I do that?" she breathes.

"No!" Ahbni says.

"Yes," Pip counters. A glance to my other side tells me that my wife is also staring up into the darkness. Even in the light of the emergency backups, the mingled orange and red from the exit signs, I can see the grim cast of her features. "I don't think we need to hold hands anymore."

I am reluctant, *deeply* reluctant, to let her go. We need to know if the magic will hold once I do. I reach across the table and pick up an unused paper napkin from what looks to be one of their finished meals and hold it out in front of me.

"What are you——?" Ahbni asks, but chokes on the rest of the question when I say a Word of Burning.

This time, the magic is strong enough that a flame immediately appears on the corner of the paper, flaring bright before withering to a wimpish coal and wisp of smoke. I reach out and take Pip's hand again, and the flame leaps back up, flaring as bright as a pitch-dipped torch. A terrible, faint green glow flashes between her lashes, and she gasps like she's been punched in the gut.

"Proximity is still important, but touch is stronger," I whisper.

"*Lanjakodka*," Ahbni curses. "This can't be real."

"'fraid so," Pip mutters, staring down at the table.

I can see her eyes flashing over the cards, can see her trying to work out the way in which what just happened did so. And how to fix it—how to keep it from happening again. The players all lean backward, confused, unsure of why she's peeking at their cards so intently.

"Todd? Todd? You okay?" the Frenchman asks the other fellow at the table, and Todd shakes his head, swallowing hard.

"Not so good with dark spaces," Todd gulps. His free fingers scrabble at the table top, knuckles white. He looks ready to bolt.

"We must fix this, before people start to panic and someone is harmed, Pip," I whisper to my wife.

"Here," Pip says, leaning over Todd's shoulder. "Play this one."

"I can't. It's not my turn," Todd protests.

Pip snarls in frustration. "Who's next?"

"Me?" the young woman called Kora says.

Pip slides around the table, stumbling a little in the low light, and says, "That one. That reverses the last card played, right?"

"Right."

"Play it."

Tentative, staring up at my wife through her smudged glasses with an expression that clearly states that she thinks Pip is crazy, the young woman lays down a card with an image of a blue bottle in a field of equally electric blue lightning. Another, static-cling sort of shiver crawls across my skin. Pip's eyelids flutter as she sucks back a pained gasp, that same faint green glow flaring in her eyes for a brief second. Elgar groans and catches at his chest.

The darkness splutters, and sparks, and then, with a mechanical whine, the lights surge back on.

"*Merde*," the Frenchman gasps, and folds his hand. "I'm done."

"Good idea," Pip says. "Maybe stop playing altogether."

"Perhaps it is best to get *everyone* to stop playing," I suggest. It's entirely possible that the cards around us have started to soak up the magic we seem to be shedding in our wake, and only those of the players closest to us will be affected. But better not to take that chance.

"Oh my god," Elgar hisses, tensing up, his knuckles going white around the cuffs of his cardigan as he stares up around us. His right hand keeps twitching toward his hip, like he wants to pull his knife, and he keeps moving it back to his cuff to keep from making a bigger scene by brandishing a weapon in a crowd. "Oh my god. What does that *mean*?"

"It means," Pip says grimly, "that the leak is getting worse. We should—"

A deep, rattling *boom* fills the hall. It originates from somewhere above us, and is followed by an earth-shaking crash and crunch. The population of the lower levels screams, high and discordant, as one. The floor tilts under me, and I clutch at the card table, sending the little paper squares scattering, to keep on my feet. Ahbni goes down hard, but Pip and Elgar manage to clutch at chairs and remain upright. Kintyre and Bevel look as placid as if they're standing on a streetcar.

The shaking lasts perhaps twenty seconds in total. The lights flicker again, and the room fills with the rattle and crash of furniture overturning; the high, terrified noises of the people; the sickening thud of bodies hitting cement. The air fills immediately with cement dust, chalky and stifling and impossible to breathe. I bury my chin and mouth in my sleeve, reaching for my wife, who is reaching back, clutching me as the world around us tremors. The four card players dive under the table for shelter against the raining dust and pebbles.

And then, as suddenly as it began, the shaking stops. The room is quiet, each person there waiting, waiting to see... The walls groan. One corner of the room buckles slightly, the tiles of the ceiling cracking under a shift in pressure and weight. It holds. Thank the Writer, it holds.

People start coughing. Standing. Calling for friends, and medical attention, and help. Kintyre and Bevel each stand on chairs, scanning the crowd, searching, searching... but no, of course he's not here. The Viceroy would never endanger himself thus.

Green light flares, once, through the new cracks in the ceiling. Oh, no. Upstairs. All those people who had no time to flee, no warning. Who must have been crushed by... by whatever has happened above us. Writer, we need to get out, get *up*, get to where I can see what's happening, where I can assess our options.

"What was that?" Elgar asks, voice shaking.

"You wanted a trap?" Pip answers. She huffs in frustration, punching her own thighs. She is wobbling again, eyes glassy, clearly in pain from whatever magics were just used to accomplish the cave-in. "We're in a trap. And it looks like the bastard just sprang it on us. Look at the escalators, the elevators, the emergency stairs. All cut off. There's rubble everywhere. *Fuck.*"

"Save one. That path is clear," Bevel says, pointing back the way we came, to the escalators. "We should scout it first, though, before we send people up it."

"Agreed," I say.

Pip is having trouble finding her balance, and as much as I wish I could be the one to support—or even completely carry—her, my greater strength is needed for Elgar. He is wincing with every step, holding his shoulders and neck tight, and I feel a vicious stab of pleasure to realize that his injuries have been aggravated. Good, let the blind fool suffer. I am not feeling charitable toward him at the moment.

"Right," Kintyre says, hopping down from his chair. "It looks like the most secure and easily defensible area is there." He points at the ballroom. "Mr. Reed, take the womenfolk and head inside. Forsyth, Bevel, and I need someone who knows this realm to scout for escape routes with us."

"The womenfolk?" Ahbni repeats, aghast.

"Time and a place, Ahbni," Pip says between gritted teeth. "I'd rather Forsyth was with Elgar and I went with Kin and Bev, though."

Bevel shakes his head. "Protect the Writer. I believe you capable."

Pip, clearly annoyed that he's trying to pander to her vanity, snorts and turns to gather up Elgar as well as the four card players still cowering under the table. Whatever backlash she experienced while the upper stories were brought down upon us seems to have left a mark. I do not know how severe it was, what with her being cut off from my view by the dust, but she is mincing, holding her ribs tenderly, grimacing with each step. The green in her eyes lingers, a glowing rim around her iris. I do not know how much more Pip's body can take before the magical runoff does her a permanent injury, and that terrifies me.

Ahbni and Pip leave first, Elgar and the little pack of card players close on their heels. In the distance, I can see that the doors of the ballroom have been blown off their hinges, the whole wall singed and seared, the metal in them warped and half-melted, dusted with virulently green ash. Between us and them, lining the walls, the doors to all the other small panel rooms have been flung back, left hanging open like gawping mouths, giving the room a gap-toothed grimace. In the center of the open space, the gaming tables are overturned, the chairs thrown to the side, bags and satchels abandoned, food and drink spreading across the concrete.

The people are still, though, startled and hunching down, waiting to see what might happen next.

I see a few bodies amid the tables and rubble, too, and hope that they are not dead. Though, better dead than injured and abandoned to their pain. I wish to go to them, to help, to see. But the safety of my family is paramount, and perhaps once I've got them ensconced in a safe place, Bevel, Kintyre, and I can come back to see what can be done. Hopefully, by then, we won't have to, though, and the emergency personnel will have arrived and given aid.

Kintyre has Foesmiter drawn, and Bevel has the Shadow's Cloak wrapped around his free arm in an impromptu shield. I unsheathe Smoke and together, we head toward the escalators.

There is a *snap* and a sizzle, and a shower of sparks suddenly rains from above. People gasp and yelp. The lights flicker once more, and then cut off again. Only the red and amber glow of the emergency beacons light our way. Was the power cut off in the massive crash above us, or is this more magic? Is this the Viceroy's attempt to draw us out, or stalk us?

I wish I could stop guessing, stop thinking in circles, stop trying to anticipate. It's exhausting. I wish to just *know*. I was always a Shadow Hand more at home behind a desk than out in the fields and castles and taverns, and now I am reminded why. I much prefer to read the reports of action, than to participate in it.

We make our way, quiet and stealthy as we are able, toward the escalators.

The food court seems abandoned, though I hear the harsh whispers of those hiding in the small booths as someone soothes a crying child, and someone else hisses medical instructions to another. The blue glow of phone screens being used as flashlights breaks up the darkness of the booths and carts. Good, it seems that these people, those that are left here, are safe and sane enough to care for one another.

Again, a pang of guilt for leaving them behind surges in my breast. But I am not their lordling; their safety is not my purview. Not until the safety of *all* can be assured.

We inch up the escalator slowly, ears straining for any sound that might give us warning that an attack is coming. The escalator is not functioning, the power cut along with that of the lights. I keep my eyes aimed at the ceilings and shadowed corners around us, not putting the Viceroy's love of the dramatic out of my mind, knowing that he does prefer to be literally above everyone and everything.

Nothing. Nothing. Damn it, why does he wait?

When Bevel reaches the top of the stairs, he pulls Kintyre to an abrupt stop beside him. "Aw, hells," Bevel whispers, and the moment I'm in the foyer of the convention center, I see why.

The grand glass doors have been entirely blocked with

what used to be the floor above us. Jumbled boulders of concrete ring the escalators and fountain—which has gone quiet—cutting off access to all of the exits. The remains of tables and chairs from the Dealer's Room above are sprinkled around the space, splintered and twisted, pebbled with abandoned wares and an avalanche of loose papers from destroyed books, and comics, and artist's prints.

Syrupy afternoon sunlight streams in from the glass ceiling above us, now visible with the floor brought down.

"We could climb up there, break a window," Kintyre says, pointing to the mountain of rubble and debris. "Get out that way?"

"I don't trust it," Bevel says. "It doesn't look stable enough. And we'd be exposed and easy to pick off. I say we head back downstairs and regroup."

"Agreed," I say again, morose, and we descend the still escalator once more.

"I hope nobody is in that mess," Bevel says, as we pick our way back down into the gloom of the lower levels.

"We must hope that they all escaped. And if some did not, there is nothing we can do for them now," Kintyre comforts him with more wisdom than I am used to hearing from my brother.

"I despise that there's collateral damage," I add quietly. "And I hate that I am relieved that Alis isn't among them."

"Where is she?" Bevel asks.

"Not here, thank the Writer. She stayed with Pip's parents," I say. I pull my phone out of the pouch strapped to my sword belt, and bring up Martin's contact information. "It may be on the news by now. They must be scared sick."

I feel my whole body drop with disappointment when

I look at the screen, however. "No signal." I hold the phone up to the open air above our heads, watching the bars, but there's nothing. "Either the concrete is blocking it all, or it's been cut off on purpose."

"What about outside help?" Bevel asks.

"Someone outside would have called for rescue personnel, yes," I reassure him, replacing my useless phone in its pouch. "But it might take a few hours to get everything safely cleared and get inside. It might take *days*."

"Then we assume we are under siege," Kintyre rumbles.

I point at the fountain. "At least there's water. It might be heavily chlorinated, but it will be safe to drink. And food, for a few days, in the food court, and in the... the bags down in the gaming room from the... uh..." I cannot say it, and instead, swallow heavily.

"We'll search," Bevel says. "I promise. We will get ourselves secure, and then scout for survivors."

I can only nod jerkily. "This way," I say, and point at the ballroom. "I dislike the openness. Collect what provisions you can, and rally those able to move. I would much rather we all weathered this siege in the ballroom, where there are only three entrances to guard."

"Yeah," Bevel says, echoing my sentiment, and shooting me a cheeky grin when I turn to look at him in surprise. Kintyre moves to obey me, and then pauses.

"I don't even know what half of this stuff is..." Kintyre says, poking his nose into a cabinet filled with pizza slices. "Is this travel bread?"

"Of a sort," I tell him.

"Oh, hello," Kintyre adds, addressing someone who is behind the counter.

"He-hello," that someone says, standing. It's Ichiro, the liaison, his face smeared with dust-cut tear tracks, his bright volunteer shirt stained with what appears to be someone else's blood. "Is it safe to come out?"

"For now," Kintyre says, and helps him limp around the counter.

The answer of whose blood is on his shirt becomes clear when the skinny volunteer from the Green Room follows after him, the back of his forearm showing a long, deep defensive wound that is matched by the one on his forehead. Clearly he'd raised his arm to protect his face from some sort of flying debris. There are paper napkins stuck to the edges of the wounds where Ichiro had tried to stop the bleeding.

"Come on," Kintyre tells them. "Grab whatever you think we'll need—water skins, bandages, ointments, what food you can, and we will set up a camp in the far room there."

"Water skins?" the skinny volunteer echoes, looking dazed. He was probably concussed by whatever caused the gash to his arm and forehead. All the same, the two lads obey, and a handful of other people—a mix of all ages and ethnicities—emerge from behind the counters and under carts at their urging.

Bevel goes over to a mother holding her sniffling baby tight to her chest—they are both extremely dark-complected, their hair in matching tight braids along their scalps, their eyes both wide, white, fearful circles in their faces. The side of the mother's face and the backs of her hands are covered with fine cuts from protecting her child.

"Here," Bevel says, and takes the babe from its dazed mother. The child, like all children around Bevel Dom, immediately ceases to fuss and stares up at his face in fascinated, charmed awe. "There now. Much better, isn't it? You're all right now, wee thing. Look at you. Regular Queen of the Pirates, you are. Follow us."

The mother, as charmed as her child, stoops for the

always present diaper bag and shoulders it. I know the weight of such bags intimately, and watching my brother-in-law cradling someone else's baby, I find I miss mine fiercely. But again, I am glad she is not here. Others emerge from the shadows in the corners, from under gaming tables. Everyone sports defensive cuts and bruises, everyone is covered liberally with dust, but it seems as if no one save the skinny volunteer is deeply, dangerously wounded. Good.

Kintyre leads the caravan, shuffling and limping, to the ballroom. A dozen more people emerge from the side rooms, about a third of them in volunteer shirts, and another third in cosplay. Several are thankfully carrying plastic first aid kits.

When we reach the ballroom doors, we see that there are about a hundred people altogether. Several of the able-bodied men and women help Kintyre yank the main doors closed behind us. They mostly fit, even if they cannot close all the way.

Bevel leads his ragtag refugees to the corner of overturned and trampled chairs to the left of the stage. The stage itself is empty, Elgar's club chair overturned. The projector screen is crumpled on the stage floor, the fly gallery above it a ragged mess of hanging wires and ropes.

"Best nobody goes up there," he says, peering up at the rigging from the lip of the stage. "Is there an exit at the back?"

"Yeah, into the corridors," one of the volunteers says, and Bevel nods.

"Right, take some folks and block it up best you can with chairs or whatever you find. Anything to make it so that if someone comes in that way, we'll hear it, and they'll have to go slow."

"Yeah, but... I mean, who are you trying to keep out?"

Bevel just stares at her evenly, until she swallows hard,

nods, and does as she's asked, fear and curiosity on her face. Kintyre would have shouted to get it done. But Bevel has always been more subtle than his trothed.

Kintyre, done with the doors, crosses the room to Bevel. He scoops the child out of his trothed's hands, placing her back in her mother's embrace, then wraps his arms around Bevel's shoulders and pulls the shorter man tight against his chest. He lowers his face to Bevel's neck, whispering something in his ear, or simply taking in the scent. Then Kintyre pulls back, just enough for me to hear: "We've just vanished, and they'll never know..."

Kintyre says it in a long, hitching rush, and suddenly, I feel horrid for intruding on what is clearly a deeply personal moment.

"I know. It's torture," Bevel soothes back, his hands sweeping down my brother's spine. "It's awful. But you have to keep moving. These people need us."

"Yes. Yes, of course."

We join Pip, Ahbni, and Elgar where they are seated in a small clump, looking shaken and anxious. Ahbni, especially, looks as if she is about to vomit. Shock can be vicious, and I cast around for a blanket and some water. I find the latter, and take the Shadow's Cloak from Bevel for the former.

"Thanks," Ahbni says, but it is hollow, automatic. She is staring at the wall, seeing nothing, teeth chattering. Her fingers curl into the layers of fine cloth.

"Right," Pip says, and nods to herself, firm, shaking herself from her own shocked funk. "Right. Okay. Okay. So, now what? What's the plan, my brawny boys?"

"You need to rest," I tell her, and she shakes her head, then winces. She looks feverish, and is still shaking slightly, sweat beading on her forehead and upper lip as she tries to hide how difficult even walking to the ballroom had been. "Don't argue. That is our first priority."

"Rest, and then what?" Pip asks, mulish. "Forsyth, we can't just... it's not *working*. Everything we're doing, it's just endangering people, it's just making things worse. We don't know where he is, and if we keep blundering around, then who else is going to get hurt?"

"Do you know of any other way to draw out the Viceroy?" Kintyre says, impatient.

"Maybe... I don't know..." Pip says and looks over at Elgar. "Maybe if you Wrote—"

"Absolutely not!" I shout. "Pip, this is *killing* you. You think you are fine, but you are *not*. You grow weaker with each fit, with each use of magic, and I cannot allow—"

"It's my choice to make!" Pip shouts right back. "And if it's between me and all these people—"

"What of Alis?"

"You think I'm not thinking of our daughter, too?" Pip counters.

Ahbni makes a strangled, pained keening noise and screws her eyes shut. "Oh my god, you have a kid. I forgot you had a kid. I just... I didn't... It's *real*, and you have a *kid*, and real people are getting hurt, and I just..." she trails off, choking on her own realization.

"It's 'real'?" Bevel says, bemusement evaporating into concern. "Are you well?"

Ahbni trembles, her voice shaking as she turns to him. "You're actually him, aren't you? You're not just cosplaying Bevel Dom and Kintyre Turn. You're not just a family member he based the character on. You're actually *him*."

Silence hangs between us as we share glances, debating, wordlessly, what truths to tell, and which to keep hidden.

"Yes," I say finally, because I do not see the point in lying to her. Not if she is to be our ally in this. Not if we must trust her.

"Oh god," she breathes, and staggers back a step. Her chair falls sideways behind her and she climbs backwards over it, as if she fears that the moment she stops looking at us, we'll vanish. Or attack. "Oh, god... I *can't*..."

And before anyone can ask her what it is that she cannot do, she spins on her heel, the cloak and her scarf flaring out behind her, and runs out of the ballroom.

THIRTEEN

ELGAR

"Son of a bitch!" Lucy snarls, turning in circles just outside the ballroom like a bloodhound seeking a lost scent. "It's like she walked across the threshold of the door and just... ceased to exist."

Kintyre, already taller than everyone else, rocks up onto his toes, as if the extra height will reveal Ahbni and her violently pink scarf between the forest of tumbled concrete and furniture.

"He's taken her," Lucy says, with absolute finality. Elgar's scalp crawls. "He's taken her to get to us. Fuck. *Fuck.*"

"Maybe she's just ducked into the washroom, or...?" Elgar offers, hoping. "Someone must have seen—"

"Ahbni," Lucy says, grabbing the arm of a passing blue-shirted volunteer. "Where'd she go?"

"Who?" the volunteer asks.

"The guest liaison—dark hair, very pretty? Pink scarf?" Forsyth urges.

"Ichiro's the guest liaison," the volunteer says, and looks at them like the stress of what is happening has snapped their minds. "I can get him for you."

"The other liaison, the girl," Lucy insists. "Where has she gone?"

The volunteer shakes off Lucy's hold. "I don't know who you mean."

The pronouncement should have been more ominous than that, Elgar thinks. If he'd been writing it, there would have been a clap of thunder, or a flicker of lights, or something more than just the volunteer's bland truth and distrustful expression.

"Look, some of the ConComm are looking for you," the volunteer says when everyone has finished glancing at each other to check that, yes, the rest of the heroes had heard that, too, and yes, they're all equally surprised. "You guys seem to know what's going on."

"Slightly," Forsyth dissembles.

"More than slightly," Kintyre corrects, trotting up behind him with a grin. Forsyth rolls his eyes and sighs hard.

"Well, you're in costume, too, so maybe you already know, but we think that..." The volunteer stops and shuffles, hunches in, suddenly mortified by what they have to confess. "We sort of... um... think that the... the costumes are coming to... life?"

"They what?" Lucy asks, eyes going wide.

Forsyth makes a thoughtful sound. "Yes, that makes sense."

"It makes sense?" Elgar can't help but repeat.

"Pip is still here, still shedding magic."

Lucy grimaces. "Like fleas, awesome. Make me sound like a plague carrier. No, go on. I love this analogy."

"*Bao bei*," Forsyth chides her, and Lucy huffs.

"In what way are the costumes—?" Lucy begins to ask, but the approach of someone else cuts her off.

"Hey! Something's wrong with my prop!" a cosplayer shouts.

"Has everyone but me forgotten the girl in the pink scarf?" Kintyre groans. "I think we have more to worry about than—"

"It's not a prop anymore!" the cosplayer says, and Elgar turns to get a better look at the woman in the costume. She is dressed as some sort of spaceship crew member, though he doesn't know from what franchise.

"What do you mean, it's not a—?" Lucy starts, but is interrupted by a bright flash of blue streaking across the ballroom, accompanied by a sizzling *zing!* The blue light slams into a bit of empty wall, juddering the entire structure, and leaves a scorch mark as wide as a man's chest smoking in the wallpaper. There's already a second scorch mark right beside it.

"What in the seven hells is that?" Bevel yelps, stumbling back a step and colliding with Kintyre's chest. Kintyre just steadies him there, his own eyes wide and on the wall.

"Holy shit," Lucy breathes. "Can you—can I see that?" She barely waits for the cosplayer to hand it over before she snatches it away and is aiming across the same empty stretch of ballroom to fire her own bolt of energy at the wall. Her aim isn't as good as the cosplayer's, though, mostly because her hand is shaking. "Holy shit."

"Pip," Forsyth says urgently. "Ahbni."

"I know, I know. Just... the magic is pooling again. That has to be it. The cards, now this?"

"This is good?" Kintyre asks. "Instead of Players' props, these people will be armed with real weapons. They can defend themselves. Let's go find the girl!"

Elgar wonders idly if Kintyre will want to sleep with her if he saves her. And then he wonders what Bevel would have to say about that. *Well, commitment doesn't always mean monogamy. Maybe—*

"No, this is definitely not good!" Lucy replies. "Anything can go off by accident! We should ask them to put all their weapons away somewhere."

"And when the Viceroy comes, and they're separated from them?" Bevel challenges, and Lucy dithers.

"What's going on?" the cosplayer breaks in, her chin

wobbling and her eyes filling up with tears. "Why is this happening?"

"Oh, god. Someone needs to give a speech," Lucy says. "One of those Inspirational General ones."

"We-well, it wo-won't be m-m-me!" Forsyth stutters, alarmed.

Elgar realizes that four sets of eyes—five, including the cosplayer—have fallen on him.

"Me?" he asks, mouth suddenly dry with apprehension.

"We owe them the truth, I think," Lucy says. "Don't we?"

"That the land of fairy tale and story books has come to life?" Kintyre asks.

"They deserve to know what we're facing. *Who* we're facing," Lucy adds quietly. "They deserve to be prepared. So what's happened to Ahbni won't—" She cuts herself off, eyes still darting around the room, as if she can find the girl if she just looks hard enough, looks *again*.

"We kinda are," the cosplayer replies, and gestures behind her, at the small knot of people who are also dressed up. Elgar stares at them for a moment, trying to decipher what she's trying to get them to understand. In the end, it's the two card players—Kora and Turtle—who make the jigsaw puzzle pieces of understanding slot into place. As the crowd in the room huddles together, it's those two, who've had longer to come to grips with the idea of magic suddenly becoming real, who have collected together the group of costumed folks.

"Right, who's got weapons' experience?" Kora asks the group, and a few raise their hands. "Even if it's just stage combat?" A few more hands go up.

"Weapons' experience," Bevel repeats, sounding bemused. "This is a rare thing?"

"Is there no militia? No standing army? No knights in

the Overrealm?" Kintyre adds.

"Sort of," Lucy says. "But it's different. Civilians don't need to defend their crops from raiding barbarians, or their daughters from untrustworthy lordlings. If any study a kind of martial art, like, um, shooting or grappling, then it's a hobby, not a necessity."

"If we have no army, then at least that one's a natural general," Kintyre says, pointing to Kora.

"Good thing, too," Bevel agrees. "We can't be everywhere at once."

A very young boy dressed as a Magical Girl is looking up, seriously, into Kora's face, gripping a wand that is sparking and spitting out a slowly falling stream of gold glitter that vanishes before it can accumulate on the hideous carpet. Turtle is marshaling everyone wearing any sort of uniform, checking their ray-guns and phasers and staff-weapons and rifles. Blue-shirted volunteers surround those who seem to have no protection, those not in costume.

"Who's got magic?" Turtle calls, and several people put up their hands. "Anyone with cards or spellbooks?" A few more people make themselves known, including Ichiro. The Frenchman with the cane confers seriously with him, both of them pulling hard-bound game books from their bags to look something up.

"What are they doing?" Elgar asks, watching order form out of terrified chaos.

"What geeks do best," Forsyth says, hand on Elgar's shoulder, squeezing once. The spark of creative connection jumps between them, but it's welcome this time. "Acting as a community. Come, shall we see what we can do to edify them?"

"You don't think Kintyre and Bevel can... get him?" Elgar says slowly.

"This magical earthquake? This is just the Viceroy's

first foray. He's trying to cause a panic. And people suddenly realizing that magic is actually a thing will definitely do that," Lucy says with a firm head nod. "We're all experienced enough to know that this can't possibly be his endgame. Not yet. And we gotta make sure they know what might come after them if they need to defend themselves. Elgar, that speech?"

Elgar balks. "So, what, I just stand up on a chair, tell them that magic is real, and that we're canceling the apocalypse? That wrath and ruin descend, but today will not be that day, and also, lend me your ears?" Lucy, at least, snorts at his lame attempt at a joke. "It takes days to craft a speech that good."

"It's not a *speech* speech. It's an explanation. It's a... a call to arms, perhaps," Forsyth says.

"What, this crowd against the *Viceroy?*" Elgar asks, and it finally hits home what is happening with the group of cosplayers. They're marshaling for war. "Oh, my god, no. He'll tear through them like tissue paper."

"And would you rather they sit here, ignorant and afraid?" Kintyre challenges.

"Better armed and aware, than not, even if they don't believe us," Lucy adds.

Elgar looks out over the crowd. One of the blue-shirted volunteers had taken over organizing the food and water, making sure that everyone is hydrated and fed. Most of the people who needed first aid are now bandaged. The wailing baby has stopped, preoccupied by a couple of cosplayers in skimpy metal bikinis shivering under coats lent to them by other people not so affected by the intense amount of air-conditioning the building is still apparently pumping out, despite being on the emergency generators.

As for Elgar, a day full of running, falling, tumbling, stress, more running, sneaking, and yet more running, is catching up to him all at once. He slumps into a chair. Everything aches, from his shoulder blades upward, and his scars itch.

"I wish I hadn't left my pain meds upstairs," Elgar moans.

"I'm sure someone has something," Lucy dismisses. "Come on. Talk to them."

"Why me?"

"Because they know who you are," Forsyth presses. "Because they will listen to you."

"I'm not sure what I should say to—" An explosion, followed by a loud, monstrous, echoing, bone-shaking roar interrupts Elgar. "Thank god."

"Thank god?" Lucy screeches. "For an *explosion?*"

Elgar tries to be cheeky with his answer, even as he grabs hard onto the seat of the chair to keep from being rocked off his feet by the resulting tremors. "No speech necessary now!"

"Unbelievable," Lucy groans.

"'S how I would have written it," Elgar offers. "Best way to write yourself out of corners is to make something explo—"

A second blast rocks the room.

The crowd screams.

"Stop talking!" Lucy shouts, slapping her hand over Elgar's mouth. "Oh my god, stop talking!"

"Get those people away from the walls," Kintyre shouts over the building roar coming from outside the room. Foesmiter is already in his hands, and Elgar allows himself one moment, just one small one, to be dazzled by the vision of the Great Hero of Hain, his proudest creation, standing before him in all his battle-ready glory. Forsyth, clever enough to know when his brother's orders are best followed and when they should be ignored, obeys.

Bevel and Kintyre make a dash for the main doors of the ballroom, waving off those few members of the security team who had taken it upon themselves to investigate. The civilians look relieved to be told to hang back.

"Can I keep this?" Lucy asks, gesturing with the raygun prop, and the cosplayer yelps an affirmative before another crescendoing roar sends her scrambling back to the knot of people in the middle of the room.

Because the roaring... the roaring is getting louder. Getting closer. It's a continuous rumble punctuated by a thunderous screech, like a rusty pulley, and the leather flap of what sounds like enormous bat-wings. Overcome with curiosity, Elgar shakes out of Lucy's grip and moves to stand just behind Bevel, to the side, where he'll be shielded by the wall.

Kintyre and Bevel themselves open one door, and pause in the threshold. They don't look stunned, per se, but they look... concerned.

"What on the Writer's green backside is that?" Bevel asks, and Kintyre shrugs, fingers clenching and unclenching around his sword. Bevel slings his bow off his body and nocks an arrow. "In the eye, do you think?"

Kintyre nods. "Quick, before brother's wife sees."

Bevel smirks, sardonic and cheeky. "Pip's soft-hearted, but I don't think even she'd want to tangle with... whatever that is."

"Manticore!" someone just behind them says, and Elgar glances back just long enough to realize it's the shorter of the two men who had been playing the card game that had accidentally doused the lights earlier. Todd? Todd, right. "It has the ability to control other creatures."

"Other creatures?" Kintyre echoes, and Todd points to the abandoned food court. Just past the massive lion with bat-wings and a scorpion's tail is a parade of monsters working their menacing, slow-paced way across the overturned tables and chairs. One looks like a massive, half-rotted leaf on legs, with praying mantis arms.

"King Reaper," Todd explains, pointing to that one. His finger shifts to a man-high, deep red saurian quadruped. "Kavu Predator."

"Are such monsters common in the Overrealm?" Kintyre asks Todd.

"They're not *real*," Todd insists instead. "At least, they're not supposed to be."

"I suddenly miss Capplederry, like, a lot," Lucy shouts, coming up behind Todd to see what everyone's staring at. "What are you waiting for, Bev? Shoot 'em!"

Bevel and Kintyre exchange another knowing smirk, and Bevel lets fly.

The bolt strikes true, and the manticore howls, tail lashing, pawing at its head before it falls down sideways, dead. The King Reaper stops to inspect the corpse with what might have been eyes, or might have been spiders.

"Good lord," Elgar says, and though he hasn't been religious since he lost his Aunty Lilah, he crosses himself and steps back from the door.

"Let me try," Lucy says, shoving to the front of the group. "I'd like to save your arrows if we can."

She levels the ray-gun at the King Reaper and fires. The first bolt goes wide. Out of nowhere, the air crackles with a whiplash of gleeful laughter. It is unexpected, high and harsh, and Elgar can't find the source.

Pip cringes and fires again, the noise grating, but it's clear her hands are shaking in earnest now, and that bolt misses its target, too. The laughter, now piercing and echoing around the rafters of the hall, crescendos. The third shot hits the Reaper square in the chest, and then Pip stumbles backward as the monster crisps up and turns to leafy ash. She claps her hands to the side of her head and shouts: "Shut up, you mad asshole!"

Elgar's guts clench as he realizes it's not one of the creatures laughing.

"Clever toy," Bevel says, and snatches the ray-gun from her hand. Good thing, too. It only takes him one shot to get used to the kickback, and then the Predator is keeled on its side, howling through a wound that's eating through its flesh, then ribcage, then internal organs.

The air fills with the acrid, gorge-lifting tang of burnt flesh and curdling blood. Elgar jerks the collar of his shirt up to cover his nose and mouth.

Pip slaps her hands over her ears, eyes screwed shut. "Shut up," she hisses, over and over again. "Shut up, shut up, *shut up!*"

It's only then that Elgar realizes he recognizes the laughter. Poisonous and sticky, like venom and honey, it's exactly how he'd written it to be. A shivering, sickly horror squirms up Elgar's spine. He wraps his arms around himself, shuddering with the way the voice makes the very marrow of his bones resonate, like a humongous gong rung in the deepest canyon on Earth.

"I hesitate to say that that was easy, but—" Kintyre begins, and this time, it's Elgar who stops him, placing his own palm over his creation's mouth.

"No," Elgar says hurriedly, ignoring the way his hand tingles. "No, don't say that. Ever."

Which is when, of course, three more flares of acid-green light spark into flames in the middle of the gaming floor.

"Oh. My new pets! Such a shame. No matter!" a voice booms across the echoing, empty cement box of the convention center. *His* voice. Elgar has only heard it once before, in the hospital, but he knows it intimately. He's been hearing it in his own head for decades. "There are thousands more monsters to summon forth. Such fertile imaginations, the Writers of this world. Such creatures they envision. Such *deaths* they design!"

"The monsters are all headed this way. We have to get you away from the innocents," Bevel hisses over his shoulder at Elgar.

"What do you mean, awa—*ay!*" Elgar yelps as Bevel grabs his wrist and yanks him out into the open floor and along the wall. His bare hand, where it's wrapped around Elgar's skin, tingles and sparks the way Forsyth's does when they touch one another. Elgar wrenches his head around to watch the three gouts of flame resolve into three more creatures he has no name for. The movement sends hot pain shooting up the back of his neck, still not totally healed from the whiplash, but running for his life and keeping the things that are trying to kill him in sight is worth it.

Kintyre is just a few steps behind them, and this time, the monsters don't stalk slowly across the floor. One is some sort of legless crawly thing, until it launches itself from a pile of tables and spreads horrific, spiny wings. Elgar thinks he'll be forgiven the girlish shriek he lets loose as it bears down on them, its wide-open maw ringed with rows and rows of fangs.

Kintyre stops, spins around on the balls of his feet, and flings himself back in the direction of the creature. Foesmiter does... does something too quick, and too bright to see, and then the monster is nothing more than quivering chunks of carcass on the cement floor. The laughing overhead redoubles.

"Run!" the Viceroy howls, still unseen, still menacing from above, in glee. "Go on, you fat, stupid, worthless old man! You think they can protect you?"

"Don't listen," Bevel hisses as he yanks Elgar behind one of the food court carts. "And keep your head down."

Bevel takes the moment's respite to sling his bow back over his chest and raise the ray-gun. He peeps over the top of the cart to watch what Elgar assumes is Kintyre hack and slash at the two remaining monsters. The air fills with the stench of loosed bowels and fresh meat, the sounds of boots scraping on concrete and claws shrieking against rebar. Kintyre's grunting huffs mingle with the shrill cries and howls of the monsters. Elgar isn't sure what's worse. Not knowing what's happening, or only hearing it and imagining the worst.

The surreality of the situation is punctuated by the fact that Bevel Dom, bard, fantasy knight and seventh son of a seventh son, is clutching a futuristic laser-weapon in his hand that he's—after just a few shots—completely comfortable with. Sure, Elgar had written him to be extremely proficient with any targeted range weapon, but the picture of Bevel, in his battle leathers and Dom-amethyst short-robe, with his fingers wrapped around a high-sheen, chrome cosplay prop that *literally magically works* is enough for him to want to screw his eyes shut, and pinch himself hard until he wakes from this wacky, awful nightmare.

Elgar's neck hurts, and his pulse is so fast and thready that he can feel it jumping in the hollow of his throat, clutching with taloned fingers at his lungs, prickling in beads of sweat at his hairline. He swallows hard, trying to beat back the fear, trying to trust the fact that it's Bevel Dom protecting him. He should trust his own creation. He should have more faith. But a year of knowing Forsyth Turn, and several months of friendship with him, has also taught Elgar that his creations, while heroic and clever and strong, are also human. And that means *fallible.*

"It's the papers," Bevel snarls as he takes aim over and over again, firing off bolt after impossible bolt from the ray-gun. The roars and howls of dying beasts are punctuated by crackling flames and the slick, poisonous laughter of the Viceroy. "There's no end to these monsters. He'll just keep summoning them, again and again."

"Words of Burning!" Elgar gasps at him. "Forsyth made them work before."

Bevel shouts out to Kintyre that he should try to burn what paper he can with the Words, but his trothed is too caught up with keeping the monsters at bay to waste his breath on Word magic.

Bevel burns what paper his Words can reach nearby, the syllables of it gorgeous and syllabant and hissing in Elgar's ears. They *sound* like fire. Elgar scrambles on his hands and knees to shuffle every paper within arm's length onto the pile. Bevel has to keep popping his head up to shoot at the monsters, though, his attention divided.

"Get back inside, you fools!" Kintyre calls over the din, and Elgar wrenches himself to his knees, clinging to the side of the upset hot dog cart to see what he's talking about.

At the far side of the room, the large doors to the ballroom have been thrown back.

"What are they doing?" Elgar hisses. "They're going to get killed!"

From this distance, it's difficult to distinguish individual faces, though Lucy and Forsyth are distinctive enough in the forefront of the rush. Like football linebackers, the group of be-weaponed cosplayers surges out onto the floor, ray-gun blasts sizzling and filling the room with the tang of ozone and even more burnt flesh. Magic swirls and pulses through the air, some of it the watercolor swirls of his own creations, some very clearly the recreation of effects he's seen on television, in film, in anime and comics.

"No!" the Viceroy sneers from above and all around them. "No!"

"Clever Forssy," Bevel says with a panting grin as he

pops back down behind the cart, taking a moment to rest.

"What? Why? What's he doing?"

Bevel's grin gets wide and ever-so-slightly goofy, his dark blue eyes shining with mirth and adrenaline. Elgar chokes back a startled sound. He knows that Bevel loves action, but he never realized that this is what his creation would look like in the midst of a heated battle. Elgar had spent so much time detailing the way the armies moved, the way the villains gestured, or the arc of Foesmiter and the bend of Bevel's bow, that he hadn't spared much description for the faces of his heroes. He never realized that Bevel would be so *happy* to be fighting for his life.

Is it because they're in the midst of doing exactly what Elgar has written Bevel for—to support Kintyre, to protect the innocent, to cross swords with evil? Like Forsyth, who is most content when he is behaving as a spymaster, who is most *himself* when in the pursuit of information, is Bevel most himself when in mortal peril? Or is it that he is fighting beside his trothed? His *hus-band?*

Kintyre comes sliding around the side of the cart on his knees, grinning like a little boy. He steals a second of their reprieve to wrap one large arm around Bevel's shoulders and draw him up for a windblown, breathless kiss. It's quick, and chaste, but it leaves them both pink-cheeked and giggling like children.

"Useful to have a bookmouse for a brother, eh, Bev?" Kintyre asks, releasing Bevel to shift over to the cart and watch the action.

"*Why?*" Elgar asks again.

"Look," Kintyre grunts, impatient. "Don't you see what they're doing?"

Elgar looks. "Burning the paper."

"Means Forssy figured it out, too," Kintyre says, and he sounds approving. Elgar tries not to goggle at a

Kintyre Turn that *approves* of anything his brother does, much less speaks *admirably* of him. And he's heard it twice now in as many hours. "He's using the resources at his disposal. There's no way he could have burned them all with his Words fast enough. But with an army..."

"But they're not an army," Elgar protests.

"They're the best we've got in a pinch," Bevel says. "And if they're going to kill monsters and burn paper, and use up all of the Viceroy's resources so he's forced to show his hand, then I won't be turning them away."

"Is that what we're doing?" Elgar asks. "Trying to get him to show his hand?"

"Or his face," Bevel says with a casual, sideways shrug.

It's Gallic, and arrogant, and Elgar can't remember if he'd ever written that gesture onto Bevel himself. He doesn't think so. It's yet more proof that his creations are more human, more complex, than he's suspected. It's odd. Eerie. Unsettling. Uncanny.

"We can't hit him until we *see* him," Kintyre says. "And we won't see him until he's exhausted every other avenue first. It's what he does."

A thought occurs to Elgar. "Like him going after Ahbni?"

Bevel nods, spares a second to peek up at the battle, then ducks back down and runs a hand through his sweaty hair, pushing it irritably off his forehead. "Find her, and I bet we find the Viceroy."

"But we're not *looking*. We're just... sitting here! Like sitting ducks!"

Bevel offers him another cheeky grin. "Well, it's not like he's gonna come out otherwise, with Forssy stuck to your side like a cockleburr."

"Oh my god. I'm *bait*?" Elgar shrills. "Again?"

"Can't fight what we can't see," Kintyre says with an

unapologetic shrug that matches Bevel's.

"You guys are... are... *assholes*," Elgar says, and then stops to blink. Huh. That's... that's what people have been saying about his work for years, and yet he hasn't really... honestly, it hadn't occurred to him that his creations might actually be... exactly what people called them. *Boorish. Narcissistic. Shallow.*

"There's no point in changing what's proven to work," Bevel says. "One way or another, the Viceroy wants you dead. So if we stick to you, and wave you under his nose, he's eventually going to have to stop puppeteering fictional monsters and come out to do the deed himself."

"Oh god," Elgar says with a groan. He covers his face with his hands, mortified and terrified, all at once. He wishes that he had stayed over with Forsyth and Lucy. At least they seemed to *think through* their plans before implementing them. Even if they sometimes do over-think them.

"Bev, let's start moving toward the army," Kintyre says, apparently confident that their conversation about *dangling Elgar like a worm* is over. "Burn what we can see as we go."

"They're *not* an army," Elgar protests once more, weakly, but he is utterly ignored.

"I don't like that we might miss some," Bevel says. "But that's better than sitting here, letting the monsters creep up on us. If nothing else, we can keep the creatures distracted and let the army finish the flush."

"They're not an *army*," Elgar repeats, a little louder.

"Right, I'll take point; you take rear. Let's head down that way." Kintyre points to a side aisle clear of hazards. "Push him to the back when you reach the army, and I'll take its head."

"Right," Bevel agrees.

"They're not an *army!*" Elgar shouts. "They're just...

just *fanboys*! Smelly, sweaty, self-important, vacant, *playing* at heroics and sucking back too much Mountain Dew fanboys! You're going to get them killed if you encourage them to do more than they're capable of!"

Bevel and Kintyre both frown at Elgar, faces darkening.

"How dare you demean their bravery?" Kintyre grinds out. "They are doing this *for you*. For love of *you*, Writer."

And there, right there. That is it, that is the fear that has been fluttering in Elgar's chest since it became clear that the Viceroy would target anyone and everyone close to him in order to traumatize and torture Elgar, to literally scare him to death. Juan, and Linux, and now Ahbni? There it is, pinned down and labeled. Finally.

Dread that someone is going to *die* and it will be all his fault. No, not dread. Apprehension. Anxiety. Dismay. Consternation. *Terror.*

"*I never asked them to!*" Elgar chokes. His eyes are burning. He can't seem to get a full breath. He feels shaky, hollow, and yet completely filled up with something sharp and boiling.

Kintyre's frown turns less disapproving, more puzzled. "You didn't have to."

"I... what?" Elgar says, and it's a sob. He touches his face, and yeah, he's crying. He is actually crying.

"You can't control who loves you, or why," Bevel says gently, as if Elgar is a foolish toddler who's never been taught this before. Maybe he *is* a fool. "And if they choose to put themselves in peril for love of you, you can't control that, either."

"But I don't want... I don't *want* them to!" he protests.

"And yet, there your army stands. There it *battles*, in your name."

Elgar wrings his hands, desperate to make his heroes

understand. "But they're *not an army!*"

"Of course they are—look at them," Kintyre orders with a scowl. He draws Elgar up to his knees, so the three of them can look out over the convention hall floor together.

The cosplayers have spread out from their knot by the door. Lucy and Forsyth are still in the forefront, generals directing the fighting. Those with offensive weapons are doing their best to damage the monsters and creatures that keep springing up, hydra-like, from the sediment of papers, cards, figurines, comics, posters, and anything else the Viceroy can draw from. The attackers have ranged into a semi-circle, protecting what appears to be several staff-wielding wizards, witches with house-robes and wands, a whip-thin Asian boy dressed in some sort of red, Chinese-inspired armor making elaborate hand motions and tumbles, and a masked video game character.

For those in the center of the circle are making *fire.*

And in the middle of all, Ichiro, the blue-shirted liaison, tosses something up into the air, catching it repeatedly. When it lands, he checks the item, and produces a puff of flame from his hand, burning whatever is nearby. Some of the tosses and flames are large, some are whimperingly small.

"He's rolling dice," Elgar breathes, stunned by this realization. Ichiro Eiji is literally *rolling for their lives.*

Flames shoot from futuristic pixilated guns, from the tips of wands, from the ends of staffs, and, in Ichiro's case, his bare hands. As the offensive circle inches forward, the flame-wielders follow behind, spreading out so they cover not just the floor in front of them, but moving toward the sides of the hall, too, picking out whatever paper they can see and reducing it to ash. With each step, fewer and fewer monsters spring to life. The ones that have been slain dissolve into swirling, ink-splotch smears of acid-green magic as the Viceroy clearly abandons sustaining their existence, now that they are no longer any use to him.

"They do this for you," Kintyre says gravely. "Do not tell them their valor is for nothing. Do not make yourself worthless in their eyes."

Elgar wipes at his face with his abused cardigan cuffs. "I am, though."

"That doesn't matter," Bevel intones. "*They* believe you worthy. They believe in what you Wrote—in heroes, and magic, and fairy tales that always end with laughter and the victory of good over evil. The very least you can do is respect that."

"I respect my fans!" Elgar hisses, indignant.

"From one storyteller to another," Bevel says, clapping his shoulder. "It sure doesn't sound like it. Now, get ready to move."

All three men rise to their feet, crouching, watching the byplay of the monsters and the magicians.

"Ready? Now!" Kintyre says, and sprints toward the next convenient pile of rubble and furniture to hide behind.

"Why are we sneaking if I'm supposed to be bait?" Elgar says when they're crouched again. His shoulders are burning, the pain radiating down his arms, squeezing at his lungs, pressing at the bottom of his skull.

"Bait for the Viceroy," Kintyre says, pointing at the nearest creature—something out of the black lagoon, for all Elgar knows. "Not bait for a hungry behemoth."

"Fair enough," Elgar chokes.

"Move toward the flame-wielders," Kintyre says.

But before they can move again, Ichiro calls out: "Natural twenty!"

As one, the flame-wielders run toward the outer walls of the hall, and the offensive rangers duck behind pillars and tables. Only Forsyth and Lucy stand their ground, swords drawn and faces grim as they become the sole focal point for a dozen horrible beasts. Forsyth raises a hand, and though Elgar can't hear the Words of Shielding, he can see the air waver and glimmer around the two of them, like a thin layer of ice overlaid by spring-thaw water.

Ichiro holds out his hands, palms pointed down at the floor, and, screwing up his sweating face, screams: "I cast *Fireball!*"

"Duck!" Bevel shouts, hauling Elgar back behind a jagged outcropping of concrete.

"What's he going to do?" Elgar gasps, eyes watering from the sudden jerk on his ruined arm.

"Don't know, but everyone else is ducking, too, so it must—"

The rest of whatever it was Bevel was going to say is lost in the roaring *fa-woosh* of every piece of paper in the room catching fire, explosively, all at the same time. The remaining monsters squeal and screech and keen, shriveling up into charred nothingness before scattering like fireflies in the smoke.

The papers pop and snap, yet none of the broken wood or abandoned cloth around them catches. The flames surge, dancing red, and orange, and white-hot at their very hearts. And the moment their fuel is spent, they snuff out in curling black clouds that has everyone coughing and hiding their faces in their sleeves and collars.

Bevel and Kintyre are on their feet and halfway across the room before Elgar has even managed to get a clean breath. He trundles after them, limping, his shoulders burning.

"Impressive!" Kintyre calls out as they jog closer to the ragtag army.

"Oh, thanks, bro!" Ichiro pants, flexing his fists and grinning fit to burst. "But man, it's easy if you're a level-five Evoker. It's a wizarding sub-class, see? And you get a special ability called 'sculpt spell,' which lets you blast or burn things without causing as much collateral damage. I mean, yeah, a big old Hollywood-style fireball would have been just as effective, but not if we wanted to, you know, not set fire to everything else and kill everyone horribly."

"I'd like to learn that," Bevel says, approvingly. They are just a few steps away from Ichiro now, everyone feeling loose-limbed and confident that they are in the eye of the hurricane.

"Sure, man, we can roll up a character for—*hurk!*"

Something wet and hot splashes across Elgar's face so quickly that he doesn't get a chance to see what it is before he stumbles back, hands up. He reels, eyes screwed shut, spitting it out of his mouth. It tastes like pennies.

"*Fuck*," Elgar hears Bevel snarl, and then there are hands on his shoulders, drawing Elgar back, and away again. He's pushed down amid a jumble of chairs and tables, with no care for bashing his limbs.

"Ow!" Elgar says, indignant.

"Shh!" Bevel hisses back.

"What happened? Why are we...?" he trails off when he finally gets his eyes clear. It takes a second to focus them, to really see what he's looking at.

Red-and-black splatters on a blue field resolve themselves into... *dear god*, blood on a headless torso.

FOURTEEN

FORSYTH

have watched people die many times.

I stood over my father as the light flickered and snuffed in his eyes. I grasped my mother's hand as she struggled to breathe against the chest infection, and ultimately failed; when she went still and let out a rattling sigh, and I prayed for the inhale that never came. And I was there when Lanaea was struck down by the Deal-Maker Spirit, though I did not see the precise moment her Book was Shelved.

I've never seen decapitation, though; never gone to the execution grounds in Kingskeep; never even watched a chicken being beheaded for dinner. It's quicker than I thought it would be, and I will call that a blessing only because it means that Ichiro didn't suffer.

Pip gasps, sucking in a deep breath, immediately turning her face into my chest. Wrapping my arms around her, I watch the body crumple like paper. The head spins once in the air, and I squint against catching the expression on the face. I do not want to see. I do not want it to feature in my nightmares.

"Holy fucking fuck!" Elgar yelps. His voice echoes in the vast hall and covers the sound of the head hitting the floor. Thank the Writer, for if I had heard it, I don't think I would ever be able to get that out of my nightmares, either.

"What... how...?" Kintyre says, Foesmiter up, scanning

the room for what has done this horrible thing. A puff of ash and sparks, directly behind Ichiro, is the only clue. Some monster that I had missed, that I had failed to see, had struck the young warlock from behind. And then burned.

This is my fault. Again.

"Fuck, is this Station Five?" Pip whimpers against my jerkin, her face pressed against the lump that is the Shadow's Mask.

"I thought we agreed that the Stations didn't apply?" I ask her.

"I didn't think so, but now I... Forsyth, what do we do now?"

"Retreat and regroup," Bevel answers, herding Elgar back toward the ballroom.

"No!" comes a scream.

At first, I think it's one of the ashen-faced, silent, horrified cosplayers around us, but then the scream happens again: "No! Let go! Let me go!"

The voice is shrill and panicked, and it is not coming from the people around us. A grunt of physical struggle catches my ear, and Pip and I both turn to look over at a pile of unremarkable, overturned tables at the same moment. We are just in time, too, for through what appears to be a tear in a veiling spell, an elbow emerges—an elbow clad in mint green. It is followed by the rest of the arm: wrist and hand, shoulder and neck; long dark hair, loosed from its braids; a violently pink scarf.

"Ahbni!" Pip shouts, and takes a few running steps toward the young woman before Kintyre blocks her path. "What the hell, Kin? Get out of the way!"

"Wait," Kintyre says, and remains blocking Pip. "If she's pulled back in, you're not going with her."

"Yeah, that's not something I need to do a third time," Pip says, her fingernails biting into Kintyre's arm.

"But we can't just... someone, help her!"

Something has hold of Ahbni's other arm, dragging her back, and she skids and slides on the cement and ash as she struggles to escape. Bevel leaps forward and grabs her around the waist, yanking her out of the tear in nothingness.

When she is free, he tosses her aside, and she trips and falls hard to the ground. Bevel wasn't rescuing her, I realize; he was getting her out of his way. Bevel aims the ray-gun into the tear and fires, but whoever was there is gone already, lost to sight once more.

"Damn you to all seven of the hells!" Bevel snarls at the open air.

"Gee, fucking thanks!" Ahbni says, wincing as she struggles to flip onto her hands and knees. Bevel grunts and helps her to her feet.

"Are you hurt?" he asks, perfunctorily. Something about his abruptness niggles at me. Something about her shirt, and her phone, and the timing of her escape from the Viceroy. The fact that she is a guest liaison, and yet isn't. Something that—

"No," Ahbni says, and that's all she manages before my wife is barreling into her, wrapping her in a hug and simultaneously patting her down, looking for blood or bruises.

"Jesus Christ, are you okay?"

"I'm fine," Ahbni says, pushing Pip off and blushing. "Thank you, but I'm fine."

"Tell us what he has planned," Kintyre says, stepping up now. "Tell us how to get at him."

"Give her a few minutes, Kin—" Pip starts, pushing past me, but my brother cuts her off.

"We don't have a few minutes. There, on the floor, lies our first casualty of this war"—he points to Ichiro's remains with Foesmiter—"and the longer we stand around squawking, the more opportunity we give to the villain."

"Just give her a second to get her—"

"She is not Alis," Kintyre snaps. "She needs no babying. You are not her mother. Now, girl, his plans!"

"But I didn't—" Ahbni tries again. She cuts herself off, staring wide-eyed at the shocked crowd around us.

"Back to the ballroom," Bevel says, and it's loud enough, has enough command to it, that those few people still lingering around Ichiro's corpse start and turn away.

I am uncertain what is more respectful. Do we leave his body, and his head, where they lay? Or do we fetch them into the room? *Drag* them? And who among us would take up these tasks? I cannot leave it to my brother, can I? To ask him to haul away yet another body of yet another short-term companion because that is how our Writer constructs his plots, and I am too squeamish to accomplish the necessary task?

"Tell us what you know," Pip entreats Ahbni, looking into her eyes, brown to brown.

"But what if I do that, and he—?" Ahbni starts, then cuts her eyes toward the ballroom.

Here, I speak up. "We have to believe they can protect themselves."

"A bunch of civilians with fancy flashbangs?" Elgar snarls. His anger is unexpected. And Bevel and Kintyre both look moderately shamed. Interesting. "Haven't we just proven that they *can't?*" He points at Ichiro's remains, and the slowly widening pool of ichor glinting ruby in the emergency lights.

"I don't like our chances without all of us together," I explain. "We need brawn, yes, but brain in this instance, as well. And Pip's access to magic. Back into the ballroom with you," I hiss over my shoulder to the last lingering fellow in a blue shirt. "Get them all back inside, lock and bar the doors, don't come out. Keep everyone quiet. Do not attract attention."

"But—" the volunteer protests.

"Now." I say it in my Shadow Hand voice, and the blue-shirt obeys swiftly and silently.

The rest of us wait until the con-goers are shut away before exchanging serious looks.

"What we need is some more support," Bevel says. "No more untrained..." His gaze strays to Ichiro. "But they're all in Hain."

Elgar's eyes glint suddenly, a grin pulling at the side of his mouth. "Does anyone have a pen?"

"No," I say immediately. "There are enough people in danger here—"

"It's not utterly unreasonable," Pip says. "It's practically... heh, practically tradition at this point. Post-Station Five, pre-Act Three opener?" She is trying to be light about it, but her posture is weary, her eyes wandering to Ichiro at every spare second. She leans gingerly against a pile of rubble.

"You mean that damned dragon?" Kintyre pouts, and Ahbni's eyes go large and fearful.

"*Dragon*," she chokes.

"Wyndam, too?" Bevel muses.

"I don't think weakening Pip is wise at this juncture—" I begin.

Elgar steps up into the knot of people looming over Ahbni, elbowing right into her. Ahbni grunts, and drops her eyes. They snag on something behind Elgar, presumably the splatter of Ichiro's blood that paints his shirt in an arc like a morbid pageant-queen's sash.

"If we're not Writing out the next generation of heroes, then we have to do *something*. This isn't working. It isn't going to get him to show his hand." Elgar sneers down at Ahbni. "Now, come on, sweetheart. Stop stalling and—"

"Whoa, whoa!" Pip interrupts Elgar. "Hey now—"

"*Sweetheart!*" Ahbni hisses, eyes narrowing and venom in her voice. "You self-important douchewaffle!" She lashes out, trying to strike Elgar, but Kintyre jerks her to a stop before she can reach him.

"Hey now!" Elgar yelps. "You brown girls are violent!"

"No!" Ahbni corrects. "Just sick of your shit!"

"Come on, Elgar," Pip groans. "Don't escalate—"

"*Chitthu Pooka!*"

"Enough!" Kintyre snarls.

Ahbni cringes away from his voluminous anger, half-hiding behind Elgar, as if he will protect her from Kintyre's ire when he's so incensed himself. It is an odd choice—I would have assumed Ahbni would choose Pip as her shield.

"Now, Kin, no need to play Lord of the Hall here," Bevel admonishes, and Elgar protests over him, squawking indignantly over the insult.

"Quiet, everyone!" I shout over the sudden racket of every voice trying to be heard over the others. "Please!"

"Quiet, yourself!" my creator snarls. "I think the time for talk has passed, Forsyth! We need to—"

What we need to do, I do not know, for Elgar chokes off mid-sentence, eyes bulging out and jaw suddenly clenching.

"Elgar?" Pip asks, sheathing her sword and reaching for him as he tips backward on his heels, reeling, eyes rolling up in his head. "Elgar!"

She gets her arms on his wrists and, together with Bevel, lowers him safely to the ground.

"What happ—?" Kintyre starts, but then Ahbni starts *laughing.* "What have you—?"

She is grinning with manic glee, nostrils flared and arm shaking. And in her hand, Elgar's dagger—*Kintyre's* replica dagger—is soaked with gore.

"I am not your darling, your sweetheart, or your coffee fetcher!" Ahbni screeches. "You will treat me with the respect I deserve!"

"Jesus Christ," Pip breathes, and scrambles to get Elgar turned onto his stomach.

The stab wound is bright with blood, a red flower blooming at an alarming pace across his shirt and down his back.

Pip presses her fingers to Elgar's throat. "Still breathing," she says, "but his pulse is thready. We need to... we need to... *fuck, fuck*! We need a first aid kit, we need to... pressure on the wound! Bevel!" Bevel obligingly strips off his short-robe, balls it up, and jams it against the wound.

Pip screams for someone to find a paramedic in the crowd, for a doctor, for a paladin or healing mage. But even from here, even with her body between mine and Elgar's, I know that it is futile.

I know it in my bones. In my skin. In my blood. I feel the truth of it in the air.

It freezes me in place.

"Elgar," I gasp, my chest heaving, lungs burning. I cannot seem to get enough *air*. "Pip?"

Pip looks up at me across the expanse of her despair. She is red up to her elbows. Her chin trembles, her eyes filling with tears. She blinks, and salt water runs down her cheek, stained black by her eyeliner and mascara, like war paint, like a tattoo, literal marks of her mourning.

I know already. I know. We are losing him. He will not live.

"We are not stupid, vapid, screaming fangirls!" Ahbni is still screeching, near-incomprehensible through her fury. "We are not here to boggle young nerds and trick them into falling in love with us! We are not in costumes just to get your attention, and if some of us want to dress sexy, well then, we can! It makes us feel powerful, so fuck you for trying to prude- and slut-shame us all at once! Fangirls are legion. Fangirls are powerful! And screw you for telling anyone, least of all us, otherwise! How dare you take my money and then spit in my face?"

"Jesus, Kin, get her under control!" Pip snarls at my brother, and Kintyre shakes himself out of his horrified gawping. He swings his big, meaty arms around Ahbni's elbows and across her stomach, pinning her to his chest and lifting her off the floor.

"I hate you!" Ahbni screams, and in her hand, the bloody dagger quivers, splattering the floor. "I hate every-thing about you!"

"That's no reason to *stab* him!" Pip shouts up at her.

"Isn't it? Violence is the only language idiots like him speak! This is me, punching up!"

"Violence is *never* the only recourse!" Pip growls. And then suddenly, she sits up straight, looking Ahbni dead in the eye. "Where are you from?" Pip asks, her voice shaking, a non sequitur as my wife leaps in her usual fashion to a conclusion that is just beginning to become clear to me. "Where do you live?"

Her face filled with triumph, Ahbni hisses: "*Detroit.*"

All at once, the niggling at the back of my head set-tles. The truth comes clear.

Too late. Oh, too late, Forsyth, you utter useless fool!

"The troll was *you*. All this time, it was you. Your new ga-gaming p-p-partner... n-n-no. You—" I choke, having trouble speaking around my own self-recrimination.

"You... you *brought* him here. How could you?" Pip challenges, staring at Ahbni with horror and regret, both. Blood drips from the tips of her fingers, splashes against the floor. "Your eyes aren't even green. How could you *choose* this?"

Ahbni grins, triumphant. "I've done what no one else could! I've silenced a monster!"

"He's *getting better!*" Pip screams, cradling Elgar's body. "He's growing! He's *trying!* You can't just—just—*execute* people who don't think like you! You can't—"

"And I'll be rewarded for it!" Ahbni shouts.

"By him?" Kintyre snarls, tightening his hold. His biceps strain against his shirt as Ahbni writhes, feet flailing in the air to no avail. "Are you stupid?"

"I'm not stupid!" Ahbni protests, her pride pricked.

"You've gotta be!" Pip seethes. "You don't think there are any corpses in the rubble upstairs? You don't think that he intends to kill every single person in this building? Really? You don't think we're all next? That the Viceroy isn't out to kill *all* of us? It's what he does. He won't stop until he's laid waste to this entire building and everyone in it. He's a sick, sadistic fuck."

"But that's not... that's not what he..." She blinks, and swallows hard, eyes darting around the room. Her shock is real, I think, and not an act.

"You didn't put two and two together?" Pip asks. "It's in the books!"

"Well, I've never read them closely!" Ahbni protests.

"But you know you hate them all the same," Pip hisses. "How can you claim to critique if you're only reading for what will support your—?"

"He said that—"

"Not the point right now!" Kintyre snarls. "*Help the Writer.*"

"It pierced his lung, I think," Bevel says, his voice shaky in a way that I've never heard from my brother-in-law before.

"For fuck's sake, Forsyth, stop standing there!" Pip snaps at me.

Am I just standing here?

I am.

My feet don't seem to be moving, even though I command them to do so. My hands twitch at my sides, as if I am already pressing them to the wound to aid Bevel, but they are not on Elgar's body. They are not dipped in the blood of the man who invented me. My breath comes shallow and sharp. Swollen with grief, a hot fist of anger and surprise, my heart is struggling to pump blood through the constriction of seized terror that afflicts my veins. I try to speak, try to lick my lips, try to *anything*, and the most I can do is blink mechanically and let my mouth flop open, let out a harsh, low "*haaaaa*" sound that wavers and stumbles as I run out of breath.

The look on my creator's face might have been comical if it weren't so horrifying. Slack jaw, wide eyes, surprise and pain pinching the sides of his mouth white and thin. He is propped on his side, Pip and I before him, Pip pressing her knees into his belly to give Bevel leverage, and Bevel behind, jamming his increasingly red-soaked robe against Elgar's back.

"Forsyth, *please*," Pip sobs, face upturned and pale with her own grief, cheeks wet with her own terror. "*Do something.*"

The "please" is what knocks me back into my own body, into the moment, and I drop to my knees beside Elgar. I fear—I *expect* him to be dead already, but Elgar blinks up at me, smiling dopily through what must be his unbelievable agony.

"Hi," he chokes, a bubble of red spittle popping with the vowel.

"Hush," I say to him, and then, one hand laced tightly with Pip's free one so I can draw upon her magic, I recite all the Words of Healing to which I am privy.

"It's too deep," Bevel grits out in a whisper, his voice

tight. When I look up at him, I see sweat beading across his forehead. The tendons of his neck stand out, he is clenching his jaw so hard. His shoulders bulge with the effort of stopping the bleeding. "Forssy, it's too much."

"No!" Pip cries. "No, just... try harder!"

"*Bao bei*," I say softly. "Th-the ma-mah-magic isn't-t st-stron-ng enou-gh h-here. And th-the Wo-Wo-Words can-n only do-do-do s-so mu-ah-ch."

"No! Don't stop Speaking them! Keep going!" my wife orders, snot on her upper lip and her cheeks now splotchy, her eyes swollen with her tears. "If we can... Elgar, just hold on." She turns her head back toward the ballroom door. "Isn't one of you guys a fucking healer? Come on!"

Someone inside the room yelps, and the sound of feet pounding toward us rings out, but they are going to be too late. Too late. Kintyre drops down beside Pip, grips the ball of our tangled fingers, and recites the Words of Healing in tandem with me.

"The bleeding is slowing, but not enough," Bevel grinds out. "Kin."

"Where's Ahbni?" Pip asks, and we both start when we see that Kintyre has bound her to a piece of protruding rebar with her own pink scarf. She is straining, working to get away, but the knot is too efficient, the material too thick.

The Words seem to bring Elgar back to himself enough that he is able to focus on our faces. He squints at me thoughtfully, then slides his gaze to Pip. He doesn't linger long on her, turning his head slightly to take in Bevel instead. He squints at him, too, and then finally, his eyes settle on Kintyre.

I shouldn't feel overlooked, or offended. I know I shouldn't. But it feels, suddenly, very much like being the ignored and forgotten younger son once again, skipped over in favor of Kintyre. Bright, shining Kintyre, who does everything the wrong way and yet still holds the greater affection of the world.

Elgar has had a year with me, I tell myself, squashing down my jealousy for his attention, and regretting all the times I had pushed him away, and the time in each other's company we had subsequently lost. *He has had mere hours with Kintyre and Bevel. Do not begrudge him this.*

Elgar lifts a hand, half-curled, toward Kintyre's face. Without ceasing his drone of Words, my brother takes it and presses the old man's palm to his cheek. He doesn't wince at the usual jump of electricity between creator and creation, and I wonder if it's because Kintyre is hiding his reaction or because the strength of the unnatural feeling is fading as Elgar drowns slowly in his own blood.

"Weren't... s'posed to... love 'im," Elgar grunts, and each word brings red foam to his lips.

The pronouncement is startling, shocking, and though I can't speak for Bevel or Kintyre, I feel as if Elgar has just slapped me in the face. How could he choose to use his last breaths on this? To decry the happiness that my brother and his trothed have fought so hard and so long to make their own? How controlling, how spiteful must Elgar be?

"Stop talking," Pip insists. "Just breathe. Just keep breathing."

Kintyre's eyes narrow, becoming even icier, his lips curling inward as he bites them to keep from wasting these last few moments in shouting.

Elgar's mouth melts into a beatific smile, and he blinks so slowly that I fear for a moment that his eyes may not open again. When they do, he focuses hard on Kintyre.

"Glad you... do, though," he says.

The reversal hits Kintyre so hard he grunts like he's

been punched in the gut, the breath whooshing out of him. His expression breaks into a sunrise, and half a moment later, crumples into sorrow.

"Don't go," he implores. He lets go of Pip's hand to grasp Bevel's wrist, desperate for a connection with his trothed at this moment.

"Glad you're... all loved," Elgar hisses. "L'cy... do me... f'vor?"

"Anything," Pip vows.

"Love the books ag'in. Write 'em if they ask."

"What? No!" Pip gasps in horror. "I can't! I'm an academic! I don't write fiction! You do it! Stay, and write more!"

Elgar makes a slight motion with his head that might be a shake. "You *care*. P'tect Hain with tha... tha TV... bring F'syth."

"I... I will. I vow," Pip says, and then gasps as something invisible seems to clutch hard at her chest. She coughs, eyes screwing shut, and when she opens them again, they glow violet. For just a moment, just one very brief second, *violet*.

What does it mean? I do not have time to wonder, to ask, even. I have no time; there is *no time*.

"F'syth," Elgar moans.

"I'm so-sorry," I say, and I can't seem to make my voice get any louder. It's a harsh, low whisper, choked by sorrow and the onset of grief, and all things that I never said to my creator, and now, never will. "Elga-gar, ple-please, for-for-forgive me."

He smiles dopily, eyelids drooping, and the corner of his mouth peels back in a grimace that, even now, he is clearly attempting to disguise as a smile. His teeth are red with frothing blood, and a tiny ruby stream of the stuff escapes from the quirked corner of his lips.

"For?" Elgar whispers.

"I'm a f-fu-fuck up, aren't I? A c-c-co-omplete and utt-er t-t-tit. I m-made eve-ry single wr-wr-wr-wrong choice there wa-was to make. I was over-overconfident and b-buh-blind." I sob, grasping Elgar's other hand tight, where it is pinned against the floor. "Oh, f-f-for-forgive me. Elgar, p-p-p-pluh-please!"

A man dressed in white healer's robes shoves, sudden-ly, in between Bevel and I, uncapping a phial and dump-ing its glowing blue contents over Bevel's fingers, against the wound. Most of it runs down his arms, ineffectual.

"Try again!" Pip implores him.

"No, m'boy," Elgar mutters. "No, no, no..."

"Stop it!" Pip sobs. "Just... stop it. Come on, Elgar. It's your magic. You made it up. It should be working on you!"

"Last sec'rt," Elgar says, grinning now, mischievous-ness warring in his eyes with the pain. He takes a deep, bubbling breath, gathers his strength to speak clearly. "Viceroy has no love in him. His mother, she lov'd 'im, but... m'be 'cause I nev'r unnersood what's mys'lf."

"No..." Pip says. "Elgar, no, don't say that."

The healer dumps out another phial, but it is diluted in the blood. It's not working. Nothing's happening. It's like the liquid is still just a prop. It's infuriatingly ineffec-tual and each uncorked phial smashes what little hope we are clinging to just that much more.

"Fans... people I pa-pay—a-agents, PAs, but... but not real love. Not... not fam... family."

"You're *our* family," Pip says fiercely, grabbing his hand alongside mine. "We love you."

"Do... you?" Elgar asks, a dribble of blood appearing at the lower corner of his mouth. "All 'f you?" He tries to roll his head to the side to see Kintyre.

"Absolutely," Bevel says, and there are tears on his cheeks now, too, fat and rolling, and I can't recall ever having seen my brother-in-law cry before. Not even when I stepped into the Overrealm for the first time, when I thought I'd never see them again. "Always."

"Oh," Elgar says, and it is a great gusting woosh. Blood splatters his lips. "Tha's nice. No... na nice... *copacetic.*"

He exhales then, long and slow. It goes on forever, for an age, for an eon. Silence rings through the hall. Even Ahbni's struggles have stilled. We watch, each of us, eyes wide and breaths caught in our whole, unharmed lungs. We wait.

But his chest doesn't rise again.

Bevel is uttering Words of Healing, Words of Comfort, Words of Reversal, over, and over, and over, the first prayer I have ever seen anyone offer up to our creator. Pip's eyes flare violet with each Word, whites showing all around.

"I hear them," she whispers, licking her lips. "Forsyth, I *hear*—"

And then, like a tap being shut, the flow of Bevel's Words cuts off. He sits back on his heels, lowers his head, heaves a wrenching groan, and *howls.*

"Oh god, *no,*" Pip blurts, tears and snot mingling and bubbling on her lips. Her voice is like a crack of thunder; it shatters the moment, the stillness. She turns into my arms, thumps her forehead painfully against my sternum, presses her mouth to my jerkin, and *screams.* Her hands fist in my sleeves, and she cries: "Stay! Stay! Oh god, don't go, don't go!"

"I'm here," I assure her, my own hands coming up to cradle the back of her head with no concern for the blood I'm smearing on her skin, her clothes, into her hair, into the dips and valleys of her scars. "I'm not going anywhere."

I'm not sure if it's the truth, though. My extremities

have begun to tingle. My breath feels shallower, less real. Like I'm not getting enough oxygen from the air. My ears have begun to ring with a high, tinny whine. And under that, I think I hear... I hear a voice, calling out.

"Wyndam," Kintyre breathes, and his eyes are glassy, his posture loose. Bevel looks the same. Dazed and staring at his fingers, he licks his lips over and over again, chasing sensation.

"Don't fade," she moans. "I couldn't stand it if—"

"*Bao bei*," I choke, panic rising hard and fast, burning in my throat. "Alis!" I scrabble at Pip's shoulders, trying to force my fingers to curl, to grasp, to *hold on*, but they are dead weights at the end of my wrists. My skin washes cold, and hot, prickling and sweating, and no, Writer, no, I don't—I don't want to—I don't—

"I don't want to go!"

"I forbid it!" Pip shouts, and she grabs my face in her bloody hands, holding hard and tight. It should hurt, but I can barely feel it. She looks up, eyes flaring violet again, lashes spiked with tears. "You stay! You all *stay!*"

The command hits me behind the heart hard enough that I sway on the spot. I hear Kintyre and Bevel grunt. Feeling returns to my body like a stone dropping through my stomach. I gag and gasp, light-headed and nauseous. Kintyre flops back onto his arse with an ungodly belch, and Bevel covers his mouth with his hand, pressing the other against his stomach and swallowing hard.

"What did you—?" Kintyre tries to say, and has to stop halfway through to gulp and gasp. "Pip, how did—?"

In the periphery of my vision, the healer jerks back into motion. His face is still covered by his hood, but he is focused on the blood on his hands. He too retches, but it must be from the gore.

"Did we almost...?" Bevel asks, and his voice quavers. "Are we going to vanish?"

"No," I whisper over the top of my wife's head. "Not anymore."

Relieved, Bevel drops the blood-soaked short-robe and wraps his arms around his trothed. Kintyre is white-faced and shaking, eyes wide and shocky. Bevel pulls Kintyre down, arms around his head, hiding his trothed's face against his own neck. Kintyre heaves a massive sob and clings to Bevel like a drowning man. I stand. Or try to. My knees wobble; my spine cannot seem to unbow. There is nothing nearby for me to clutch to stay upright. I sway.

Splayed on the floor, hateful and obscene, Elgar is still and breathless.

His eyes, blue and frightened, still stare up at the ceiling. His hands are lax at his sides, his legs flopped akimbo. His stomach and chest are bare and splashed with red. The hole in his back seeps blood like a spring in a glade, still, and it is too much. It is *disrespectful*.

I lean down, shaking, wobbling, and gently, respectfully, lower his eyelids for him. My fingers don't seem to want to work, and it takes me much longer than I am proud of to unpick the knot keeping my sash tied tight around my hips. When I have it free, I shake out the length of Turn-russet silk. The golden thread shimmers in the overhead lights, and, beside me, Kintyre sucks back a sobbing gasp.

Lightly, gently, I kneel and lay the length of cloth over Elgar's form. Clothing his nakedness. Blocking the harsh overhead glow from his face.

And then a noise from behind us grabs my attention.

At first, I think it is the Viceroy, come to finish us all while we're distracted by death, but then I realize it is the sound of whimpering, and fabric tearing. Ahbni scrambles to her feet in my periphery. She is shaking, shocky as well, her makeup running down her face with her own tears. As if she has *any right* to weep when she was the one who murdered him.

"You!" I hear myself roar, and I am on my feet before I really register that I intend to stand. Then two sets of strong arms wrap around my shoulders, pressing, gripping hard, holding me back. "No!"

But they are not strong enough. They are not stronger than my rage, than my agony, than my *grief.* I will *kill* that bitch for this. I will... I will—

I know my brother's fighting techniques better than he thinks I do. I've watched him spar. I've read Bevel's scrolls.

I drop to my knees, startling both men and working against their hold. My arms slip through their hands, and I dash forward from my crouch like a sprinter.

"Forsyth!" Pip shrieks when I break free. "Stop!"

Ahbni doesn't expect me to go for her. Perhaps she expects me to stay at Elgar's side, perform the first aid exercises that are meant to pound life back into a body. No. I do not feel like fighting for a life already extinguished, not today. Today, I am going to revenge it.

She dives for the dagger, which Kintyre had foolishly left on the floor when he'd forced her to drop it. Overconfident arse. No matter. I am faster than a child with a weapon she does not know how to use.

Her long curtain of hair makes it hard for me to get purchase on her neck, and she slips away at first, screaming in terror when she realizes what I mean to do. That I mean to harm her. To *end* her. She slashes wildly, amateurishly, at me with the dagger—defiled, bloody, *desecrated*—and I slam my forearm against her wrist. The blade clatters away. Ahbni backs up a step, then another, hands up and shoving, slapping at me, and I don't *care.* I don't care. Let her slap and scratch all she likes.

It's easy, Writer. It is so easy to sweep a leg out, to trip her. She falls backward, eyes wide, whites showing all around, but she doesn't land. I fist my hand in her shirt, right above her throat. With all the force of my rage, I slam her down against the cement floor. Her head bounces, there is a loud *crack*, and Ahbni convulses. I crouch over her, knees pressing her arms into the ground as her hands flail uselessly, like leaves in a strong breeze on the end of a fragile twig. So easy to snap.

The skin of her neck is silky—smooth to the touch, I note absently—when I wrap my hands around it and *squeeze*.

"Stop him!" Pip sobs somewhere behind me. "Kin! Stop him!" And then Pip is beside me, Elgar's blood still warm on her hands as she scrapes and scrabbles at my wrists. "Enough! Forsyth, please!"

But my vision is hazed with red, with rage, with agony, and all I can see, all I *want* to see is the way Ahbni's face is turning red, and puce, her tongue growing fat in her mouth, her eyelids fluttering, those pretty false lashes flicking up and down as her eyes roll in her head and her heels keep the tempo of her death, beating on the floor.

Pip shoves hard at my shoulders, but I will *not* be swayed. I will not. I am the Shadow Hand of Hain. I am the Lordling of Lysse. I am the arbiter of justice, of what is right, and I say that this loveless, heartless bitch must *die*.

Pip sways back, and then, balling her fist, cracks me hard across the jaw. Those months of preparing Pip for a physical fight, those hours in boot camps and martial arts classes all turn against me, condensed into a single blow. I am thrown off the girl. I lose my grip on her throat. I lose my grip on wakefulness.

Black swims up and over my eyes, stars dazzling in

the periphery, and I feel a hard, crunching jolt as my right elbow slams hard into the concrete floor. And, just like that, I am down, on my back. I try to rise, hands curled into talons, determined to finish—I will *finish*—but a blow to my stomach lays me flat, knocks all the air from me, and I flop back, gasping and hacking and trying not to choke on my own vomit. Pip stands over me, her face like a thunderstorm, hands on her hips like a conquering giant. I try to kick her ankle, feeling petulant, *wronged*, but she shifts out of my reach. Horrible *bully*. Just like my brother!

How dare she stop me?

"How dare—" I hiss and cough, but I cannot *breathe.*

I roll onto my side, reach again for my prey, but Pip is between us. Her back is to me now, and she has Ahbni cradled against her chest, rubbing her back and helping the bitch *breathe*, the Writer-be-damned *traitor*. Ahbni is coughing worse than I am, sucking and struggling. Pip is pressing the fabric of her shredded scarf against a gush of red on the back of Ahbni's head.

Ha! A touch for me, then, at least!

If I could just—but Kintyre steps between us, and I snarl at him, wordless and infuriated by my frustrated goal.

"Lay back, and do not even *think* of moving," my wife threatens, craning her head around to meet my gaze. "I will not hesitate to knock you cold, Forsyth Turn. Don't think that I won't."

My revenge stymied for the time being, I bare my teeth at her in a soundless threat, and lay back, hands out, belly exposed, subdued. I know very well how to play submissive to my brother, how to pretend contrition or acquiescence, how to portray one thing while plotting another. And Kintyre, thick-headed, trusting *fool* that he has always been, *believes* me.

Kintyre swings away to crouch beside Pip, the soft-hearted, softer-skulled, blasted *buffoon.*

"Have we not all learned our lessons about sparing the villains?" I snarl at them both, from the ground. When Kintyre makes no move to stop me, I sit up. "*Have we not* invited disaster enough?"

"You don't get to say that after you tried to... after you... how could you?" Pip says, her voice harsh and graveled with her choler and disappointment.

"Pip," I say, holding my hands out to her, wanting to pull her into my arms, to feel her warmth, to know that her heart beats and her lungs work because they are doing so right against my own flesh, where I can *feel* it.

"No," she says,. "No. You don't get to... not after you... oh my god, I am so angry with you I could... don't you dare touch me right now!"

"End her, so that we may finish this!" I shout. "Come now! She is Bootknife! She is the sidekick that one must destroy to summon forth the final antagonist! Do not *coddle* her!"

"She's just a confused kid who thought she was doing the right thing," Pip insists.

"Pip, *please*," I shout. "I know you want her to be good. I know you see much of yourself in her and are desperate that she be only misunderstood, but her eyes are not green! She entered into this venture of her own volition. She made this choice!"

"And so, what, you'll kill her for it?" Pip asks.

"Of course!" I say. "Hainish justice dictates—"

"This isn't *Hain*!" And her derision, her hatred is worse than a slap in the face, a punch to the gut, a crack across my jaw. My wife *hates me*, and it stabs, and stings, and burns. At first, I am indignant, filled with an incandescent righteousness, for how dare she judge me so harshly when all I was doing was avenging my creator, the man who would be my *father*, when she would do the same to anyone who harmed Martin or Mei Fan or *wai po*.

But the truth is, she did not. Pip did not try to harm Ahbni for hurting Elgar.

Kintyre, startled by Pip's harsh words, stares at my wife. "She murdered Elgar Reed," he says. "The punishment for murder is death."

"Not in the Overrealm, it isn't!" Pip says. "You can't just—"

"Do you really think she'll regret it?" I ask. "That she will meekly go to jail and become reformed? Pip, do not be a *fool*."

"Overrealm justice for a crime committed in the Overrealm!" Pip insists.

"You cannot call to witness two people who do not exist!" I say, punching the air in the direction of Bevel, still guarding Elgar's corpse. "And I will never support you in this. Let me finish what I started!"

"No!"

"*Yes!*" a voice howls, but it is not mine. It is not Kintyre's, not Bevel's, nor even Pip's.

It comes from behind us, where the healer has stood this whole time. His white robes dissolve into black smoke, leaving nothingness in its wake. There is nothing there.

"Yes!" the healer's voice echoes again, and I know it now. Know it for what it is. It is the Viceroy's.

"Go on," he says from nowhere, and everywhere. "Go on, Forsyth Turn. Kill her."

"You *want* your protégé to die?" Bevel snarls, and the ray-gun is once again in his hand, aimed at the sky, waiting for the opportunity to fire it.

"*My* protégé?" the Viceroy sneers. "Reader, surely

she was *yours*."

Pip makes a horrible gulping sound, screwing her eyes shut and shaking her head once. A hit, for the Viceroy, and a palpable one. "She wasn't," Pip hisses.

"You already thought of her as such. Young, moldable, teachable. She wanted you, you know. Wanted to save you from your oafish husband, your chained existence as wife and mother."

"I *don't need saving!*" Pip snarls. "This is what I chose!"

"Is it?" the Viceroy chuckles. "Or is it where I put you? My little puppet. My little mole in the Turnish house."

The scars on Pip's back flare briefly, and she arches in pain, clenches her fists and jaw. "You like your little puppets, too. The trope is that the villain disposes of the sidekick the moment they stop being useful, but you held on to Bootknife for years and years. He was hot-headed and temperamental, and you kept him because you *liked* him."

"Because I had put so much work into him. But her? What does she matter to me?" he challenges.

"After all the work you must have put into getting her on your side?" Pip counters, arguing for the value of a life that only she believes has any.

"Do you really think I'd need to coerce her?" the Viceroy sneers. His tone is both invasive and intimate, and so very wrong. "The people in your world are so filled with hate. I barely have to lift a finger to incite them to fury and violence. They murder each other in the streets and call it policing. They threaten and stalk and harm each other in messages, and texts, and through avenues of communication that we couldn't even begin to fathom trapped between our covers, in our neat little worlds. Do it, Lordling. *Do it.*"

"No," I say, and stand, hands deliberately flexed at my sides. Empty. "No, I shan't." Not if it is what the Viceroy wants.

"*Do it!*" the voice shrieks, and the emergency lights flicker. "Coward!"

"I am not the coward! Why do you not show yourself?" I shout back. "Why sneak around us like this?"

Kintyre turns to blink oafishly at me. "Forsyth," he says. "The Viceroy always sneaks. You know this."

"He does?" I ask, staring goggle-eyed at my brother, floored by his insight. I shouldn't be. I keep forgetting that my brother isn't actually as much of a fool as I have led myself to believe.

"Yes," Bevel chimes in. "He never steps in himself until he's certain the day is his."

"No, that's not right," Pip says, face screwing up in confusion. "The first time I was there, he came down the stairs into the Rookery. He showed himself. He fought Forsyth and I in person."

"Then he only did so because he was certain he had already won," Kintyre explains. "He'll never show himself when he thinks there's a chance he might lose. He waits. He sends others."

Pip looks down at Ahbni, still unconscious, but breathing.

"Okay," Pip says, more to herself than to us. "Okay, braniac. You're the smarty-pants here. Figure it out. Enemy's weakness revealed. What do we do with it." She chews on her thumbnail for a moment, nervous, eyes flicking back and forth as she stares at nothing, lost in her own head, in her own internal, mental Excel. Then, suddenly, with a jolt and a gasp, she looks up, and straight into my eyes.

Again, that violet flare passes from the rim of her iris to the pupil, like arcing lightning.

"The Stations!" Pip hisses. "We're at Station Six, the crisis point and the squeeze on the protagonists. There are seven in an Elgar Reed quest. The Viceroy won't reveal himself right now, because he hasn't won yet. We're not at the end of his game. We're not at the end of the... we're not at the apex of the plot, the climax." Pip lays Ahbni's head against her thigh, and holds her hand slanted upwards in demonstration. "We're only here." She points to her knuckles. "He'll come out here." She points to the tips of her fingers. "But if we wait that long, we fall into his trap. Into the predictability."

"Is that a bad thing?" Bevel hisses, and I can see his own mind racing to catch up with her. "We always win in the end."

"Yeah, but this isn't a story anymore. And the author is dead," Pip says softly. "Does this make us free of authorial intent? The Viceroy can die now, because he was always meant to live? Can I finally escape what it means to be a woman in Hain? Is... the stasis cracked? Will what worked before work still? Can we rely on Kintyre winning the day *because* he always wins the day?"

"What do you mean?"

"Forsyth Turn is one of the good guys," Pip says. "In the books, he has the capacity, the means, the motivation, the intelligence to go dark, but he never does. Why? Because the author wanted him to be a good guy. And yet, the moment Elgar... you went for Ahbni like a madman."

"That's not the same," I protest.

"But it's different enough. The narrative has *changed*. It's fractured. You win, but he gets away. Every time. But this isn't like the other stories," Pip cautions.

"Isn't it?" I ask, catching on to where her thinking is leading her. "Are we not still characters in a book? Are we not still beholden to how we were Written?"

"Yeah, but then you wouldn't have attacked..." Pip

begins, looking up into my face, and swallowing hard on the rest of her sentence at what she sees there.

"Would I not have, *bao bei?*" I ask softly. "I am a kind man, but I am also a just one."

"I'm just saying that we can't rely on this going our way this time," Pip says with a sour, pinched look on her face, which means my comment will not go unremarked upon or un-discussed later. "This is the third book in the trilogy. We might defeat the Viceroy, yes, but not without someone else dying. Not without one of the heroes falling, to make the narrative more poignant. And you'd do that, wouldn't you, Elgar?" She looks over at Elgar's remains, her own body slumped with misery and grief and exhaustion. "We all have heirs. There's a protagonist to take up our mantel and avenge us. Wyndam, and Alis, and the Lady Gyre, and Lewko Pointe. There's a new generation ready to step in. *Fucking* trilogies." The violet sparks again.

"So, one of us is going to die?" Kintyre asks.

"If we let the narrative play out?" Pip says. "Maybe."

"What do we do?"

Pip turns to me, grinning. "We hack it."

The violet has infused the whole of her iris now, like the green did when she was under the Viceroy's sway. Whose power is this that shines out of her gaze now? Whose magic? Whose *intent?*

And just like that, I know. *Yes, of course!*

"Pip, yes," I say, seizing her shoulders. "Elgar passed the series on to you. You are the Writer. You can *change how the story goes.*"

Pip blinks for a moment, startled, and then her mouth curls into a wicked, fiendish grin devoid of all joy.

"We get him *now,*" Pip snarls. "Get him to come out. Get him to break his pattern. Get him to fight for himself. And then we kill the motherfucker."

"How?" Bevel asks.

"Threes!" Pip says. "Forsyth, it's a trilogy! The third book!"

"Ah!" I say, understanding what she's aiming for. "I see!"

"I don't," Kintyre grumbles. "What are you on about?"

Pip grins, but it is a knife slice of clever smugness. "*His name.*"

"Varnet, son of Edvane," I call into the open air, lacing my command with Words of Compulsion, Words of Obedience, the kind of dark and dangerous Words that only Shadow Hands know. Pip grips my hand, gives my Words power and possibility, sends them into the air with a faint purplish curl of watercolor magic. "I compel you with your first name to appear before us, stripped of your glamour!"

The air around us shivers and tingles with ozone. The emergency lights flicker and crackle. A low chuckle builds like fog around us, echoing in the rubble. From the direction of the ballroom, I hear people begin to shout and panic once again.

Bevel's eyes widen as recognition settles there. He places a hand on Pip's shoulder, fingers brushing her bare nape. His own voice heavy with the Shadow Hand's less savory Words of Revelation, Words of Dominance, and Words of Binding, he shouts: "Viceroy, former right hand of King Carvel Tarvers, betrayer and traitor, I compel you with your second name to show yourself, to come before us unarmed!"

Kintyre starts and looks around, eyes wide. "I don't know his other name!" he hisses.

"I got it," Pip says, and sets Ahbni's head down on the ground gently to stand. Her chest is splotched with blood, a grim waistcoat to go with her elbow-length red gloves. She throws her head back and bellows: "Child and Heir of Solinde! By the Deal-Maker magic carved into my bones, put there by your own hand, I compel you to appear before us!"

The laughter careens up into an incredulous screech. "How do you know her name? How do you *know*?" the Viceroy squeals.

"Show yourself!" I shout.

The laugh condenses, tightens, crystallizes. Just over my left shoulder.

I spin around, snap the tie holding Smoke into its sheath, and heft the sword. Then I stumble back a step when the Viceroy wraps one gloved hand around the sword's tip. "My dear Lordling Turn," he hisses, "all you needed to do was ask."

FIFTEEN

FORSYTH

I slash the blade at his face. The Viceroy dodges backward, laughing with a manic grin that is cartoonish in its grimacing horror. Pip bolts across the floor to intercept him, sword flashing, and once more, I am grateful that my wife enjoys exercise and jogs so often. But her sword work is clumsy, and she telegraphs her movements too easily. He dodges her, as well.

"Ah, Mrs. Turn! Where's that implausible spawn of yours? Is she well?" the Viceroy asks conversationally, skipping backward, as if we had met on the street in passing instead of in the midst of pursuing him with blades drawn. His footsteps leave acid-green scorch marks on the cement, magic bolstering his retreat, making him fleet and nimble.

"You don't get to talk about her," Pip snarls, slashing at him again.

"Oh?" the Viceroy asks, eyebrow cocked, and he spins hard on the ball of his foot, doubling back and skidding to a stop over Ahbni's supine body. He straddles her shoulders, hands on his hips, and giggles.

Kintyre and Bevel, who had been pacing us to try to find their own opening, spin quick to face him, weapons high. Bevel fires the ray-gun, but the Viceroy deflects it with a spluttering ball of phosphorescence.

"Ah, ah," he says. "Mind yourself. You wouldn't want to harm her, now, would you?"

"I thought you didn't care about your new sidekick," Bevel challenges.

The Viceroy sighs in delight, as if just looking at Bevel is as relaxing and refreshing as a hot cup of coffee on a chilly morning. We are all sweating and red-faced, stinking of adrenaline and desperation in this airless, lightless concrete box, but one glance at Bevel's face and the Viceroy looks like he has just stepped out of the most pleasant springtime meadow.

"Oh, Bevel," the Viceroy says, voice dropping to a seductive register, and it is close, *intimate*. "Hello."

In an instant, he's abandoned his perch over Ahbni, and is pressed right up against Bevel's body like a lover. Bevel tries to flip the gun around, to aim it at the Viceroy's head, and a tendril of green magic wraps itself around Bevel's wrist and wrenches his hand behind his back, jamming it upward so hard I can hear Bevel's shoulder *pop*. A flare of green flame consumes the ray-gun, and the prop melts right out of Bevel's hand, pooling in a puddle of hot plastic on the floor and filling the room with the acrid stench of burning chemicals.

My brother-in-law only grimaces and grunts, grinding his molars together, not giving the Viceroy the satisfaction of voicing his pain.

"I've *missed* you," the Viceroy whispers. His hand on Bevel's cheek is tender, and light, but also strong; his fingers brush the lower lid of Bevel's left eye, seeking out the scar that Bootknife had left in the furrow under his eye two decades prior, when Bevel had been young, and strong, and handsome. "You've gotten older, but your eyes... your fine, blue eyes are the same. Oh, Bevel, what a cruel mistress Time is. Look at you and Kintyre—old men. White hair and wrinkles and sagging faces. I should pluck out your eyes now, before they are lost behind cataracts. Would you thank me for it, preserving your one true beauty? I think you would."

"Get off him!" Kintyre snarls.

"Tut tut, Great Hero of Hain," the Viceroy teases. "So *jealous*. You've shared him often enough before. Surely you can't object to letting me have a taste?"

The Viceroy, golden eyes on Kintyre, slowly and deliberately leans forward and bites Bevel's bottom lip.

"Aren't you sick of playing second to this brainless barbarian?" the Viceroy smears against Bevel's grimace. The rest of us dare not try to attack now, lest he use Bevel as a shield, or decide to kill him immediately and toss him aside. "Join me, Bevel. I'll cast off the girl. I'd rather have you instead."

"Rot in all seven of the hells," Bevel sneers, turning his head as far away as he is able.

The Viceroy sighs dramatically and pushes Bevel back hard. Kintyre is there, though, keeping him from breaking his arm in his fall, getting his trothed immediately back on his feet. The Viceroy paces back to Ahbni, daringly presenting his back to us.

"So, I am stuck with this one, aye? Well, as Mrs. Turn rightly pointed out, I *have* invested so much time in her. It would be a waste to just toss her and her delightful, delicious hatred aside quite so callously. She needs a more appropriate name, though, don't you think? Something really *Hainish*. What do you think of Whisperblade? She did slide your dagger into our creator so quietly, so very *neatly*. And it was so very *appropriate* that she killed him with the knife you stole from my dear Bootknife."

"It was never his blade to begin with!" Kintyre snarls. "It wasn't mine, either."

"Details, details," the Viceroy dismisses.

"Or you could just not," Pip offers. "Come on, Vicey-wiessy. There are so many other raging lunatics in the world. MRAs, internet trolls, people who don't believe in feminism, alt-right Nazis. Why use *her*?"

"Why?" the Viceroy laughs. "Because she asked me to. Because dear sweet Maddie knew her from an online forum, and I could *taste* the anger in her words. Because she gave me refuge from your police in Detroit. Because I knew she could make you love her. Because she reminded me of you." He pauses, cocking his head in a theatrical show of thoughtfulness, one finger pressed to his lips. "You know, Reader, I think she reminds me entirely *too much* of you. And do you know what I've always wanted to do to you?"

Pip takes a shaking step backward, hands up to cover her face, to fend him off. "*No*," she grunts, guttural, primeval.

Ahbni is, as far as I can tell, still unconscious from the blow I delivered to her head. It's been so long now that it's possible her brain is even swelling, that I dealt her irreparable damage. At the time, it didn't seem like a concern, but seeing her limp and gray-faced now, her chest rising jerkily, with the Viceroy's blade poised by her jugular, a flash of guilt pierces my heart, swift and deep.

Oh, Writer's balls, what have I done? She cannot get up and run. She cannot even protect herself.

A flash of something slim and metallic green and small in the Viceroy's hand catches my attention—the glint off a blade. An arc of motion too fast to really see, and far too fast to stop. A splatter of red on the concrete.

"*No!*" Pip screams, lunging for Ahbni, hands out to stopper up the gaping smile ripped in her throat. But the Viceroy's blade is raised again, and I tackle Pip to the side, out of the way. The blade comes down on the back of my boot, nicks the heel, and I roll Pip and I over and over until we are far enough away, out of the reach of the blade, before yanking us both upright.

"Come back here!" the Viceroy shouts. "Do as I say!

Obey me!"

"Never," Pip snarls.

"You are *mine*," the Viceroy roars. "You never stopped being mine. And I will turn everything you touch to *ash*. I will take it all from you until the only person you can rely on is me. You and I will be the only ones who know what really happened, who know the *truth!*"

Dread punches me like an icy fist in the solar plexus, and I gasp for air as Pip's face drains of all color. I want to tell her to run, to flee, but where would she go, that the Viceroy would not follow? Where could I send her that he could not find? The only way to protect Pip and Alis now is to end the Viceroy.

"I'm not... but I'm not important to the narrative!" Pip shouts. Her eyes are glued to Ahbni, though, sucking on air, eyes open and rolling wildly, blood frothing on her lips.

"Don't look, *bao bei*," I urge her. "Don't watch."

"We need to—"

"There's not enough—"

Before I can even say it, Ahbni's convulsions cease. Her body drops flat against the cement, limbs flopping. Her eyes stare upward, blank.

Dead.

"Oh god," Pip sobs, her voice a harsh and rasping thing. "Oh god, no. Why would you—you didn't need—I thought... I thought you just wanted *Elgar*," Pip says, and her whole body is shaking now. She swallows, heavily, over and over again, and I am too filled with grief for her sorrow to feel much else.

"I wanted my revenge on him, yes, but I had that the moment I first had you in my grasp. The woman who knows more than he? The woman with power? Ha!" The Viceroy laughs, gleeful at her horror.

"I thought... I don't..." Pip whines.

"What use have I for a fat old man? You think I couldn't have killed him the moment I found him?" the Viceroy sneers. "For months, I knew where he was! He slept safe and unaware, oblivious as a pig to the slaughter knife above his head. He lazed about in ignorant luxury like the fat king he was. And I *watched*, and I *knew*."

"Then... I don't..." Pip gasps. She is inching away from him, and I step between them, between her and this man who wants to steal my wife, my best friend, the mother of my daughter, this man who wants to rip her away from us. This man who wants to steal Bevel from my brother, who seeks to take Kintyre's power and fame, who hates the House of Turn with all he has. "Why wait?"

"It was not enough to simply *kill* him," the Viceroy says. His eyes have begun to take on a hint of acid green, his hair and clothing lifting in the beginnings of a cyclone of air that swirls around him alone. His mother was a weather witch, and in his manic fury, the elements struggle to bend to his whiplash will. "Not enough to kill you *all*! I want you *humiliated*. Defeated in the way that you forced on me! Unmanned and frustrated at every turn. *Cornered!* I wanted him *running* scared, and I want you all helpless. And now, here he is! Dead before his audience, broken on the floor, *nothing*, and you failed to save him!"

Pip takes a step toward the Viceroy, but I will not be moved.

"And *you*," he snarls at her, eyes burning green. "I want you broken, so I may put you back together again in my image!"

The Viceroy's feet leave the ground, his toes brushing the concrete as the wind carries him higher, higher, until he is hovering in midair like an anime villain.

"Oh, how stereotypically melodramatic," Pip sighs,

and I have to press down the ridiculous urge to giggle. Only my wife could sound so put out and annoyed in the midst of such deadly peril.

"*And*," the Viceroy punctuates with another flare of acid-green flame crackling around his fist, "I needed him to lead me to you."

"Leave off Pip!" Kintyre shouts, yanking the Viceroy's attention back to him and Bevel. "*I'm* your archnemesis!"

"You?" the Viceroy says, and it is followed with a howling gale of hysterical, painfully shrill laughter that makes the Viceroy's eyes pop, the tendons and veins on his hands and face strain and stand out against his flushed flesh. "*You are nothing!* You are an oaf with a sword and a swagger, and little else! You have *never* been a match for me! I am faster, cleverer, more powerful! You have only won because I have been *Written* to lose! You? Do not insult me. You are not my equal, Kintyre Turn."

He swings his lizard-gaze around to stare me dead in the eye, licking his chops.

He stares, brutal and broken. And the last floating pieces, the last itching lack of understanding smoothes into place, soft and silky, whispering the truth. I know, now. I understand. I understand *everything*.

"It's me," I say, the revelation sweeping down my body like ice water had been poured over my head. "All this time, Elgar thought he was Writing the tale of a villain being rousted by a hero, and it wasn't that at all, was it?" The Viceroy grins at me, eager for me to explain, eager to gloat. "It was never that. Kintyre's adventures were the surface. But underneath it was a... a *spy* novel. The Shadow Hand and the former Right Hand of the King. You hate House Turn, but it was never *Kintyre* you plotted against."

"No!" the Viceroy agrees. He licks his lips again, as if

my revelation is the most succulent feast he's ever consumed. "He got in my *way*, but it was never him I wanted."

"It was me," I gasp. I turn to my wife. "Pip. You came to me because I am the Shadow Hand. You were brought to Turn Hall because... he threw you at me because... not to get at Kintyre, but because it's *me*."

"It's you, what?" Bevel asks through a clenched jaw.

My body shaking, the words ripped from the deepest, darkest part of my gut, the answer falls like lead from my dry mouth: "*I'm the Main Character.*"

The Viceroy throws back his head and howls, dancing a circle in the air. "Yes! Yes!" he screams. "And now I will kill you and end this story *forever!*"

"But you'll die!" Pip says. "I don't understand. If you end the story, if you destroy it all, doesn't that mean that you'll—"

"And what point is there to life in this stinking, horrible realm, anyway?" the Viceroy sneers. "Mother is not here! We are at an end, Main Character. For you are clever. You have outmaneuvered me at every twist. Every turn. Every turn, but one!"

"Which is?" I ask, stepping neatly into the pause the Viceroy leaves, because he so dearly wishes to tell us, and any hint of what he is planning is one extra advantage to our side.

The Viceroy's palms start to crackle and swirl with a particular spell that I have dreaded seeing since the moment Pip began to suffer her nightmares. "I still have that which you value under my control."

The magic flows toward Pip, and she barely has a moment to take a step back before it has her in its grasp for the third time.

"No, wait—" Kintyre shouts, bounding toward Pip, trying to get Foesmiter between the two of them. As if the magic from his sword will do any good. It is already too late.

For here is the thing I feared. *Again.*

Here is the thing that Pip and I never discussed a protection from, because there is none. Here is the thing that kept me awake every night, even as the pain of the magic runoff kept her. Because I am no warlock, no spell-caster, no witch. The Words I know have never worked in the past, and the spells I practice are small things of divination and warding.

The only protection, the only thing that has saved Pip from this in the past is her own will.

And that?

That I believe in *strongly.*

I grasp her hand hard, and together, we stare down the Viceroy. Her eyes are taking on that horrific, telltale tinge of green again, the acidic color swirling out like venomous ink from her pupils, but she is grimacing and blinking hard, forcing it to slow. The purple beats it back.

"I'm here for you," I whisper in her ear. "Tell me what you need. I am the Main Character. I can make it happen."

"A Word," Pip says, trying to grin around the grimace that the war inside her own flesh causes. "A powerful Word. A Last Word."

"Let me think," I say. "The mask will have the right one, if I just had—" I plunge my free hand into my jerkin, but Pip suddenly stops struggling.

She sways back on her heels, wrenching my arm where our fingers are entwined. Her irises are entirely violet. The scars on her back shine so brightly that I can see the individual leaves glowing green through her clothing as they ripple and flutter, as if the ivy is growing in real time. It spills over her flesh, down her shoulders, twining around her arms, curling under her wrists. But she doesn't look blank, or stunned, or forcefully stilled, or any of the things she is when she is under the control of the Viceroy.

No, Pip is relaxed, loose-limbed, and *grinning*.

The Viceroy lands on the concrete with an audible *thunk*, his short hair whipping around his head and a grimace on his face. He shakes his hands out, flexing his fingers, cracking his knuckles, and glares at Pip from under his eyebrows.

"Yield!" he commands, and Pip actually snorts at him.

"You know, the definition of insanity is doing the same thing over and over again and expecting different results," Pip says with a malicious grin. "Not quite the appropriate idiom for this situation, but close. I won't let you puppeteer me a third time. You see, in this world, with the rules that Elgar wrote into it? Third time really *is* the charm."

The Viceroy slings a bolt of magic at Kintyre, desperate and wild-eyed, but Kintyre deflects it with Foesmiter. Bevel, his ray-gun gone, draws his own sword. He is grinning, too.

"You don't understand, do you?" Pip tries again, for she is my wife, no matter how much magic writhes under her skin, and she will always prefer to talk her way out. " You see a damsel, you put her in distress, I defy your expectations, and you don't understand *why*."

"It *does* work!" the Viceroy snarls, but he sounds unsure now.

"You're stupid," Pip says, but her tone is almost gentle. "Don't look at me like that. In the end, you're still just a character. He never fleshed you out, did he? Gave you just enough will to want, but not enough freedom to evolve."

"I killed him!" the Viceroy seethes. "I am free from the story!"

"No. The one person who could have given you more, given you what you wanted, set you free, Written you love and a family—you had him fucking *murdered*."

The Viceroy's golden eyes widen, horror creeping in at the edges. "You're wrong!" he howls. "This... this isn't... this wasn't supposed to..." The Viceroy casts around, eyes wild and darting, hands clenched in his hair as the revelation that Pip is no longer his to control makes him stumble and stutter. "This is not how it ends!"

He slings exploding spells around, but before I can do much more than duck them, a lasso of bright golden magic whips over his head and pins his arms to his sides.

"This is exactly how it ends, you unbelievable as-shole," says someone with a faint French accent from behind the Viceroy, and from the doors of the ballroom, the man with the cane leads the magic-wielding cosplayers out onto the floor. Among the gathered are all *The Tales of Kintyre Turn* cosplayers.

Three Kintyres, two Bevels, a Bootknife, and what appears to be a slew of folk in Turn-russet stand with their weapons drawn and their faces grim alongside the young lad dressed as a Magical Girl. The loop of glittery restraining magic holding the Viceroy captive emanates from the lad's bright pink plastic wand.

"Ichiro was my *friend*," the video game cosplayer with the fire-gun sobs, her face splotchy and swollen.

"*You* yield, Viceroy," Bevel—*our* Bevel—challenges, and a worried murmur ripples through the assembled fans, echoes of the villain's name on the air. The Boot-knife cosplayer looks absolutely disgusted.

"*Never*," the Viceroy snarls. "I'll die first!"

"We can arrange that," Kintyre says with a sharkish, dimpled grin, and the three Kintyres behind the Viceroy step closer, brandish their props-made-real with echoed "Yeah!"s and fist pumps.

"Not easily!" the Viceroy snarls, and with a flex of his arms, he breaks the loop of glittering gold and throws the lad back hard. The Frenchman dives for the boy, and they tumble to the cement floor together in a wheel of limbs and cane; both sit up unharmed at the end of their spin.

Only one of the Kintyre cosplayers has the gumption to lunge at the Viceroy, and the young man certainly has the muscle to pull off my brother's physique. He whacks the Viceroy hard on the shoulder, amateurish and, unfortunately, with the flat of his blade. Incensed, the Viceroy turns and with another hot pulse of magic, flings the man across the room to land, groaning, amid a jumble of furniture.

"They don't know what they're doing. They're going to get themselves killed," Bevel says, and then, roaring to pull the Viceroy's attention off the fans, attacks.

Steel blades flash, the magic-users call spells, and Bevel and Kintyre bob and weave, dodging friendly and malicious fire alike in order to get at their archnemesis. But the Viceroy is swift, his footing fleet, and where he stays on the ground, he leaves acid burns behind. The fans score some hits—with such overwhelming numbers they must be lucky at least some of the time—but not enough to do any real damage. The Viceroy bleeds from a cut on his cheek and another on his forearm, both wounds defensive, and his jeans are charred on one leg.

"Forsyth, the last Word!"

"Buy me time!" I shout, and yank the Shadow's Mask from my jerkin. But I do not have the time to don it. The Viceroy, watching me, screeches in fury and throws bolts of magic from his hands, intent on stopping me.

I expect Pip to try to manipulate the magic to give me space. What I do not expect is a literal *volley* of spells to spring from the ballroom door and surge toward the Viceroy. He throws up a quick shield and dodges just as much as he is able. Stunned, I look toward my benefactors.

The magic-users have gathered together, talking rapidly and chanting. Spells pop around the Viceroy's head, flashbangs and flares of fire that have him distracted and dazed. The Kintyres and Bevels work to cover the gaps my brother and his trothed leave when they duck and weave around the Viceroy's vicious magical defense. Some swords bounce off his invisible shields, but they do so less and less often, until the Viceroy's arms, and torso, and face are covered with gashes and scratches and slashes, each bleeding freely. The blood pools under him, and the Viceroy is slipping in the gore, losing his footing and straining for the sky.

"He's exhausting," I say rapidly. "Pip, he can't sponge up enough magic. He's going to make a mis—"

Before I can even finish the word, it happens. The real Bevel gets in low beside the Viceroy and slashes viciously at the back of his knee, hamstringing him. The Viceroy shouts and crumples, and instantly the other two Bevels are on him, each of them kneeling on his arms, holding his hands still so he cannot cast.

"Ha!" our Bevel cries, triumphant.

"Forsyth, find that Word now. I need you to—" Pip shouts, then she stumbles forward, a grunt tugged from her chest as she claps her hands on her sternum.

The Viceroy wriggles his hand free. He flings his open fingers at Pip, then fists them hard, and Pip stumbles again.

"Oh no you don't, asshole," Pip snarls through clenched teeth, looking up. I follow the line of her glare to see that the Viceroy has his hand flung at her chest, and he is trying to... to suck the magic back from her. "You're not getting this back. This power is mine now."

Closing her hands on what appears to be utter nothingness, Pip *yanks*.

The Viceroy makes a shrill, keening cry. "Stop, *stop!*"

"No, no," Pip says with a grin, and yanks again. "This is my magic now. This is my power. My strength. You may have wounded me, cut me, scored me, scarred me. But you have brought a kind of magic into this world which makes the inherent, the inborn, the innate *manifest*. And what I am is a *fan*, Viceroy. Varnet, son of Solinde, weather witch and Deal-Maker. I take things, and I appropriate it. I borrow the voice of another to speak my own truths. I clothe myself in another's power until I have grown steady on my own legs, and have learned to wield my own. You may have put the vines in me, but they don't belong to you, not anymore. You can never control the interpretation of a piece of art once you release it into the world. You cannot control the way it affects others. This interpretation is *mine now*."

Pip yanks a third time, and then, whatever it is she is grasping gives way. She jerks back, and I rush to get behind her, to hold her up, to keep her from crashing into the ground. Her eyes roll up in her head, her whole body slack, as the ivy scars wriggle and writhe all over her body, purple-swirled green glowing out from under her eyelashes.

The Viceroy spasms and jerks, his own eyes rolled up in his head and his mouth foaming.

"He's having a fit!" one of the Kintyres shouts. "Get off him! You don't hold down an epileptic!"

The fans scramble away, even as the real Kintyre says, "No, don't—" and surges forward to pin the Viceroy in place. It is too late, though. The seizures have passed, and though he is dazed, the Viceroy is present enough to slug Kintyre in the face and kick him back. My brother grunts, surprised, and rolls back, flipping with the momentum of the blow and regaining his feet.

Even without the magic to bolster him, the Viceroy is quick. He skitters across the floor. Something glitters in his fist, and I realize that it is that damned dagger again.

"I wish I hadn't bought that fucking thing!" I snarl, chasing after the Viceroy. He crawls away as fast as he is able, leaving a bloody smear in his wake.

"I won't live without magic again. It *hurts*," he cries.

"I... I never..." Pip says, all confidence and color draining from her expression. She stumbles back against my chest, and I wrap my hands under her elbows to hold her upright. "I never meant to..."

The Viceroy bares his bloody teeth at us. "You *tortured* me!"

"You started it!" Pip snarls back.

A woman dressed in light armor, carrying a staff and a pouch of what looks like tiny phials of potions skids to the floor, kneeling in Ahbni's blood and pressing her hand firmly against the wounds of one of the Bevels. It is the healer. The *real* healer.

"Healing spell, healing spell," the woman mutters to herself, digging through her satchel before crying out triumphantly and dumping a viscous teal liquid onto the bleeding gash. A quick glance around the room shows me that there are other cosplayers dressed similarly—paladins and clerics and holy druids—all performing the same office. Healing what can be healed, saving those who can be saved. I am grateful, suddenly, that the magic has spread so far that their potions and spells seem to be working. I wonder what had really been in those phials before the leaking magic altered them. And then I have no more time to wonder, for my attention is wrenched back to the battle before me.

The Viceroy dodges around Kintyre and lunges for Pip. "Give it back to me!"

But I am there first, Smoke swift and sure, to hamstring his other leg. The Viceroy howls as he collapses, hands barely catching him and palms already slick with blood, so that he slides forward onto his face. It becomes clear to me that the Viceroy will not be escaping this encounter alive—not because any of us will kill him outright, but because he is bleeding to death in small, ghastly increments.

Crumpled on the ground in the center of a spreading pool of ichor, the Viceroy peers up at Pip with pleading eyes. "Please," he says. "Please, it hurts so much."

"No," Pip says back, crouching by his side. "No, I won't give it back. But I'll help the hurting. I'll make it quicker, if that's what you want."

Ah, damn my wife and her compassion, anyway. She is too close to the monster, and before I can say much more than, "Pip, move back—" the Viceroy's got one hand clamped hard on Pip's wrist.

She screams like she's being scalded and tries to jerk away, but her boot slips in the puddle of his blood and she lands hard on her arse. Bevel grabs her by her shoulders, and a hard stomp from Kintyre's foot snaps the Viceroy's wrist instantly. The villain grunts, and curls in on himself.

We are not fast enough. The magical, watercolor ivy has leapt off of Pip's flesh in tangible, glowing vines, and is curling around the Viceroy, lifting him from the ground. Like its real-life counterpart climbs a trellis, this magical ivy curls up his body, straightening him, supporting him. Pip, limp and panting in Bevel's arms, can only watch in horror as the ivy growing at a rapid, unnatural pace from her own flesh pierces and digs under the Viceroy's.

"No, no, no, no," Pip moans. I can see her growing weaker by the moment. Something cracks and snaps, and the Viceroy's wrist straightens and pops back into place.

He flexes his fingers, grinning as his yellow eyes take on a greenish hue.

Desperate to sever them, I slash Smoke through the vines. They part like fog around the blade, unharmed, and coalesce again like nothing happened. Kintyre copies my actions, but his magical sword is no more effective than mine.

"Ah, that's better," the Viceroy sneers as the cuts on his face seal up slowly, red gashes becoming pink scars, white tissue shriveling up and flaking away in a matter of seconds. "Stand, woman. Come to me."

Pip does stand, but it is under her own power. Bevel helps her to her feet, tucks an arm around her waist to keep her upright. "This isn't going to end the way you think it will," Pip gasps. "You're the villain. You can't win."

"Can't I?" the Viceroy spits back at her. "What was it that you said earlier? You all have heirs, don't you? That makes you disposable, in the narrative. The horrible father that pushes the hero out the door, wasn't it, Forsyth Turn? Or perhaps the tragedy that the young protagonist needs to avenge?"

Kintyre turns to look at me, poleaxed. "How does he know all that?"

The Viceroy scoffs. "Kintyre Turn, do you think that I cannot *read?*"

"The runes of Hain differ from the alphabet here, though," I say.

"Juan was an excellent teacher," the Viceroy sneers. He makes a motion quite like a shrug, and it sets the vines rolling and dancing happily around his frame.

"And what did you read, then?" Kintyre asks, stalling as his eyes dart over the writhing foliage, looking for a gap in the arboreal armor.

"Why, only the very best academic material," the

Viceroy says. "From the very cleverest of scholars this Overrealm has on offer."

Pip understands what he means a moment before I do, and she lets out a choked cry of horror. "I put it on the Internet," she hisses. "The full text of my dissertation."

"What?" Bevel asks.

"Her thesis," I answer grimly. "Pip's entire treatise on how the stories in Elgar Reed's world work."

"Hundreds of pages, too," the Viceroy says. "So long-winded, my dear. Took me simply *ages* to work my way through it."

Pip's mouth is working, gawping like a fish, but she says nothing. Fear prickles the underside of my skin, and I don't know what to say. I don't know what to do. Our one advantage, and the villain has been cheating with it the whole time.

"Do you understand now?" the Viceroy says, raising his arms and summoning another wind to lift him off his slowly healing legs. "I know everything you know. You *taught* it to me. You have been stymied at every turn because I knew before you did that you would make it."

He turns a grin toward Kintyre. "And now, I think, it is time to do that one thing that Our Glorious Creator would never do, would never have Written. You say I have doomed myself by killing him? Fine—but now he is not here to undo my actions, either."

The Viceroy raises his arm, and the ivy around it swirls and spins tightly into a cone—no, a lance! The grin on his face splits wider, and the Viceroy giggles in delight as the wind around him picks up to cyclone speeds. I am thrown sideways, struggling to stay upright where I slip in the slick blood puddled on the ground, and Kintyre raises his arm to keep the wind out of his face, out of his eyes, to keep the Viceroy in his view.

"Kin!" Bevel bawls over the rattling hiss of the wind.

I slam against one of the nearby piles of rubble, Smoke flying from my hand, a sharp *crack* reverberating in my side as one of my ribs snaps. Pain, burning and sudden, paints the edges of my vision black, sets stars dancing in the middle. I suck in a breath to scream and something in my chest clicks. I cough, but no blood comes up—there's a mercy!—and struggle to my knees, struggle to breathe around the pain and the way the air seems to be snatched away from my lips by the Viceroy's building tornado.

"Die!" the Viceroy shrills. "Here is your Final Chapter, Kintyre Turn! *The End*!"

Kintyre, spun about by the whipping wind, his hair blowing in his eyes, cannot seem to get his bearings. He swings Foesmiter wide and high, but he is too slow.

Too, oh Writer, too—

The Viceroy's ivy lance slams into Kintyre's gut.

"No!" Bevel screams, and leaps into the wind to shove Kintyre away. It seems like only a second later, a *microsecond*, but the damage is done already. I don't know how deep the wound is. I don't know how... how...

I struggle to my feet, hands clutched over my side, breathless and... my heart has stopped, I'm sure of it. The fierce ache in my chest is cardiac arrest.

Bevel spins Kintyre in midair, and my brother falls on his trothed, limp-limbed and flopping. Bevel scrambles out from under him, blood already splashed up his chest. The cyclone approaches, and Bevel wraps his hand into Kintyre's belt, determined not to be ripped away. He is pressing on a wound in Kintyre's stomach, but the force of the gale is so strong, it keeps pushing his shoulder back. Blood spins into the air in tiny droplets, like morbid rain.

Cement dust and splinters of broken furniture swirl

up into a deadly cloud. It swallows my brothers, and my enemy, and my wife, whole, obscuring them from my gaze.

"Pip!" I cry. "*Pip!*"

Another sound shatters the keening scream of the wind and the high-pitched whine of the Viceroy's laughter. It is a deep, dark thrumming, like drums, and motorcycle engines, like angry cats. A throaty *boom* shakes the room, and cuts through the Viceroy's cyclone like the fallout from an atomic bomb. The wind stutters to a stop, and I stagger, wincing and grimacing as I try to keep my feet under me. I had been braced against the push of the wind, and must reach out to the rubble to steady myself. Another *boom*, and the dust and blood fall to the ground, revealing a grisly tableau.

Kintyre is sprawled on the ground, spread-eagled, his hair a tangled mess. But I can see his face, and he is... thank the Writer, he is blinking, he is *blinking*. He is still alive! Legs thrown over his hips, straddling him, a half-naked Bevel presses his own shirt against the wound, packing it as best he can and leaning down low over Kintyre, Speaking Words of Healing straight into his ear. And Pip...

Oh, Pip, I think, stumbling forward a few steps before the cutting pain in my side forces me to stillness with a frustrated grimace.

Pip is *flying*.

The ivy is doubling back, surrounding her, answering *her* call now. *Her* fury. Bending to *her* will. Behind her, over her shoulders, the vines weave together, leaves flaring bright, into a pair of violently green wings. Green... and *violet*.

I had once compared Lucy Turn Piper to an angel. We had been in the Lost Library, and she was standing in a shaft of light that struck her at such an angle it appeared as if she was wreathed in wings made of golden light. Seeing her now, hovering a few handspans above the floor, glaring down at the Viceroy with all the holy fire of the righteous in her eyes—eyes that glow completely green, the color blotting out the iris, and whites, and pupils all—I am reminded that, in the Overrealm, angels are creatures of fury and terror. Angels *avenge*.

"Enough now," Pip says, and the boom is in her voice. The Viceroy, too shocked to even speak, crumples to the floor and gibbers.

"The Author is Dead," she intones, "but Authorial Intent lives. I control the afterlives of the characters, *not you!*"

The Viceroy wriggles and writhes like a worm on a hook, pleading, slurring.

My wife turns her powerful gaze on me, and holds out her hand. Who am I to disobey the command of such a creature? I stumble forward and take it. As soon as our palms kiss, the pain in my side eases. I can't decide if it's terrifying or arousing that my wife has become some sort of emerald valkyrie. I simply feel *lucky*.

"How lucky am I that I got to fall in love with you twice?" I say, and lift Pip's hand to my mouth, kiss her knuckles softly once, twice... and a third time, because there is magic in threes.

And then I don the Shadow's Mask for what I know will be the final time, and turn to face what is left of the Viceroy.

The truth of being a spymaster is that sometimes, one must do terrible things in order to preserve peace. To keep the kingdom healthy, one must sometimes wield a surgical knife. While I preferred to run my network from the warmth and safety of my private study in Turn Hall, there were those of my predecessors who were more inclined toward getting their hands messy.

Reaching deep into the magical memory banks of the mask, I pull up and download into my mind the most terrible and dark deeds of those who came before me. Until now, I had avoided filling my head with the horrible knowledge they had amassed, content with fooling myself into believing that I could preserve the freedom of my kingdom without recourse to dark deeds and darker spells.

But now?

Now, I tumble every Word ever Spoken, ever Heard, ever learned, ever developed by a Shadow Hand—Bevel included—into my mind, and soak them up, eager and parched.

The Viceroy doesn't even look up at me, doesn't even consider me a threat, until I am standing directly over him.

"What are you—?" he begins, and then realizes I am wearing the mask. "N-no!" he stammers. "You can't!"

"And yet," I say softly, memorizing the way the smooth, cool silver of the inside of the mask brushes my cheek for the last time, "you are the one who named me more threatening than your archnemesis. You were the one who acknowledged me as such. Not I. You are the one who claimed the Shadow Hand as your great enemy. And by the rules of the narrative, that makes it so, does it not, Reader?"

"It does, Main Character," Pip intones solemnly.

Words have always been my power. Words have always been my domain. So I slip up to him and whisper Words of Unbinding, Words of Unraveling, Words to Loosen Knots. Words that, backed with my newfound understanding of physics and biology, I can use to not only Reverse, but also *Unmake*.

"Oh my god," Pip breathes, her face taking on a beatific expression even as the tears slip down her cheeks.

"Forsyth, the Words. They're so *beautiful.*"

At first, the Viceroy simply stares up at me like a trapped prey animal. And then he grimaces. The cuts on his face reappear. His legs jerk. His wrist breaks. His eyes fly open as he understands what is happening. He begs mercy; I ignore him. I tell his joints to dissolve, his bones to liquefy, his cells to let go, his protein strands to unravel.

His final scream of defiance ends in a whimpering pop as all that the Viceroy was froths into nothingness and boils away.

Silence, glorious and pregnant, fills the room.

Only to be broken by Bevel's breathy: "Holy *fuck.*"

SIXTEEN

FORSYTH

Bevel's shock is momentary. He wrenches his attention back to his trothed, shouting Words of Healing and Words of Repair, and Words of Replenishment.

"Forssy, c'mon, help me," Bevel begs, and I kneel beside my brother to add my Words to his.

"The magic can't stay," Pip says, and she sounds punch-drunk and woozy. "It's building. It's going to—I can't—"

"Just give me long enough to save him," Bevel sobs. "Please."

"I can't—"

"*Please!*"

"Forsyth," Pip says, and she is grimacing when I look up at her, her skin growing brighter and brighter. Dear Writer, I think she's going to explode. Actually *explode*. "Forsyth, I can't hold on to it!"

"He breathes!" I say. "Kintyre breathes, the bleeding slows. He'll live."

"You can't just—" Bevel protests.

"She must, Bevel. She must—"

Pip swallows hard and grinds out: "Think of home."

"Home?" I ask. "Victoria?"

"*Turn Hall,*" my wife says. "Hain."

The name is enough to conjure my memories of the place. It was the scene of some of my greatest sorrows, but also some of my greatest joys. The room where Pip's first words to me were, "*Oh, it's you.*" Where my daughter first slept in the cradle of my House. Where Bevel confessed his love to Kintyre, and where Kintyre returned to live as husband to him. Where they guarded Lysse, and bid Wyndam, "well come," and offered sanctuary and occupation to Caerdac and Bradri. Where Pointe and I had whiled away long hours, sparring and laughing, and where, in the rosy dawn light of the first day of the new year, we sat on the front steps and shared a pipe, and confided to each other our Solsticetide wishes.

"That's perfect," Pip whispers, and then, struggling against some monumental weight that only she can feel, she raises her free hand. She points a single finger, raises it just above her eyeline, then draws it down slowly.

A bright white light follows, a rip in the veil of the skies, and the sound of the fabric of the realms tearing is like silver bells and shattering glass and the gleeful, high-pitched giggles of my daughter.

"Father!" a voice calls through the portal.

"Wyn!" Bevel shouts back.

"Bevel! You're alive! You're all right!"

"For now," Bevel lies to the lad. Bevel looks up at us, his features grim.

"Wyndam?" Pip says, and already she sounds better, like a pressure valve has been released. "Stand back!"

"Aunt Pip?" the lad yelps, but there's a scuffling noise that I assume is my nephew complying.

"Come on, Bevel," Pip groans. "Grab Kintyre. The opening is going to close any moment."

"I can't..." Bevel chokes, startled back into his own body, staring down at Kintyre's chest as his lover struggles for breath. The shock has set in, and Kintyre is fighting his own body now. Fighting to live. "Moving might kill him, and Mother Mouth won't come in time."

"Agreed," I say, pulling off the mask and replacing it

in my jerkin. "But staying here—the healer is powerless now. The Words are only air."

"Uh, hello?" Wyndam calls from the other side of the portal. "Aunt Pip, what's happening? It's closing!"

"I know!" Pip calls back. "Bevel, you have to go."

And she's right. The two ends are starting to stitch back together, the rip in the fabric of reality healing over, the entry point getting smaller and smaller. The glow on her skin is starting to become unbearable to look at. We are out of time.

"Not without Kin!" Bevel snarls.

"But you'll be trapped here, forever," Pip insists. "The magic will be gone for good. This is it. This is your only chance. What about your family?"

"Kintyre Turn is my family," he snarls with bull-dog-gish stubborness. "And I'm *not leaving him!*"

"Bevel, I can't—" Pip gasps. The creak of branches in a breeze is the only warning that I get. I duck quickly, and just in time, too, for Pip's ivy wings fold over her shoulders, the tips reaching into the tear. The gash closes hard on Pip's wings and she skids forward a half a pace, eyes screwed shut, teeth clenched, fighting the pull of the Deal-Maker's magic. Another booming *crack* fills the room, echoing across the ceiling.

Pip's wings are splintering. They are cracking at the shoulders, the wood too fresh to break cleanly, the leaves being torn from their stems and sucked into the por-tal. Pip's hair flies across her face, and I throw my arms around her waist, hold on to her, anchor her body to the floor as best I can.

"I've got you," I whisper in her ear, warm, sure.

Pip throws her hands toward the portal, and the ivy twined around her arms skitters off and away. With a final resounding *crack*, both of her wings snap off and vanish into Hain.

"There," Pip pants as we both back away from the opening. Her hands are fisted against her stomach; the separation must be making her nauseous. "The magic is back where it belongs."

I press a relieved kiss to her temple. She sinks to the ground, hugging her middle, squinting back tears of immense pain, face flushed and countenance windblown. She has never looked lovelier to me, and I have never loved her more than I do in this moment.

"Bevel!" Wyndam shouts through the portal, which is rapidly shrinking now. "What's happening?"

"We're staying," Bevel shouts back. "Writer, Wyndam, I'm sorry! We're staying!"

"What?" Wyndam and Pip both shout in tandem.

"Goodbye!" Bevel shouts, tears spilling over his lashes and rolling down his cheeks, cutting paths through the blood and the sweat and the grime smeared there.

"Goodbye? Bevel—"

"Wyndam, be a good lad! Marry that girl Caerdac and have a Happily Ever After, and know that Kintyre and I love you very much!"

"I... goodbye!" Wyndam returns, and Writer, he is crying, too. The pain in my side is lessened, but it still hurts when my breath catches, and the burning at the back of my eyes grows so intense that I can feel the tears pushing their way out, rolling down my face as well. "Goodbye. I love you both, and... wait, Caerdac's a *girl?*"

Pip laughs wetly as the portal closes with a final, soft *pop.*

There is a moment of stunned silence, and then Pip laughs a second time, weak and pained-sounding.

"Classic epic fantasy trope," she whispers. "The girl disguised as a boy."

"Is that it?" Bevel asks miserably. "Is that all of it? Is the magic gone now?"

"Almost gone," Pip says softly, and then opens one of her fists. Pip holds up a single sprig of ivy, still writhing and curling and glowing bright green. She reaches out and presses it hard against Kintyre's wound. I bend down over her hand and whisper the strongest Words of Healing, and Repairing, and Recreating that I know. And, as of just a few moments ago, I do know rather a lot of them.

We watch as the blood stops flowing, and the sides of the wound inch together. It doesn't close, not completely, but it seems to be enough to keep the wound from being fatal. Kintyre's breathing evens out, and he relaxes back into Bevel's arms, eyes closed in a true sleep.

Above us, a thin siren wail pierces the silence. A flashlight beam sweeps down the escalators, and a voice calls, "Anyone down here?"

"Help!" Kora shouts, from the door of the ballroom, and races toward the escalator, waving her arms wildly. "We're down here, and we need medical help!"

The next few moments are a blur of emergency personnel in dayglo vests, and the commotion of shouting voices, people crying, and loud assurances that everything will be all right now.

I am exhausted, and all I can do is wrap my hand in Pip's and hold on.

I come back to myself when my wife untangles her hand to shove at Bevel.

"Hey, you lump. Move."

Bevel snaps his eyes up to her, horrified. "No. No, I—I can't! I..."

Pip points at the people ranged around us, clutching medical bags, grim-faced but hopeful. "Ah," I say. "Bevel, you need to—"

"I won't leave him!" Bevel snarls. "I won't... I won't be where he's not."

"Jesus fucking Christ!" Pip snarls back.She grabs him

by the shoulders and hauls him back as much as she can. His hands flail up, red to the wrists, and I gulp in horror. "Move so the paramedic can get in!"

"The what?" Bevel yelps, caught off guard by Pip's insistence and manhandling. "Is that a healer?"

Pip grins at him. "Better. I promise."

"Fuck of a Dead Dog Party," Pip says from the other side of the hospital room. She's leaning against the wall, arms crossed over her stomach, watching Kintyre as intently as the rest of us.

She looks better than the rest of us, too, having been the only one of us well enough to escape the paramedics' roving eyes and slip up to our hotel room for a shower and a change of clothes. The fire department has cleared the tower for occupation, though only the out-of-town guests with no immediate way home have been allowed to remain. Pip has brought me clothing, as well, and it feels nice to have a soft shirt over my wrapped ribs. Pip even stopped at one of the clothing shops between the hotel and the hospital to buy Bevel some jeans, a t-shirt, and a cozy red hoodie. Bevel still has blood crusted in his hair, though, and under his nails. A scrub in the waiting room washroom sink can only achieve so much.

"A what?" Bevel asks, moving as if he will glance back over his shoulder, but never quite managing to complete the gesture. He cannot tear his eyes away from his trothed's face.

"Usually, at conventions, the committee who put on the con get together to finally relax once the con is over. Hang out in someone's suite, eat pizza, drink the leftover booze, actually get time to meet the guests. Celebrate the end of the con and fight off sleep. Dead Dog Party."

"Sounds exhausting," I say.

"Usually is," Pip agrees, and she lifts her eyes enough to send a twinkling look of fatigued mirth in my direction. "This is the best one I've been to yet, though."

"The best?" Bevel splutters, affronted.

"Yeah," Pip says, and steps forward to rest a kindly hand on his shoulder. "'Cause Kintyre's gonna be fine."

Bevel reaches up and clutches at Pip's hand. He blows out a hard sigh, and if it ends on a bit of a sob, it is not my place to point it out.

I shift in my chair, trying to find a comfortable position, and failing. Though we are not supposed to use our phones in the hospital, I am being abysmally selfish and naughty, and am monitoring the media feeds, both social and mainstream. So far, it seems that only vague reports of what happened inside the convention center are surfacing. No one cornered the fans, nor did we threaten them to keep what they saw secret. If they care to tell the world that they experienced magic, real magic, while suffering a traumatic experience in an airless, lightless building, I am certain that it will cause no harm. Even if others believe them, there is no longer any magic in the Overrealm—no one would be able to recreate the experience or spells.

So far, the news is reporting it as either a homegrown terrorist attack or a crazed murder spree perpetrated by yet another maladjusted, entitled white man. Fifty-seven casualties are reported, including Ichiro Eiji and Ahbni Rebbapragada. Elgar's death is, of course, the headline.

My heart aches to read of it, and I put my phone away.

"I've called my parents," Pip says into the beeping silence of the hospital room. "They're going to come here for a few weeks, while we all get healthy enough to travel. I've already arranged a room for them, and Bevel can take the spare one in our suite that was for... uh..." She trails off and swallows hard, the sound shaky. She turns away and dashes at her eyes.

"That's extravagant," I say. "Two flights and an extra room?"

Pip shrugs. "The con's insurance is paying for it. Though I have no idea how it all got pushed through so quickly."

I grin sharkishly and waggle my phone. "None, *bao bei?*"

Pip returns my grin, though hers is a little more wilted around the edges. "None."

We lapse back into silence after that, and Pip shuffles her chair a little closer to mine, so that she can rest her head on my shoulder. I carefully lift an arm and wrap it around her, drawing her close and reveling in the scent of her skin, the heat of her cheek through my shirt, the soft warm puffs of breath against my collarbone. "I miss Alis," she whispers.

"Me, too. But I'm glad she wasn't here."

"Me, too." Pip drops a peck on my neck.

"You don't have to stay," Bevel says, without looking up. "I can mark the vigil alone."

Pip and I exchange a glance and sit up.

"Do you *want* to be alone?" Pip asks.

"Yes," Bevel says, but he sounds uncertain. "No? I just—I feel *useless.*"

"What would you prefer we were doing?" Pip asks, gently, and it's not meant as a challenge or an unkindness. She honestly wants to help him.

"*Magic,*" Bevel says. "Why couldn't you have cured him before you—?" He cuts himself off with a frustrated noise. "No, I know. Just getting rid of it was the clever thing, but I just..."

I understand his frustration, and anger. It is justified. I know Pip is wracked with guilt over the fact that she was so focused on keeping the magic away from the Viceroy that she didn't stop to consider that she could do more for Kintyre, not until it was rushing past her and she had just enough presence of mind to snatch a tendril out of the air, to claw back just a little.

"He will live," Pip says. "And he will be *fine*. All the doctors say so." She leans forward and lays a hand on Bevel's shoulder, aiming for comfort, but he jerks out from under her touch.

Pip sighs, not hurt by the rebuff, and sits back again.

"Perhaps we may try an experiment?" I suggest. "Pip, can you fetch that pen on the doctor's chart? And some scrap paper, if anyone can find some."

We cannot. We search for a few moments, and Pip suggests we ask the nurse for some. But then I remember what I shoved into the bag with my bloodied clothes and the Shadow's Mask: the paper that Elgar used to summon Bevel and Kintyre into the Overrealm.

"Wait. I have some," I say. I pull the wad of crumpled paper out. Carefully, I smooth it out on the end of the bed. It reads:

The Reader had the magic of the Viceroy inscribed on her bones, in her muscles, in her flesh. And while only the power of the Deal-Maker Spirits could rip a portal through the veil of the skies, the Viceroy was descended of one of the strongest: the weather witch who was his mother. His magic was Deal-Maker strong, and so were all the spells he had ever woven. He was a warlock in full possession of all the magic afforded to him by study and blood alike. That strength, that power, lived on in the corporeal essence of the Reader. Her husband could draw upon it—and so, too, could his maker, when he touched the Reader.

And so it was that the Writer placed his hand on the bare flesh of the Reader, cupping his palm over her scars and leeching the magic still held dormant there, releasing it, tapping it. And with that magic, that power, the Writer did what only a Deal-Maker had been able, in the past, to do.

He reached through the veil of the skies and pulled.

Through the rip stepped Kintyre Turn and Bevel Dom. They were attired for battle, armed with all their best and most treasured weapons and armor, and in the pocket of Kintyre's jerkin, he carried a flask of the best dragon whiskey Drebbin had to offer. They came, ready to fight, ready to protect, ready to finish the final battle between good and evil. Ready to win.

Pip sucks in a wobbling breath, and then reaches out and touches the very corner of the paper with the tip of one finger. I am not certain what she expects to happen. That it will crumble to dust, or electrocute her, or catch on fire, possibly? That perhaps magic will be made manifest in this bringing together of Writer and Reader?

Nothing happens, though. Nothing at all. Cautiously, tentatively, she takes the paper from me and smooths it over her thigh. The pen barely leaving a mark in her hesitance, Pip writes just below Elgar's last line:

And with the excellent care of the hospital staff and the miraculous medicines of the Overrealm, Kintyre Turn completely healed by one o'clock in the morning, east-

ern standard time, and woke up.

Heaving a shaking sigh, Pip puts the pen back on the bedside table, and holds up her phone. We all watch breathlessly as the phone switches over from 12:59 to 1:00. Three sets of eyes dart immediately to Kintyre. We wait. The machines beep out their steady, rhythmic music. I am forced to exhale and inhale again.

At 1:03, Pip puts her phone away. She folds up the paper with Elgar's writing on it, and presses it into Bevel's hand. Her eyes are brown; not green, not violet, brown.

"I guess it was too much to hope for," Bevel says quietly. "That the magic would linger long enough for just one more spell."

"It was worth a try," Pip says.

"Yes," Bevel says sadly. "But this world isn't a story. This world isn't anything like the one I come from."

"Not to be persnickety," I say gently, "but this is exactly the world you come from. And it's not so very different from Hain."

"Oh, shut it, Bossy Forssy. You don't have to keep indirectly apologizing for trapping me here," Bevel snarks. "I chose to stay, didn't I? I chose to... anyway, I *chose*."

"You did," Pip says. "And I just want to let you know that we'll be here to help you adjust to—"

A tap on the doorframe makes Pip sit up ramrod straight and snap her mouth shut, like an errant child caught out by her governess. Standing in the doorway is a middle-aged man in the dark blue uniform of the Toronto Police Service. His hair is flecked with gray, his gaze tired but direct, and for a moment, he reminds me strongly of Rupin Pointe—upright, kindly, worn out by his duties, but also firmly and nobly beholden to them.

"I'm sorry to interrupt," the man says, "but I'm looking for Lucy and Syth Piper?"

"That's us," Pip says, eyes narrowed warily.

"Ah," he says, and shifts, picking at the side of his trousers with one fingernail, clearly uncomfortable. Clearly about to impart news he'd rather not. "I'm afraid that I need someone to... to come down to the morgue with me to identify the body, please."

The body. As if the creator of my whole world could be reduced to so pithy and hollow an epithet.

"I'll go," Pip says, rising stiffly from the uncomfortable hospital chair. "You've got a broken rib."

"No," I say, putting a hand over hers. "No, please, I... I want to do this. For him."

"Okay," Pip says, and tries to pretend she's not relieved that I've volunteered.

The morgue is in the basement of the hospital, and the room is chilly in a way that has very little to do with the actual temperature. There are far more than three bodies laid out on the gurneys in orderly rows in the room. And while this is the closest hospital to the convention center, it cannot be the only one to which the casualties—both living and not—were ferried.

The police officer stops me just inside the room and introduces a similarly weary-looking fellow.

"Detective Khouri," I say, holding out my hand for him to shake.

"Mr. Piper," the detective says. "I apologize that we're meeting again like this."

"Yes," I say, not liking the feeling of being on the back foot.

"You know, I tried to look you up, after the hospital," the detective says, hands in his pockets, emanating a friendly, casual air. It doesn't fool me—I am too familiar

with the spark of curiosity in his eye, see it too often in
the mirror, to fall for it.

"Oh?" I ask, matching him tone for tone, raised eyebrow for raised eyebrow. "And what did you find?"

"Not very much, I'll tell you," Khouri puffs out in a
chuckle. "You must be a hell of a spook, for you to be so
un-existing."

I raise my other eyebrow at his invention.

"What?" he asks. "That's a word."

"Certainly," I allow. "If you say so."

We both crack a grin at one another, aware that our
respective positions and duties will allow this conversation
and line of inquiry to go no further. He will never know
who I am, not really, and he accepts that. He believes that
I do not really know what he's been investigating all this
time, and I will let him continue to believe it. Whether
he is aware that I am allowing him this fiction, I do not
know, but I don't feel like pressing the issue.

"Wanna tell me what actually happened in that hole?"
the detective ventures. "Just between you and me? One
agency mook to another?"

I allow my mouth to curl into what Pip calls my
"*enigmatic Cheshire Cat grin.*" Khouri sighs and scrubs
his hand through his hair, chuckling and shaking his head.

"Right, then. On to the grim stuff, then. This way, Mr.
Piper." His cheerful demeanor falls away, solemnity taking
its place. "Normally, a detective from Toronto would be
walking you through this," he says as we wind our way
to the back corner of the room. "But I wanted to be on
hand to close out this case personally. We're still searching
through the deceased to find the, ah, the *stalker*, but I'm
starting to wonder if he got caught in the blast."

He looks askance at me, and I offer him nothing.

"Right, then. I guess I should take that as a sign that I
won't find anything?" he asks, but he's not really directing

the question at me, not now.

A doctor with a clipboard and a face mask, her hair bound back in a colorful hijab, nods respectfully. "Mr. Piper?"

"Yes."

"We just want you to confirm the identity of this man." She gestures to the body under the sheet. It bulges upward almost obscenely, and it is clear that it is nude. "You only have to look at his face. You don't have to say anything if you don't want to. Just a nod is enough. Are you prepared?"

Am I prepared? My heart flutters hard against my cracked rib, and I wince and press my palm down hard against it to relieve the ache. Khouri's wise dark eyes follow the gesture, and I can tell that he's cataloged that I am injured. Perhaps this humanizes me in his eyes a little, for his expression softens a fraction.

"N-n-o," I husk out, honestly. "Bu-but let-t-t us be-be-gi-i-in all th-th-the sa-me."

Thankfully, no one comments on my stutter. The coroner reaches out, and gently, respectfully, folds back the sheet.

They say corpses look like they're just asleep. But when I reach out and lay my free palm respectfully on Elgar's forehead, the spark of *not right*-ness that had accompanied every other touch we've shared is absent.

Elgar is not sleeping. He is dead.

"Mr. Piper?" the detective asks, tugging my attention back in his direction. I blink hard, and realize that I am weeping, silently, gently. "Is this Elgar Erasmus Reed?"

I clear my throat once, twice, and finally croak, "Yes. Yes, he was."

"Thank you," the coroner says, and waits for me to step back before she replaces the sheet. She hands me the clipboard, and I sign an attestation to Elgar's identity, and then my own.

"How long is this paperwork gonna stay in the system?" Khouri asks me, once we are back by the doors and within the realm of levity again.

"L-l-ong en-enough for it to mat-ter," I tell him, truthfully. "Af-af-after th-th-at..." I shrug, wiping my face clean.

Khouri nods, understanding. "Appreciate that. And who should we inform?"

"Hmm?" I ask, puzzled.

"Who should we call regarding, ah, arrangements?"

"Oh," I say, realizing what he means. "L-et me ju-just..." I fumble my phone out of my pocket. "His PA Hua-Juan will be th-the best-t-t. I c-c-can—"

"No, we'll call Juan. I have his info already, so I can start there. I'm sure his agent had something in place, right?"

I nod, not trusting my tongue. I have no idea what sort of arrangements Elgar had made. We were never close enough for him to tell me that sort of thing, and I am struck with the sensation of a pit opening in my chest, hollow and unfillable. So many things that I never knew about him, that we never had the time to discuss, or share, or learn. And now, I will never know them. I will never be able to share them.

"One last thing," Khouri says, waving me to stay by the door as he steps over to the coroner's desk nearby. He retrieves a big, plastic ziplock bag and tumbles a length of fabric out into his hands. "We retrieved this with him. It's beautiful, clearly handmade, and I wondered if... I've had it released from evidence, if you'd like to keep it." He shakes out my Turn-russet sash, the golden thread glimmering in the low fluorescent light of the morgue. As far as I can see, there is no blood on it, no stains.

All the same, I say: "My mother made it."

Khouri holds it out to me wordlessly. I fold my hands behind my back.

"No," I say. "Ask Juan to bury him with it. He'd appreciate that."

"What about Ahbni?" Pip asks me later that day, when Bevel has fallen asleep with his head pillowed on Kintyre's arm. We are sitting squashed together in one of the narrow hospital chairs with the lights off, as reluctant to be parted from one another as Bevel and Kintyre.

"She was... *collected* with the other victims," I say, tilting the screen of my smartphone so she can see that I am following the progress of those who had survived through the legal and medical system. And if I am giving some of them nudges to give them better care or quicker processing time, then what of it? We have all suffered, and it is within my power to make their suffering come to an end more quickly.

I owe them all that, if nothing else.

"It seems... cheap," Pip says.

"Cheap?"

"Or maybe just... really stereotypical? The villain disposing of the traitor once they're done using them." Pip is quiet for a long moment, picking at her cuticles. "But she still died. She was a person, and this isn't a book—people aren't all bad, or all good. She could have... I could have—"

"Pip," I interrupt gently. "*Bao bei.* You cannot hold yourself accountable for every evil of the world."

"But was it my fault?" Pip asks quietly, voice barely audible above the hush broken only by Kintyre's monitoring machines. "I mean, no intelligent, rational, passionate human being stabs someone whose values she disagreed with. And just a few hours before that, I was praising her for her passion and dedication to the cause, and... all right, so I'm a bit of a fool, a bit old-fashioned! So I'm not a perfect feminist; I'm not a perfect person. But I listen, don't I? I listen, and I learn, and I try. I let others teach me!" she hisses. "So why couldn't she...?"

"Zealots are zealots, no matter their gender or creed," I remind my wife. "And when someone twists and manipulates their values to spur them into violence, you cannot blame yourself for sharing those same values. The values are not the issue—the issue is how psychopathic narcissists weaponize them. The Viceroy was good at manipulating people. It is what he did. He did it his whole life. He worked his way up to the Viceroy of the King by it. Carvel Tarvers is not a bad man. He was duped. Everyone was duped. And we cannot blame the victims of a manipulator for being his victims."

Pip sniffs and buries her face against my neck. "I liked her," she says.

"I know," I say. For what else is there to add?

In the end, it is Juan who handles all the funeral arrangements, on behalf of the family—well, *us*—if only because he is in Seattle already to sell his condominium. Elgar's agent has requested that he lay in state long enough for his legions of fans to be able to pay their respects, and the funeral parlor agrees. The length of time is just enough, we hope, for Kintyre to wake and for us to attend the funeral. The doctors agreed that my brother should be kept in a medically induced coma for a few weeks at least, to allow the trauma in his abdomen to heal enough that the regular work of sitting, eating, and, *ah*, digesting would be no strain upon him.

Bevel remains faithfully stalwart, walking to the hospital every morning for the start of visiting hours, and only leaving when the pitying nurses send him back to the hotel. He passes the time with children's primers, learning to read and write this new alphabet, regaling the sleeping Kintyre with increasingly confident stories as his skills improve. He learns how to navigate a computer tablet, revels in the discovery of electric razors, delights in pizza, and pretends that he is not having vicious, horrible nightmares that keep him up half the night.

Martin and Mei Fan fly in a few days after what Pip has dubbed the "Fucking Trilogy Wrap-up," bringing Alis with them. My daughter is, at least, a healthy distraction for my brother-in-law as he frets.

At the end of the second week, Juan flies to Toronto to finalize some paperwork that, unfortunately, requires my actual signature. He brings Gil with him—a handsome, older man with all the slick charm of a Hollywood denizen—and introduces him to Pip and I when we fetch them from the airport as both his boyfriend and the executive producer of *The Tales of Kintyre Turn* television series.

Blast and drat. I had forgotten about that bothersome thing.

"A what?" Bevel asks. We are in the hotel room when I tell him that Juan and Gil have arrived, and are settling into their room, and that they would like to discuss some things about our creator's estate with us. "A *television* series? Based on our books?"

Bevel knows what a television series is by now, but I had not told him that Elgar's series was in the process of being adapted.

"Yes. And I think you should be there," I explain. "Have a say."

Bevel scowls. "They'll have to come to the hospital, then."

"I'm certain Kintyre will be fine sleeping alone for a

few hours."

"No," Bevel says, and lifts his chin, mulish. "In Kin's room, or no meeting."

"If that's what makes you feel safest," Pip agrees, sticking her head out of our bedroom. Alis slips away from where Pip had been dressing her, delighted to run into the middle of the room in only her nappy and a dimpling grin.

"Come here, sweet girl!" Bevel says.

He hefts Alis into his arms to plant raspberries on her bare tummy as she kicks and squeals, "Bev, Bev, Bev!"

"Yeah, so not helping to get her geared up for a day at the zoo with her grandparents," Pip scolds him fondly. "If you're gonna get her all riled up, then you dress her."

"Yah, sure," Bevel says, standing from where he'd been moping on the suite's sofa.

"Yah, yah, yah!" Alis echoes.

"Wr-Writer grant me patience," I say fondly, only stumbling a little over the oath. Bevel pretends not to notice. It is the least he can do, when I have been similarly ignoring his own emotional difficulties with his usual cussing. "Now my daughter really will grow up speaking like a Bynnebakker blacksmith."

"Best kind," Bevel says, deliberately thickening his rural accent. "Yah, girl?"

"Yah!" Alis obediently agrees.

"Traitor," I grumble at her, then lean forward to kiss the tip of her nose. "Off you go, then, you rotten turncoat. Let your Uncle Bevel dress you while I let Juan know where to meet us."

Gil cannot stop staring at Kintyre, which is very slowly putting Bevel into a *state*. Juan is at least more subtle. His eyes cut back and forth between both men, but his face stays carefully blank.

"Juan?" Pip prompts gently, bringing his attention back around to those of us who are awake.

"I... uh... there was a will," Juan says. "Syth Piper and family are the main beneficiaries." He hands a document to Pip. Her eyes flick over the contents, and then her mouth drops open.

"Holy Tallulah," Pip says, eyes wide. "This is an *absurd* amount of money."

Gil snorts, shoving his hands in his pockets and finally tearing his eyes off my brother, only to have them latch on to me. He squints, brow furrowing, eyes darting over my frame, my thinning ginger hair, then back to Kintyre, and, ah, yes. There it is: the moment he understands what he's looking at. To be fair, the only version of Forsyth he knows at the moment is a bratty eleven-year-old. "And there'll be more once the TV series is out," he says, clearly avoiding the topic he'd really like to discuss. "Royalties from the show, plus a cut of the merchandising, plus the surge in book sales from people who want to read it before they watch it."

"*Bao bei?*" Pip asks me, and I am pleased that I had anticipated this, at least.

"I have already set them up with bank accounts," I answer her unvoiced question. "It will be very easy to ensure the royalty payments are funneled into my brother's reserves instead of our own. And of course, I shall set aside enough of it to ensure Alis's education is paid for, and her life a comfortable one."

I have only a tiny twinge of guilt as I recall that I had once rebuffed Elgar this very offer in person. Had I not, would our relationship have been different? Would we have been closer before the Viceroy had begun to terrorize him? Would he have felt safer coming to me? Could we have stopped the Viceroy sooner, before he... ah, but down that path of speculation lies self-recrimination and madness. What happened has happened, and even if magic still existed in the Overrealm, I still could not have brought the dead back to life. There are no Words strong enough for that.

"And there's the matter of the... the house," Juan adds. "The estate is yours, Mr. Piper, but if you don't mind, I'd like to... there are a few mementos I'd... if that's okay, I mean. And you'll need to hire someone to clean it—the police have been through it for... for evidence. I can give you Elg—Mr. Reed's... uh... the weekly cleaning service's number," he finishes shakily, his voice damp. "Though I don't think I could... help you sell it. I couldn't stand it."

"We shan't be selling it, I don't think," I say, with a meaningful look at Bevel. "I find myself in need of two houses, suddenly."

"Is your manor not large enough to accommodate just two more?" Bevel asks, and I realize that we haven't yet given my brother-in-law an accurate impression of what my station is, and what dwellings are really like in the Overrealm. How ridiculously inflated the housing market is in urban British Columbia.

Pip snorts. "'Manor,' my arse, Bev. No one has manors. It's too expensive to keep staff. Our whole place could fit inside the Great Hall, with room to spare."

"Ah," Bevel says, looking baffled, but not adding anything else.

When it seems that no one else has anything to add, I thank Juan and Gil for coming all this way to hand-deliver this news, and promise to meet with them to finalize the handovers with the lawyer tomorrow afternoon.

Juan shakes our hands, and goes. But Gil lingers beside Bevel, looking as if he's just discovered religion.

"Forgive me," he says. "But I can't... I just... listen, you are uncanny. Elgar never said that he based his characters on real people, and you and... this guy"—he waves at Kintyre—"you're just perfect. Your accent. Your bearing. You even have that little scar under your eye." He points to it, and Bevel jerks back, away from him. Less because Gil was coming at his face with a pointed finger, and more because Bevel is still horrifically self-conscious about the mark. "Right, sorry. I just... look, here's my card. Come to set, okay? I'd love to have both of you on set when he's on his feet again. Just... come consult, or something?"

"Consult?" Bevel turns to Pip for explanation, the way he does whenever he is confronted with something particularly Overrealm-ish.

"You're familiar with the Kintyre Turn books?"

Bevel grins and snorts. "Intimately."

"Then come to set. Please. See how TV magic is made."

"There's no such thing as magic," Bevel snaps, and it is churlish, mutinous. He is still angry about that.

Gil, however, seems unaware that he is poking the Bulldog of Bynnebakker and keeps on. "Oh, this is going to be fun. I like you... Bevel." He forces a business card into Bevel's hand.

"I make no promises," Bevel grunts at length.

"No, I get it," Gil says. "I do. I don't... let me be clear, I don't want you to replace Elgar, okay? Nobody can do that. You're not runner-up to him. But you... you both... please. When he's up and around. What a resource you could be. Just think about it?"

"I will," Bevel reluctantly promises.

Gil takes the time to shake everyone's hands, and then rushes out after Juan, grinning like Alis when confronted with a whole mountain of paper to crumple to her heart's delight.

"Well," Pip says, slumping into the chair beside the bed. She reaches out and brushes a lock of hair off my brother's forehead. "That was a circus. You sure missed something just there, Kintyre Turn."

Bevel hands me the business card, and I explain the process of getting in contact with Gil, if he wants to.

"Should I?" Bevel asks, sitting on the edge of the bed and laying a hand on Kintyre's knee. He is rarely out of physical contact with his trothed for long. I do not know who this is meant to comfort more, but I suspect that it is not the man asleep in the bed. "He wants me to help."

"Only if you want to," Pip says, grinning up at me. "Consider his offer, Bev. Once Kin's up and at it, you two will want to do something to keep you busy. I know you don't miss being Shadow Hand, not the way Forsyth does, but you're going to have to find some way to occupy yourself. This might be a good opportunity."

Bevel chuckles a little to himself. "You know as well as I that Kintyre Turn will never be content with simply telling people how things must look or happen. He will pick up the prop sword and wade into the choreography himself." Bevel groans and rubs his forehead. "And I will have my hands full with the ruddy great brute while he does, won't I?"

"Will that be so bad?" Pip asks softly. I look away from Bevel to find her patting Kin's arm. "Just like old times, right? Just like that time with the King's Players."

"Yeah," Bevel croaks. He swallows hard, clears his throat, and then adds: "I'm dying for a pipe. I'll, uh..." He gestures awkwardly at the window over his shoulder, indicating his intention to go to the courtyard. He was quite put out to learn that he was not allowed to smoke indoors, at Kintyre's bedside.

I wait for Bevel to exit, then take one of the seats. Pip offers me the paperwork from the lawyers to read and, ah, yes, I do see the reason for her outburst. That is a veritable flock of zeroes.

"He passed the series on to you," I say, conversationally, as I peruse the rest of the document. I will read it seriously later, when we are back in our hotel room. "Why did you not speak up?"

"I haven't made up my mind. I... Juan and I are emailing, a bit," she confesses. "Mostly about the legal stuff, but they've mentioned wanting a new story consultant. I didn't say anything because... I don't know, it will be good for Bev and Kin, don't you think? To have a link back to Hain, to Turn Hall?"

"Or it may break their hearts," I point out.

Pip bites her bottom lip and nods, looking away from me and back to Kin, where he is quiet and still. I rifle through my memories, but I cannot think of an instance when he hasn't been rambunctious, fidgety, opinionated, or loud. He even grumbles and shifts in his sleep, and more than once when we were adventuring together, his restlessness would wake me.

"Will you do as Elgar asked? Will you write more stories? Of Wyndam and Caerdac?"

"No, I couldn't. I... I'm the sole repository of magic in this world now," Pip says softly. Her voice is reverent and sad. "You understand, right? I will never Write. Never. I couldn't bear to hurt anyone we love. Even unknowingly. Even accidentally."

"Very well," I say softly, pulling her against me. "No one is forcing you to do it. However, as you are now the keeper of Elgar's Authorial Intent, if the series is to happen, you should accompany Bevel into the meetings. If only to... ensure that nothing goes awry."

Pip is quiet for a long, long moment. "You're saying I should be the midwife?"

"It may help you," I suggest, deciding to try another

tack. "It may offer... closure."

Pip chuckles at my poor attempt to replicate the cadence and tone of our therapist.

"It's not... it's not a bad thought. After all, according to the Viceroy's summoning spell, I am the person who knows the most about the series," Pip says. But she smiles thinly, still a little too hurt by the events of the past three years to really make light of it. "What's your opinion of Newfoundland?"

"I hear they have a vibrant filmmaking community and many fascinating museums and award-winning restaurants for me to take Alis to while you're on set," I answer, as lightly as I am able. "I have experienced one coast of my adopted nation. I should rather like to experience the other."

Pip scuffs her feet, chews on her bottom lip, looks at the floor, and says: "I'll think about it."

Kintyre is allowed to wake at the end of three weeks. It is a longer process than I thought it would be, for even after the medicines that held him in stasis have been lifted, he dozes in fits and starts. And when he is finally, properly wakeful, he is confused about where he is, and what's happened. It takes him several days to be able to stand and walk unaided, and even then, they make him depart the hospital in a wheelchair. He is dour, and grumpy, and hates the clothing Pip has procured for him. He wants Turn Hall, and dislikes all the food just to be contrary.

But Alis greets him at the door to our suite, standing on her own and holding a ridiculous bouquet of Gerbera daisies so large it obscures her face. Kintyre smiles for the first time in my presence since he woke, and against the doctor's explicit orders, he scoops my daughter up to

smush kisses on her cheeks. Alis is startled, as she barely remembers Kintyre, and Martin laughs and steals her
away, distracts her with Library before she can decide she
wants to have a proper cry about what just happened.

Kintyre lets Bevel fuss him into a seat on the sofa,
and takes the offered glass of wine—also against doctor's
orders, when Kintyre is on the pain medication he's been
prescribed. But old habits die hard, and Bevel is still mild-
ly distrustful of the tap water.

"I'm never going to see him again, am I?" Kintyre
asks softly, eyes on his lap as he wraps a careful fist
around the stem of the glass. "Wyndam. My son." He
is looking at his niece. "I'll never see him again. Or... or
Caerdac, and Bradri, or Pointe, or... any of it. Will I?"

"No," Pip says gently. "I'm sorry."

"Can you... can I have some time with Bev?" Kintyre
asks softly.

"Yeah," Pip says. "C'mon, Mom, Dad, let's go back to
your room."

"Come, sweeting," I say, holding my arms out for my
daughter. "Let's go."

"Bye bye bye!" Alis says over my shoulder when
Martin passes her over. She opens and closes her fingers
adorably, apparently forgetting that, just a moment ago,
Kintyre was a man to be suspicious of.

I do not know what Bevel and Kintyre discuss, but
they are in their room when Pip and I return several
hours later, Alis flopped, dead asleep, over Pip's shoulder.
The next morning, Kintyre is more gracious, more patient, more generous, and I offer Bevel a thankful handshake when Kintyre isn't looking.

"So this is how the adventure ends, yeah?" Bevel asks
as we all pack up the following day. "How all our adventures end? The Happily Ever After, and all that?"

"Surely not all, Bev," Kintyre says with a smirk, waggling his eyebrows at his trothed and pinching his bottom hard, and... uhg, yes, I am absolutely glad that we have settled that Bevel and Kintyre will be moving to Seattle. I definitely could not live with my brother making *that* face at his trothed in the same house. Not even in the same town. Yes, a whole different country is a very suitable distance between me and *that*, indeed.

I must be making my own face of disgust, because Pip laughs at me, free and joyful in a way that I haven't heard in months. Alis takes the opportunity of her mother's distraction to "help" us pack by pulling our pajamas out of the suitcases and throwing them on the floor.

I despise flying, so of course my brother simply adores it. It took some jigging within the airline's system, but I managed to get us all on the same flight and seated together. Kintyre flirts shamelessly with the flight attendants, using his injury to procure a pencil and paper so he can sketch what he sees out his window, and Bevel grumbles and giggles, and generally is quite pleased with the world now that Kintyre is back by his side.

We part ways with Martin and Mei Fan at the airport—they're taking their car back to Victoria—and the rest of us hire a van service after they've handed off Alis's car seat. The drive from the Vancouver airport to our home takes three hours, but it is better than taking a second plane to Victoria, I think. Kintyre is starting to look a little gray around the edges, and being sat in one place without having to do the shuffle through the airport is good for him. Additionally, the van drops us all directly at our own doorstep, which is convenient. My ribs twinge as I help the driver unload our admittedly few bags, and then Bevel and I steady Kintyre as he steps out into my driveway for the first time.

He looks up at the house with a critical eye, his gaze sweeping across the windows of the upper story, the lush landscaping that Pip lovingly tends and which has been left to grow out of all control in the weeks we've been absent, the cheery front door Pip insisted we paint Turn-russet.

"'Small," Kintyre sniffs, and Bevel pinches his arm.

"Yow!" Kintyre protests, and then laughs, his mock-disapproval melting away. "Looks nice, actually. A place that's all your own."

"Exactly," I say. "And soon enough, you will have one for yourself, as well. For now, let us get you settled on the sofa, hm? Give you one of those lovely little yellow pills."

"Yes, please," Kintyre sighs. He's rarely so polite as when he's in pain and someone else is in control of his potions. I steer him toward the door, and Bevel drops back to let me unlock it, then I take Kintyre's hand and help him across the threshold.

"Well come to my home," I say, and squeeze Kintyre's fingers. "And well met."

"Temporarily," Pip says, coming in behind us.

There is a bit of a squeeze as we all drop our bags on the bottom of the stairs and kick off our shoes. Pip sets Alis down on the floor. Our toddler is squirmingly full of energy after being forced to sit on airplanes and in vans all day. She has nearly mastered walking without needing to cling to something, and she is off like a crossbow bolt toward her reading chair.

"This is cozy," Bevel says, as I help Kintyre get comfortable in the corner of our sofa. He runs his hands appreciatively along the backs of our reading chairs, the edge of the book shelf, the dusty mantelpiece. "Kinda Turnish, but not too grand."

He stops and looks up with wide eyes at the large painting of Turn Hall that hangs above the sofa. Elgar had commissioned it from one of the fellows who did the artistic design on the *Lord of the Rings* films as a gift to mark Alis's birth.

"Oh," he breathes, and Kintyre cranes his head up and around to get a good view of the painting as well.

"Huh," he says. "Good likeness."

"Indeed," I agree. "I wasn't sure how I felt about it at first, but I must say it's become my favorite wall hanging in the house. It reminds me of home, but it does not try to replicate it."

"The Turn family tapestries wouldn't fit in here," Kintyre says gamely.

"And I wouldn't want that horrific tapestry of the Bloody Battle of Bigonner, anyway," I point out.

Bevel chuckles. "Yeah, I hated that damned thing, too. Who in the hells wants to stare at that sort of thing over dinner?"

Exchanging a knowing look, Kintyre and I both smile, and at the exact same time, say: "Father."

"Right," Bevel says. "Well, I need coffee. Anyone else?"

He's become a bit of an espresso fanatic since Pip introduced him to it. He loves the efficiency and variety. Kintyre hates the noise of it all, the grinding and the beeping and the whirring.

We can see into the kitchen from the living room, and I chuckle when Bevel slaps his palm on the countertop in a fit of pique. "This hells-damned contraption is different in every place I've been. Show me how to make it sing."

Alis demands to be lifted "up up up, 'Lis up, Bev!" and my brother-in-law complies, hoisting my daughter onto his hip so she can smack the counter in imitation.

"Oh, lord," Pip groans, but she is smiling.

I find that I am smiling, too, a great wide stretch of a thing, probably foolish and dopey-looking, but it feels so good that I cannot begin to imagine ceasing. The tight knot of grief in my chest unfurls and softens and warms, just a bit.

It doesn't dissipate completely.

I don't know if it ever will, though I hear that, eventually, one stops thinking about a beloved friend's death, that you think of them first every moment, then only once an hour, then once or twice a day, then once a week... but never lose the deep, bone-weary ache of their absence entirely. The knot doesn't dissolve like potions ingredients in a cauldron, but rather unclenches, just a bit, just a little, slowly and over a lifetime.

Pip laughs, and kisses Alis's cheek, and pulls the quality coffee beans out of the freezer. "I can't believe I'm introducing Kintyre Turn and Bevel Dom to the pleasures of domestic appliances in the twenty-first century. Jesus. Ha. Just think of the *fan fiction*."

EPILOGUE

Pip sets her new, ever-present leather satchel down on the floor of Turn Hall's foyer. The sconces are unlit, the elaborately woven silk wallpaper lacking its usual jewel-like gleam in the false gloaming. The house is silent, hushed, holding its breath. Waiting for its inhabitants to arrive.

She stares upward at the grid of steel pipes, cables, and massive shuttered lights, and I follow her gaze. It is very odd to be stepping into my own home, only to look up and find that the ceiling is gone. There is no second floor to this Turn Hall, no rooms at the top of the stairs, no apartments. The grand staircase continues upward, splits at the wall, where it always has, and then flows further up to the left and the right. But those staircases end in metal railings and yellow warning signs.

The library is off the foyer, to the left as it always has been, my private study behind it. To the right is the morning parlor, which leads to the salon. There is no grand hall further back, though, no ballroom-cum-gymnasium, because none of Kintyre's scripted adventures are meant to happen in what were once the most important rooms of the house for me. Kintyre's suite of rooms exists on another part of the sound stage. Mine do not exist at all.

Kintyre's life did not happen in the same places mine did.

I set Alis down on the freshly swept floor—even the

pattern of the marble mosaic is perfect, eerily and exactly as I recall it—and she immediately makes a break for the staircase.

Alis is now so confident in her walking that she rarely wants her parents at all. She has tumbled headlong into her "just so" phase, and Bevel has become a horrible enabler. Stairs must *always* be climbed.

"Ah, ah!" I say, and direct her toward the library instead.

"Want—" she starts, and then cuts herself off mulishly when I shake my head.

"Don't let her wreck anything," Pip says, grabbing up her satchel and following after us. "I promised we wouldn't wreck anything."

"Me good!" Alis protests.

"I am watching her," I tell my wife, and Pip pinches my arm when she catches me rolling my eyes.

The library, too, is exactly as I recall it. Alis's penchant for climbing seems to be satisfied by one of the chairs by the fireplace, so I take a moment to peek into the set of the study. Here again, everything is eerily right, and just that little bit wrong. A crystal whiskey decanter set sits on the credenza, but it is not my set. The blotter is green, but not Carvel-green. Everything is close, but not correct, and it is enough to make the whole place feel flesh-shiveringly eerie. Though perhaps that might also be the chill from the air-conditioners and the high ceilings.

Newfoundland in January is bleak, and gray, salty and snowy and gorgeous. Air-conditioning wouldn't be needed in the studio at all, save for the fact that the professional-grade stage lights are apparently extremely intense.

Pip has been teaching me a lot about the film industry these past few months, since she has taken a hiatus from her position at the University of Victoria. This past half year has been a crash course for Pip on how television is made. She's diving into readers and textbooks like the education enthusiast that she is, as well as the behind-the-scenes videos on DVDs. She approaches her task with all the fervor that has, in the past, gone into her academic studies. Thus, she was fully prepared when we relocated to St. John's just after the start of the Overrealm's new year. Our house in Victoria is currently being looked after by my in-laws, and occasionally rented by short-term stay travelers, while we ourselves have taken a very charming set of rooms in a flat on Jellybean Row.

"This is uncanny," I say.

"I thought so, too," Pip says.

"Mama, book!" Alis demands once she's properly seated in the wingback chair that is at once mine, and formerly mine, and not mine at all. We have trained our daughter well.

"Be gentle," Pip says, and pulls a much-annotated and post-it note-ed *The Serpent of the Sleeping Vale* from her satchel, handing it to Alis. As if our daughter is ever anything but utterly gentle with books.

Content with just one of the eight be-flagged books Pip jokingly refers to as her "Neo-Excels," Alis opens it up—upside down—and starts quietly flicking through the pages, pausing to run her fingers along each of the illustrations she comes upon.

"Bevel did a good job describing the rooms in the scrolls," Pip says, patting her satchel. "The art department said it was nearly as good as having a blueprint."

"Yes, and I see that he's been very good at sticking his nose into the artistic designer's work, too," I say, pointing to a sheaf of illustrations and photos that have been left on an out-of-place director's chair against a wall. They have Bevel's telltale chicken scratch all over them. His writing of the Overrealm alphabet has improved, but his penmanship has not. "They must have been making the changes over the holiday break."

Pip nods. "They haven't filmed any of the interiors yet. Gil says they wanted to do all the locations stuff outside while the weather was nice in the fall. It gave them time to tweak. I guess Kintyre got a bit vocal about a few things, too."

I snort. "Why does that not surprise me? Bevel's prediction has rung true."

"Juan says he's on set as often as he can be," Pip agrees. "And Kin said the other day that 'heroes don't just quietly retire.'" She snorts.

"Ah yes, Bevel said something similar," I reply. "Let me see if I can remember the exact wording... ah, he said that 'being a lord was a nice break, but I like adventures. It's nice to tell stories again. But we're not actually in danger, so it's really the best of both worlds.'"

"At least they're staying out of trouble," Pip says. "More or less."

"Agreed. At least until their surrogate gives birth. And then, I think, the trouble will be all theirs."

"Or doubled," Pip laughs. "God, *twins*. I don't know if I should point my finger and laugh at them, or just start crying. *Two* babies that are a mix of Kin and Bevel. God help the Overrealm."

"*Cousins!*" Alis shrills delightedly, as she does every time someone mentions the forthcoming addition to the Turn family tree.

"And what do *you* think of the set?" Pip asks, standing in the middle of the library, hugging her satchel and staring at me nervously. "You haven't said."

"I think," I say, reaching out and tugging my wife into my arms, dropping an appreciative kiss on her forehead, "that this is an excellent treat. Thank you for arranging for us to have the set to ourselves today."

"But how it *looks*—"

"*Bao bei*," I say. "I don't care how it looks. It is an interpretation; it will never be entirely correct. And I am fine with that. This adaptation cannot tarnish my memories of my childhood home."

"Okay," Pip says.

"And I'm *ecstatic* that we are here, supporting you as you do this," I say. "I know that it has been difficult for you, learning to love the books again, finding your way through the darkness of our experiences and into this light. I adore that it is you who is midwifing the show. It is appropriate. You, the Reader who wields Authorial Intent."

"Mmmm," Pip says, and leans up for another kiss. "I love it when you speak in poncy capitals."

"Gar Gar!" Alis shouts suddenly, and we are both startled enough that we separate and turn to her. She is standing in the chair, the unwieldy novel clutched in one hand, pointing with the other at the portrait over the library fireplace. A portrait of, ah...

"My father," I correct her. "But the resemblance is remarkable. Well spotted, sweeting."

Preening under the praise, Alis turns in a joyful circle.

"We sit on our bums in chairs," Pip reminds her, and Alis plops down onto her bottom and resumes staring at Algar Turn. However, upon closer inspection, I realize that I was the one in the wrong.

While this is the location the portrait of my father has hung for decades in the real Turn Hall, *this* painting is, indeed, of Elgar.

"M-my good-goodness," I say. "It... A-Alis wa-was right."

Pip looks up and gasps.

"Well," I say, moved. "Th-that's a b-b-bi-bit of a ni-ce tri-ri-but-te."

"Yeah," Pip says, and tucks herself under my arm,

wrapping her arms around my waist, staring up at the portrait with me. "Are you happy?"

"Yes. And you?"

"Yes," Pip laughs, and winks at me. "Though, I'm the only person I know whose in-laws have an ISBN number. Do you think Kintyre and Bevel are?"

"Kintyre has joined a dojo in Seattle, and has decided he wants to be a stunt man when he grows up. And Bevel Wordsmith has discovered fan fiction. I think they are both as happy as they will ever be, in the Overrealm."

Pip laughs. "He wrote the scroll-sagas to learn one sort of writing. It makes utter sense that he would write fan fiction here to learn another. Did you know that Elgar's publisher is absolutely *hounding* him for a contract?"

"Oh?" I ask, because of course I knew. I was the first person Bevel came to with the offer, asking me to interpret the legal jargon for him.

"Yeah, apparently all his fan fiction is the stuff that happened around the eight books Elgar wrote, and of course, he's got the voice nailed down."

"Naturally," I say. "As it is his own."

"Elgar's agent, Kim, is going bananas for it. They want to make an anthology. They will call it *The Untold Tales.*"

"Will he do it, do you think?"

"It'd be good for him, if he did," Pip says. "I really think that. And he's had two meetings with them already."

"Well, then," I say. Alis rockets off the chair, and into my knees, reaching up to be included in our hug. "A third meeting will decide it, then."

"Of course. Third time's the charm," Pip says, and kisses first Alis, then me, sweetly. I curl my arms over her shoulders, press her close to me, and kiss her again, a little less sweet this time.

"It always is," I say. "Three quests. Three confrontations with the Viceroy. Three little Turns in this room right now. We even won the day by threes."

Pip grins and kisses me silent. Then she stops and pulls back, her brow wrinkled prettily as she considers what I just said. "Wait, what three things did we use?"

"Swords, and Words, and hacking," I say. "Your cleverness, my skills, and Kintyre and Bevel's brawn."

Pip blinks up at me, suddenly grinning, eyebrows arched high with mirth. "Huh," she says, brown eyes twinkling mischievously. "Fucking trilogies."

THE END

ACKNOWLEDGEMENTS

My first set of thanks goes to the original team who championed this series, my former agent, Laurie Mc-Lean, and Ashley, Voule, Cal, Winter, and Kisa of Reuts Publication. I think we made something really awesome together, folks.

Cory (Kora), Todd (Todd), Cheryl (Turtle), and Bob (Bob), who won the right to name a character in this book from a contest, but who didn't know their characters would become vital ones. Thanks!

To my beta-readers, Cory and Ashley, who help me sound more clever than I really am.

Alix Malorie and Anna Tan, who did marvelous de-bloat edits and sensitivity reads.

Devon Taylor-Black for creating the tabletop campaign the characters play in this book, so that I knew it would be a viable setting and adventure when I described it. Devon has also been a tireless champion of this series, and an insightful, thorough beta-reader who isn't afraid to tell it like it is. Thanks must also go to her husband, Gavin, who is also a huge supporter, her son Taran, who allows me to cuddle him and tell him stories, and baby Aurora, who arrived like a good omen as soon as her mother had turned the manuscript back to me.

Adrienne Kress, who has been there to hold my hand, to get me to just shut up and put something on the page, and who sees my work as what it could be instead of what it is, and thus helps me see it that way, too. (Is it Monday? Are we Famous yet?) And for Adrienne's Atticus, who was the inspiration for Linux, and who I would never hurt that way, little buddy.

Sunny Hope, who egged me on with word sprints, and GIFs of kittens, and virtual soup and wine.

Nicole Spurrell, my wonderful cousin and, thankfully,

willing translator.

Mike Perschon, who believes so strongly in my work that he teaches it to the next generation. And to all the students and faculty of Grant MacEwan University for inviting me to speak to you, and to share my love of Hain with you.

Liana K, for late-night academic conversations that helped me figure out the arc of the characters' journeys and reminded me of the point of these novels when I was floundering in the plot.

Julie Czerneda, for her unwavering love of this world and these people, and her child-like glee every time I put a new book in the series into her inbox.

Christian Stiehl, who helped figure out what kind of D&D character Ichiro would play.

Jay Hunter for helping me figure out which cards to deploy.

Elize Morgan and her, "GO! GO! GO!"

Mad Lori, who is always great for a chat when I just need to get my head elsewhere for a bit.

Mom and Dad, for supporting me while I pursued this small bit of happiness. And a second batch of thank-yous to Mom, in particular, who has been a tireless and generous proofreader for me for years. I am so grateful to her for that. If you find a typo in this book, it's only because it managed to hide while she was circling all its cowering brethren. (No, seriously, I mistype a lot.)

Aunt Brenda, who calls me and gives me a lovely book report each time she finishes one.

And lastly, to my Readers. Thank you for sticking with me, and Forsyth, and this world, for as long as you have. We are both so humbled, so flattered, and so pleased.

ALSO BY J.M. FREY

(Back)
Triptych
City By Night
The Dark Lord and the Seamstress, a coloring storybook
Hero Is A Four Letter Word,
short story collection
"Whose Doctor?" in *Doctor Who In Time And Space:
Essays on Themes, Characters, History and Fandom,
1963–2012*
"How Fanfiction Made Me Gay," in *The Secret Loves of
Geek Girls*
"Time to Move," in *The Secret Loves of Geek Girls
Redux*
"Bloodsuckers" and "Toronto the Rude" in *The Toronto
Comic Anthology vol 2*
"The Promise" in *Valor 2*
"TTC Gothic" in *Amazing Stories vols 1-4*
Lips Like Ice, as Peggy Barnett
Time and Tide

The Accidental Turn Series
The Untold Tale
The Forgotten Tale
The Silenced Tale
The Accidental Tales,
more stories from the Accidental Turn series

The Skylark's Saga
The Skylark's Song
The Skylark's Sacrifice

ABOUT THE AUTHOR

Photo by Marion Voysey

J.M. Frey is an author, actor, and professional smartypants. She's appeared in podcasts, documentaries, radio programs, and on television to discuss all things geeky through the lens of academia. J.M. lives near Toronto, surrounded by houseplants because she is allergic to fur. She's a tea and wine nerd, and her life's ambition is to one day set foot on every continent (3 left!)

Her debut novel *Triptych* was nominated for two Lambda Literary Awards, nominated for the CBC Bookie Award, was named one of *Publishers Weekly*'s Best Books of 2011, was on *The Advocate*'s Best Overlooked Books of 2011 list, received an honorable mention at the London Book Festival in Science Fiction, and won the San Francisco Book Festival for Science Fiction.

www.jmfrey.net

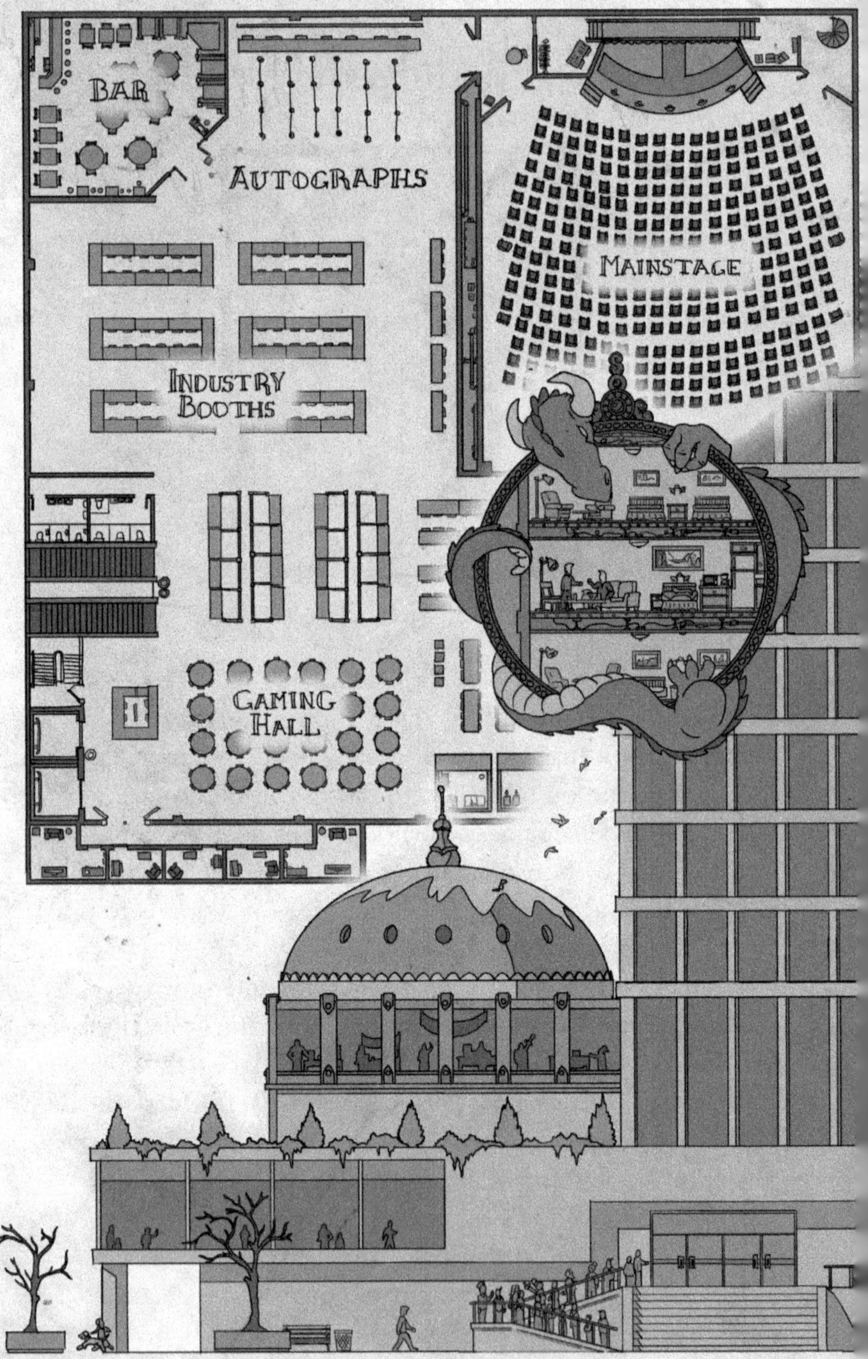
BAR
AUTOGRAPHS
INDUSTRY
BOOTHS
MAINSTAGE
GAMING
HALL

www.ingramcontent.com/pod-product-compliance
Lightning Source LLC
Chambersburg PA
CBHW072037190726
48294CB00005B/1295